THE
KILLING
ART

THE KILLING ART

Jonathan Santlofer

WM WILLIAM MORROW *An Imprint of HarperCollins Publishers*

HarperCollins books may be purchased for educational, business, or sales promotional use. For information please write: Special Markets Department, HarperCollins Publishers, 10 East 53rd Street, New York, NY 10022.

FIRST EDITION

Designed by Betty Lew

Printed on acid-free paper

Library of Congress Cataloging-in-Publication Data

Santlofer, Jonathan, 1946–
    The killing art: a novel of suspense / Jonathan Santlofer.— 1st ed.
        p.   cm.
    ISBN-13: 978-0-06-054107-1
    ISBN-10: 0-06-054107-5
    1. McKinnon, Kate (Fictitious character)—Fiction. 2. New York school of art—Fiction. 3. Women art historians—Fiction. 4. New York (N.Y.)—Fiction. 5. Painting—Fiction.   6. Painters—Fiction. I. Title.

PS3619.A58K55   2005
813'.6—dc22   2005043421

05 06 07 08 09 ❖ / RRD 10 9 8 7 6 5 4 3 2 1

For my mother, Edith,

who always encouraged me

Verily I say unto you, that one of you will betray me.

— MATTHEW 26:21

The one struggle in art is the struggle of artists against artists . . .

— AD REINHARDT, MEMBER OF THE NEW YORK
SCHOOL AND ONE OF THE "IRASCIBLES"

Here (in New York) is where the showdown fight goes on — it's bloody and real. No illusions about social morality high or low. The artist is his brother's enemy like nowhere else. . . . New York is a slash across the belly. You know your friend has a knife and will use it on you.

— CLYFFORD STILL, MEMBER OF THE NEW YORK
SCHOOL AND ONE OF THE "IRASCIBLES"

Prologue

December 22, 1978

Is it the chemical vapors that are causing his eyes to tear, or the impending loss?

He plucks the pen off his desk, starts to write what will be the last entry in this journal—if one could call it that. It's just a spiral notebook, begun some years ago, a place to record just a fraction of life's disappointments; and now, a statement of regret, an apology and explanation, though there is no real way to sum it up. A few sentences become a paragraph, then another, his hand shaking as he writes, and yes, the tears on his cheeks are emotional, not chemical.

Enough. He slaps the notebook shut, reaches for the whiskey bottle, sees it is empty, stands, sways a bit, unsteady on his feet, opens the small fridge, and without thinking exchanges the notebook for a bottle of vodka, takes a swig, considers his many losses, then lifts the metal can off the floor and picks up where he left off. He tilts the can and watches the clear liquid spill onto yet another painting—this one slit down the center with a palette knife, canvas sagging and folding like old flesh— the piece, made years ago, beloved at the time, though now, so long after its creation, nothing more than pigment and canvas coupled with regret.

And who would mourn its loss? The critics? Collectors? Other artists?

A drunken, bitter laugh.

He reaches for the bottle of vodka, another long pull, leans back against the wall, takes in the peeling paint and ratty furniture of the Lower East Side tenement he despises, so far from the scene—the Cedar Street Tavern, the Club—places he'd stopped going to long before they became history without him.

The "new American painting" it was called back then, when the scene got going and a few of them caught the media's eye—first Jackson Pollock, "Jack the Dripper," according to *Life* magazine, a miserable drunk who pissed it all away, then, in turn, the various members of the self-anointed in crowd—Mark Rothko, who was always depressed about . . . something, and that son of a bitch Robert Motherwell, and the others—but why bother to think about them, most of them dead now except for the king, Bill de Kooning, who was still going strong long after the movement's star had faded.

He thinks back on his career. Career? That's a laugh. But there was a moment, wasn't there? One article, a bit of praise, and then . . . nothing.

Was it something I did? Something I said?

A conversation—angry, bitter words—tugs at the recesses of his mind. But it's no good. Impossible to remember after all these years—and all the drink.

Fame? He no longer cares.

For years he wondered why it had come to them and not him, why he had failed where they had succeeded, but when he discovered the truth, what was he to do—tell a world that no longer cared? And who would believe him?

Nowadays, when he can get out of bed, he paints houses from nine to five, and at night is too tired, or too drunk, to put brush to canvas. Ironic.

Decades of paintings—mostly large, bold color, heavy paint, disjointed abstract figures, ugly but brilliant, some would say, and did at one time—stacked against walls, crammed into wooden storage racks, collecting dust, suffocating, begging for exposure, the chance to hang on a wall, to be appreciated.

He moves unsteadily among them, turpentine soaking the bottoms of his work shoes, rubber soles making sticky, smacking noises, eyes closed as he caresses paint and canvas with fingertips roughened and stained from years of exposure to pigment and resin—a blind lover's touch.

He opens his bloodshot eyes, looks away from the paintings at patterns of ice crystals on the panes of his tenement window, mini-abstractions as beautiful as any art.

Another winter. Christmas only days away.

Memories flood his alcohol-infused brain: Winking holiday lights, decorated store windows, holding the hand of a beautiful child who became a drug-addicted woman, a life even more despairing than his own.

My fault?

No time to figure that one out. Another face has taken shape in his mind—a portrait of innocence.

He stares at the far wall as if he can see into the connecting room, and hesitates for just a moment.

Yes? No? There is still time to change his mind.

But how to heal the heart?

Impossible.

It's better this way.

The baptism is complete, the gallon tin of turpentine, empty; he pitches it into a pile of oily rags, wobbles, almost falls, swipes a few tears from his cheeks, takes a deep breath of the turpentine-tainted air, strikes a wooden match along the edge of his paint table, opens his fingers and watches its lazy, lethal decent toward the studio floor.

A sound—a collective gasp, a Greek chorus sighing—before the red-orange stalagmites undulate like a roomful of drunken belly dancers.

For a moment the artist imagines he is painting, capturing these flamelike figures, all this color and drama, on canvas.

But he is wrong.

He has become part of it, one of them: shoes melting, pants smoldering, lungs constricting and gasping, throat burning, his flesh simmering.

CHAPTER 1

To the artists of the New York School painting was their life, their soul, their raison d'être. For them, the 1930s and '40s were defined by cold-water flats, hard work, heavy drinking; painters hanging out in bars and coffee shops, arguing about the latest trends and ideas—creation over completion, painting as an event—but most of all, it was a time of intense friendships and camaraderie.

Kate McKinnon stared at the sentences on her computer screen, then glanced at her watch: 2 A.M. She'd gotten used to working on her book late at night and into the morning hours, a time when most normal people were sleeping. Since Richard's death sleep had been an intermittent visitor at best, the days and nights yawning in front of her.

A year ago, her life had been nearly perfect; but now, when she tried to reconstruct it, the events, memories, were fragmentary and scattered, like shards of a mirror she had carelessly dropped.

Had she really been a married woman, an uptown mover and shaker, a bona fide member of New York's elite? It felt like another lifetime, and the transformation she had gone through to get there—Queens cop to society grande dame—like something that had happened to someone else.

Kate pushed away from the desk, stretched her slender, almost six-foot frame, and ambled quietly down the hallway of her Chelsea loft, paused a moment to peek in on the one-year-old curled in his crib, son of her protégée Nola, the two of them having moved in with her when she'd sold the uptown apartment to pay taxes and debts accrued after the demise of her husband's once-lucrative law firm.

Kate leaned against the doorjamb, taking in the baby's dark curls, his chest rising and falling. Had it been only a year? It seemed forever—or yesterday. If it were not for the baby, she would have little idea of time passing.

A *dark alleyway. A dead body.*

Kate squeezed her eyes shut, but the image of her husband—*a broken, toppled scarecrow, cops and medical examiner huddled over his body*—intensified.

A deep yoga breath, eyes still closed, searching for another image, and there it is, the one she was after: Richard, tall and handsome, smart and rich. The chance to start over. Exchange a cop's uniform for Armani, a row house for a penthouse, go back to school, pursue her first love, art history, earn the Ph.D., write the first book.

Ten years of marriage. Close to perfect.

Perhaps, if she were honest, only perfect through the lens of loss and melancholy. But God, how she missed that imperfect marriage.

Memories jitterbugged through her brain, impossible to hold on to, already starting to blur. *Is this what a life together is reduced to?* Kate felt tears burning behind her lids. But no. She would not allow herself that indulgence. She'd had enough tears.

She wondered how Richard would feel if he could see her now, living in a downtown loft, with a baby named for him just down the hall?

Pleased, she thought.

They hadn't been able to have children of their own, though they'd tried. And when they finally gave up, Kate devoted herself to charity work, nurturing dozens of kids through the educational foundation Let There Be a Future—one of them, a once troubled teen from a Bronx housing project, Nola, asleep in the room just beside her baby. Funny, thought Kate, how she had unexpectedly gained a daughter, and a son, a reason to go on living when she had come so close to giving up.

Outside, garbage trucks were clanking and grinding, something she had rarely, if ever, heard when she lived on Central Park West, but it did not bother her. She was here now, in her new home, in her new life, still trying to figure it out, and determined to be happy.

Black and white acrylic paint on the palette. Brushes lined up. Simplicity itself. Just like the plan.

Well, okay, the plan is not so simple. No, the plan is simple. First one. Then another. Work my way up to the prize, that's it. Slow and steady.

Yes, a simple plan. It's the paintings that are complicated, or will be, for some. But that's the fun part, isn't it?

A warped smile.

Music turned on, an old Michael Jackson CD, *Thriller;* brush dipped in black paint, then white, mixed to create a cool gray, not quite right; more black, an image starting to take shape, a few details added. The artwork, a balm, takes the edge off pain, tamps down anxiety, dulls the recurring nightmares that do not wait for sleep.

An hour, maybe two, passes, one of the painted images finished. Time for a break. Sit back, assess the work, and the plan.

Will they get it? Does it matter? Were the other pictures received—and what did they make of them?

No way to know. Not yet. Impossible to think it through with this pain, this damn pain.

When was the last pill? Can't remember. Just breathe. Feel the diaphragm expand. That's it. Hold it. Now, let it out, slowly.

Again, breathe. Give it time.

Patience.

Practically a motto, for art, for life.

A damp paintbrush plucked from the edge of the palette, drawn along the cheek, an imaginary painting: smooth flesh, features redrawn.

What's the use?

Back to the painting. The one completed image stripped down to essential black and white, no color necessary, the replication slightly skewed, a facsimile—like this life.

Painting: A way to order the world, and manipulate the viewer.

Order. Yes. Necessary to the plan.

Music turned up. An improvised moonwalk, awkward, though the performer believes it is perfect.

I can play the role any way I want. And why not? It's my turn now.

A lifetime of acting—and so good at it.

Over the years, the history has been researched, incidents that led to tragedy charted, assembled, and duly noted, and though none of these facts has been verified, the actor believes he has actually lived and experienced them—a justification for revenge, for setting the record straight, all of it processed through a mind distorted by deprivation and pain.

Is it true?

Yes? And no.

But true enough.

Does it matter if what drives one is real or imagined, true or false, good or evil?

What matters is that it propels one forward, supplies nourishment for existing.

Some people create. Others destroy.

It's a game, you see—though the others do not yet know they are playing.

But the game is for . . . who?

Me? Them?

The actor waits in the wings to perform.

The role: normalcy. Challenging, for sure, but one that has been labored over, perfected. Though right now, alone, there's no need to put on the mask. That will come later. A special performance. Tonight.

Makeup. Costume. Smile. Frown. Laugh. Cry. Turn it on. Turn it off.

Lights! Camera! Action!

So easy.

Except for the pain.

Fuck the deep breathing.

Another pill. Head thrown back. Eyes closed.

3 A.M.

Notes on her book in hand, Kate tiptoed down the hallway careful not to wake Nola and the baby, curled on a couch in the living room, and switched on a small lamp—the room, her collection of young artists' work, cast in a soft light. The modern masters—Picasso, Léger, Braque, de Kooning—were safely ensconced in museums, all donated, the thought of making money from the art she and her husband had collected impossible, even if she could have used the money.

Of course the sale of the Central Park West apartment had been profitable, but more than half of it had been snatched by the IRS, another sizable chunk to take care of Richard's employees, who had lost their pension plans when the firm collapsed. Sure, the law firm had had insurance, but the company was refusing to pay—murder and embezzlement, they argued, rendered the agreement null and void. It infuriated Kate that they would try to find a loophole, though, in fact, she wanted no part of it—*blood money*—the way she saw it.

And it wasn't like she was poor, there was enough in the bank to keep her comfortable for the rest of her life, though her days of blowing wads of cash on designer outfits and Jimmy Choo shoes were over, which was just fine with her; money and status had never been her thing. She hadn't cared much for the trappings of wealth, the fancy cars and an apartment way too big for the two of them, and she didn't miss them. What she did miss was her husband, and the things they had shared: indefinable moments spent together, talking, laughing, making love, the way you could sit in a room beside another human being and feel that he knew you without ever saying a word.

Kate glanced up at the artwork, details and color lost to the shadows, and a memory flashed across her brain: the Color Blind killer, an unexpected, surely unwanted assignment, tracking a psychopath with the

NYPD, and only a year after the horrors of the Death Artist. And yet, on some weird level, it had helped her cope—temporarily at least—with Richard's death.

Now, *Thank God*, she was starting over, taking care of a young mother and baby, working on a second book and the PBS series she had been hosting for several years, *Artists' Lives*. Like her book, it would focus on the New York School of the 1940s and '50s and include interviews with the few surviving artists of the period, along with experts in the field.

Kate read over a few of the pages she had written and made some notes.

The garbage trucks had stopped whining, the loft, unusually quiet.

A picture of her father in his blue uniform came into her mind, her uncles, a few of her cousins, too, all in the same uniform, crowding the living room of the Astoria row house where she grew up, cigarette smoke clouding and smudging a few details, but the event all too clear—the day after her twelfth birthday, her mother's wake. Then, another image, fifteen years later, of herself in that same blue uniform chasing runaways and homicides on the Astoria force—until she met Richard, and her life had changed.

But it had changed again.

Lately, in bits and pieces, Kate had been trying to say good-bye—to that old life, to her old self, even to Richard—though she wasn't sure she really wanted to, because . . . then what? Who would she be? A woman alone—which wasn't so bad. She'd always been strong and independent, had maintained her own life even when she was married. But it was different, wasn't it, knowing she had someone to come home to, a buffer against the harsh realities of life? It was as if her safety net had been pulled out from under her, and if she stumbled, who would be there to catch her? She guessed she would have to catch herself, or simply not fall—though with her leap-then-look attitude toward life, she thought she'd be better off investing in a suit of body armor.

Kate pushed the thoughts from her mind and went back to her writing, a few more notes on her book, an hour passing. Back down the hall.

Notes typed up. A shower. As she toweled off, she caught a glimpse of herself in the mirror—her new look—which still surprised her.

When was it—a month ago?—that she had passed the mirror in a store window and spotted a tall dreary woman in staid, conventional clothes, a sad-looking creature without spark or verve? That did it. Never mind if she was crying on the inside, she would not go out in the world looking like a middle-aged frump. Not that she would go for an Extreme Makeover—anesthesiologists and surgeons bullying her into a nose job and breast implants. Forget that. She simply exchanged her tired Jackie O look—beige cashmere sweaters and slacks—for bright cotton pullovers and basic black jeans, started mixing them with funky jewelry and her old high-end designer accessories. But the biggest change was also her biggest splurge, a birthday gift to herself—since no one else was about to give her such an extravagant one: a new "do."

Gone were the classic shoulder-length tresses with subtle streaks of gold that had been her signature for the past ten years. Now she was sporting that tousled bed-head look, classic Jane Fonda in *Klute* meets Meg Ryan in almost anything, her thick mane hacked off, falling now just past her ears, half in her eyes, curling over the back of her neck, but-tery blond chunks mixed in with her natural russet color. Her uptown friends thought she'd gone mad, but men in the street were doing dou-ble takes, and Nola thought she looked ten years younger and twenty times cooler.

For this particular transformation she had gone to the meatpacking district, yesterday's no-man's-land that had become oh-so-chic in the last few years, to the hippest of the hip new hair salons, this one owned and operated by a celebrity hairstylist, who had assessed her through horn-rimmed glasses, sighed as if she were hopeless, then got to work with two gorgeous male assistants, washing and cutting and coloring and blow-drying.

The cost? Unspeakable. Kate wouldn't tell anyone, it was too embar-rassing. But the next day she made donations to three of her favorite charities, and vowed not to spend a cent on clothes or jewelry for the next six months.

The truth? She loved her new look. And now, glancing in the mirror, she smiled at this "groovy" new chick and wondered who the hell she was.

In the bedroom, she slipped into her jeans and T-shirt. Outside her windows it was still dark. If she left now, she could miss the traffic and make it to Phillip Zander's Long Island studio with time to spare.

Kate stepped into a pair of ankle-high boots and zipped them up.

In her office, she retrieved her tape recorder and notes, then glanced at the reproduction pinned above her desk, a typical Zander painting— a funky, funny female figure created from dismembered body parts coming together in paint on canvas that usually buoyed her spirits and made her smile, though at the moment it seemed more sinister than jolly, and Kate could not imagine why.

CHAPTER 2

Standing inside the gleaming white cube that was the Modernist Museum, one would never guess that the space had once been a nineteenth-century printing factory. The floors were some sort of poured polyvinyl plastic as smooth as ice, the pipes and hardware hidden behind pristine fourteen-foot-high walls, lighting that was state-of-the-art, benches like minimalist sculpture that practically screamed *Do not even consider sitting on me!*

Detective Monty Murphy stood before the painting feeling slightly queasy. The almost life-size canvas, one of Willem de Kooning's *Women* series, a wild fusion of figure and abstraction created out of supercharged brush strokes, had been slashed vertically and horizontally so that the disjointed figure on canvas was now truly mutilated, flaps of canvas flopping gracelessly out of the frame.

"We've only had this painting for six months—*six bloody months!*" The museum director, Colin Leader, originally from the north of London—though his accent was as high-toned as the Prince of Wales's—could barely control his rage.

Murphy had recognized the painting immediately and, unlike most cops who would not know a de Kooning painting from a John Deere tractor, was almost as upset as the director, though he did not show it. In his six years with New York City's Art Squad he had witnessed plenty of willful destruction as well as the disappearance of several great artworks, some of which, he knew, would never resurface. "And you say the painting was in one piece when the museum closed last night?" he said, his voice calm.

"There was an opening last night, very crowded, in the front of the museum, in our New Works Gallery. I guess someone could easily have slipped back here, into the permanent collection." The museum director sighed. "But a guard made rounds before he left—and this would have been hard to miss."

Murphy unconsciously played with the rubber band on his wrist, a nervous habit he'd acquired some years ago, then stood back and took in the painting situated in its own niche. "Could someone hit the lights?"

One of the crime scene crew, dusting the area for prints, hit the switch, knocking out a strip of spotlights. The painting nearly vanished into the shadows—it would have been possible to pass it without noticing. "You said a guard was in here?"

"Most of the guards were up front for the opening. But there was one in this area, not specifically in the niche, but in the room."

"He here today, the guard?"

"The police have already talked to him. He's very upset. I was going to send him home—but I can get him."

"The museum receive any threats lately?"

"Threats? No, of course not."

"No disgruntled patrons or artists?"

"We've had a couple of recent board member resignations. Policy disagreements. But these things happen. Of course there must be thousands of artists who harbor a grudge against the institution for one reason or another. Ever hear of the Guerrilla Girls?"

"Feminist artists—lobby for more women to be included in museum and gallery exhibitions. They wear gorilla masks to hide their identities when they protest."

"You're well informed, Detective."

"I do my best."

"Well, a few of them obviously infiltrated the opening last night, planted stickers on several patrons' backs."

"You don't mean someone actually let in a group of women wearing gorilla masks?" asked Murphy, unconsciously switching the rubber band from one wrist to the other.

"Of course not. They were probably invited guests, just part of the usual art crowd. No one knows who is or isn't a Guerrilla Girl—and without their masks, well . . . They must have had the stickers with them, slipped them out discreetly, patted someone on the back, then simply merged into the crowd."

"And no one saw them do this?" Murphy had to ask, though he could well imagine it would not be hard to get away with. He'd done his research, spent his share of on- and off-duty hours at museum and gallery openings, and could picture the scene perfectly: the artists, gallerists, collectors, and curators, all in their requisite black costumes, packed into the room, basically ignoring the artwork—God forbid anyone should say, *Oh, that's a nice painting*—when they could be making connections, chatting up a potential gallery exhibition or sale, oblivious to everything but career moves.

"If anyone saw anything, they're not saying," said Leader. "If you ask me, it's a criminal act."

"No," said Murphy, then nodded toward the slashed de Kooning. "*This* is criminal. So, what was their beef with the show?"

"They claimed we were excluding women."

"Were you?"

"No, there were women in the show, but the ratio of men was, um, a bit higher."

"Do you happen to have one?"

"One—what?"

"One of the stickers."

"No. They were all torn off and discarded."

Convenient, thought Murphy, eyeing the museum director. "Do you remember what it said?"

"It had our logo on top, and below it said . . ." Leader glanced at the ceiling. "'Hormone imbalance.'"

Murphy suppressed a grin. "I'd like the names of those ex-board members."

The director frowned. "I don't see what—"

Murphy leveled a cool stare at Leader, his pencil poised over his notepad. He was a big man, well over six feet, intimidating when he wanted to be, though his face had yet to harden into the cynical mask most cops developed by forty—Murphy had two years to go. His father, a lifer, had the mask from day one. As a kid, Monty always wondered what he'd done to piss off the old man. His mother—who waited tables in a local Italian dive and was an old-movie buff who'd named her son for the actor Montgomery Clift—left his father the day after Monty graduated from high school.

"Walter Bram," said the museum director. "But Mr. Bram is in on an extended trip around the world, and has been for months."

"And the other?"

"Cecile Edelman." Leader's brow furrowed. "I can't tell you her specific complaint. I would have to say it was a series of policy disagreements with the other board members."

"Such as?" Murphy used the back of the pencil to scratch at the stubble on his chin.

Leader leaned in toward Murphy. "I do not wish to speak ill of Ms. Edelman, but she is an extremely wealthy woman and can be—how shall I say it—a tad spoiled if things are not done *her* way, if you get my—" Leader stopped speaking as an elderly black man in a gray uniform came into the room. He signaled him over with a snap of his fingers. "Clarkson, this is Detective Murphy."

Murphy asked, "You were stationed here during last night's opening, correct?"

"That's right," answered Leader. "Clarkson was back here all night."

Murphy hooked the man by the arm and walked him down the hall. "I know you're feeling bad about this, Mr. Clarkson."

"Clarkson's my first name. Clarkson White."

"Got it." Murphy offered the man a warm smile. "Look, anything you say is between us, Mr. White."

The old guy glanced down the hall at Leader, then back at Murphy. "How's that?"

"I'm not regular police, Mr. White. I'm with the Art Squad. I only care about the painting, not museum politics. You hear what I'm saying? I'm not going to repeat this to your boss."

"Nothing to repeat."

So much for playing Good Cop. Murphy pulled himself up to his full height and peered down at the guard. "Mr. White. Last night someone got into your area and destroyed a painting. Either you were asleep on the job or not here—or, worse, you were in on it."

"Are you crazy?!" White jerked to attention. "I've been working here since this museum opened its doors, before that, at the Metropolitan Museum. No way—"

"Take it easy." Murphy laid a hand on the older man's arm. "Just tell me what happened."

White took a deep breath. "You've got to understand. When there's an opening there's not enough guards to go around. We've been complaining for a year now. But they don't listen—say they can't afford more guards. Joey, he's one of the younger guards, he comes and gets me, says they got some trouble up front, something about some stickers being put on people's backs and he needs another man, I tell him I can't leave my station because I'm the only one back here, but he says, 'Just for a minute,' looks around, says there's no one back here anyway, which was a fact. He shuts the lights, and we cordon off the area, and I go up front with him, and we were trying to figure out who it was slapping those stickers on people's backs, and before you know it, maybe an hour passes."

"This was when?"

"Just before closing. When they started flashing the lights to let folks know it's time to go home, I said good night to Joey and I came back here, and . . . I didn't look around. It was late. And I was tired. And the lights were already out, so . . . I just left."

Murphy nodded, then headed back to the gallery. "I'll need to speak with the rest of the guards," he said to Leader, "your curators, too, and anyone else who had access to this room."

"Detective, there were hundreds of people here last night."

"You have a mailing list for the opening?"

"Of course. But it's not going to do much good. We do not check names at the door. A guard simply takes your invitation. People bring guests, or pass their invitations along to friends."

Fuck. How could he possibly interview hundreds of people who had attended an art opening, maybe half of them without direct invitations? Not to mention the fact that he had no support from the goddamn NYPD. *Art Squad.* What a joke. Nowadays? In New York? Unless it was a terrorist threat to blow up the Metropolitan Museum of Art, no one would care. For the past year and a half, Murphy *had been* the art squad. He'd be lucky to get a few rookies to work with him on the case. An expensive painting slashed might make headlines, but carry weight with the department? Forget it—not when you had slashed bodies to deal with. And it wasn't as if Murphy could make a decent argument for art–versus–human life, but still, weren't a culture's artifacts worth more than one man on the force to look after them? He guessed not.

Murphy sighed, came in for an up-close look at the destroyed artwork. The slashes in the canvas were neat and clean. The conservators would be able to put it back together, patch the back, match the paint where it had been cut and it could look okay to the naked eye, though it would no longer be worth anything—nothing the museum could barter or sell if they needed funds. He closed his notepad, leaned to the left of the destroyed painting, and read the wall text:

Willem de Kooning, *Untitled* (1959)
Oil on canvas.
Gift of Katherine McKinnon Rothstein.
In memory of her husband, Richard.

CHAPTER 3

It was a little past 8 A.M. as Kate drove through East Hampton, then Amagansett, the once bucolic Long Island towns that managed to retain their quiet beauty despite the influx of new money, which had transformed the sleepy hamlets into a weekend and summer playground for the rich.

The roads grew a bit narrower and winding as she made her way toward Zander's studio in Springs. She passed the Pollock-Krasner house, which she thought looked lonely, a museum now, a monument to the artist Jackson Pollock, who had burned too brightly, and too fast. She turned onto Accabonic Road and found herself at the famous Green River Cemetery, and without thinking, pulled to the side of the road.

No grass, barren trees, probably not the best time of year to visit a cemetery, thought Kate, though something had drawn her here—her book, or her own tragedy? She wasn't sure.

She stopped at the poet Frank O'Hara's grave, recalled his senseless death, run over by a dune buggy on the beach, a life of promise cut way too short. He'd been one of the first to write about the artists of the New York School—she had his reviews and essays at home, and referred to them often.

A life cut short. She could not help but think about her husband, not quite forty-five, and gone. Would she ever get used to the fact that Richard was not coming back?

Kate glanced around at the markers and gravestones, so many of her artist subjects buried here, and had an image of them, underground, comparing notes on their paintings. She hoped at least some of them, the ones who had not experienced fame in their lifetimes, had somehow learned of their lasting impact on the history of art.

Kate had never been one to put much stock in the idea of an afterlife, though this past year she often found herself talking to her dead husband and hoped he could hear her.

She walked a bit more, pulled her jacket tighter, cold air off the bay bringing a damp chill to the winter air, and when she found Jackson Pollock's marker she wiped the dirt off and thought about the tormented genius, and his wife, the painter Lee Krasner, buried close by, who had survived him and dedicated so much of her life to his memory and legend. Was that how the woman had continued to live? That, plus her own artwork, Kate guessed.

A few more minutes of sodden earth and gravestones, evoking memories of this dead artist and that one—Ad Reinhardt, Elaine de Kooning, Jimmy Ernst—all of them bringing to mind her own loss, and Kate had had enough.

Back on the road, the chill still with her despite the blasting of the car's heater, she found the turnoff that took her down a smaller wooded lane, and finally came to another, this one narrow and gravel covered, which brought her to Zander's property.

The old wooden house, set back from the road, was not particularly imposing and looked as if it hadn't been repainted since the artist bought it in the 1950s; but it was the barn, adjacent to it, which the artist had converted into his studio, huge and impressive, that captured one's attention.

Zander was already at work, though Kate apologized for being early.

"Never too early for me," said the artist. "I don't sleep much. It's true what they say about babies and old people—both up before sunrise, both drooling. I'm thankful I haven't reverted to the diaper stage. Not yet." The old man chuckled, his bright blue eyes as alert as those of a twenty-year-old.

The sun had cut through the early morning clouds and was streaming in through the windows and skylights, dappling light across an expansive space free of furniture other than a few chairs and a couple of long tables covered with tubes of paint, bottles of varnish, tins of turpentine, brushes upended in coffee cans. An ad hoc office sat in a far corner: a desk with a computer, shelves stacked with books and magazines that featured the artist's work, binders with slides and transparencies of his paintings. It was here that Zander's assistant took care of the day-to-day details of the artist's extensive career.

There was a smaller paint table on wheels, topped with a glass palette, a few brushes and paint tubes, which Zander could manipulate by himself. He had it beside him now, as he worked on a large painting propped against the wall.

Kate was excited to be back in the studio with a true living legend — the last of the Ab Ex big boys, an artist up there with the best of them, his work in every major museum here and abroad.

Phillip Zander was a Polish immigrant who had come to the States in the early 1930s, settled in downtown Manhattan, and made the sacrifices necessary to become an artist—no normal job or any sort of normal wage—and had managed to make it through the Great Depression with a combination of frugality and single-minded determination to be a painter. After the early deaths of his good friends, the painters Arshile Gorky and Franz Kline, Zander had cleaned up his act, exchanged tea for alcohol, vitamins for cigarettes—and apparently it had paid off. He was now ninety-four, though, with his shock of white hair and relatively clear skin, he looked closer to seventy.

Kate checked the small video camera that had been set up in Zander's studio for the past few weeks and switched it on as subtly as possible. The artist would not allow any actual cameramen, reminding Kate that after Jackson Pollock had been filmed painting, the artist, feeling like a fraud, had gone on a bender from which he'd never recovered. But Kate had persisted, finally convincing Zander to allow just one small video camera to film her interviews and the occasional moment of him working.

This was their second interview. The first had centered almost entirely on Zander's artwork, the wild abstract figures he'd become famous for—disjointed jigsaw-puzzle body parts meshed into thick, acid-colored paint, intentionally crude. At the moment, there were over a dozen such paintings lining the walls of the huge barn studio—paintings for an exhibition of the artist's new work that was to be held in the spring.

"It's going to be a great show," said Kate.

"Who needs another show at my age? But the art dealer, he kept asking until I finally gave in." Zander looked happy and self-satisfied when he said it.

"The figures look like they could dance. But maybe it's the music."

Ella Fitzgerald was scatting in the background, and the barn's high ceilings created concertlike acoustics.

"To have music all day," said Zander. "It's one of the best reasons to be a painter. Even when I was broke I bought records, the big ones back then, seventy-eights, not like those tiny things they have today. You know, Mondrian, the Dutch painter, when he came to this country, to New York, in 1940, the guy was an absolute miser, but he bought a record player because he loved American jazz. Even named his last paintings for it.

"*Broadway Boogie-Woogie* and *Victory Boogie-Woogie*," said Kate.

"Exactly," said Zander. "Which reminds me—" He was off and running, one story after another. How most of the artists had met on the WPA, twenty minutes on the economics of the period; the artists' shared poverty, how they would hang out in cafeterias—first Stewart's on Twenty-third Street, later the Waldorf, and Bickford's—talking all day, nursing five-cent cups of coffee; eventually trading the cafeterias for bars—the Cedar, on University Place, the most famous—coffee giving way to booze, talk to arguing.

"We even had nicknames for one another," said Zander. "Ad Reinhardt, the Monk, because of those black, minimal paintings he made. Mark Rothko, the Rabbi."

"And what did they call you?"

"Me?" Zander laced his thick-knuckled fingers together and glanced up at the ceiling. A moment passed. "Judas?"

"Really?" Kate scrutinized his face for any hint of irony. "Why?"

"Oh . . . I'm kidding." He barked a laugh.

Kate wondered. It had not sounded as if he were kidding, but she did not have time to pursue it—Zander was already into another story, this one about the painter Arshile Gorky.

"Imagine, coming to America from Armenia when you're fifteen, teaching yourself to paint like Cézanne and Picasso. Oh, he was a very impressive guy. Of course that wasn't his name. He just adopted it, said he was the grandson of the Russian revolutionary Maxim Gorky, which we all believed—at first." Zander grinned. "Of course we were all busy reinventing ourselves. It's a very American idea, isn't it, to re-create who you are?"

True enough, thought Kate, the poor girl from Queens, who had been a cop, then a New York mover and shaker, and was now starting over for the third or fourth time. She ran her fingers through her cropped hair and nodded.

"Of course Gorky's life was a tragic one," said Zander. "His wife running off with his best friend, the artist Matta, his battle with cancer, a car accident that left him partially paralyzed, and a studio fire. How much could one man take?"

Kate knew the story, pictured Gorky's death scene, which she'd read about. The artist had hanged himself in his studio, scrawled a message on a crate of his paintings: *Goodbye my loveds.* "If only he'd lived a few more years," she said. "He'd have seen how important his art became to so many—how famous he was going to be."

"Fame," said Zander, a touch of bitterness in the word before he launched into a discussion of how they had each finally gotten their first exhibitions and become famous. "De Kooning was the first to exhibit, then me."

"And Sandy Resnikoff, right?"

Zander nodded; his eye twitched.

Resnikoff, Kate knew, had been as big a part of the New York School as Zander, as big as any of them, but he'd left the scene early to live the rest of his life in obscurity, in Rome—an artist who quit at the top of his game.

"You know," said Zander. "One time, Bill de Kooning, he was invited to the Rockefellers for dinner, and he said something like: 'Mrs. Rockefeller, you look like a million bucks.' That still gets me, telling Mrs. *Rockefeller* she looks like a million bucks!" Zander barked another laugh.

Kate laughed, too, then segued back. "I met Sandy Resnikoff, very briefly, when I was in Rome, a little over a year ago, just before he died."

"Oh?" Zander swatted at his twitching eye. "What did he say?"

"Not much. He was very ill at the time. Basically, I just got to say hello. I didn't even see his paintings. But I'm planning to go back to interview his daughter, to get more background for my book."

"You're including Resnikoff in your book?"

"Why not?"

Zander looked down at his hands. "Oh . . . I don't think there's much story to get there."

"Do you know why he left New York?"

"Who knows why anyone does anything," Zander snapped, then softened his tone. "Look . . . by the time Sandy left, the group was beginning to disperse."

"Exactly why did the group break up?"

"It was . . . complicated."

"How so? I'm trying to get a sense of what happened to the New York School, the exact incidents that split the group."

"People grow apart." Zander folded his arms across his chest.

"But there was a camaraderie between the group, wasn't there? A sense of one for all and all for—"

"Why must everyone romanticize that time?" Zander snapped again. "Do you think we were all heroes?"

Kate was about to say yes when the front door to Zander's studio swung open and a young man burst through, long hair flopping into geek-chic black glasses, droopy mustache, ratty-looking hooded sweatshirt hanging off his thin frame, sleeves practically to his fingertips. He dumped Pearl Paint and New York Central art supply bags onto the floor. "Hey, Phil, how's it going?"

"You remember my assistant, Jules."

"Yes, of course." Kate had one of those maternal urges to hold the kid under a shower, then drag him off to the barber, get him a shave and a haircut.

"Hey." Jules gave the old artist a warm pat on the back, scooped CDs out of his backpack and displayed them: Lauryn Hill, Norah Jones, Mary J. Blige. "Thought you might like these. They're sorta cool, but mellow."

"I think the boy spends every cent I pay him on music. He's a regular music junkie."

"I admit it," said Jules. "Rap, hip-hop, opera, jazz, old Motown, you name it." He hummed along with Ella for a moment, his voice light and sweet. "I make my own CDs, too, some acoustic stuff, some dance—like Moby, only hipper, though lately I'm into grime."

"Grime?" asked Kate, thinking he looked like a poster boy for whatever it might be. "Is that a group?"

"It's a kind of music," said Jules. "Brit rap. Basically, a mix of Jamaican dance hall and English rave—the Streets, Dizzee Rascal—both Brits. They're the masters right now." He cut across the barn.

"You mind if I change the music? I've got something new you might like."

Zander nodded. "As long as you keep the volume down."

The assistant switched the CD, then exchanged heavy winter gloves for latex ones, started squirting oil paint onto a second glass palette, swirling brushes in tins of turpentine.

"He lives for music, that one."

"Who's this singing?" asked Kate, enjoying the mix of gospel, soul, and something else not quite identifiable.

"Antony," said Jules. "Antony and the Johnsons."

"Oh, for a minute I thought it was a woman."

"Antony's neither man nor woman, like a castrato. Cool, huh?"

"Very," said Kate.

Zander glanced over at his young assistant with affection, then shouted, "Not so much cadmium red. It's expensive."

"Cheapskate," Jules shouted back.

"The young," said Zander. "They've never known hard times, never had to scrimp and save, to choose between buying dinner or tubes of paint."

"Speaking of hard times," said Kate, "I'm going to be interviewing Beatrice Larsen."

Zander glanced up at her, then away. "Beatrice? Why?"

"Same reason I want to know more about Resnikoff. I don't want my book to be all superstars—like you." Kate added a smile. "Did you know her, Beatrice Larsen?"

Zander hesitated a moment. "Yes. She was part of our crowd, for a while, but . . . Where is she living these days?"

"Tarrytown. I've spoken to her on the phone, but haven't actually met her yet. She lives alone. Paints every day."

"Good for her," said Zander. "Of course she's a youngster."

Kate smiled. Beatrice Larsen was eighty.

"All set up," the assistant called from across the barn.

"You mind?" asked Zander.

"Not at all," said Kate. "As long as I can come back."

"Of course," said Zander, then pushed himself up from one chair, and with the aid of his assistant settled into another in front of an unfinished painting with a nascent figure, a blob for a head, no features, maybe a torso, thick slabs that looked as if they might become legs.

Kate shut off her tape recorder, popped the old tape out of the video camera, and exchanged it for a new one.

At the door, she had the odd sensation that something was about to go wrong. *But what?*

She turned to watch Zander lift a brush, study his painting, and consider his next move.

Kate received the call on her cell phone just after she'd left Zander's studio: her painting, the de Kooning she had donated, slashed.

Thoughts ricocheted through her brain—*Who would do such a thing, and why?*—as she made it back to the city in record time, speeding when she could, weaving in between cars on the Long Island Expressway, cutting off and taking the smaller, though less crowded service road, even running a couple of red lights, checking her rearview mirror for patrol cars, and completely forgetting that she had planned to stay out on Long Island to attend a party at a friend's home that evening. Now, as she cut through a ring of police cars and vans and crossed the maze of walkways heading toward One Police Plaza, she thought: *At least it's not a body.*

Detective Montgomery Murphy's office was not at all what Kate had expected.

Yes, it was boxy and beige, but little of that innocuous wall color was visible. One wall was floor-to-ceiling art books, the rest plastered with art reproductions, Manet and Monet, Pissarro and Cézanne, Picasso and Braque. Only the space above Murphy's desk was reserved for case-work—Polaroids of stolen artworks set up in a perfect grid, ten across, five down, case numbers written on them in bold black marker.

The good-looking detective was not what she had expected either. Despite the two-day growth of beard that darkened the lower half of his face, and the rumpled hair that made him look as if he'd just fallen out of bed, the guy was handsome.

Of course Kate knew about the NYPD Art Squad, though she hadn't had dealings with them since neither the Death Artist nor Color Blind cases had involved any art theft or vandalism.

Murphy indicated a chair, and watched as she slid into it, surprised that in person Kate McKinnon was even more striking than she was in pixilated television color; taller, too.

"Good to actually meet you." He dragged a hand over the dark stubble on his cheeks. "I watch your show, which is pretty much required in this line of work."

"Hell of a compliment," said Kate.

"Let me give that another shot: I like it. How's that?"

"Don't strain yourself," said Kate. She offered the detective a half smile, patted her new hair, crossed her legs, and tried not to look as if she somewhat enjoyed the idea of being a minor celebrity.

Murphy plucked at the band on his wrist.

"You trying to remember something?"

"What—?" Murphy followed Kate's glance to the rubber band. "Oh. This? No. Just a habit." He reached for a folder, opened it, and spread photos of the slashed de Kooning painting onto his desk.

"Jesus." Kate took a deep breath as a memory played: Richard raising his placard, offering the winning bid at Sotheby's for the painting, the moment so real, so alive in her mind. The idea that a girl from Queens could actually own a masterpiece, one she had studied and loved, truly amazing—though right now she was trying hard to deny those feelings. "It's only a painting," she whispered to herself.

"What's that?"

"Never mind." She played with the ring on the chain around her neck, Richard's wedding band. "Who would do something like this?"

"Just what I was going to ask you." Murphy snapped his rubber band. "Can you think of anyone who would single out *your* painting for destruction?"

The question seemed absurd. She forced a joke, trying hard not to feel anything—the loss of the painting, the memory of Richard. "Maybe they hate my TV show."

Murphy did not laugh; he could tell she was fighting emotion. He scooped the photos back into the folder.

"Maybe it's just random vandalism," said Kate, "like the attacks on Michelangelo's *Pietà*, or Rembrandt's *Night Watch*."

"Could be," said Murphy. "But most people steal paintings, not destroy them." He chewed his lower lip, mulling something over before he spoke. "Two weeks ago a Jackson Pollock got cut up at a law firm, one of those big corporate collections. The Pollock painting is with the lab before it goes for restoration. I'll send your painting as well—see if they can find any similarity in the knife cuts, check for crossover residue, particles, hairs, anything that might match up."

Kate sat forward. "You're thinking there's a lunatic out there who slices up paintings?"

Murphy wasn't sure about anything. He studied her a moment, then looked away. It wasn't just that he watched her television show and knew her reputation as an art expert, but the job she'd done with the so-called Death Artist and Color Blind cases was on its way to becoming legendary, and he sort of hoped she'd want to work with him, turn him into a legend before it got too late. "I need to check out a couple of things— a disgruntled ex-museum patron, the Guerrilla Girls."

"The Guerrilla Girls? No way. They don't destroy works of art."

"Hey, they were in the museum the other night slapping stickers onto patrons' backs."

"That doesn't mean they stayed to slash a painting." A few years back Kate had written a piece about the group, gotten to know several of the women—artists and curators who donned gorilla masks and moonlighted as peaceful revolutionaries—and they had gained her respect. "Look, I know a few Guerrilla Girls—and it's just not their style."

"Maybe not, but I've still got to check it out."

"How? They're a secret society."

"You just said you knew some of them. How about setting up a meeting?"

Kate thought a moment, then reached for her cell phone. She chatted a few minutes and, when she got off, said, "One of the Guerrilla Girls is going to call me back—you'll get your meeting."

"Fast work," said Murphy.

"Figure it's easier for me to set it up than have you hunt them down like animals."

"Why not? They're g——"

"Please," said Kate, her hand out in front of Murphy's face. "Just don't say they're *gorillas.*"

Murphy swallowed the word. "You interested in seeing your de Kooning painting before it goes to the lab?"

Kate considered the question. There was still time to back out of this, cut her losses, go home, work on her book, kiss the baby. But she said, "Yes."

The Modernist Museum was the brainchild of a self-made multimillionaire who deplored New York's Museum of Modern Art after trying, and failing, to become part of its board of directors, and so took revenge by creating his own museum—enlisting his rich friends, Richard Rothstein among them, and convincing them to purchase and renovate the old factory just north of Canal Street, and only a block and a half from the Holland Tunnel—an unlikely home for the collection of art he frequently overbid MOMA to get for his institution. When he died of a heart attack less than six months ago, Kate was in the process of donating her paintings, dividing them among several New York museums, and gave the Modernist her de Kooning because she knew Richard would approve.

Closed since the attack on the painting, the museum had the air of a graveyard, the art on the walls like relics from a prior civilization that no one cared about, including Kate, who did not acknowledge them as she headed down a cool white hallway that stretched out in front of her like some exaggerated surrealist painting—or was it simply the way she was feeling?—her nerves on edge since she'd received the call. The idea that her painting had been attacked felt so . . . She rolled the idea around in her mind. *Personal.*

At the end of the hall was a pair of naked cut-off legs jutting out of the wall. Had Kate not known they were the work of the contemporary artist

Robert Gober, she would have been startled, but even with that knowledge they were disconcerting in the nearly deserted museum. She and Murphy stepped around them and headed down a concrete staircase to the basement storage area, where the de Kooning was draped with heavy opaque plastic, a guard pacing in front of it like a sentry.

Murphy lifted the plastic off and Kate was immediately sorry she had come. The sight of the slashed painting was much worse in person.

The museum's director, Colin Leader, whom Kate knew, though not well, nodded at her with appropriate solemnity. "Senseless," he said. "Absolutely senseless."

"Not usually," said Murphy, with a snap of his rubber band.

"What is that supposed to mean?" said Leader.

"Just that most people do things for a reason. They might seem insane to you and me, but they've got their reasons."

Kate thought about the psychopaths she had pursued. It was true—they fully believed what they did had purpose and reason.

"Conservation has viewed the painting," said Leader. "Work will begin almost immediately."

Kate eyed the flaps of hanging canvas. "Is it really possible to repair this?"

"They'll glue the painting onto new canvas, repaint the slashed areas. The cuts are fairly clean. I've been told the painting can be made to look the same, although—"

Like Humpty Dumpty, thought Kate—*it will never be the same.*

"Restoration will have to wait," said Murphy. "This is evidence. After the police finish with it you can have it back."

"And how long will that be, Detective?"

"I don't like to make promises," said Murphy. "It just makes people disappointed." He snapped his rubber band.

For effect, thought Kate. She threw him a look. The habit was beginning to get on her nerves.

Martin Dressler, curator of Twentieth-Century Painting and Sculpture, greeted the group with a knit brow and pursed lips. "I can't bear to look at it," he said, removing his horn-rimmed glasses dramatically, though

Kate knew his feelings were genuine—there were few people in the world who loved art the way Dressler did, another reason she had given the painting to this institution. When he took Kate's hand, she saw there were tears in his eyes.

"I'm sorry," he said, resetting his specs and running a hand through his thinning gray-brown hair. "I know you must feel worse than me. It's just such a devastating loss."

Yes, it was a loss, and Kate felt it, though she had lost too many people in her life and knew the difference between objects and human beings—no matter how great the object.

"If you no longer need me," said Leader, "I have a meeting."

"Just one thing," said Murphy. "I was wondering when the museum was planning a press release."

Leader pinched the bridge of his nose. "I was hoping we could keep it under wraps for a few days. At least until I have informed my board. I would hate for them to read about it before I tell them."

"A million-plus painting, destroyed," said Murphy. "That's news. I'd do that press release ASAP."

Leader nodded solemnly.

Dressler watched his boss leave before he spoke. "If our esteemed director thinks a little acid-free glue and a few dabs of oil paint can repair *this* . . ." He frowned. "And worrying about what the board will think, well . . . I don't mean to sound . . . it's just that museum politics always seem to come first. But I guess that's why I'm a curator and he's the director."

"Meaning?" Murphy kept his tone light, but he was watching the man.

"Nothing, really," said Dressler. "It's just that I love art—the first and foremost reason I became a curator."

"And the second?"

"Excuse me?"

"You said that was the *first* reason you became a curator. I was wondering about the second." Murphy tugged at his rubber band.

"Oh." Dressler almost smiled. "Because I was a lousy painter."

"You wanted to be an artist?"

"Well, yes. I went to art school, started out in studio art. I could draw and all, but I didn't have the drive, the need—not that everyone with the drive and need should be making paintings, if you get my drift." The curator rolled his eyes. "Eventually, I realized it was enough for me to simply be around art. And in this job I get to know the artists, choose paintings for the museum, handle great artworks—and that's as good as it gets." He eyed the destroyed painting and his face sagged. "Sometimes."

"Ever get any hate mail?" asked Murphy.

Dressler considered the question. "The last time was for a show of Picasso's erotic etchings. Some people found the show offensive. Several even canceled their museum membership. Good riddance, I say."

"What about the Guerrilla Girls?"

Kate turned away from the slashed de Kooning painting to give Murphy another look.

"What about them?" asked Dressler.

"They ever bother you?"

"Not really. I guess a few of them were at the opening, incognito, if that's what you mean?" He grinned. "Funny, isn't it? I mean, the Guerrilla Girls are incognito *without* their masks. But I can't see *them* doing *this*." Dressler glanced back at the destroyed painting and seemed to remember something. "You know, there was this one odd thing, but I don't think . . ."

"What's that?" asked Kate.

"It's nothing, really, certainly not a threat or hate mail. Just that I received a curious little painting about a week ago. I don't think it means anything, but . . . it has a fragment of this painting, the de Kooning—or something quite like it—replicated in it."

"For a show you're curating?" Kate asked.

"No. This was entirely unsolicited. That's what made it odd. And there was nothing enclosed with it—no announcement, no artist bio, nothing."

"You still got it?" asked Murphy.

"It's back in my office," said Dressler. "Follow me."

CHAPTER 4

Kate and Murphy regarded the painting, which lay faceup on the curator's desk.

"You see. There." Dressler pointed it out. "Right at the top. Like I said, it's not quite your de Kooning, but a kind of variation."

"Yes," said Kate, taking it in, trying to make sense of it, thinking it did, indeed, have a resemblance to her de Kooning.

"Some artist thinking postmodernism is new," said Dressler. "Putting all sorts of art imagery together, willy-nilly. Lots of artists were doing this in the eighties—but the idea's gotten a bit stale."

"And nothing accompanied this?" asked Murphy.

"No," said Dressler, "absolutely nothing."

"This other image," said Kate, "at the bottom. It looks very much like a Franz Kline painting."

"Yes," said the curator. "A bit generic-looking, but I agree." He straightened up, his eyes widening. "Good grief! We have a Kline in the museum—two, in fact. Do you think—" He did not wait for Kate or Murphy to respond, immediately going for a museum phone. "Connect me to the guard in American Post-War Abstraction." He waited a moment. "This is Mr. Dressler. Is everything all right in there? With the paintings, the Franz Klines, in particular—the large black-and-white paintings on the west wall." Dressler let out a breath as he replaced the phone. "Guard says all is well with the Kline paintings."

"Look, Mr. Dressler, I don't think we should go off on some conspiracy theory," said Murphy. "This painting you received might not mean a damn thing. But for safety's sake, maybe you should take those Franz Kline paintings off display for a couple of weeks."

"I'll have to speak with Colin," said Dressler, "but, yes, it makes sense to be prudent."

Murphy glanced back at the small black-and-white painting on the curator's desk. "So why did you keep it?"

"Excuse me?"

"This painting. Why'd you hang on to it?"

"Oh." Dressler seemed to be thinking the answer through. "Well, I'm a curator, Detective, an art lover. I couldn't just throw it away, could I?"

"But a minute ago you referred to it as *stale*."

"Did I?" Another pause. "Truthfully, I don't know. I just set it aside, and . . . forgot about it."

"You have any glassine I can wrap around it?"

Dressler produced a piece of the translucent acid-free paper that was used to protect artwork and Murphy laid it on top of the painting. "Think we'll take this, if that's all right with you."

"Oh, fine," said Dressler, drumming his nails along the edge of the desk. "Absolutely fine."

Kate's cell phone was ringing as they stepped out of the museum. She listened a moment, cupped her hand over the mouthpiece, and turned to Murphy. "You still want that meeting with the Guerrilla Girls?"

"Sure. When?"

Kate made a quick survey of the neighborhood, then spoke into her phone. "There's a coffee shop right across the street from the Modernist Museum, that okay?" She turned to Murphy and said, "How about right now?"

The coffee shop was the usual Greek affair, only a quarter of the tables occupied, the lunch-hour rush over, several of the waiters leaning on the counter, bored.

Kate and Murphy had just settled into a red vinyl booth with a clear view of the street when a black van pulled to the curb and two women got out. Well, maybe they were women, one could not be absolutely certain with their bulky black jackets and heads completely encased in rubber gorilla masks.

As they came through the door, the few patrons swiveled in their direction, and the bored waiters did double takes.

The Guerrilla Girls slid into the booth, facing Kate and Murphy.

"Thanks for coming," said Kate. "You're both looking gorgeous."

"You wouldn't consider taking off those masks?" asked Murphy.

"I asked them to come," said Kate. "I don't see why their identities matter."

Murphy let it go—for the moment—watched as the women shed their jackets. They were both in black tees, slender feminine arms exposed, one woman in tight hip-hugger jeans, the other in a short black mini and fishnet stockings, the contrast with their gorilla masks somewhat disconcerting.

"Call me Frida Kahlo," said the one in fishnets.

"Georgia O'Keeffe," said the other.

Kate smiled. She enjoyed the fact that the Guerrilla Girls used the names of dead women artists, something that brought to mind the various roles women had played in the history of art. But she was also aware of why they needed to remain anonymous—to protect themselves from art world retribution. She was certain they had agreed to the meeting to defend any slander against their group.

"Okay," said Murphy. "Here's the deal. A painting was destroyed at the Modernist Museum last night and—"

"And you think *we* did that?"

"Well, a few of your Guerrilla Girls were slapping stickers onto patrons' backs during the opening."

"Stickers are one thing, Detective. But we do *not* destroy paintings. We're artists, not vandals."

"So you admit that someone—some Guerrilla Girls—were inside, at the opening?"

"I admit nothing," said the Frida Kahlo. "But I guess it's possible. That show is a scandal. There are—what? Two women in it—out of forty! It's an outrage."

"That show deserves one of our special awards," said the Georgia O'Keeffe.

"Awards?" Murphy was staring at the women, trying to see through the eye slits in their masks, but it wasn't possible.

"Yeah. Maybe our Norman Mailer Award for Sensitivity to Issues of Gender Equality. We've bestowed that more than once. You ever hear of Brice Marden?"

"Of course," said Kate. "One of the art world's superstars."

"And an award winner for his sensitivity, too," said the Frida Kahlo, shaking her gorilla-hooded head. "He once said in an interview that he wasn't sure it was a good thing for him to be represented by a woman art dealer. Can you believe that? That man is lucky we *don't* do violence."

Kate almost laughed. She liked the way these women went about things, with humor and spunk.

"Listen," said the Georgia O'Keeffe, "we do posters, letter-writing campaigns, billboards, magazine spreads, occasional picketing, but that's it. Our aim is to get more women and artists of color into exhibitions. We're about inclusion, not exclusion."

Murphy asked, "So how many Guerrilla Girls are out there?"

The two gorilla heads looked at each other.

"Have no idea," said one.

"Could be hundreds," said the other. "Probably thousands."

Murphy figured they knew pretty much who was and who was not part of their secret society. "You have meetings, don't you?"

"Yeah, like about every twenty-eight days. Once a month, you know."

Murphy looked baffled. Kate leaned toward him and said, "Menstrual cycles."

He blushed and spoke quickly. "And you've got a newsletter, right?"

"*Hot Flashes*," said Georgia, fanning herself. "Fact is, I'm having one right now. These masks are suffocating."

Kate stifled a laugh.

"So you have meetings and a newsletter," said Murphy, "but you don't know how many of you exist?"

"I'm sure you can get a hold of the mailing list, Detective, and persecute the thousands of women—and men—who receive it," said Frida.

"Look," said Murphy, winding the rubber band around and around his wrist. "I'm not trying to persecute anyone. I'm just trying to get some truth."

"You want truth?" Frida leaned forward, her gorilla mask only inches from Murphy's face. "Until the Guerrilla Girls started to make the truth public, there were almost no women artists represented by the most influential art galleries anywhere."

"Or included in museum shows," Georgia chimed in. "In 1985, the Museum of Modern Art had a show, An International Survey of Painting and Sculpture, and the curator, a man, said that the work represented the most significant artists in the world. There were one hundred and sixty-nine artists. And only thirteen of them were women."

"And nearly all of them white," added Frida before Murphy could respond. "And you know what that curator said? He said any artist who was *not* in the show should rethink '*his* career.' Now that's what I call *balls!*"

"If I had 'em I'd be king," said Kate.

"Right on," said Frida.

Murphy shot Kate a look and sighed. "Here's the thing—someone got inside the museum and destroyed a painting."

"Like I said, Detective, Guerrilla Girls don't do that." Georgia looked at Frida. "I think this meeting is over."

"Hold on," said Kate. "Detective Murphy is not accusing you, or any of the Guerrilla Girls. It's just that it appears some of your members were inside the museum during the opening."

"And you think that makes them guilty of defacing artwork?"

"No, not at all," said Kate. "I was just thinking maybe someone saw something odd or unusual."

"Nothing odd or unusual about that show," said Frida. "Like most, it was all *men*. But I'll ask around, see if anyone noticed anything." She tugged at her fishnets. "But I'm telling you again—a Guerrilla Girl would not do anything like that. It's just not our thing."

"You can't control all of your members," said Murphy. "Hell, you just admitted you don't even know who half of them are. Maybe one of the Guerrilla Girls went *ape*." He sneered a smile.

"How about . . . went *bananas*?" Frida suggested, not allowing his comment to get to her.

"Touché," said Murphy flatly. "But you get my point. Someone could have decided to do something the group does not sanction, like take all this anti-male stuff a step further."

"We are not *anti-male*, Detective." Frida Kahlo's voice went strident. "We are simply trying to amend art history in favor of the women who have been left out."

"Well," said Murphy. "Destroying a painting by one of America's most famous and successful male artists might help tip that scale, now wouldn't it?"

"I'm not sure that was fair," said Kate once the Guerrilla Girls had taken off in their van and she and Murphy were out on the street. "There's not a shred of evidence that the Guerrilla Girls were involved in this."

"All I know is they were inside the museum and protesting the exhibition."

"The group has been in existence for twenty years without a single violent act."

"Always a first time," said Murphy. "Look, I'm not attacking the Guerrilla Girls as a group. But all you need is one lunatic."

Kate knew he could be right, but didn't feel like admitting it. She switched back to the small black-and-white painting, staring at it through the transparent glassine. "So there's a fragment of a de Kooning painting—or a *sort* of de Kooning—and of a Franz Kline painting, two of America's greatest abstract expressionist painters. But these other images . . ." She tapped her lip. "I don't know how they relate."

"It's worth taking to the lab, see what they can turn up. Obviously, it's no good for prints anymore, but—"

"You know," said Kate, "since it's already contaminated, it can go to the lab later. But right now, I have a better idea."

CHAPTER 5

The Delano-Sharfstein Gallery, in a turn-of-the-century town house, was a quiet oasis of refinement sandwiched between the high-priced Calvin Klein and Giorgio Armani shops on upper Madison Avenue. Unlike so many art galleries that were streamlined and pristine, Delano-Sharfstein had retained its original circular staircase, inlaid floors, ornate plaster ceilings, and woodwork that seemed to emit the scent of old money, all of which had come by way of the Delano half, Mert Sharfstein's former partner, who had died several years earlier. Sharfstein, meanwhile hailed from the wrong side of the Dayton, Ohio, tracks, though one would never guess it—his suits were Savile Row, his shoes Italian leather, his elocution pure Cary Grant.

Sharfstein had been a mentor to Kate when she'd gone back to earn her Ph.D., and their friendship had included Richard's working with him to acquire several important artworks. Sharfstein catered to the very very rich, though he welcomed anyone with style, wit, class, or good looks.

Taking note of his staff, Kate thought any one of the young men and women could have stepped out of an Abercrombie & Fitch catalog—all of them scrubbed American beauties. Years ago, Kate had accused Mert of discriminating against the homely, and he'd snapped back: "No one, *no one*, buys from the ugly!"

Sharfstein welcomed Kate with a hug, then turned and grasped Murphy's hand. "Ah, the handsome Detective Murphy, it's been too long."

"What?" Kate glanced from Sharfstein to Murphy. "You two know each other?"

"Indeed," said Sharfstein. "Montgomery has, on occasion, sought out my expertise."

Kate shot Murphy a look.

"Hey—" He plucked his rubber band. "You didn't ask."

"Art police," said Sharfstein. "What a concept. Now if I were running the squad, I'd send you fellows out to artists' studios, take away paints and supplies from the bad ones, and slap all those nouveau impostors with hefty fines."

"I seem to recall the Nazis did something like that," said Kate.

Sharfstein dismissed her comment with a wave of his hand and led them into his office—a large room outfitted like a pasha's treasure trove, paintings and antiques everywhere. "I imagine this visit is more than casual."

Murphy removed the glassine from the painting, and Sharfstein literally sniffed at the canvas. "It's not oil. I'd have to guess it's acrylic."

"That's easy enough to test," said Kate.

"So what's this about?" asked Sharfstein.

"If we told you, we'd have to kill you," said Kate.

"Funny," said Mert through pursed lips.

"You'll know when we know," said Murphy.

"Always a man of mystery," said Sharfstein, studying the painting.

Kate pointed out the de Kooning image, and asked the art dealer if he agreed.

"Yes." Sharfstein nodded. "Though it's more in

the *style* of de Kooning, one of his *Women* paintings, than any actual painting."

"And here"—Kate pointed at the bottom of the painting—"Franz Kline, yes?"

"Yes," said Sharfstein. "Though, again, a facsimile."

Kate plucked Sharfstein's magnifying glass off his desk and ran it over the painting's surface. "What's that?" asked Kate, finding a tiny isolated fragment.

"It doesn't look like much," said Sharfstein. "Maybe the beginning of the de Kooning figure? It could be something that was meant to be painted over."

Kate stared at it another moment and agreed. "So what do you make of the painting? In general, I mean?"

"Dreck," said Sharfstein.

"Oh, come on, Mert. It's got some charm. And there's been a lot of care put into it."

"Care does not mean quality, my dear."

"I didn't say it was the fucking *Mona Lisa*," said Kate. "Just that who-ever made it spent time doing it."

Sharfstein raised an eyebrow. "I sometimes wonder who brought you up, my dear."

"Wolves," said Kate. "But let's stick to the paintings."

"This postmodern stuff leaves me cold. Always a mishmash of styles rolled into one." Sharfstein stared at the painting, then looked up at Kate. "Hold on. This de Kooning fragment, it's rather like *your* de Kooning painting—the flashing eyes, the breasts, not *literally* your painting, or any real Willem de Kooning, but still—"

Exactly what she had thought. The man had an eye, and a memory, which was why Kate had suggested they show it to him.

"And the same is true of this Franz Kline—more an approximation than the real thing, and yet . . . it reminds me of one Kline in particu-lar . . . " Sharfstein gazed into space, then back at the picture. "*Downtown El.* That's the one."

The title touched something in the back of Kate's memory, but at the moment she was too preoccupied to get at it. "What do you think of Michael Jackson's face?" she asked.

"I try *not* to think about Michael Jackson's face," said Sharfstein.

"And what about the tunnel?" asked Murphy.

"Good question. Maybe some American precisionist painter—Sheeler or Demuth, but it doesn't look like them." Sharfstein shook his head. "It just looks like . . . a tunnel."

"What about the image above it?" asked Murphy. "The framed piece of cake?"

"I think it looks more like a wedge of cheese," said Kate, tapping her chin. "Cheese . . . hanging over a tunnel?"

"The cheese tunnel?" said Murphy.

"How about the Brie Tunnel?" said Sharfstein.

"Or the Dutch Tunnel," said Murphy.

"Dutch Tunnel," Kate repeated. "What about . . . the Holland Tunnel?" She thought a moment. "A facsimile of the de Kooning painting above the Holland Tunnel . . . Wait a minute—the Modernist Museum is only two blocks from the Holland Tunnel." Kate's adrenaline was pumping.

"What about this?" Murphy indicated the long white form. "It looks like a centipede or something."

"Or a dragon?" said Sharfstein.

"Maybe," said Kate. "A medieval one, out of an illustrated manuscript."

Not any illustrated manuscript I've ever seen," said Sharfstein. He reached for his magnifying glass and ran it over the length of the image, then put it aside and began rotating the painting this way and that, upside down and sideways. "Wait a minute . . ." He stood back, took a deep breath, and turned the painting again, this time horizontally. "This is no dragon," he said. "It's a map, a map of Long Island."

CHAPTER 6

Marci Starrett replaced the phone and joined her husband at the table, where they were sampling a fine sherry. "Kate's not coming," she said.

"That's too bad," said her husband. He had a pleasant, still-boyish face that would be hard to describe, regular features, eyes pale blue. "Nothing wrong, I hope."

"I don't really know, but I didn't want to push her."

The caterer and staff were busy preparing the usual hors d'oeuvres and finger foods in the kitchen; the household staff fluttering about, setting up small stations for eat and drink.

Marci Starrett refilled her husband's glass. She was an attractive woman, somewhere on the road between sixty and seventy, impeccably groomed.

Nicholas Starrett took a sip of the sherry and said, "Delicious." He glanced out at his backyard view—frost on the ground, a semi-frozen pond, rolling hills, a Hallmark winter scene that never failed to soothe him. "Coldest December I can remember on Long Island in a long time. We should have stayed in Palm Beach."

"We'll be going back in a few weeks, dear. I didn't want to stay away that long, especially from Kate. Not yet." Marci frowned. "I wish I could persuade her to come to Florida with us."

"Doubtful she would leave that baby."

Marci Starrett smiled. "It's done a world of good for her, hasn't it? Really, I've been so worried, but I think she's finally pulling through."

"Much of it thanks to you, my dear."

"Oh, Nicholas, that's absurd. I simply did what any friend would do."

Her husband knew this to be untrue. Marci had been an exceptional friend. He smiled at his wife, then shifted his glance to the latest addition to their impressive, ever-expanding art collection—a series of photographs by an artist who, a few years back, had gotten himself in a lot of trouble with a photo of Jesus Christ floating in urine. These new photos were large-scale Cibachrome morgue shots, horrifying, he thought, though his wife seemed entranced, and it had been her turn to choose the art, which was the way they worked it—something he liked, something she liked, something they both liked. And Marci hadn't much cared for his last choice, the Andrew Wyeth boating scene. Perhaps, he thought, she was getting back at him, poking fun at his conservative taste by choosing something outrageous. But that was fine. He adored his wife and just about everything else in his beautiful, flawless life.

"You don't like the new pictures," said Marci.

"They're fine, dear," he said.

"Oh. Speaking of pictures, there's something I have been meaning to show you." She excused herself and returned with a painting, black and white, on loose canvas. "What do you make of this?"

"Some artist's idea of a unusual exhibition announcement?"

"But it's an actual painting." Marci held it between her thumb and forefinger, then flipped the canvas around. "There's nothing on the back. A very odd announcement, if you ask me. It arrived yesterday in a plain brown envelope, no return address, no nothing."

"Maybe it's some sort of teaser." Nicholas Starrett sighed. He was not in the mood to look at some inane piece of art that had been sent to them. "I think it's quite annoying that anyone—galleries, artists—can simply get one's address off the Internet these days and send us anything."

"But look at this, darling." Marci Starrett jabbed a well-manicured index finger at the anonymous painting. "This is why I wanted to show it to you."

"What is it, dear?"

"*Look.*"

"Oh," he said.

"*Oh?* Is that all you can say?"

"What would you like me to say, dear?"

"Something more"—she waved a hand through the air—"emotional."

"Why would I want to get emotional?"

It was Marci Starrett's turn to sigh. She took in her husband's boyish face, the total lack of guile. Really, how could she be annoyed with him? He was right. It was silly to let such things get to you. "It's just that it looks very much like *our* painting, darling, our Franz Kline painting."

"Yes, dear, I see that."

"And you don't think that's odd?"

Nicholas Starrett considered the question. "Perhaps that's why it was sent to us. Some young artist doing art-about-art, including our painting, thinking we'd be interested in buying it."

"But we don't have to buy it, dear. It's been sent to us, free." Marci Starrett turned the painting to face her. "You know, I rather like it. I think I might even frame it."

"If you like, dear." Nicholas Starrett finished his glass of sherry and smiled.

Marci Starrett lay the painting aside and glanced at her watch. "Oh my, I'd better start preparing myself for the party."

CHAPTER 7

Kate shut her cell phone. Of course Marci had understood. She always did.

Kate pictured her friends Marci and Nicholas in their Water Mill home, the pond and manicured landscape that had helped to soothe her so many weekends over this past year. She stared through the taxicab's window, headlights of oncoming cars streaking across the glass. Winter days, she thought, way too short. She missed the sun, days at the beach with Richard.

Kate replayed her parting conversation with Detective Murphy.

You have any interest in seeing the Jackson Pollock painting I mentioned—the one that got cut up at that law firm?

She'd almost said yes, adrenaline still pumping from the dissection of that odd little painting, the way she'd always felt when she was on a case. But she was finished with that; she had a new family, and a baby, to think of—though she'd had to fight the part of her psyche that wanted to see it.

A phone call had saved her. José, one of her foundation kids, had been in a fight, fractured his arm, and she wanted to make sure he was all right.

But as the cab cut out of Central Park and headed uptown, she could not get the slashed de Kooning painting out of her mind.

———

The pills have taken effect. A half Hydrocodone, a pinch of Valium, just enough to take the edge off the pain, off the anxiety, too, while the mind remains clear. Everything is under control; the plan in order. Step two. Or was it three? A moment of doubt. *Three. Yes, three.* The actor takes a step forward, paintbrush poised like a microphone.

"I'd like to thank the ladies and gentlemen of the academy, my high school drama teacher, all the *little* people out there who have made this possible." A deep bow, a histrionic swipe at tears, the voice a high falsetto and saccharine sweet: "You like me, you really like me."

Another bow, followed by a shrieking laugh, high-pitched, almost out of control, that dissolves into a wheeze, then a gasp.

Okay, calm down. Calm down. Breathe. Breathe.

Eyes closed. The mind a blank white sheet.

There you go.

This is not the moment to lose control, just moments before the play begins. The lines have been rehearsed, everything perfectly planned— route, entry, where to hide, how to leave. A dry run last week, and no one took notice.

The cruel blindness of others. One can count on it the same way one can count on insensitive wisecracks or looks of shock or half-hidden laughs.

Fuckers.

Another deep breath. *No time to think about that now.*

Concentrate on the plan.

It's time to get ready.

The costume has been laid out, along with the necessary accessories. More than an hour to get it just right.

Now, go over the checklist.

Route. Check.

Gas tank full. Check.

Arrival time. Check.

Departure time. Hmm . . . variable. Check.

Gloves. Check.
What else?
A laugh.
The knife, of course.
Check.

José had already been released from the hospital, his arm—just a hairline fracture—set in one of those new plastic air casts, which he proudly displayed, explaining how he could take it off at night, and how he couldn't wait to show it to his friends.

They were sitting in the cramped kitchen of the Medinas' railroad flat, Kate sipping a cup of café con leche that Anita Medina had made for her. She had shooed her two daughters, José's younger sisters, out of the room, and a television was now blaring in the background.

"That one," said Mrs. Medina, standing over the stove, aiming a spatula at her thirteen-year-old son, "always looking for trouble." She was a pretty woman, probably no more than thirty-five, though her eyes were tired and old.

Kate glanced at José as she put her coffee cup down. She didn't know what to say. It was true, the kid was always in trouble, sassing his teachers, getting into fights; but a smart kid, too, IQ off the charts, and a talented musician. Still, the way he was going, the teachers in Let There Be a Future would not put up with him much longer. And Kate had seen what the program could do—offering a handful of kids special attention, less crowded classrooms, encouragement and preparation for college, if they wanted to go. For many, it had been the opportunity for a new life.

Kate had been hands-on since the first day she'd walked into one of the classrooms. Talk about timing. Just after her third miscarriage, tangled in the red tape of adoption, and here they were—dozens of kids who needed her help. It became her passion, dedicating herself to the program and the kids, and had given so much back—all those surrogate children, whom she loved.

"Tell him," Mrs. Medina said to Kate, "that he will be kicked out. Am I right?"

Kate tried to catch José's eye. She did not want to lecture him, but she didn't want him to blow his chance either.

José glanced up with piercing dark eyes that made him look a lot older, then shrugged. Kate pictured herself at his age—the Saint Anne's Catholic School uniform, plaid skirt that she'd hike up to become a mini, spending a half hour in the girls' room putting on the lipstick and mascara her father forbade her to wear, and that the nuns were forever scrubbing off.

"He runs wild when he should be the man of the house," said his mother.

Big job for a little boy, thought Kate, though she didn't say so.

"It is two years now since Enrique, his father, passed on." She sighed heavily. "It is not easy, but I do the best I can."

"I'm sure you do," said Kate, thinking about her own loss, how much easier it was for her, having some money, a nice place to live. She thought back to the Astoria row house where she'd grown up: single bed, the plain chest of drawers her mother had lined with brightly colored contact paper. Her mother—tall, like Kate, beautiful at one time; dead, by her own hand, before forty; and the last visit; the talk of shock treatments, which was both mysterious and terrifying to a twelve-year-old; all of it as clear as the cracks in the plaster wall she was now staring at.

She switched her gaze to José's cast. "How are you going to play the drums?"

"No problemo." José plucked a spoon and fork off the table and did a dazzling ninety-second set. He grinned, and Kate could not help but smile back, even though she wanted to shake him, to say, *You've been given a chance, don't fuck it up!*

Instead, she took the opportunity to tell José about Willie, a foundation graduate who had become like a son to her, who had grown up in a housing project and was now a famous artist selling his paintings and

traveling around the world, and about other kids who had made something of their lives. "You can do that, too—something special with your
music, if that's what you want."

"Trouble," said his mother. "That's what he wants."

Nola was hunched over her computer, books opened to color reproductions of paintings, spread out on the desk.

Kate lifted the long dreadlocks away from the young woman's cheek
and planted a kiss.

"Weren't you supposed to go to a party on Long Island?"

"Too tired. I bailed. I'll get all the gory details from my friend Blair
first thing in the morning, I guarantee it." Kate was referring to one of
her old society pals, one she did not see very often these days.

"I don't know how you can stand that woman."

"Oh, Blair's not so bad. Under that Chanel suit beats a heart of
gold—at least twenty-four karat."

Nola laughed.

"The baby sleeping?"

"Yeah. But I should get him up soon or he'll never sleep the night."

"I'll do it." Kate glanced over at Nola's art history books with a bit of
pride, her protégée following in her footsteps. She considered telling
her about the slashed de Kooning painting, but did not want to think
about it and deal with all of the requisite feelings, not now. "You eat anything?"

"Not for hours. I'm starved."

"I'll see what we have in the fridge, or order out. Anything you're
dying for?"

"Yeah. Food."

Kate headed down the hallway, glad to be home, though a sense of
foreboding clung to her. *Is it the destroyed de Kooning painting? Richard?
Thinking about my mother's suicide today?*

Perhaps her brain chemistry had changed. She'd read studies that claimed the brain chemistry of rape and torture victims actually altered, that they became programmed to expect the worst.

Kate shrugged off the bad feeling when she saw the baby. He'd hoisted himself up by the bars of his crib, was standing and grinning.

"What a big boy you are." Kate lifted him out and hugged him. A string of drool leaked from his lip onto her blouse.

"Lovely." She plucked a tissue from a nearby box and patted his mouth. He pulled back, let loose with a raspberry, more drool spattering her clothes.

"No spitting, sweetie," said Kate, carrying him into the kitchen while he kept up a steady stream of sputtering half words.

There wasn't much in the fridge other than baby food, and she wasn't in the mood for strained pears and pineapple, doubted Nola would be either. "Takeout," she said, giving the baby another squeeze. She could not believe the depth of feeling the child stirred in her.

She kissed his forehead, still fighting the sensation of dread that, no matter how hard she tried, would not go away. There was something she had seen today—other than her slashed de Kooning painting—that was still in her mind, waiting to be processed, but she couldn't get at it. *I'm just too tired*, she thought. *Let it go. Just let it go.*

CHAPTER 8

The house, a sprawling country manor, is nestled among tall naked trees and soft sloping hills, down a long drive with a gated entry to keep out unwanted cars—though it does not deter the lone pedestrian. There is no one checking names, no guards on duty.

The research has been scrupulous, the dry run only a week ago.

The couple, rich art collectors, are famous for their Friday-night dinner parties, a coveted invitation, though easy enough to crash—walk in, mumble a name they will never remember, the assumption being that one must have come as a guest of so-and-so. These sort of people would never cause a scene, never ask: *Do I know you?*

A manservant answers the door, white-haired, stoop-shouldered, a character out of an old MGM comedy of manners, the party under way, the late arrival premeditated, the hosts, across the room, huddled with a few guests.

Even better than planned, no need to give the old coot any name at all. "Went out for a smoke. Didn't want to disturb the others. Gross habit. I keep promising myself I'll quit."

The servant is distracted, keeping an eye on the hired help, the bartender and girls with trays, not part of the regular household staff and therefore, to him, not entirely trustworthy.

The hallway is wide, a few steps down into the first of several living rooms, one emptying into the other, art everywhere—covering walls, on pedestals, hanging from the ceiling.

Eyes narrowed, taking it all in, remembering the layout, where the prize is to be found. But it can wait; patience, always a virtue.

The guests are almost as artfully arranged as the paintings—small clots of privileged natives in beautifully tailored, mostly black clothes.

A thought—*Kill them all*—while crossing the room, head down, with an attitude of *I belong here*; spots a group, watches them gesture and laugh, all the confidence they display. *The fucking in crowd.*

Okay, act the part. Get closer. But not too close.

"The show at Art Specific, you must have heard about it—photographs, life-size, black and white, supersharp focus. Old people. Nudes. Bodies like relief maps. Flesh like crinolines. I don't know how the photographer ever convinced them to shed their clothes. I know I wouldn't." This from the New York socialite Blair Sumner.

"Oh, I would," says a young man beside her, paint under his fingernails. "In fact, I already did. Took it all off for that guy who photographs hundreds, thousands of people clustered together, nude. You know, Spencer Tunick. The guy's a genius. I was one of, oh, I don't know, a few hundred men and women, standing stark naked in Grand Central Station. What a high. All that flesh. Tunick goes all over the world convincing people to participate—London, Barcelona, Helsinki."

"Helsinki? Now that must have a been *chilling* affair," says Blair with a smile.

The young man doesn't seem to get the joke. He barrels ahead. "After you've seen the first thirty or forty naked bodies, all those tits and asses and cocks and balls, you stop being shocked." The artist turns and looks at the people around him, one at a time. "Imagine. All of us. Right now. Naked. No secrets. Everyone instantly equal."

"Some more equal than others," says a man in a houndstooth jacket.

"Seriously," says the one with paint under his nails, the artist. "No clothes, no labels to hide behind."

Blair says, "I'll keep my labels in place, thank you very much."

The hostess, overhearing, steps in, places her well-manicured hand on the arm of the man with paint under his nails, and with her long tapered fingers and blood-red nails gives him the gentlest squeeze. She likes to invite a few artists to her gatherings, the more controversial the better, just to make sure the crowd does not get too sleepy. "I think it best we keep our clothes on," she says, and laughs.

A kind woman, maybe.

The host ambles over. "What's all this about shedding our clothes?" His boyish face is lit up by a third martini. "Is Jeremy suggesting we strip?" He laughs, one of those teeth-clenched laughs through the back of his nose.

The hostess, the woman with blood-red nails, kisses him on the cheek. *The husband, right. The two of them, owners of the prize.*

"Are those new?" Blair gestures toward a series of large-scale color photographs.

"Yes," says the hostess. "Gorgeous, aren't they?"

"A bit ghoulish," says the man in the houndstooth jacket.

"Please say that again," says the host, looking at his wife, but smiling.

"I *heard* him, Nicholas." She pats his cheek affectionately. "Nicholas doesn't like them, but it was my turn."

"Are they actual morgue shots?" asks Blair.

The intruder, standing apart, gazes up at these grotesque pictures of the dead, and feels something between a chill and a thrill.

"Andres Serrano," says the artist, showing off his knowledge. "He's the *Piss Christ* guy."

"Do you think an artist has to be a provocateur to be important these days?" asks Blair.

"Yes." "No." The host and hostess reply at exactly the same moment, and laugh, then the hostess turns to Blair and asks, "How is Kate?"

Kate?

"Lazy," says Blair. "I'm afraid I couldn't persuade her to make the trip tonight."

"We shouldn't push her," says the hostess. "It can't be easy. She and Richard were such a close couple."

Yes, a kind woman.

"You coddle her," says Blair. "Me, I'm a graduate of the kick-in-the-pants school."

Now that one is a real bitch.

"Give her time," says the hostess.

The intruder turns away—*Keep walking, pretend you belong here*—heads down another flight of stairs that leads into the large room, almost like a museum or gallery. Three walls of perfectly lit paintings, a wall of glass looking out onto that picture-postcard winter landscape, a few of the guests admiring the art: a Warhol *Mao*, a late Picasso, a Plexiglas sculpture suspended by an almost invisible wire from the ceiling, and, on a wall by itself, a large black-and-white painting.

Bingo!

"Franz Kline," says a man, who whispers to the woman beside him. "I heard they paid a small fortune for it."

"No other way you can get your hands on a painting like this," says the woman. "Unless you steal it!"

They do not acknowledge the intruder, who stands several feet away from them gazing at the painting.

Franz Kline. One of the New York School's major players, dead at the age of fifty-two, a brief, powerful career that is about to take another hit, the painting's bold broad brush strokes already suggesting ways to slash it.

But not yet.

The intruder slips away, a swift turn through another door, down another staircase, into the basement, that perfect hiding place—a storage closet, cartons stacked up, light fixtures, cleaning products, folding chairs, the back part of it an el.

Wait. Be patient. Breathe.

Again: *Wait. Be patient. Breathe.*

A mantra. Repeated. Over and over.

1 A.M.

No longer any noise from above.

Hospital-type booties, latex gloves, on. A rag lifted from among the cleaning products to wipe down the railing as the intruder heads upstairs.

The room with the Franz Kline painting is empty now, no sign there has been a party, everything in order, cleaned up, the moon shimmering through the wall of glass, just enough light to work by.

Exacto knife out, poised in front of the painting, then in.

A fierce tug through sixty-year-old canvas and paint, up, then down. Flakes of cheap house paint, the kind Kline preferred, crack off and flutter to the floor.

It sends shivers through the body, this defiling of great art, so pleasurable.

Suddenly light appears from above. Nicholas Starrett, in pajamas and slippers, at the top of the stairs.

"What the— My God—are you mad!? This is a Franz Kline. A Franz Kline! One of the greats, a masterpiece, worth millions—" He hurries down the staircase, fists out in front of him, trembling with rage.

Not the plan. Not the plan. But there is no time to think. A trapped animal's reaction: a jab into the man's gut—up, then down. And, beneath the anxiety, there is an involuntary shudder of something distinctly pleasurable in the loins.

Nicholas Starrett's flesh surrenders more easily than the Kline canvas. He grabs his belly as blood spills through his fingers, soaks his silky pajamas. His pale blue eyes open wide with shock as he stumbles forward into the wrecked painting and drops to the floor.

The car, just off the road in a thicket of trees, has been waiting, winter coat still inside, tossed onto the back of the driver's seat.

Key in the ignition, shivering, heart beating fast.

Oh, God. What happened? Images stutter through the mind like a silent movie.

The alarm, which has gone off as the back door was opened, shrieks in the distance like a scream directly inside the brain. There is no time to think, no time to answer questions.

For a moment the mask cracks, and memories, like maggots, bloom in the wound.

Where the fuck are the pills?

A vial retrieved from a pocket, a pill swallowed without water.

Head back. A deep breath.

With gloved, shaking fingers, the ignition key is turned, foot heavy on the accelerator, the car jerks forward.

But as the nerves settle, thoughts clarify. *Was it really so wrong? After all, isn't the owner, the possessor, as guilty as the artist?*

A reasonable argument: *Punishment for adoration.*

Hands steadier now, mind clearing, strength drawn from a realization: *I am capable of doing anything.*

A smile twists the lips, while the mind thinks it through: *This changes nothing. The plan is still the plan. The sequence still in order.*

True, this particular act was meant to be saved for last. Though, to be honest, there was a fear of not being up to the task. And now, there is nothing to worry about.

Alternating hands on the steering wheel, a momentary struggle tugging off bloody gloves, then one hand drops to the edge of the waistband. Another shiver of pleasure.

The actor has to admit it was . . . something: The piercing of flesh so much more thrilling than slicing through canvas. Another shudder.

Really, it's better this way. This simply adds to the plan, gives it more depth and meaning. It's a role to be savored and played . . . again. And again.

Practice makes perfect. Isn't that what they say?

"Help me." He looked down at his torso and belly, his guts spilling out.

She reached out, shivering, but it was too late.

Somewhere, someone was whistling a familiar pop song, *"Smooth Criminal,"* and there were other people there now, cops, bent over the body, a modern-day pietà.

No, no. This can't be.

The whistling had stopped, though the song continued to play inside her head. It was singing, wasn't it? Or was it a cry—or a scream? Where was it coming from? Angels? That's what it sounded like. Yes, there they were, peeking out from between painted clouds in a painted sky, the scene black and white, like the painting from the museum, which was suddenly undulating before her eyes, the de Kooning fragment breaking free of the canvas, and that song starting up again and Michael Jackson's painted face, shimmering, lips not moving, but singing.

But it wasn't singing, was it?

It was crying.

Crying.

Kate awoke with a start and switched on the lamp. She was breathing hard, her nightgown sticking to her body.

Crying. The baby.

She pulled herself out of bed. The dream—Richard's body at the end of that dark alley, cops huddled over it, all mixed up with that slashed painting—still playing in her mind.

Nola was in the baby's room when she got there, agitated, the baby in her arms. "He's been crying for fifteen minutes. I changed him and tried a bottle, but he won't stop."

Kate took hold of the baby. "Shhh . . ." She whispered into his ear. Then to Nola: "Go to sleep, honey. You have class in the morning. It's okay, I'll get him back to sleep."

"You sure?"

Kate nodded and rocked the baby. She liked having him in her arms. She touched her lips to his forehead to see if he was warm, but he felt normal. She wondered if he'd had a bad dream, as she had.

She walked the baby to the far end of the loft and back, bare feet padding on wooden floors, unconsciously humming a bit of the song from her dream.

Finally, the baby fell asleep. Kate put her face against his cheek, breathed in his fresh smell, then laid him into his crib, that damn painting still idling in her brain—Michael Jackson's face, and the fragment of her slashed de Kooning, the tunnel, and the Franz Kline fragment that looked so familiar, though she could not figure out why.

CHAPTER 9

Nola was busy cramming books into her backpack with one arm, balancing the squirming baby in the other.

Kate scooped the infant out of her grip, his chubby legs doing a jig. "Easy there, tiger." She settled the baby into his high chair, then stirred applesauce into powderlike cereal.

"I don't know where Diane is."

"I'm sure she'll be here soon. Go to class. I've got it covered."

"Thanks." Nola kissed the baby, then Kate.

When Nola had given birth, Kate had made her a promise—that she would make it possible for Nola to complete her studies and earn her degree. And she'd meant it. She would make sure Nola earned that master's in art history and go for a Ph.D., if she wanted one. The truth? Kate loved being depended upon, feeling as if the child sort of belonged to them both.

She was saying, "Yum-yum," offering the toddler spoonfuls of the applesauce cereal mix, when the phone rang. She hooked the receiver between her shoulder and ear and continued to feed him.

It was her friend Blair. No doubt ready to recount every bit of gossip about the party. Kate readied to have her ear bent for a good half hour.

"I have some bad news," said Blair. "It's about last night . . ."

Kate felt her muscles tense.

"Nicholas," said Blair. "He's . . ."

"What?"

"He's . . . been killed."

"Oh my God—" Kate dropped the spoon, goop spattering her and the baby, who laughed.

"Sometime after the party. A break-in, apparently." Blair's voice was shaky. "Nicholas must have interrupted them. The police just called me. They're questioning everyone who was at the party."

Kate was stunned, speechless.

"Kate. Did you hear me?"

"Yes, I—" Kate stared at the sweet-faced baby in front of her, trying to make sense of the news. *Nicholas Starrett. Dead.* "Is Marci all right?"

"Yes, fine. Unharmed, I mean. She's here, in town."

Images were flooding Kate's mind, making it difficult to concentrate.

"Kate. Are you there?"

"Yes. I'll speak to you later, Blair. I've got to call Marci."

The nanny was calling from the hallway, and Kate met her halfway, kissed the baby's cheek, and handed him over without speaking.

Kate might have had trouble recognizing the old woman seated on the couch were it not the Starretts' plush Park Avenue apartment. The usually elegant, perfectly clothed and coiffed Marci Starrett appeared to have aged ten years overnight.

Was this how I looked when Richard died?

Kate did not want to turn this into her tragedy, but could not separate it.

Marci Starrett looked up at her and started crying, and Kate embraced her. By the time the woman lifted her head from her shoulder, Kate's sweater was wet through.

"Thank God my sister could drive me in. The police wanted me to stay out there, but I just couldn't. I had to get away. You understand, don't you?"

Kate understood perfectly. She had sold the Central Park West apartment and the house she and Richard shared in East Hampton as soon as she was able—the thought of staying in them, memories everywhere she looked, impossible.

"I just—" Marci grasped Kate's hand. "I'm not sure I can—" She swallowed and tried to catch her breath. "It seems impossible. I mean, where is Nicholas when I need him so much?"

It was the exact sentiment Kate had felt at Richard's funeral—that the person she needed most in the world was not there for her.

"The painting, a stupid painting."

"The painting? What do you mean?"

Marci blew her nose into a tissue. "The Franz Kline, the one we bought a few months ago, it . . . this, this person was destroying it, and—"

"Your Kline painting?"

"Yes." Marci drew a long breath. "*Downtown El.*"

Downtown El. The black-and-white painting, the fragment of the Kline in it, flashed in Kate's mind. *Oh my God. Of course!* What she had been trying to remember. How could she possibly have missed it? Was she so unconscious, so self-involved these days that she wasn't capable of seeing anything?

There were questions buzzing in Kate's brain, but Marci was sobbing again, her thin shoulders quaking.

Kate's recurring nightmare was starting up again, too, flickering like a movie—Richard's broken body, and that dark alleyway closing around her, suffocating her. She put her arm around Marci, needing the human contact almost as much as her friend. The woman felt frail, breakable.

Marci looked up at her with red, swollen eyes. "How did you do it, Kate? How did you . . . recover?"

It took Kate a moment to understand the question, and then another to find her voice. "I don't know, Marci. I'm still . . . figuring it out."

Marci Starrett looked directly into Kate's eyes. She spoke softly, but with an urgency that unnerved her. "You won't let whoever did this get away with it, will you?" Her fingers tightened on Kate's wrist. "You can help the police, I know you can."

Kate did not answer. She was thinking about Nicholas Starrett being murdered and the painting—that damn Franz Kline painting. How could she have failed to see it, to connect the picture to her friends? If only she had.

The morning, which had started out clear, had turned overcast, low clouds hugging the tops of Manhattan skyscrapers. Kate had left her Chelsea loft so quickly that morning, she'd forgotten gloves and scarf, but barely felt the cold now as she headed along Park Avenue.

She had not been lying to Marci when she said she was still figuring it out—Richard's death, and how to live her life. Yes, she had moved and taken in Nola and the baby—all of it new and exciting and filled with promise. But still, her life, all of it, felt like a work in progress. So often it would simply overtake her, a feeling of utter disbelief that she was a widow; and though she had seen her husband's body on a steel slab in the morgue, had shoveled dirt onto his coffin, she still could not grasp the fact that he was dead, and never coming back.

How did you recover, Kate?

The truth? She's thrown herself into her work. And right now, as she slowly took in the broken Manhattan skyline, she realized she would do it again.

She'd made the decision back at Marci Starrett's apartment, seeing her friend's pain, feeling it, too, and the way it had stirred up her own bad memories. But it was more than that, and she knew it.

It was guilt.

If only she had recognized that painting. Put two and two together. It all could have been different.

Damn. Kate flagged down a taxi and folded herself into the backseat. She gave the driver the address and took a deep breath, considering what she was about to do.

CHAPTER 10

One Police Plaza.

Office of Clare Tapell, Chief of Police.

Kate looked past files and folders, locked eyes with her old Astoria boss, years of history between them; they did not have to say much to understand each other.

Tapell was pacing. "You sure you want to do this? So soon after—"

Kate cut her off. "I'll stick with the paintings, and with Murphy," she said. "Homicide can do their thing. Murphy and I will give them anything we find."

Whom was she trying to kid? It was a simple fact: Find the person who slashed the painting, you found a killer.

"Nicholas Starrett's homicide belongs to Suffolk," said Tapell. "They're in with Brown and Perlmutter right now."

Kate pictured Floyd Brown and Nicky Perlmutter, Brown the head of Manhattan's elite Homicide Squad, Perlmutter a detective under him. They'd both worked Richard's case.

"The Starretts spend half the year in the city. Suffolk wants the NYPD to work with them." Tapell let out a sigh. "But I can't spare the manpower. I told Brown to put them off."

"Well, I work for free," said Kate. "I can assist Murphy, help him gain entry with a few art experts."

"Murphy's been doing this for some time. He can handle it," said Tapell, though she knew he could use the help, the recent budget cuts having reduced the Art Squad to a one-man department, his former partner now assisting the understaffed Robbery Division.

Kate took in her former boss, dark eyes, dark skin, no makeup other than lipstick, the rigid posture that summed up her personality. "Look, Clare. The NYPD has called on me twice—twice—in the past two years."

"I believe it was *you* who called us," said Tapell.

"The first time, yes." The image of the dead girl flashed across Kate's mind. "But not the last time, with the Color Blind case. Brown came to me, remember? And I broke the case—actually, if I remember correctly, both cases." She let that sink in. There were other things she knew about Clare Tapell, a few less than squeaky-clean deals her old boss had made to get where she was, but she didn't think it was necessary to remind her—they both knew. "You owe me this one."

Tapell stopped pacing. "I thought you liked your civilian life."

"Nicholas Starrett was a friend."

Tapell sagged into the leather chair behind her desk. She'd known Kate for twenty years, knew she would not stop pushing until she got what she wanted. She'd known Richard, too, and in her own way was grieving for him. "I think you're crazy, but if it's okay with Murphy—" She sighed. "I'll go along." She knew that cops did not like ex-cops, civilians, as far as they were concerned, meddling in their cases. But Kate had proved herself, that much was fact. "But it's in no way official. Unless you want to give up your writing and TV show and be fully reinstated." Tapell raised an eyebrow, making the question both serious and ironic.

"I'll stick with unofficial," said Kate.

Floyd Brown massaged his temples, a headache setting in. With a deskful of his own cases, the last thing he needed was to deal with an out-of-town homicide.

Suffolk County detective Gene Fuggal seemed not to hear him. "All I'm saying is this Starrett fellow lived in Manhattan—"

"But he died in East Hampton, Detective."

"Water Mill," Fuggal corrected.

The same back-and-forth had been going on for a half hour. "Still not our jurisdiction." Brown signaled Perlmutter with his eyes: *Help me out here.*

"Tell you what," said Perlmutter, rising out of his chair to his full six feet four inches. "Anything we get, we'll be sure to give you a call."

"You know, the wife's back here, in Manhattan. Tried to stop her, but she bolted."

"Doesn't really matter," said Brown. "Unless she killed her husband."

Fuggal scratched his nearly bald head. "Well, you know what they say—wife dies, look at the husband, and vice versa."

Brown puffed air out the side of his mouth. "We'll talk to Mrs. Starrett. Like Detective Perlmutter said, anything we get, we'll give a holler."

"Could have been for hire," said Fuggal.

Brown looked at the short, overweight cop, figured he didn't have a lot to do on the east end of Long Island—couple of unsolved murders that they'd probably never solve; the last Brown had read about was a big scandal having to do with some rich guy organizing a police sting to arrest a bunch of guys who were hooking up in the parking lot beside the thirty-million-dollar property he'd bought without knowing it was the area's major gay pick-up scene.

"Think you've been watching one too many *Sopranos* episodes," he said. The Starretts, Brown knew, were big New York money, philanthropists who gave to practically every institution in the city—arts foundations, hospitals, the New York Public Library. According to his chief, who had asked him to stay away from the case, the mayor wouldn't take kindly to Marci Starrett being harassed. "Seems more like a case of bad timing. Someone slicing up their painting, the vic interrupting."

"Maybe," said Fuggal, continuing to scratch his scalp, which was turning pinkish red. "I've had my best men examine the crime scene.

Called in detectives from the surrounding towns as well to have a look. Don't you worry, Chief Brown, I'm giving this priority."

"Oh," said Brown. "Real good." He knew what that meant: *Contamination*. Brown had lost count of the times it had turned out that items and evidence discovered at a crime scene—cigarette butts, footprints and fingerprints—turned out to have been left by the cops who had traipsed through it. Brown could just about picture the scene by now—a forensic pathologist's nightmare. He gave Nicky Perlmutter a look.

Perlmutter took the Suffolk cop by the arm and led him toward the door. "We'll be in touch."

Detective Monty Murphy had already gotten the call from Chief Tapell, and was now attempting to act nonchalant about having McKinnon on board.

He still hadn't shaved, and Kate thought his thick black hair looked even more rumpled this morning. He rubbed at his eyes.

"Tired?" she asked, settling into a chair.

"Insomnia," he said, which he blamed on his wife, his high school sweetheart, who had left him a year and a half ago for some high-finance guy, taking their eleven-year-old daughter along with her, the trio now living in the guy's Southampton mansion—though this was not entirely true. The insomnia had started a couple of years earlier.

"Sleep's overrated," said Kate, meaning it as a joke; but from the look on Murphy's face she could see she'd drawn attention to her situation.

"Hey, listen," said Murphy, swiping at his mess of hair. "I've been meaning to say I'm sorry about your—"

"Forget it," she said, cutting him off. "So, what do you have on the Starrett case?"

He handed her a folder. "Jacket on the painting. *Only*. The murder is somebody else's department."

"So they tell me." Kate slid the pictures out of the folder, a half dozen photos of the slashed Kline—that damn painting she should have recognized right away, what she had been trying to get at from the moment she'd seen the odd little black-and-white painting, and later, with Sharfstein. "Mert Sharfstein nailed it," she said. "*Downtown El,* remember?"

Murphy nodded. "And there's more. According to Mrs. Starrett, she and her husband received a painting—one that had their Kline painting replicated in it."

Kate had not thought to ask her, the moment with Marci Starrett too emotional. "Like the one at the museum?"

"I don't know. I haven't seen it. It's still out in Water Mill."

"Well, what are we waiting for? We should see it. Right away."

"Suffolk PD is sending a car out to the Starretts' home to fetch it. They'll fax us a copy soon as they get it."

"Fax it? Are you kidding? Let's go out there."

"Brown's not going to approve that, and neither will Tapell. It's not our jurisdiction."

"Fuck the jurisdiction."

"Maybe *you* can." Murphy leveled a stare. "But I actually work here."

Kate knew he was right. *Nicholas Starrett's homicide belongs to Suffolk.* What Tapell had said; plus she'd agreed to stick with Murphy, and to the paintings. Kate tried to tamp down her adrenaline, but it wasn't working. "I really want to see those paintings. Both of them—the slashed Kline, and this painting the Starretts received."

"Patience," said Murphy, playing with the omnipresent rubber band at his wrist. "Let's not get ahead of ourselves."

"Why? You want to sit around and play with your . . . rubber band?" Kate sighed. "Sorry. I know you're between a rock and a hard place. But if the Starretts' Kline was slashed in the same way as the de Kooning—and they received a painting like the one Dressler did . . ." She paused, thinking it through. "Then we could be looking at something pretty weird here, right? Something . . . premeditated." Kate considered her own statement. *A psycho out there slashing paintings—and people?*

Could it be? She studied the photos of the Starretts' slashed Kline, the flaps of canvas hanging out of the frame. "The cuts look clean, same as the cuts in the de Kooning, but there's no way to be sure without seeing it."

"Not true," said Murphy. "Suffolk lab will be able to tell us what kind of knife was used. We'll compare it to our lab's findings on the de Kooning. The two labs can tell us a lot more than our naked eyes would at the scene."

True enough, thought Kate, but the lab couldn't tell her what the scene *felt* like. She spread the photographs out on Murphy's desk and tried to get a sense of it. One of the pictures included just a bit of a taped outline on the floor. She closed her eyes.

"You okay?"

"Fine," said Kate, realizing Murphy thought she wasn't able to take it in, when it was just the opposite. "I was trying to see it, the scene," she said. "If the victim was discovered just below the painting, then there probably wasn't much of a struggle, or a chase." She closed her eyes again. "The assailant slashes the painting. The victim interrupts. The guy stabs him."

"Probable scenario," said Murphy. "But as you can see, they've made a point of not showing us the entire scene. This is the Art Squad version of the crime."

"You mean the bullshit version."

Murphy almost smiled. He was starting to see another side to the elegant art lady he'd watched on PBS—the one the cops all talked about, the one who could chase down psychos without losing her cool.

At least that's what he thought.

It wasn't easy for Kate to picture her friend as just another victim, though necessary if she was going to do this—and she had been a cop long enough to know she had to do it. Detachment: the name of the game. And she had already started the process, referring to Nicholas Starrett as simply *the victim*. "I imagine the same knife was used on the painting as the victim, so that the timing of whether the vic or the painting was attacked first can be easily established."

"You're saying is, if the vic's blood shows up imbedded in some of the slashed canvas, then the man was attacked before the painting. That it?"

Kate nodded.

"Which tells us what?"

"For one thing that it's going to be damned hard to keep this as a job for the Art Squad. And if the victim was stabbed *before* the painting, it might indicate that the *man* was his target, and the painting second." Kate took a deep breath. "When will we get the lab results? Fibers? Any DNA?"

"When we get them," said Murphy, playing his rubber band like a banjo. "*If* we get them."

"Could you stop doing that?"

"What?"

"The rubber-band thing."

"Don't think so," said Murphy.

Kate rummaged in her bag, came up with some gum, folded a couple of pieces into her mouth, and popped it loudly.

"You gonna try and annoy me with chewing gum?"

"Hadn't occurred to me," said Kate. "So you're saying we won't be seeing lab results?"

"We'll see them on the painting, for sure. On the vic, I don't know."

"Doesn't make sense," said Kate.

"Welcome to the Art Squad," said Murphy.

Kate sighed. She'd play this little game of red tape and departmental jurisdiction for a while. Then she'd go back to Tapell, if she had to, play hardball. "So what did you find out about the Jackson Pollock painting—the one you mentioned that was slashed at the law firm?"

"I didn't. I called after I last saw you, but neither partner was in."

Kate was about to say they should go see it when the fax machine started buzzing and an image inched its way out of the machine.

"Well, this sucks," said Murphy, staring at the fax. "It's a mess."

"Yes, it's bad, but there's something here, maybe paintings. I'm not sure." Kate squinted at the mass of gray and black tones trying to make it out. "That could be the Kline painting, at the top, see? And . . . a portrait, maybe, down here, at the bottom. I'm not sure. Can't Suffolk take a decent digital picture and e-mail it to us?"

"It's a thought." Murphy made a call to Suffolk. "Yeah, they can do that," he said, shaking his head as he replaced the phone. "If some doofus named Clyde goes home, gets his digital, brings it over to the Starretts', blah, blah, blah. It's like talking to *Mayberry RFD*. But I told them to get us the original, by helicopter. And they agreed. It should be in our hands in an hour or two. Less time than if we went out there."

"Except that we still don't get to see the scene," said Kate.

"Give it up," said Murphy. "And from what I hear, the rookies first on the scene contaminated the place—and the vic's wife did too."

Kate didn't bother to tell Murphy it was easy enough to separate Marci Starrett's fingerprints and DNA, as well as the rookies', because she knew he knew it. She could see he was just playing by the book. And maybe it was better this way: Did she really need to see the outline of the body on the floor, the stains in the rug, smell the stale blood in the air?

"You want to see something?" asked Murphy. "Then come on. Let's go to the law firm, the one that had their Jackson Pollock painting slashed."

CHAPTER 11

Norman Brandt thumbed through stacks of papers on his desk, then systematically opened and closed drawers.

Murphy leaned over the lawyer's desk. "You didn't throw it out, did you?"

"I would have told you that over the phone, Detective, when you called. No. I just put it . . . somewhere." He ran a hand through his thinning hair. "My wife says I lose everything." He smiled. "Guess she's right." He tugged on suspenders already under serious pressure from his impressive belly, and crossed to a wall of dark wood bookshelves and cabinets.

"Do you choose your own art?" asked Kate. The pieces on display included a suite of elegant Ellsworth Kelly flower drawings and a dazzling Richard Diebenkorn landscape. Everything about Brandt's offices telegraphed cool refinement, except Brandt.

"We have an art consultant who does that. Me, I know what I like, but what's the point of buying art if you're not going to make a return on your investment, right?" He looked to Kate for approval.

"I usually tell people to buy art with their head *and* their heart." Kate wanted to add *if they have one*, but resisted. She indicated a blank wall with a hanging hook still in place. "Is that where the Pollock was hanging?"

Brandt nodded as he continued to open cabinet after cabinet, one revealing cut-glass canisters of liquor. "You want a drink? Oh, guess you can't," he said to Murphy.

"On duty, right? Isn't that what they always say?" He cocked an eyebrow at Kate, looked her up and down. "But you're not a cop."

"No, thanks," said Kate. She had explained she was consulting after Brandt recognized her from her television show.

"So it was you who found the Pollock slashed?" asked Murphy.

"Nope." Brandt shook his head while he poured himself a drink. "Cleaning lady. Called the security guard from the lobby to come up, and he called us."

"Any suspicious characters hanging around your offices you can remember?"

"Suspicious characters? Yeah. Most of our clients." Brandt snorted a laugh. "Criminal law, you know."

Kate did know. Richard occasionally had a client who had made him nervous—though it was not a client that he should have been worried about in the end. She pushed the thought from her mind. "How did you say you received the painting, Mr. Brandt?"

"It came to the firm, not me, simply addressed to Brandt and Seligson."

"You still have the envelope?" Murphy asked.

"Tossed it. Sorry." He lifted the Scotch. "You sure you won't join me?"

"Positive," said Kate. "So, the painting?"

He took a sip. "It arrived a few days before the incident, before the Pollock was slashed. Man, was that ever a shock. You know how much that little painting cost?"

Bye-bye, investment, thought Kate.

"And nothing else was touched?" asked Murphy.

Brandt shook his head. "Weird, huh? Some freak who hates Jackson Pollock?" He snapped his fingers. "Wait a minute. I know exactly where I put it." He put his glass down and plucked a coffee-table-sized art book—*The Complete Works of Jackson Pollock*—from the shelf. "In here."

Kate saw the edges of the canvas even before Brandt opened it.

Brandt was saying something about why he'd put it inside the Pollock book, but Kate and Murphy weren't listening. Their eyes were riveted on the black-and-white painting the lawyer had just laid onto his desk.

"It's quite a bit like our Pollock—the one that was slashed," said Brandt. "But hey, Jackson Pollock, he's just a bunch of expensive drips, right?" He tapped the black-and-white painting. "I thought maybe the art consultant had sent it over for consideration—you know, another piece of art to buy? I kept meaning to call and find out. But I forgot all about it—until you called." He glanced at the painting. "Must be hard work, copying all those drips—harder than making the original, if you ask me." He rolled his eyes.

Kate nodded without thinking. She was staring at the design beside the faux Pollock, trying to decipher it. "What do you make of this?" she asked Murphy.

"Jasper Johns, maybe? He painted letters and numbers, maps and such, right?"

"Yes, but not like this." She walked around the painting to view it from all sides, careful not to touch it. "It looks like letters. All the same letters. B and S, repeated," said Kate. "Over and over."

"Oh. I never noticed that," said Brandt. "B and S. Well, that's us. Brandt and Seligson."

With the carefully wrapped painting from the law firm with them, Kate and Murphy were anxious to get back to One Police Plaza and compare it with the others. But when a call to the station confirmed that the Starrett painting had not yet arrived, they realized they weren't far from the home of that ex–museum board member, Cecile Edelman, and they jumped at the opportunity to kill a bit more time.

There were four doormen in the lobby—the first greeted them, the second used the intercom, the third accompanied them to the fourth, who operated the elevator, which transported them up to the Edelman apartment. Kate felt like she was back on Central Park West, only grander.

A short, stocky maid with a heavy Slavic accent guided them through a foyer and into an imposing living room filled with art.

Kate was immediately drawn to a large canvas—a distorted rag doll of a woman, arms and legs triple-jointed, painted in wild acidic color.

"I see you are admiring my Phillip Zander." Cecile Edelman strode across the room, perfectly groomed, slim figure draped in fine wool slacks and beige cashmere sweater—the sort of uniform Kate used to wear, and did not miss. Edelman was probably in her seventies, though at first glance you'd never know it—her face was Botox-smooth—but her hands, bony and liver-spotted, gave her away. "I can't believe we've never met," she said to Kate. "Between the art world, the museum, and your television series, I would have thought . . ." Edelman eyed Kate from bottom to top—the black boots, jeans, heavy canvas coat cinched with a thick belt, finally the hair. "Does someone else dress you for the show? You look so . . . different."

"I'm afraid this is the way I'll be appearing for the rest of this season. It's my new look."

Edelman's Botoxed brows tried—impossibly—to arch. "Well, don't you let anyone say a single word about your appearance, dear. I think you look very . . . *with it*."

Kate could see it now, the stacks of letters PBS would be receiving: *What's with her hair?* She glanced back at the Zander painting. "I'm interviewing Phillip Zander for my show."

"How fabulous! My art group watches religiously. Afterward, we dissect the paintings you've shown, though we have our own art teacher, a man who is both an artist and a teacher, and well . . . he doesn't always agree with your critiques."

"Fine with me," said Kate. "I hate a yes man—unless he's saying yes to *me*." She tapped Cecile Edelman on the arm, and the two women chuckled. Murphy hung back, admiring the way Kate loosened her up.

"Your collection is remarkable," said Kate, taking it in: a wall-sized

Mark Rothko in deep reds and purple, a large black-and-white Robert Motherwell—one of the artist's *Elegy* paintings—and two Warhols, a *Marilyn* and a portrait of the lady of the house—a multimillion-dollar art collection. But what stopped Kate was something less known—a dynamic, abstracted figure in a landscape. "Is this a Resnikoff?"

"Indeed it is," said Edelman. "Hardly anyone recognizes his work anymore. He's not very well known."

"But he was," said Kate.

"It was the first artwork my late husband ever owned. His father gave it to him for his eighteenth birthday. I believe Morton's father may have known the artist, and bought it directly from the studio. At the time, Morton hadn't liked it very much and sold it. But years later, after his father died, the painting showed up at auction and Morton bought it back—at twice the price. Morton was a sentimental man."

Kate smiled. "You know, I'm quite interested in the neglected artists of the New York School. I'm planning to visit Resnikoff's daughter in Rome, get a bit more personal history on the man for a book I'm writing."

"How wonderful," said Edelman. "Morton, my late husband, would have been thrilled." She placed one of those telltale hands over her heart. "He's been gone almost two years now."

"Is that why you left the Modernist Museum board?" asked Murphy.

"No." If Cecile Edelman was frowning, it was hard to tell—her forehead did not move. "I imagine your visit has something to do with that awful business—the de Kooning painting. Oh, my—that was *your* painting, wasn't it, dear? I'm terribly sorry . . . though not surprised."

"Why?" Kate and Murphy practically said in unison.

"It's just that the museum has become, shall we say, lax."

"In what way?" asked Murphy.

"In all ways. If you ask me, the museum has lost its . . . vision."

"And that would be the director's job," said Murphy, referring to his notes. "Colin Leader."

"I was on the search committee, along with my late husband, that hired Mr. Leader. I thought Colin showed tremendous promise. He had, after all, taken a small Australian museum and turned it into a major player almost single-handedly."

"But you lost faith in him?"

"You could say that, but . . ." She waved one of those bony hands.

"The art world can be exhausting," said Kate. "You give and give and give to an institution, and for what?"

"Exactly," said Edelman. "When you've worked so hard for a place, and it lets you down, well . . . Morton and I gave quite a bit to the Modernist, and I don't just mean money, though of course we did give plenty of that. But we also gave time and energy, and . . . heart."

"I know *exactly* what you mean," said Kate.

Murphy pretended to study a painting, barely suppressing a smile. He was enjoying Kate's performance and was afraid he might blow it if he didn't turn away.

Cecile Edelman sighed dramatically. "But when a museum director is not quite what you thought, and your opinion is no longer valued, well, what can you do? You either get the director to leave, or *you* leave—which I did."

"And Colin Leader didn't try and stop you?"

"No."

Odd, thought Kate. The loss of a board member meant a loss of museum revenue.

Cecile Edelman seemed to read her mind. "It appeared that Colin was getting money elsewhere—new board members, I imagine. He certainly enjoyed the social aspects of the job, the contacts, the people he got to know." She leaned in close and whispered, "I don't like to talk, but lately, and quite often, there was alcohol on Colin's breath—at more than one meeting—which is fine if one has come from lunch, but I'm speaking of meetings at nine in the morning." The eyebrows attempted to rise again, but failed. "I tried to persuade a few of the board members to think about replacing him, but he's made some very strong alliances among a few of the newer businessmen on the board—Floyd Lattin, an investment banker, and particularly with Henry Lifschultz. They play golf together. I saw them out on the green at the Maidstone Club in East

Hampton. More than once. Mr. Lattin or Mr. Lifschultz must be the member. It certainly couldn't be Colin."

It was clear that Cecile Edelman, who said she did not like to talk, *did*, and would have continued if Murphy's cell phone had not started ringing. "The painting," he said to Kate. "From Suffolk. It's in."

CHAPTER 12

Kate and Murphy stared at the painting. "No question." Kate's adrenaline surged as she laid the painting from the law firm down beside the one

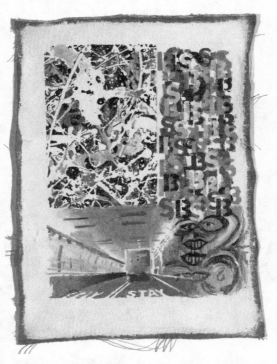

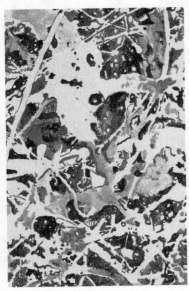

from the Starretts. "The same artist made both of these paintings. And the one sent to the Modernist Museum as well."

"You sure?" asked Murphy.

"Well, I wouldn't swear it on a Bible, but look at them. They're both painted on loose linen, about the same size, both just black-and-white paint—probably acrylic, like Mert Sharfstein said—same kind of paint handling. Yes, I'd say it's the same artist." She focused on the painting from the law firm. "Here's the reference to their Jackson Pollock painting that was slashed."

"And then, beside it, we've got the initials that stand for the law firm, *S* and *B*, repeated," said Murphy, drawing a magnifying glass over them.

"And the two repeated images—my de Kooning, which was slashed at the Modernist Museum, and

the Holland Tunnel that appears to represent the location. Norman Brandt received this *before* the Jackson Pollock was slashed at his law firm," said Kate. "Which means that it *was* some kind of warning— it was meant to alert Brandt and Seligson to the fact that their Jackson Pollock painting was going to be attacked . . ." She could feel her adrenaline ratchet up another couple of notches.

"Which, of course, they had no way of knowing at the time." Murphy was plucking his rubber band.

"No, they couldn't possibly have known. But it also predicted the *next* attack—the de Kooning painting at the Modernist Museum."

"So the law firm gets the painting, which contains the two images of what is about to get hit—the Jackson Pollock and what will be hit *next*—the Willem de Kooning." It was clear that Murphy's adrenaline was pumping along with Kate's, the two of them seeing it, understanding it. "Then Dressler, the curator at the museum, gets the next one, which also has the two paintings that *will* be hit—your de Kooning, plus a prediction of the next attack—the Franz Kline, along with a clue to *where*—Long Island."

"Exactly." Kate took a deep breath as it crystallized in her mind, then looked at the painting that had been sent to the Starretts. "That means *this* painting not only shows that the Starretts' Franz Kline painting will be attacked, but also tells us what will be *next*."

Murphy stared again at the painting that had been sent to the Starretts. "Okay, so we have the Kline painting and Long Island, there in the top half."

"But who's the dude down in the corner?" he asked.

"If I'm not mistaken," said Kate, "it's Franz Kline himself, a portrait. I'd say it's just one more clue about the identity of the painting that was going to be slashed." An image flashed through Kate's mind; it was not of the painting, but rather of her friend, Nicholas Starrett, dead at the foot of the painting. She did not have to see a crime scene photo to imagine it. *Detach,* she told herself. *And concentrate.*

"Then this—" Murphy tapped the image to the right of the Kline portrait with a gloved finger. "This must be the prediction of what's next, right?"

"Right," said Kate. "And I wouldn't swear to it, but I'd say it's a Hans Hofmann."

"The next hit." Murphy's voice was just slightly above a whisper. "A Hans Hofmann painting."

And maybe its owner, thought Kate, but she did not want to say it out loud. "Let's get this over to Mert Sharfstein. He'll know for sure if it's a Hofmann painting—and maybe even help us figure out which one."

Gabrielle Hofmann Lifschultz thought Bonnie, her usually frisky, often poorly behaved Doberman (the dog was forever eating the cat's food, tearing up the carpet, or stealing the latest in a long succession of down comforters, then shredding it), had been acting lethargic for days—no kisses for the mailman, no barks and howls when the UPS guy made his delivery, and now, not the least bit interested in eating.

Gabrielle, "Gaby" to her friends, knelt beside the dog, lifted its snout in her hand, and gave it a smooch. The Doberman dragged its tongue over Gaby's cheek in a lazy slurping manner.

"Not feeling well, baby?"

The dog curled at her feet. Not a good sign. Gaby gave her another smooch, then called the vet and, a moment later, her husband.

———

Henry Lifschultz was only half listening, something about the dog being sick. *Gaby and her babies,* he thought, glad his wife could not see the sneering smile on his face. He hated that damn animal. "Oh . . . too bad," he said, then, "I have to work late. Probably can't get home before midnight. You know . . . I think it's best if I just stay in the city."

"Again? You haven't been home for days."

"Did you forget I'm designing a new building? It's very demanding."

That was all he had to say. Gaby immediately backed down, started apologizing. He'd almost have preferred an interrogation. Something a normal wife would do. This was pathetic. But a moment later she was saying something about leaving the dog at the vet and coming into the city to spend the night with him.

Well, forget that.

"I don't think that's a very good idea," he said. "I'm going to be *very* busy." He pictured the king-sized bed in the couple's elegant Park Avenue pied-à-terre, where lately he'd been spending a good deal of time. *Was she onto him?* He didn't think so. "Maybe next week. So, uh, what's wrong with the pooch?" he asked, switching the topic, thinking about his next call while Gaby prattled on about the dog acting lethargic, maybe having eaten something; she was taking it to the vet where it would most probably spend the night. "Well," he said, "I'm sure it will be fine." He hung up as his wife was saying "Love you," and instantly made another call.

"We're on," he said. "For tonight."

Gaby Hofmann Lifschultz stared at the receiver, feeling as if she might cry. "Love you, too," she said to herself.

Unlike most of the women her age who were forever chauffeuring kids to soccer practice or dance and music lessons, Gaby, who was childless, was bored; and now, with Henry spending half the week in the city—without her—she thought if she did not soon escape the doldrums of Greenwich, Connecticut, she was going to go crazy. She missed the art galleries and museums she and Henry had enjoyed before they'd moved to the suburbs.

Of course one might say that she and Henry lived in a veritable museum of their own.

Gaby glanced around her living room at her inherited art collection, entirely mid-century abstraction that her grandfather—the great artist and teacher Hans Hofmann—had taken as barter for classes, as well as several pieces by the late master himself.

Gaby thought back to the man whom she'd known as a child, an old man with a heavy German accent, a man who had influenced any number of the great New York School artists with his ideas about the unconscious and what he called the *push and pull* of images on the flat plane of the canvas surface.

Gaby stopped a moment to admire her favorite—a large oil, bright rectangles of color held together by a Z-shaped line that looped through the canvas—a joyous work that always made her feel good, aptly titled *Bliss*. Over the years, Gaby and her siblings had donated or sold off several artworks, but this one, she thought, she would take to the grave.

She gave Bonnie another pat and looked into the Doberman's sad, dark eyes. "You'll be fine, won't you, girl?"

Bonnie bared her teeth in a way that terrified others, but that Gaby took as a smile. She kissed the dog's head, thinking it was definitely a good idea to board the dog at the vet's for the weekend and have them do a full checkup, just to be sure.

In the kitchen, Gaby poured a little dry food into the cat's bowl. With Bonnie out of the house, the cat might actually get a chance to eat it.

Past the living room and kitchen, through the den, and finally into the mudroom, she retrieved Bonnie's leash, slapped her thigh, and whistled. "Come on, girl. Let's go for a ride." The Doberman lumbered toward her reluctantly.

CHAPTER 13

Mert Sharfstein stared at the painting, then lowered his magnifying glass over the area in question.

"Yes, it's a Hans Hofmann," said Sharfstein. "No question about that."

He turned to one of his gallery assistants and asked the young man to scan the Hofmann image into a computer and see if it could be matched to an existing Hofmann painting—the way the police searched for fingerprints.

It took the assistant a half hour to come up with a similar painting, and by then, Kate and Murphy were close to exploding.

"They're not exactly the same," said the assistant, "but similar, see?" He turned the computer screen and they all stared at it.

"Looks like a classic Hofmann," said Kate.

"Yes. The heavy slabs of paint against a washy background, the looping line . . ." said Sharfstein, who was clearly about to go further.

"Mert, please, we don't need the art history lesson, not right now." Kate leaned over the young man at the computer. "Does it say where the painting is—which museum, or—"

"Just says 'Private Collection,'" said the kid.

"I can try and reach the estate," said Sharfstein. "They should be able to help us. Give me a few minutes to see if I can locate them."

Kate and Murphy left Mert alone to make his calls. In the gallery's front viewing room they pretended to occupy themselves with the collection of minor Dutch master paintings that dotted the walls, but neither one of them could concentrate on the artwork.

Sharsfstein finally cut into the room. "I reached the estate just before they were closing. They say the painting is owned by the family."

"Where does the family live?" Kate was practically twitching.

"There's a grandson and niece on the West Coast, and a granddaughter here, back east. They share ownership of the work."

"Phone numbers?" asked Kate.

"The estate wouldn't give me that information," said Sharfstein.

Murphy looked at him in disbelief. "Give me that," he said, snatching the estate's number, and began punching it into his cellular.

"All three heirs should be contacted," said Kate.

"If you would tell me what all this is about, maybe I could help." Sharfstein folded his arms across his chest.

Murphy had gotten through to the estate, but apparently too late, an answering machine telling him they had closed for the day. He snapped his phone shut. "Damn."

Kate glanced over at the clue painting the Starretts had received, still sitting on the assistant's desk. *It's all in here, somewhere.* She looked again, realizing they had been so caught up in identifying the painting

they had not considered anything else. "What's this?" She pointed at the shape surrounding the Hofmann painting.

"Could be a map," said Murphy.

"Yes." Kate took a closer look. "It's a state, isn't it?"

"Indeed," said Sharfstein. "Connecticut. Home to so many of my collectors."

Night has fallen, the room dim, the darkness a friend—sheltering, disguising, comforting.

She will be back any minute—and without the dog. That is one sick puppy. It will have to have its stomach pumped or something, spend the night at the vet—*poor baby.*

What was that? Wind in the trees? An owl, perhaps?

Nothing to worry about. Everything is peaceful.

But there is nothing at peace in this body, every muscle tense, nerve endings attenuated, senses on high alert.

The distinct sound of the front door opening.

Ah, there she is.

Footsteps in the hallway.

Steady now.

Gaby Hofmann dropped her keys on the table beside the door, glanced down the hallway and wondered why the lamp in the living room, the one on a timer, set to go on and off, her only nod to keeping burglars away—she could never remember to set the alarm—was not on, no light splaying into the dim hallway. Had the bulb burned out, the timer malfunctioned?

Lily meowed, just barely discernible in the dark, and Gaby called out, "Mommy's home."

The cat rubbed against her leg, and she bent to pet it. "Bonnie's going to be fine," she said. "Just a tummy ache—as if *you* care." As she absently stroked the cat, she made a mental note to tell the gardeners that the Doberman had gotten into some poison they were using. They would have to go strictly organic—she couldn't risk having her babies getting ill.

Lily meowed again, scampered down the hall toward the kitchen, and Gaby followed behind her, until she stepped on something that cracked beneath her foot. Even with the lamp out, she could see the drawing on the floor, and the shattered glass.

"What in the world?"

Gaby turned into the darkened living room and knelt over the artwork—one of her grandfather's drawings—and thought she might cry.

She was carefully picking glass off the picture when she felt a presence behind her, turned, and sighed with a bit of relief. "Oh, it's you," she said to the cat. "Careful, now. Broken glass." She shooed the cat away and, when she looked up, saw the slashed painting on the wall.

For a moment she froze, then stood, terrified, and called out for Bonnie before remembering she had just left the dog at the vet.

Oh my God.

The phone in the hallway was ringing and Gaby was rushing to answer it when it happened—an arm around her throat, a gloved hand over her mouth. She started to scream, mouth half open, now invaded by fingers, her mind attempting to process what was happening—*I'm being attacked!*—swung her elbow back into another body, a gasp of breath in her ear as the hands let go, no time to look and take stock of the damage, though her peripheral vision saw the body teeter, then fall.

The answering machine had picked up, a man speaking, she could just make it out, the police, something about her painting—*How could they know?*—but there was no time to process it. She sprinted down the hallway toward the back door, had a good lead, too, and might have made it if she hadn't caught her toe in a thick ridge of carpeting—created, ironically, by the playful pawing of the Doberman who had been chosen to protect her.

Gaby Hofmann went down, hard. She was trying to right herself when she felt her head being yanked back by her hair, and something icy-hot slashing across her throat.

CHAPTER 14

The Greenwich precinct was overheated, and Henry Lifschultz was perspiring, his monogrammed shirt sticking to his chest, the smell of garlicky pepperoni pizza making him ill.

The detective, a man named Kominsky, was wolfing down a slice in between questions. "I just have a few things to go over with you."

Lifschultz barely nodded. He'd been through it all, hadn't he? A dozen times.

Kominsky reached for a copy of Henry's statement, his fingers leaving grease stains. "So you were in your New York apartment when your wife died, that right?"

"That's what I told the other detective, yes. It's right there, in front of you." How should he play it? Stern or acquiescent? He wasn't sure which would be the more effective role.

"I hate to ask at a time like this, but . . . can anyone confirm that?"

"Yes. I'm certain the doorman saw me come in. It was around eight."

"And you didn't go out again?"

"No, I was in all night."

"You call anyone from the apartment?"

"I really can't remember."

Kominsky took another bite of pizza, chewed, swallowed, and burped into the back of his hand while he made a mental note to check the phone records. "Again, I hate to ask, but were you and your wife—were you happy?"

"I don't see how—" Henry Lifschultz tugged at his collar. The overhead lights were glaring in his eyes and he felt like he was acting in some goddamn low-rent version of *Law & Order*. Even the cop, Kominsky, looked a bit like the cop on that show, Lenny. He tried to think of the actor's name, but all he could remember was that the actor had recently died. "Of course we were happy, Detective. We were very happy. Extremely happy. Why wouldn't we be happy?"

"It was just a question." Kominsky wiped tomato sauce off the corner of his mouth. "A lot of couples—"

"Gaby and I were not like a lot of other couples, Detective."

"I imagine not." The detective glanced up at the two-way mirror. There were detectives watching from the other side.

Lifschultz followed his gaze, and knew it too. He looked back at Kominsky. *Jerry Orbach, that's the actor's name.* He caught himself about to smile and exchanged it for an appropriate look of despair. After all, his wife was dead. "I'd like to go home, Detective. I'm tired, and after what's happened, I—"

Kominsky plopped the rest of his pizza slice into the trash. He knew he could not push too hard. This man—like most of the town's residents—was wealthy and connected.

But there was something off about the guy. To Kominsky, he seemed more angry than upset. That, plus the sweating.

Henry Lifschultz stood and slipped into his suit jacket.

"Sorry," said Kominsky.

"That's all right, Detective. I realize you are just doing your job."

"I meant about your wife," said Kominsky.

Henry Lifschultz got into his Jaguar and slammed the door. He concentrated on driving slowly, not wanting to attract attention. After a few minutes he stopped checking his rearview mirror—there was no sign of Kominsky—opened his collar, and took a breath. He passed one gated drive after another, manicured hills and landscaped fields, mansions that no longer impressed him now that he had his own. He was almost home when his cell phone started ringing.

"It's me. How are you?"

"How do you think I am?"

"I want to see you."

"Impossible. You shouldn't even be calling. Can't they trace this, or—"

"Don't you miss me?"

"Yes, but—I don't think this is the right time to—"

"Are you wearing them?"

Lifschultz squirmed in the driver's seat, felt the silky fabric slide across his genitals. "Um-hmm." *Thank God, the cops hadn't done a strip search. As if they would dare.* Lifschultz smiled.

"Bet they don't fit you as well as they fit me."

Lifschultz swallowed, felt himself getting hard. But no, he couldn't do this. Not now. "Look, we can't speak. Not for a while. Or see each other. I can't take that chance." He slapped his cell phone shut, slid his hand into his pants, touched himself through the silky panties, and pressed his foot down onto the accelerator.

Kate and Murphy were in Floyd Brown's office, copies of the black-and-white paintings sent to the Modernist Museum, the Starretts, and Brandt & Seligson spread out on the Chief of Homicide's desk.

"These pictures . . ." Brown looked from one to another. "You say they contain clues?"

"Yes." Kate tapped the one sent to the museum. "In this one, there's both the Willem de Kooning painting that was slashed at the museum and the Franz Kline painting that was later attacked at the Starretts' home."

She turned to the painting retrieved from the Starretts'.

"Then, in this one, you've got the replication of the Kline painting that belonged to the Starretts, and a replication of the Hans Hofmann painting, which belonged to Gabrielle Hofmann."

"A psycho who sends previews of coming attractions?" said Brown.

"Looks like it," said Murphy.

"Except they didn't find one in this case." Brown reached for the jacket he'd gotten from Greenwich PD on Gabrielle Hofmann Lifschultz. "Detective I spoke with there, man named Kominsky, says the husband's reaction was somewhat *abnormal*. Nothing substantial to go on, but they're watching him."

Lifschultz. The name resonated in Kate's mind, though she wasn't sure why.

"Could be the husband was trying to make it *look* like our guy," said Murphy. "He could have hired someone to do it—kill the wife, slash the painting—but they got it a little wrong, didn't know about these clue paintings, which would explain why none was found. The tabloids haven't gotten wind of that part—not yet—so the killer wouldn't know to include it."

"But the Hofmann painting was there," said Kate, "in the painting sent to the Starretts—and if it's true that these paintings *are* clues, then we have to be looking at the same perpetrator—and that would be some-one who planned to attack a Hans Hofmann painting."

Brown rubbed at his temples, and Kate remembered the man was plagued by headaches. She dug into her bag, came up with two Excedrin. He nodded his thanks and washed them down with his cold coffee. "I see what you're saying, but my hands are tied. The word is—

and this is coming from Chief Tapell and the mayor—that we cooperate but stay aloof. They don't want us digging up dirt in someone else's backyard. Least of all another state's."

"But both vics—Starrett and Hofmann—had places in Manhattan." Murphy ran his fingers under and over one of his rubber bands.

"But neither of them died here."

"So what do we do?" Kate folded her arms across her chest. "Wait until someone does?"

"Those are the rules, McKinnon. I didn't make them, but I've got to play by them—and so do you. Just stick to the art part, okay? Anyway, my guess is, with two high-profile vics, expensive art, and two states involved, the Feds will be all over it—and soon."

"Lifschultz," said Kate, as she and Murphy cut out of Brown's office. "Gabrielle Hofmann's married name, right? And didn't Cecile Edelman say that a man named Lifschultz was one of Colin Leader's museum cronies?"

"I've got it written down somewhere," said Murphy. "But you heard what Brown said—stick to the art part."

"Jesus," said Kate. "If I hear that one more time . . ." She took a deep breath. "A destroyed Hans Hofmann painting *is* the art part. It's part of our ongoing investigation, no?"

Murphy was twisting the rubber band so tightly, his wrist was turning red. "I guess I can have a chat with that Greenwich cop, Kominsky," he said.

"Good idea." She glanced at Murphy's wrist. "You know, you're going to cut off your circulation if you're not careful."

Murphy let the band snap back into place.

"I'll check in with you later. I've lined up an interview in Tarrytown that just won't wait, then I have to spend some time editing the next segment of my TV show." She glanced at his wrist. "I'll just leave you two alone—you and your rubber band—for some quality time."

Murphy tried to think of a sassy retort, but couldn't. He watched her walk away, slim figure, hair snatching the sun like it was setting up a monopoly of golden highlights.

His wife, his ex-wife, Ginny, was blond, from a bottle. Fake, like so many other things about her, as it turned out. But he didn't want to think about her. It was his daughter, Carol—Candy they called her— whom he missed. Almost a month since he'd last seen her. She was about to turn eleven, entering that stage where everything he said was wrong—at least she seemed to think so, their weekly phone calls more a knife in his heart than anything else. He didn't know how to handle it—kill the kid with kindness or just kill her.

He caught a glimpse of Kate as she slid into a cab, tucking in her long legs like an afterthought. No question she was a beautiful woman, but he could not think of her that way, not if they were going to work together. He switched the rubber bands from one wrist to the other.

If he allowed himself to think about it, he was horny as hell. Too bad he didn't work vice where the cops got free blow jobs as perks. Maybe, he thought, he should put in for a transfer.

CHAPTER 15

The drive up to Tarrytown passed quickly, Kate's mind preoccupied with Nicholas Starrett's murder, and the guilt that kept resurfacing in her mind like a bloodstain that would not wash away. If only she had recognized that Kline painting. But beating herself up would not change anything. Better to concentrate on those bizarre clue paintings—if that's what they were.

A psycho who sends previews of coming attractions.

But why?

A game?

Kate knew that some psychopaths enjoyed the game almost as much as the kill, got off on playing with the cops, thought they were smarter than everyone—and sometimes they were. There were hundreds, thousands of unsolved murders, some of them, undoubtedly, the work of psychopaths who were shrewd enough to plan and execute perfect crimes.

But omnipotence led to risks, she knew that, too, and hoped this psycho would make a mistake, and soon.

By the time she arrived for her meeting with Beatrice Larsen, her crew, if one could call them that—a technician and a cameraman—were set up and waiting for her; the artist fidgeting in her chair, puffing on a cigarette, making an obvious display of regarding her watch.

"Sorry I'm late." Kate took the woman's hand in both of hers. "I can't tell you what an honor it is to finally meet you. I've been a serious fan of your work for years."

The woman crushed out her cigarette, almost smiled.

Kate retrieved her notebook, turned on her small tape recorder, and glanced around the studio at the art—hybrid works that mixed abstraction with bits of popular iconography.

Beatrice Larsen was a second-generation abstract expressionist, one of the many younger artists who had made the pilgrimage to New York in the fifties, met all the greats and worked alongside them, adopting their methods of painting—as well as their lifestyle. Her studio was small, once the semi-detached garage to the smallish Cape Cod–style house beside it. Larsen was a good solid painter, but had never achieved the stature of some of her colleagues.

Kate chatted awhile, loosening the woman up, then moved around the studio, getting the artist to talk about her work, directing the cameraman to zoom in on details of specific paintings.

"You started adding references to popular culture some time ago, didn't you?"

"After abstract expressionism dropped dead," said Larsen, lighting up a Marlboro, despite the obvious wheeze Kate heard in her voice. "The abstract painters, and the critics, they raked me over the coals for it. But what the hell. De Kooning cut out a bunch of women's mouths from magazines, glued them down, and used them to start paintings and he didn't get any shit for it. Of course he was a man."

Kate went up close to one of Larsen's paintings. "I hadn't noticed this detail before. It's Madonna and Britney, right?"

"Yeah. I like burying the pictures inside the painting like that. I use popular imagery as a jumping-off place, then let it suggest all the shapes and abstraction around it."

"I can see that. It's fascinating because the painting looks almost abstract at first, but once you discover the images, it changes the way one views the painting and how it was made."

"Exactly my point," said Larsen, allowing a smile. "Funny, isn't it? Using something like that—Madonna and that Britney chick, kissing. Jesus, the media made such a fuss. Like those were the first two girls who ever kissed."

"Maybe just the first ones to do it on live national television," said Kate.

"Well, it's the second time I've used the Madonna-Britney kiss. I did another painting with it before this one. It was in that Neo-Icon show, couple of months ago, at the Whitney Museum."

"Of course. And it was reproduced in the *Times* review of the show. I remember it. Congratulations."

"For all the good it did me." Larsen shrugged. "I think the critic called me something like a post-neo-pop expressionist, or some such horseshit. I never much cared for labels." She scowled. "I'm thinking about using a picture of Janet Jackson exposing herself at the Super Bowl for a future painting. What do you think?"

"Hey, it's just a breast," said Kate.

"Exactly," said Larsen.

Kate scanned her notes, realized she had all the necessary facts and dates on the artist. What she now wanted from Larsen was reflections on the period, as well as on her life—what it was like to be an artist who hadn't had the luck, or the breaks, something edgy and personal, not the usual PBS or History Channel interview.

"So tell me, what was it like? Coming to New York, meeting all those artists?"

"It was great. I was a pretty girl back then. The boys didn't mind having me around."

Kate looked past the old woman's lined complexion, took in the steel-gray hair and eyes to match. "You're still pretty."

"Oh, honey, please." Larsen snorted. "Those days are long over. I took my looks for granted back then." She gave Kate the once-over. "You're a beautiful woman. But it won't last. Women are judged harshly. Not like men. It's the same thing in the art world. The men, they're always on top. No pun intended." She laughed, then coughed, crushed her Marlboro out in a large cut-glass ashtray filled with butts, and sucked in a breath.

Kate had read accounts of Larsen's affairs with more than one of the Ab Ex guys, and could believe them. She couldn't help but ask, "Is it true you were involved with Franz Kline?" Kate had a flash of that destroyed Kline painting at the Starretts' home.

"Oh, yes. Franz was a great guy. A boozer and a lover. One time, we're fucking, and he stops, reaches into me, pulls out my diaphragm, throws it across the room, and yells, 'Don't you know I hate sculpture!'"

Kate's mouth fell open, then she laughed. There was no way she'd be able to use that little piece of history in her film—though she'd have liked to.

Larsen cackled, then sobered. "But Franz had a sadness, too, about his wife, I guess, a ballet dancer, nutty as a fruitcake. He had to have her committed. But me and Franz, we were no big thing, though others may have thought we were." She sighed a smile. "I remember one time we were at the Cedar Bar, me and Franz, and Franz was all over me, you know." She grinned and Kate saw the pretty young girl beneath the old woman. "I can't recall who it was, some artist," Larsen continued, "said something to Franz like . . . 'Don't you have a wife, man?'" Larsen rolled her eyes. "Oh, brother. That went over like a lead balloon, I can tell you. Bill was there, Bill de Kooning, and he practically decked the guy. Bill and Franz had become very close by then, you know, like brothers—especially when they were drinking."

"So what happened?" asked Kate.

"Angry words, plus a few punches were thrown, if I remember correctly. I was into my fourth or fifth beer, I can't really remember." Larsen shrugged. "Though I don't think I saw that other artist ever again. Probably too scared to show his face. It wasn't a good idea to attack Bill or Franz. They'd become the big guns, you know, the leaders of the pack. And to make a moral judgment—in *those* days—when we were *all* screwing around? Well, that was social suicide. He must have been drunk." She waved a hand and laughed. "Of course we all were."

"What about the other painters?"

"What about them?"

"You became friends with them all, didn't you?"

"*Friends?*" Larsen's gray eyes narrowed. "The New York School was a boys' club, honey. Women were decorative. Someone to talk *at*—or fuck."

"What about de Kooning's wife, Elaine, or Pollock's, Lee Krasner? They had big careers."

"Oh, honey, please. Lee's career came *long* after Jackson was dead. And Elaine, well, she helped Bill become a star—maybe at the expense of her own career, though there are plenty of people who will tell you it was because her work wasn't any good." Larsen lit up another cigarette, took a long pull, and stared at it. "A woman chain-smoking, boozing, and fucking around, she's a bum, right? But a man . . . he's a god." Kate was trying to figure out how she could edit that line to make it usable while the old woman puffed a gray cloud toward the studio ceiling.

"De Kooning took up with a young woman, Ruth what's-her-name, after he and Elaine split up. It's always a young one, isn't it?" She gave Kate a knowing, acid-etched smile. "But Ruth was a beauty, I'll give her that. A young Liz Taylor type. A prize. She'd been with Jackson Pollock for a while, his last girlfriend, the one in the car with him when he crashed and died." She frowned. "And then, there she was on his rival's arm, on de Kooning's arm. They competed over everything—women, art, you name it. Boys will be boys, right? And they usually get what they want." She sighed. "Me? I had plenty of strikes against me. I was second generation—and a woman."

"What about Joan Mitchell? She was second generation and—"

"That bitch!" Larsen coughed and laughed. "You ever meet her? She put the men to shame—nastiest drunk of the lot. Joan ran off. Moved to France. Created a mystique. Maybe I should have done that. But I stayed here, just another ordinary American painter. Nothing exotic about that. Not so much fun for the curators to visit an old broad in

Tarrytown. Better to fly off and see one in France, right?" Larsen squinted at Kate through a cloud of smoke. "You married?"

Kate paused. "No, I . . . lost my husband." She was suddenly very aware of the video camera. No question she would be editing this out too.

"Oh. I'm sorry." Larsen touched Kate's hand, an out-of-character grandmotherly sort of pat. "I never married. Too complicated." Larsen's lips puckered around the end of her cigarette. "The way I saw it, a woman had to have total independence, especially back then."

Kate could relate to that, had pretty much gone her own way before she married Richard, and after, too, though marriage had brought its compromises.

"For a while I was like one of the boys, part of the inner circle." Larsen smiled, but it quickly turned sour. "Let's just say they made promises . . . but didn't keep them." The old artist's eyes darkened to gunmetal gray. "What the hell—it's all ancient history." Larsen watched her cigarette smoke coil toward the ceiling, break apart and fade like an old memory. "After the heyday of abstract expressionism, only the biggest of the big survived—de Kooning, Rothko, Motherwell, a few others. Kline and Pollock, they were already dead. The rest of us, we might as well have been—no one cared. Imagine, I had a sell-out show in 1959, and didn't show again until 1986."

Kate did the math: Twenty-seven years. A hell of a long wait between exhibitions.

"And that show only happened because one of the new breed, one of those *neo-expressionists* they called themselves, had been browsing through a prehistoric issue of *ArtNews*, saw my work, and *rediscovered* me. A reporter asked me how it felt to have a comeback. I said, 'Honey, I'm like one of the Grateful Dead!' The art world can be a cruel place. They love you when you're young and pretty, and then, sometimes, if you're lucky enough to live, when you're really old. But there's no in-between. You've just got to hold on—it's a long road and not a smooth one."

Kate thought about the many artists who could not hold on, who had given up and taken nine-to-five jobs, or painted in obscurity until they died, as opposed to the successes. She glanced at the paintings on Larsen's studio walls. "Some people don't leave anything behind," she said. "But you have a lifetime of paintings for history to contemplate."

"Right," said Larsen. "If anyone gives a shit."

"Plenty do," said Kate. She brought the woman back to her paintings and they spent some time discussing expressionism versus realism, and technical issues, then Kate changed the subject. "I was speaking with Phillip Zander the other day."

"Oh, that guy—he'll live forever. One of the chosen, part of the in crowd. All the right friends, Bill and Franz, Robert Motherwell." She harrumphed. "You had to be in with the in crowd if you wanted to survive." She stopped and broke into a husky, tobacco-roughened version of the sixties Motown song—"I'm in with the in crowd"—and snorted. "I was part of it—for a while. At least I *thought* so." She punched her cigarette out in the ashtray.

"But even the in crowd broke apart, didn't it?"

"Well, half of them died—if that's what you mean." Larsen's eyes had clouded a bit, as if she were looking inward. It was a moment before she spoke again. "Who knows what really happens to a group. History? It's about interpretation, right?"

"That's what I'm trying to do," said Kate. "Interpret it. Reinterpret it."

"Lotsa luck," said Larsen.

Back in New York, at the small technical studio she used at the PBS station, Kate viewed both tapes alternately, now playing on separate computer screens in front of her. She wasn't sure how she wanted to use them, individually or as a mix, possibly play them off each other, a bit of Zander, then a counterpoint from Larsen.

She did a fast-forward on Beatrice Larsen, stopped at the woman singing, "I'm in with the in crowd." No question she'd be using that.

The in crowd. Had it really been such a tough circle to break into?

Kate looked back at the screen, Beatrice Larsen crushing her cigarette out in the ashtray, saying, "I was part of it—for a while."

Kate froze the frame on the woman's scowling face.

The in crowd. The cool kids. It brought Kate back to junior high school—a shy, motherless string bean of a girl with no idea of what the future might hold.

Larsen's interview was coming to its end. "Lotsa luck," she was saying in regard to Kate's idea about reinterpreting the history of the period. From Larsen's point of view it surely wasn't the golden time Kate had always imagined. Zander, too, had tried to dissuade her from romanticizing the era.

She turned to the Zander tape, playing on the other computer screen. "Some got famous, others didn't," he said.

Easy for him to say, thought Kate, though she found it impossible to dislike the man, who seemed neither arrogant nor conceited. Maybe success had made him kinder. She had often seen how failure could make people bitter and cruel.

Late night. Darkness. The preferred hour, like a season, an arctic winter, perpetual darkness. Oh, how perfect that would be.

The place is quiet, an unlocked window providing easy access into the small house.

Shoes in booties make the slightest swishing noise, a whispered breath against wooden floors, no sound at all on the rugs, moving through darkened rooms on the hunt—a more recently acquired taste.

How quickly one adapts. And why not?

Plans are made to be altered, perfected. One needs to be flexible. To improvise. Wasn't that part of their credo? And the third act remains in place; the best still saved for last. But no need to think about that now. Not yet. Concentrate on the present. The task at hand. Everything in its own good time.

All of this considered while stealthily moving from one room to another in search of the next one—a look here, there, but even the bedroom is empty, the bed still made, no sign of anyone at home. Has there been a miscalculation?

Outside again, in the starless night, not even the hint of a moon, but the faint yellow light from a window of the smaller building, beside the house, beckons.

Of course.

A peek in the window confirms it.

The door is unlocked. A slight creak as it opens.

A small lamp illuminates the face. The sound of a wheezing snore.

Hmmm . . . No good if she's sleeping. Not anymore.

"Hi, there." Loud, up close.

The snore becomes a snort, head jerks, eyes flutter open. "Who's there?"

Just me. Death.

A finger over the lips. "Shhh. I have to show you something."

"Wh-what do you want?"

"Patience."

"Fuck you!" Starting to get up, challenging.

"What a thing to say. Haven't you learned your lines?"

The face, a mass of confusion and terror; anger, too.

Time to take care of that.

A shove back into the chair; pillow over the face.

A few sentences—a passage from writings that have been memorized—shimmer at the back of the brain. They help to justify the act.

The body squirms, breath close to that wheezing snore again, but strangled. Not long before it stops.

Pillow off, then carefully returned to its proper place.

Standing back, taking it in, calm now, the usual pain totally gone. Odd, how this new element, this act, brings such unexpected peace.

Gloved fingers close the mouth, rearrange lips to appear normal, then lift lids, attempting to keep the eyes open, though it doesn't work.

But I want an audience. That's the plan this time.

An idea: *Tape them open.*

It works.

Blank eyes to watch the show.

Now, to the paintings.

Knife in. Knife out.

One painting down, flaps of canvas hanging.

Dead eyes staring, expressionless.

"What do you think?"

Gloved hands lift dead hands, claps them together.

"Thank you. Thank you." Smiling. Bowing. "What's that? You want more? An encore? Sure. Why not?"

Knife in. Knife out. Another painting shredded.

More dead clapping.

"You're too kind."

One more painting destroyed, followed by a deep bow. "Really, it's been *my* pleasure."

Tape peeled from dead eyes, lids flap shut.

Time to go.

A last look at the artwork, the drooping skeins of canvas—*another one down*—then a quick exit.

CHAPTER 16

The loft was quiet, Nola at class, the baby already out with the nanny. Kate had been asleep—a surprise—and had not heard them leave. She took a long shower, felt a bit guilty that she was happy to have the place to herself, then made a couple of necessary calls—to Marci Starrett, then to Richard's mother, Edie, in Florida. After that, she brewed a pot of coffee, popped an English muffin into the toaster, opened the *New York Times* and spent a few minutes skimming the front page before turning to the obits, an old habit, admittedly macabre, though sometimes fun—seeing that the scientist who had invented hair spray was dead at ninety or the silent screen star whom everyone had long ago forgotten had succumbed to her final close-up.

But this morning, it was no fun at all. The very first obit stopped Kate cold.

BEATRICE LARSEN, 80,
ABSTRACT EXPRESSIONIST ARTIST

No way. Impossible. She had just seen her. A day ago. Kate read the piece, incredulous.

> Beatrice Larsen, an abstract expressionist painter of the New
> York School's second generation, died in her Tarrytown, NY,
> home. The artist was 80.
>
> Having achieved fame in the 1950s, Ms. Larsen faded from
> the art scene until her rediscovery in the 1980s. Her work, which
> is in many major collections . . .

Kate skimmed the words quickly, the idea that the woman she had just interviewed had suddenly died almost inconceivable. It must have been only hours after she'd seen her for it to have made the paper, though Kate knew the *Times* stockpiled obits; one phone call to report the death was all that was needed to get it to press.

> Ms. Larsen, who never married, is survived by several nephews
> and nieces, including the artist Darby Herrick, daughter of Ms.
> Larsen's sister, also deceased.
>
> A memorial service for Ms. Larsen, organized by Ms. Her-
> rick, will be held at the Tarrytown Town Hall, the date to be
> announced.

Kate looked for the cause of death but none was noted. Of course the woman was eighty and smoked like a fiend, and though she appeared in decent shape, she had been wheezing and coughing throughout the interview. Was it a heart attack? A stroke?

A call to the Tarrytown police revealed that Beatrice Larsen had died of natural causes. But Kate could not shake the feeling that there was something decidedly *unnatural* about the woman dying only hours after their interview. She reread the obituary, had a chilling thought, and called the Tarrytown PD again, this time posing a specific question: Had any of the artist's paintings been damaged? The desk cop she spoke to had no idea.

Another call, this one to the niece, Darby Herrick.

"I'm really sorry to bother you," said Kate, offering condolences and explaining who she was.

"I know who you are." Herrick had a strong, direct way of speaking, like her aunt.

"I can't get over it," said Kate. "I was just interviewing your aunt for a segment of my television show and—"

"Yes. My aunt was very pleased about it, and—" Herrick stopped, possibly overcome by emotion, thought Kate. "I'm going to miss her terribly."

"Yes, I'm sure. She seemed to be an amazing woman," said Kate, then asked her question. "This may sound odd, but were any of your aunt's paintings damaged, or—"

"Yes." A long pause. "How did—" Another pause. "Several were slashed—with a palette knife. I think."

Kate tried to picture it. "Several, you say?"

"Um, yes, three."

"And you said a palette knife was used?"

"Well . . . there was one on the floor, a sharp one."

"Had she ever done that before, destroyed her paintings?"

"Yes. My aunt could be very critical of her own work."

"But with a knife?"

Another pause. Kate felt as if she could almost hear the woman thinking before she spoke.

"More often Beatrice would scrape any heavy paint off the canvas surface, then paint over it and begin again. She often explained to me that she liked the idea of all that history—even if it was bad—under a new painting."

A usual practice for that generation, thought Kate. But slashing a painting was a violation of the painting's history—the opposite of what Beatrice Larsen's niece had just described. "Did you say several paintings were slashed?"

"Three." Herrick took a breath. "It was quite . . . shocking."

"So it was you—"

"Who found her? Yes."

"Are the slashed paintings still in the studio?"

"I threw them out."

"Really?" *How odd.* "Why?"

"I figured . . . if Beatrice was so determined to destroy them she wouldn't want anyone else to see them. Perhaps she knew that . . . that she was going to die and was editing her work, her legacy. I wrapped them up and immediately took them to the dump." A quick intake of breath. "Was that wrong?"

"I'm sure you did what you thought best for your aunt." Another question burned in Kate's mind: *Did you find an odd black-and-white painting?* But she didn't want to ask it. She wanted to see for herself. "I was wondering if I might come back to the studio. I'd like to spend more time with your aunt's artwork so when I speak about it on camera I'll do it justice." Kate hated herself for the lie—she had plenty of material, including pictures of Beatrice Larsen's entire oeuvre—but she needed to get into that studio.

"I'm not sure."

"You want the show on your aunt to be as good as possible, don't you?" If the woman said no, Kate would have to bring out the big guns, tell her she was working with the police—even though this was not the NYPD's jurisdiction. She was surprised when the woman agreed.

"When did you have in mind?"

"Today, if possible."

Kate had driven back up to Tarrytown before Beatrice Larsen's niece had a chance to change her mind. Sure, there was the question of authorization—Kate was clearly overstepping her jurisdiction—but her gut was telling her to move quickly and sort out the details later.

Darby Herrick met her outside the house. She was tall and thin, with wild black hair.

Kate offered more condolences as the niece led her into the studio— she was truly saddened by the woman's death—but it was obvious that Herrick did not want to talk about it, just wanted Kate in and out as quickly as possible.

The missing paintings were immediately obvious, three blank rectangles defined by paint splashes on the white walls where the pictures had been painted.

Ghosts, thought Kate. She moved along the periphery of the studio, taking notes in a pad as if writing about the paintings, but it was a ruse—she was checking for that black-and-white painting and any sign that a struggle might have occurred. There were no indications of Crime Scene having been through the studio, everything in its place, no outlined body, no powder residue. Of course there had been no need—the death appearing natural. Still, Kate could not shake the feeling that the woman's death, having come literally on the heels of her interview, was more than coincidence.

Darby Herrick tailed her. "Anything I can help you with?"

"I was wondering if your aunt employed any studio assistants I might interview about her work habits?"

"Beatrice couldn't stand anyone assisting her in the studio—except me." Herrick plucked a pack of cigarettes from her shirt pocket. "You mind?" She didn't wait for an answer, lit up and inhaled deeply, smoke stuttering out with her words. "As you saw, Beatrice didn't really need a lot of help—at least she wouldn't admit to it. She was in pretty good shape."

Then why did she die? "Yes, she seemed strong to me, which is why her death was such a shock."

"Yes." Herrick swiped at her eyes as if tears had formed, though Kate didn't see any.

"So you were close?"

"Yes."

"Did you see her last night?"

"No, I was home. All night. Painting. I ordered a pizza around nine-ish, never went out at all."

Kate had not asked for an alibi, though Herrick was providing one. She made a note to check on nearby pizzerias.

Herrick puffed on her cigarette and Kate saw a similarity to the aunt, certainly the rough edges. Perhaps the younger woman was masking her pain with the tough-girl act, though Kate wasn't sure. She seemed more agitated than upset.

"Beatrice was very independent," said Herrick. "A housekeeper came in once a week to vacuum and do the heavy stuff. And my studio is nearby. I'd make sure to stop in several times a week to bring her art supplies, cook a few meals—though Beatrice was more interested in her whiskey and tobacco than food. I've been trying to get her to quit smoking for years, but it was hopeless. She had the beginnings of emphysema, you know. I imagine her heart just gave out." Herrick glanced at her cigarette, dropped the stub to the studio floor and crushed it beneath the heel of her work boot.

Herrick's unemotional assessment of her aunt assuaged any guilt Kate had for showing up so soon after Larsen's death. It seemed an odd way to deal with grief, unless the reality had not yet hit her, but it made Kate wonder.

"Beatrice's life hasn't been an easy one," said Herrick. "Early fame and attention, then years of being ignored."

"But she had a comeback in the eighties. That must have pleased her."

"I suppose. Though she never trusted it would last."

Kate glanced over at the large wicker chair where the artist had sat for most of the interview, and felt a pang of disbelief mixed with sadness.

"Her favorite chair," said Herrick, following her gaze. "She even died in it."

"Did she often work late?"

"Sometimes all night."

"I know this must be hard for you," said Kate. "I won't be long."

"Yes, it's . . . very upsetting," she said, as if suddenly realizing she should be displaying some emotion. "But take your time. I want the interview to be something Beatrice would be proud of."

"Is it all right if I sit with the paintings for a while, by myself?"

Darby Herrick hesitated for a moment. "I guess so," she said. "If you need me, I'll be in the house, just next door."

Kate waited for the door to close, then began to peruse the studio.

Other than the three slashed paintings, which the niece had already thrown out, everything seemed to be exactly as it had been during her interview; paint table, glass palette with mounds of drying pigment, paint tubes lined up beside it. There were several palette knives, all round-edged, nothing sharp enough to cut through canvas. Kate wondered about the palette knife presumably used to slash the canvases. Had Darby Herrick thrown that out as well?

Kate slipped on a pair of latex gloves, went carefully through a bookcase, then a table beside the door stacked with letters and bills, nothing of interest other than a large manila envelope, torn open, empty. Kate lifted it with gloved fingers. It was addressed to Beatrice Larsen, no return address, a Tarrytown postmark. She went back through the letters and bills, found nothing, slid open a drawer filled with pens and pencils, clips and tacks, index cards and Post-its, riffled through its messy contents—again, nothing.

She moved to the artist's favorite chair, wicker arms dotted with paint and scarred by cigarette burns, the seat, a lumpy pillow, its covering split in a few places, also stained with paint. Kate lifted it. Nothing underneath.

Could it be that she was making all of this up, creating a mystery when there was none? It was possible, even reasonable that the artist had destroyed her own work and died in her sleep. But then why was her cop alarm going off?

Around a half wall, a storage area, wooden racks filled with plastic-covered paintings, lots of dust. Kate pushed the paintings around, peered in between them, but didn't find anything.

She turned back into the main studio, was about to pull off her gloves and call it a day when she spotted the metal trash can, lid slightly askew, a painting propped against it, which had hidden it from view her first time around.

Lid off. A mass of paint rags, squeezed-out tubes of paint—spontaneous combustion waiting to combust.

Kate reached in, pushed the rags around, plucked out a paper palette which had adhered itself to a rectangular piece of canvas. She tore the palette off, and gasped.

Her cell phone, ringing in her bag, startled her.

"I've got it," said Murphy, on the other end.

"Got what?"

"The clue painting we thought should have been there, but wasn't," said Murphy. "You know, at Gabrielle Hofmann's? Greenwich PD just delivered it. It was there, all along."

"And it's like the others?"

"Exactly," he said.

"Me too," said Kate.

"Me too—what?" asked Murphy.

"A painting," said Kate. "I'll show you."

CHAPTER 17

Kate was still breathless from her discovery and the speed-limit-breaking drive back from Tarrytown. She hadn't said anything to Darby Herrick. She'd leave that to the Tarrytown police. The autopsy, too, on Beatrice Larsen's body, which was—clearly—imperative. She'd have Chief Tapell deal with Tarrytown PD, make sure they followed through.

Murphy had the painting from the Hofmann scene laid out and wait-ing. It was covered with splotches and stains. "Crime Scene didn't even bag it," he said. "Guess they fig-ured it was already *con-taminated*. The stains," he said. "Cat shit. The paint-ing was found in the litter box."

"Obviously Gabrielle Hofmann hadn't thought much of it," said Kate.

"Guess not. Leave it to the housekeeper to find evidence rather than Crime Scene." Murphy shook his head. "There was newspaper in the litter box, too, which might help approximate the date on which Hofmann received the painting."

"Any envelope that the painting might have been sent in?"

"If so, it wasn't found." Murphy ran a gloved hand over his stubble. "Greenwich PD has already copied everything over to our lab. They're looking at the broken glass from a framed drawing."

"Blood, maybe?"

"If we're real lucky. Coroner's initial report says there may have been a struggle so they're testing under Hofmann's fingernails, checking for fibers, the usual. You know what they say: When one human interacts with another—"

"One leaves something behind, the other takes it away."

"Right," said Murphy. "Let's hope there was some interaction before he killed her."

A gruesome concept, thought Kate, to hope the killer played with the victim, but a boon to forensics. If they could just get something that might physically, or genetically, tie these murders together, it would be a start.

Kate had bagged the envelope from Beatrice Larsen's studio, which was now at the lab. "I found an envelope in the studio. I can't be sure the painting I found came in it, but it was the right size. It had been mailed to Larsen from Tarrytown."

"If it is the envelope the painting came in, then the unsub, our unsubstantiated perpetrator, had been there before, to Tarrytown; most likely to scope out Larsen's place. And mailing the painting while he was there is smart, no home postmark."

Kate had the painting from Larsen's studio with her, which she laid on the table. "This one's also a mess. But these stains are paint, not shit. The canvas was in Larsen's trash, face-to-face with a paper palette full of paint," said Kate.

"Obviously Larsen didn't care for the painting, since it was in her trash. Maybe she thought it was some artist ripping her off, using the same image she'd used." Kate pointed to the picture of Madonna and Britney kissing. "I'd just seen the image in Larsen's studio." Damn it, she thought, another death she might have prevented if they'd found it in time. But it never occurred to her to ask Larsen. Why would she? She paused a moment, thinking again about the murder having come so soon after her inter-view. Was there a connection? Kate considered it, her mind trying to get a handle on it—Why?—her blood pressure elevating.

"You okay?" asked Murphy.

"Fine," said Kate, picturing Larsen when she'd left her: a resilient old woman who had survived plenty of art wars, suddenly dead.

"So the niece says she threw out the paintings that were slashed, huh?" Murphy raised an eyebrow. "Too bad. Now that Larsen is dead they could be worth a helluva lot."

"Jesus, Murphy, the woman's barely cold."

"Hey, it's a fact, isn't it? The artist kicks and the price of the inventory escalates."

No artist like a dead artist. How many times had Kate heard that from art dealers and curators who were *supposedly* joking? And sometimes she had laughed, but not right now—not with the image of Beatrice Larsen so alive in her mind. "It's just that I met her, and liked her. But if Darby Herrick is telling the truth, the paintings she threw away were slashed, so not worth much." She sighed. "Of course you're right—her paintings are going to be worth plenty. By now some hungry curator has just read her obit and is planning the retrospective exhibition, trust me," said Kate. "They may not have been lining up for Larsen's paintings in her lifetime, but they will be now." A thought crossed Kate's mind. "I wonder who inherits the work."

"Easy enough to find out."

"And we will," said Kate, once again studying the black-and-white painting found in Larsen's trash. Globs of paint blotted out whole patches of the painting, particularly the lower half. "There's the Madonna-Britney image, and that same house, whatever it is, and it's in both paintings—Hofmann's and Larsen's—but the bottom half is a mess." She looked closer. "The next painting to be hit should be indicated somewhere in here, right? Maybe hidden under the paint stains?"

"What's this, over here?" asked Murphy. He indicated the other painting, the one found in the litter box at Gaby Hofmann's home.

"I'm not sure," said Kate. "A shield and a motto. Hold on." She went to Murphy's computer, pulled off her gloves, and started typing. "Google search," she said, her fingers tapping the keyboard.

"What are you looking for?"

"Symbols of places." She hit a few more keys.

"What's the writing on it?"

"Qui . . . transtulit . . . sustinet, I think."

"Got it," said Kate, as an image appeared on the screen. "It's French for . . . *He who transplanted still sustains.* It's the motto on the state flag of Connecticut." She leaned back in the chair. "So that's connected back to where the Hofmann painting was, in Connecticut. And to where its owner, Gabrielle Hofmann, lived."

"What's above it?"

"Don't know," said Kate. She looked from one painting to the other. "Some sort of . . . castle?"

"It's in both of these paintings, so I'd say it's a clue that's been carried over. She slipped gloves back on and lightly touched a paint glob in the painting from Larsen's trash bin. It came away clean. "This is already dry. It must be acrylic paint. If it was oil, it'd still be tacky. We could dab the stains off with a rag dipped in turpentine if it was oil, but we can't do that with acrylic."

"What about scraping or sanding them off?"

"We could, but we might scrape or sand away whatever is under them, too. I think it's a job for a painting restorer."

"Lab should be able to do it," said Murphy.

"The techies are usually up to their eyeballs in urine, blood, and hair," said Murphy, as he and Kate passed through one metal door after another. "Paint scrapings, to them, it'll be like a vacation."

Kate's cell phone started ringing as she and Murphy cut across a lab that looked like a modern-day set for Dr. Frankenstein—white-coated technicians hunched over Bunsen burners, petri dishes, microscopes.

Kate took the call in the hall, then rejoined Murphy.

"Tapell's come through. She's spoken with Tarrytown PD. Beatrice Larsen's body will be delivered to the Manhattan morgue in the morning.

Tarrytown gets copies on anything that NYPD finds, and the body gets returned as soon as the ME is finished."

"Nice work," said Murphy. He knew it would have taken him days—maybe weeks—to get the authorization. It helped having a personal friend of the Chief of Police on his side.

"We're really backed up," said the lab tech who specialized in paint, a pale guy with thick glasses and shaky hands that spoke of one too many cups of coffee. "You have the paperwork?"

"It's coming," said Murphy. A lie. He hadn't bothered, thinking he'd run into a wall because the evidence was from another locale, though now he knew Kate could break down the wall, or at least make a good-sized dent in it.

"Well, it's going to take a while to remove the paint without destroying the underimage," he said, regarding the painting. He tugged his glasses off and rubbed at his eyes. "I'm guessing it's acrylic paint, and acrylic is a polymer, a plastic. It dries almost instantly and adheres to the paint below it. It's not like oil where the layers of paint are built up over time and you can x-ray to see the underpainting."

Kate considered bringing the piece to a painting conservator. They were, as the museum director at the Modernist had noted, magicians, but also notoriously slow. "How long will this take?"

"I can't even start this for a couple of days. There's a backlog of priority stuff."

"This *is* priority. Brown by way of Tapell," said Murphy, embellishing his lie, snapping his rubber band for emphasis.

The guy sighed. "I'll do my best for tomorrow. If you want the usual prints and fibers, I'll send it over when I'm finished, but you might lose most of them when I remove the paint splotches."

"Can you have Latent take a shot at it before you get to work?" asked Murphy.

"It's going to add time."

Murphy didn't see that they had a choice. "Okay. Latent's first. Then you. Then Fibers."

Kate couldn't stand still. "What do we do while we wait?"

"Hofmann estate lawyer," said Murphy. "C'mon. I already called him."

"I thought the estate was based in Provincetown, Massachusetts, where Hans Hofmann last worked."

"Right. But the lawyer for the estate is right here, in the Big Apple."

Eric Lapinsky was a smallish dapper man with close-cropped silver hair and a hooked nose. Even in his cowboy boots, a bit inconsistent with the Brooks Brothers suit, he was almost a head shorter than either Kate or Murphy.

"I'm still getting over the shock," said the lawyer as he closed his office door. He offered seats to Kate and Murphy, then took one behind his desk. "I've been close to Gaby since she was a girl. A lovely, gentle woman. Not a mean bone in her body."

"Ms. Hofmann shared ownership of the paintings with her brother and a niece, is that right?" asked Murphy.

"Yes. And no. You see, the two grandchildren and the niece inherited the bulk of the Hofmann estate, but there was already a foundation in place at that point, which had been put together by the artist's immediate heirs—all now deceased. The foundation paid the hefty inheritance tax on the work and continues to oversee the donation of paintings to museums, as well as give away money in the form of grants. Gaby and her brother, along with their cousin, each received a few paintings of their own with the proviso that they could not sell them without the others' permission, and that profits of any such sale would be divided among them. But Gaby couldn't sell any of her grandfather's paintings that were in the estate." Lapinsky looked from Kate to Murphy to make sure they were following him.

"During his lifetime, Hans Hofmann gave his son, Gaby's father, several works he'd made and a few made by his students or friends, which were considered *gifts*, and therefore outside of the estate, and those Gaby, or her brother, inherited specifically as their own."

"And the ones Gaby inherited she could sell if she wanted to," Kate asked, "without asking anyone?"

"Correct. Though I doubt she would have. First of all, there was no need—she was extremely well off. And second, the artwork, having come from her parents, had personal meaning for her above its worth."

"Do you have a list of the work in Ms. Hofmann's private collection?" Murphy asked.

"I can have it put together for you."

"Good. I'd like to be sure that nothing is missing," said Murphy.

"Does there appear to be?"

"I don't know. Not yet."

"The paintings that Ms. Hofmann owned jointly with her relatives, what happens to them now?" asked Kate.

"They revert to the estate."

"And the others, the ones she inherited from her father?"

"I'd have to consult Gaby's will to be absolutely certain, but I imagine they will go to her husband—to Henry."

"Henry Lifschultz," said Kate.

"That's right." Lapinsky frowned.

"Something we should know about Mr. Lifschultz?" Murphy was sliding the rubber band on and off his wrist.

"I can't say I know him that well, we only met a few times. Tall, good-looking guy, likes his fancy cars and handmade suits." Lapinsky's lips curled into a sneer. "The truth? Henry Lifschultz strikes me as a man who is about as crafty as he is good looking. And by *crafty* I don't mean smart." He considered the statement a moment. "I guess I shouldn't have said that."

"It's off the record," said Murphy. "Anything else you can tell us about him?"

"Well, Lifschultz has his own little architectural firm here in Manhattan. Not doing so well, according to the tax returns—and never has. Of course the industry's depressed—that's what Gaby keeps saying in his defense." Lapinsky sighed. "But I guess he's better than her first husband. Now there was a real cad." He laced his fingers together and sighed. "Gaby is—was—a fragile, gullible girl. She had a charmed but sheltered childhood. Her first husband got plenty of money out of her before she finally had the strength to give him the boot. I helped with that . . ." He smiled. "The divorce."

"And Henry Lifschultz? You think he was taking her for a ride, too?" Murphy asked.

"I couldn't say, but . . . I hoped Gaby had learned her lesson the first time around."

"Doesn't sound to me like Gabrielle Hofmann *did* learn her lesson the first time around," Murphy said as the elevator brought them down to the lobby.

"Lapinsky said Henry Lifschultz's architectural firm could use some business," said Kate. "I think this is the right time to build my dream house."

Henry Lifschultz reminded Kate of Michael Douglas in the movie *Wall Street*—chalk-striped suit, silk suspenders, hair gelled flat across his scalp, a tan in December that spoke of Aspen or Saint Barths, or maybe just après-shave bronzer.

Kate's plan of being incognito was immediately blown—Lifschultz recognized her from her TV show. "My wife—my late wife . . ." He looked down, sighed, took a full Barbara Walters moment. "Was a fan. She watched you every week. Until quite recently, that is. Her death was quite . . . sudden." He took a deep breath, and Kate thought there was something about everything he said that felt rehearsed. Of course she was acting, too, pretending not to know anything about his wife's death. But clearly, if Lifschultz was acting, they were not in the same play.

Kate tried for a sympathetic smile, thinking the man's wife had died only two days ago, and he was back at work, though it was difficult to fault him for that—work had been her salvation. *But two days?*

Maybe he saw it in Kate's eyes. "I realize it might seem odd," he said. "I mean the fact that I'm here, working, but I just couldn't stay at home."

Kate nodded. "So your wife was an art lover?"

"Oh, quite. Art aristocracy, you might say—a long and glorious history. Her grandfather was the artist Hans Hofmann. But if it's okay with you, I'd rather not talk about that." He tugged a tissue out of his pocket and blew his nose, then shifted gears. "So, about the house you mentioned, upstate?" He looked from Kate to Murphy, who smiled and looked back at Kate. Murphy had said exactly one word since they had set foot into Henry Lifschultz's office—"Hello"—and did not intend to say another. He had no idea who Lifschultz thought he was, but was hoping to be taken for Kate's lover.

"Um, yes," said Kate. "I've got this land, upstate, in, um, Rhinebeck, about sixty acres. I'm thinking a main house, maybe a couple of smaller guest cottages."

"Nice." Lifschultz offered up a slick smile. "By the way, how did you say you found me?"

"Oh." Kate spotted a magazine spread pinned just over Lifschultz's desk. "That place you did. I saw it in *Architectural Digest*."

Lifschultz swiveled in his chair. "You have a good memory. That was, oh . . . a few years ago."

"I save things," she said.

"Great," said Lifschultz. "Let's discuss your needs." Another quick swipe at his nose.

"My needs, right. Well, there's my art collection to consider," she said, hoping to bring him back to the subject she wanted to discuss.

"Oh, I'm very good with art. Obviously. I live with it myself. As I said, my wife . . ." He trailed off.

"So she was Hans Hofmann's granddaughter?" said Kate. "You know, I saw the most beautiful Hofmann painting the other day, at the Modernist Museum. I adore the place. It may not be the Met or MOMA—not yet, anyway—but it really is a wonderful little jewel."

"How nice to hear." Lifschultz's bronzed skin seemed to glow a bit more. "I'm on the board."

"Really? The director, Colin Leader, is such a nice man. You must know him."

"Well, yes, I know him, of course, but I'm fairly new to the board and we don't socialize. Other than museum functions, not at all." He reached behind him, plucked a pad of grid paper off a shelf and in careful block letters wrote: MCKINNON HOME, RHINEBECK, NY; then asked for her home address, telephone, e-mail, which Kate supplied. He flicked at his nose, looked up, and offered a seductive smile. "So, let's get back to your *needs*."

Kate managed to talk her way through the next twenty minutes of Henry Lifschultz's questions. Yes, she definitely wanted a pool, no tennis court, high ceilings for sure, lots of wall space for paintings. By the time she finished bullshitting she was so convinced she was building a house that when she and Murphy were out on the street she felt disappointed that she wasn't.

"Lifschultz said he didn't socialize with Colin Leader," she said. "But Cecile Edelman, the ex–Modernist Museum board member, put him on the golf course with Leader, remember? Why would she lie about that? And another thing: He recognized me—right? —knew my name, but never mentioned my painting being destroyed at the Modernist, his museum, which was odd—"

"Well, the lawyer, Lapinsky, said he was stupid."

"And crafty," said Kate.

"And those sniffles looked more like a cocaine drip than sadness to me. He didn't seem all that broken up about his wife." Murphy started weaving the rubber band around his fingers. "I'm gonna talk to Greenwich PD again, see what else they can tell me."

"You think it's possible to put a tail on him?"

"You kidding?"

"No, I don't think so," said Kate.

"You talking about Greenwich PD, or NYPD?"

"I don't think we can tell Greenwich PD what to do."

"Well, you can forget telling the NYPD, too. There's no reasonable cause, no nothing. We're not even supposed to be talking to the guy, remember? Brown doesn't want us dealing with out-of-state problems."

"But if there's some sort of link between Lifschultz, in Connecticut,

and Colin Leader, in New York, maybe Brown's got an in-state problem."

"You tell him that," said Murphy. "Not me."

Henry Lifschultz hugged the phone to his ear. "You know, the PBS
lady, the one with the art show?" He listened a moment. "That's right.
She was just here. A few minutes ago, with some guy—who could've
been a cop." He sniffed. "Supposedly wants to build her dream house. I
don't know, it could be true, I guess. Maybe I'm just being paranoid, but
I don't like it." The phone felt hot in his hand. He suddenly remembered he should not be making this call from his office. "Listen, I'll call
you later." He dabbed at his nose, which lately was dripping all the time.
He'd have to lay off the coke. "From a pay phone," he said.

CHAPTER 18

Kate never got used to the smell of the morgue, the acrid odor of formaldehyde, which was leaching through her mask.

Beatrice Larsen had just been unzipped from a body bag, and the ME's assistant, a skinny guy who didn't look quite strong enough for the job, slid her roughly from one table onto the coroner's slab as though hauling a huge slab of meat, an ungainly process which Kate knew had nothing to do with insensitivity—a body stiff with rigor mortis was not an easy thing to manipulate.

The ME, one of the senior forensic pathologists, probably around forty with dark-ringed eyes above her mask, had been on duty since 4 A.M. and looked ready for a starring role in *Night of the Living Dead*.

Kate was immediately sorry she had come—the last time she'd been to the morgue was already playing in her mind. She attempted a deep breath behind her mask, but it was going to take a lot more than that to dispel the image of her husband's body on a steel slab. She stared at the cadaver, working hard to remain in the present, focusing on age spots and wrinkled flesh, then glanced over at Murphy, who was managing to pluck at his rubber band despite the rubber gloves.

The assistant tugged off Larsen's paint-stained pants, then sweater, not an easy job over stiff arms. He cut away a long-sleeved thermal tee to expose sagging breasts, then white cotton panties, bagging all the clothing for later examination, then arranged and rearranged a ruler beside various parts of the woman's naked body and shot several pre-autopsy X rays and set the film aside.

To Kate, it seemed unfair that Larsen, ignored for a significant portion of her life, should now be exposed to such a public and invasive inspection. She thought any minute the woman would sit up and protest.

She laid her hand on the old woman's arm, wanted to tell her that everything was going to be all right. Even through her gloves the flesh felt cold and waxy.

The ME tapped the Dictaphone on and in a flat monotone stated time and date, where the autopsy was taking place, and the victim's particulars—race, age, height, weight, degree of rigor, temperature of the body—then double-gloved and made the standard Y incision.

Kate flashed on Beatrice Larsen stabbing out a cigarette, proclaiming her independence, the once proud, independent woman reduced to a biology project.

It was a dreadful process that seemed to go on forever—organs removed, weighed and picked over, samples smeared onto glass slides for microscopic analysis, cataloged and recorded.

"Heart shows some weakness," said the ME. "Could be congestive heart failure, though I can't say for sure. I'll have to do some tests. Could be several contributing factors." She removed a lung and picked at it with a scalpel. "There's something here. I'm not sure what, a growth, or . . . maybe it's something aspirated. Hard to tell, emphysema has deteriorated the organ." She sliced at the lung and handed the sample to her assistant. "Clean this up," she said, then went back to more slicing and dicing.

After a while, she pulled her gloves off, dusted her hands with powder, then double-gloved again, this time examining the inside of Larsen's mouth and nose, plucking stuff out of both and depositing it onto a tray, then retracted the woman's eyelids, pin light aimed at flat irises. "Lots of broken blood vessels here, and the pupils—"

Murphy leaned in. "What is it?"

"Looks like she might have choked or suffocated. Something else, too." She swabbed Larsen's eyelids with a Q-Tip and sealed it in a small Ziploc bag.

"What is it?" asked Murphy.

"I'm not certain. Looks like some sort of residue. I'll send this to the lab. Check with them."

The assistant had hosed down the samples taken from the lung, put them through a sieve, and presented them back to the ME on a metal tray as if serving up foie gras.

The ME picked at the small nubbins. "Looks like standard pillow filling, foam rubber." She looked over at the tiny blood-and-saliva-coated blobs she'd taken from Larsen's nose and mouth. "These could be the same, but I don't want to put them through the wash until I've checked for anything else."

"Like what?" asked Kate.

"Like anything." The ME yawned behind her mask.

Kate flashed on the pillow from the artist's studio, the one on the wicker chair. "You think someone held a pillow over her face?"

"Hard to say. When we get all the lab results we might know better."

"How soon can we get those?" asked Kate.

"This isn't an episode of *CSI*," said the ME. "The tests take *real* time. You know, hours, days. Not six minutes until the next commercial." She whipped her mask off. "But off the record, I'd say it's unlikely she nibbled on a foam rubber pillow in her sleep."

Darby Herrick lit one cigarette from the other, paint-stained fingers trembling slightly as she perused the racks that held decades of her aunt's artwork, half the paintings wrapped in plastic, the others coated with a quarter-inch of dust.

The talk with Kate McKinnon was still reverberating in her mind.

Damn. She should never have let that woman back into the studio. What was she thinking? She took a deep inhale of her cigarette trying to sort it out, but her mind was as cloudy as the smoke that swirled around her face.

But what choice did she have? She couldn't have said no. How would that have looked? She sighed heavily and a chunk of ash broke off her cigarette, landed on the edge of a dust-coated painting and sparked. Herrick whacked at it furiously, sending clouds of dust motes into the air. *Shit.* Burning up her inheritance before she even got it—not a good idea, not after all the crap she had had to put up with for so many years—cooking, cleaning, errands—and now she was supposed to share it with her brother Larry, who had never done a goddamn thing for Beatrice; her brother, who was married with three kids, living in Boca Raton in a pseudo-Mexican-style house with one of those stupid above-ground swimming pools in his stupid backyard. *Well, fuck you, Larry!*

Herrick tugged a painting out of the rack and wiped away the dust. It was an early piece, totally abstract, and a good one. She turned the canvas around and spotted her aunt's inimitable signature, plus the date, 1959, a landmark year for the woman—big show, great reviews, the *ArtNews* profile which had named her "the most important woman painter of her generation." One of the paintings the museums would want for sure—but one they might never get.

She had not expected the call, a surprise and a blessing—*everyone does it . . . who's to know . . . just between you and me . . . better hurry . . . beat the tax man*—a way to make some money *before* taxes and screw Larry in the process. Why not? The first painting, the *tester,* had already been delivered, and it looked like it was a go—which meant more to come. Maybe this 1959 painting would be a good one.

Herrick put it aside, slid another small painting out of the rack and wiped away the grime to read what her aunt had written on the back: *Self-portrait. 1948.* An early piece, before her aunt's breakthrough. She wondered if there would be a market for it. She flipped it over, drew her hand over the front of the canvas, removing years of accumulated dust from the portrait. Her aunt's eyes were staring out at her when the call came asking her for more paintings, and fast.

CHAPTER 19

Miranda Wilcox was having a productive morning on the telephone—Europe, Asia, Latin America—calls to a couple of her new *vendors*, then to her most valuable art collectors, a discreet group, not the kind to be waving paddles at auctions, ones who enjoyed the hunt for works not readily available on the open market, who, thanks to Wilcox, got to own art that the U.S. government, particularly the IRS (not to mention Interpol) would be interested in knowing about—a few pieces that mysteriously disappeared just before an estate of a dead artist was settled, though the heirs hadn't a clue as to what happened, or so they claimed.

At the moment, she was speaking with one of her favorite clients—a man who never used his name on the phone, but Wilcox knew his voice—a former American businessman who had made a fortune in commodities and exchange, not all of it strictly kosher (the IRS was still waiting for its cut), now living in a small town a couple of hours northwest of Buenos Aires. "So," he said. "What have you got for me this time?"

"A Hans Hofmann. An absolute classic."

"Provenance?" he asked, inquiring about its history as a sold or bartered object.

"Never sold," said Wilcox. "It went directly from the artist to the family."

"And now they want to sell it."

"Let's just say it's . . . available. Check your e-mail. I've sent you a JPEG." She paused. "And, um, please delete it once you've had a look. Wouldn't want another collector to somehow get a peek."

"When do you need to know?"

"No later than tomorrow," said Wilcox, knowing the collector was stalling for a little time to check auction prices. "The piece has to move fast. You understand."

Wilcox sat back and exhaled a long breath. This was the part of her business she liked best. The other part, the more legit part, if one wanted to call it that—acquiring art for corporations—paid her rent, but not much more. Of course she overcharged the corporations, found them somewhat inferior examples of high-priced art, usually got paid by both parties—the buyer and the seller. What the hell, they each got what they wanted—or thought they did.

But this part was Wilcox's specialty—trading in artworks of the recently dead, selling them quickly and quietly before the estate took inventory, a little *something* for the heirs to pocket before taxes.

Legal? Illegal? A fine line, if you asked Miranda Wilcox. So what if the work slid under the taxman's radar. Really, why should the government get all the money? She was simply performing a service, and a good one, enabling heirs to retain a portion of their rightful proceeds before the IRS buzzards descended.

Wilcox jotted a few numbers on a piece of paper, did the math, figuring out her percentage. She was already feeling the buzz. Doing a deal like this always got her hot, warmth spreading through her body, a tingling between her legs.

Should she call him? She wanted to so badly. *No, better not. Too risky. Maybe. Maybe not.* Her French-manicured fingernails were tapping the phone, trying to decide, when it rang.

Another client, this one a Roman gentleman with some vague connection to the Vatican.

"So glad you called me back," she purred. "Something quite special has just come to my attention, and I immediately thought of you." *Because you're such a sucker.* She glanced at the Gorky painting that she had procured for a client in Asia who'd had the audacity to bail at the last minute. Well, that was the last time she would do business with him—unless she could get him something inferior and overcharge him, just to get even.

She glanced at the Gorky painting. It was good, not one of the artist's best, but better than half the stuff she often peddled.

"Tell me about it," said the Roman collector, clearly eager—Wilcox had left the message only a few hours earlier.

She liked a man who made decisions swiftly, who took control, did not fall apart in a crisis—like some men she knew.

"It's a rare piece," she said. "One of the artist's late paintings, filled with symbolism, very moody. A classic." *Aren't they all?* "Paintings like this rarely come on the market. I've sent you the usual JPEG."

They went through the drill—provenance, how soon she needed to know—as if the deal were totally legit, neither party fooling the other.

Wilcox looked up, surveyed the handful of artworks leaning against the wall, work that would not be with her long, work from new heirs, or pieces that had disappeared out the back door of museums—lesser works that would not immediately be missed. Her eyes settled back on the Gorky painting, mostly gray and white with scattered doodads— nonspecific symbols they were called—that the artist favored. She remembered studying him back at Vassar when she was an undergrad, an art history major filled with dreams of teaching or museum work, dreams long ago abandoned, dreams that now made her want to laugh—or cry—she wasn't sure which. She sighed, hoped the Roman would buy the painting. She detested the idea of inventory—a painting hanging around was simply too dangerous.

After the call, Wilcox tried to tamp down the adrenaline rush that always accompanied an impending sale by booking a flight to the Cayman Islands, where she would deposit her proceeds (she was strictly a cash operation, no wire services, thank you, no paper trail; and truthfully, she just loved handling all of those bills)—but it just made her hotter.

A few yards to the bathroom to retrieve her new vibrator, the one she'd imagined jamming up *his* ass while they fucked. Yes, the man had some kinky needs, things his wife would never do—his *ex-wife*. She liked the sound of that, "ex-wife," and said it aloud a few times as she kicked off her shoes, tugged her panties down, stretched out on her king-sized bed and switched on the vibrator.

The two small watercolors were wrapped and ready to go. Not major paintings, nothing that would be missed, not right away—the estate had not yet taken inventory, nor had the police. He'd acted disoriented when asked about whether or not anything else was missing, and had evaded the question. Now he slipped the watercolors into his briefcase. Later, he would simply walk out with them. The larger painting would have to go in the back of the Hummer. He would have to wait until dark. In a day or two, with the appropriate distress, he would report all of them missing.

For the past two years he had been selling off artwork, here and there, simply sneaking lesser-valued pieces out of the storage closet, first with his wife's permission, later without—something that would no longer be an issue.

But now there would be cops looking over his shoulder, and once the estate got involved, well, that would be the end of it.

He surveyed the room. *What else?*

The ink-on-newspaper by Franz Kline? Small but desirable; no question it would deliver big bucks.

Ten minutes to get the picture out of its frame, a sliced finger in the process—the blood just missing the work itself. A close call. How could he—or anyone—explain how a famous black-and-white Franz Kline had suddenly sprouted color?

The phone rang just as Miranda Wilcox came.

She laid the vibrator aside and picked up the receiver.

Another client, this one in South America, living on a sprawling Colombian plantation, which she'd gotten a look at a year ago when she'd hand-delivered a small Monet *Haystack*; the least good of the half dozen the museum owned, the other five on permanent display. This one had not seen the light of day since the museum purchased it for a reason no one could seem to remember.

She knew that all of the museums had second-rate treasures—one too many Egyptian sarcophagi or a slap dash late-period Picasso—relegated to life in a temperature-controlled basement bin.

The way Miranda Wilcox saw it she had *liberated* the Monet *Haystack*, gotten it to someone who would love and cherish it forever. Sure, the Colombian was buying class and culture—a game that had been going on for centuries—but who wasn't? And why shouldn't a drug lord have good art? Miranda Wilcox didn't see anything wrong with that.

She pictured the man on the other end of the phone—the swarthy good looks, sexy scar that ran the length of his cheek; the few nights they had spent together when she'd delivered the Monet. The truth: The guy had been a disappointment. *Foreplay? Forget it.* The guy was all slam-bang-thank-you-ma'am—except there had not been any thank-you. Plus—insult to injury—he had a small dick. In the middle of their ten-minute *lovemaking* she'd been tempted to ask—*Is it in yet?*—but she hadn't dared, not with the Colombian's temper, which was always there, just under the surface.

"One of the greats," she said, "though, um, a slightly lesser known abstract expressionist. It will make a terrific addition to your collection. Something to add *prestige*, show that you are not simply interested in shopping-list art, you know, brand names—though I'm sure this one will be joining those ranks soon enough with the artist now deceased—very recently, too. I'd suggest purchasing before the market heats up, and surely before the work goes to auction."

The Colombian grunted, obviously not thrilled with the idea of buying any artist who was "lesser known."

"You know, I also have one of the truly established greats—a gorgeous Arshile Gorky painting." She took the opportunity to create a little bidding war.

"Gorky," said the Colombian. "A Russian?"

"No, darling. Armenian. And one of the most important members of the New York School."

Another grunted question.

"No, it's not a *school*. It's a *group*. A group of painters. Really important American painters."

The Colombian grunted again.

"Yes, I know I said he was *Armenian*, but he came to the States when he was . . . like fifteen, or something, so he's considered American." She tried not to sigh. This art history lesson was becoming a big fucking bore. "Anyone who knows anything about art will recognize a Gorky painting in an instant. And trust me. It's got tremendous resale value. It's as liquid as oil."

That did it. The Colombian grunted more contentedly, and Wilcox suggested he buy both paintings, that they would complement each other, and he seemed to like that idea too. "I'd love to bring them to you, but I can't. Not right now." *All the way to Colombia for your small dick? Forget it, baby.*

Oh, hadn't he explained? He was here, in New York; he could come by later and see the paintings. If they were all she claimed he'd give her the cash and take them back with him when he returned home on his private plane.

Wilcox shut her cellular. Two deals in one day; maybe three. Could anything be more perfect?

CHAPTER 20

Kate and Murphy stared at the newly cleaned paintings. First, the one that had been in the cat box at Gabrielle Hofmann's home.

"Well, it's all here," said Kate. "Madonna and Britney, which was the clue to Larsen, and the Hofmann painting, which indicated that Gabrielle was a target."

"What's the painting next to it?" asked Murphy.

"I actually know that," said Kate. "It's a portrait of Washington Irving." She glanced just below it.

"Now I get this, too," she said. "It's Sleepy Hollow."

"As in, *The Legend of . . . ?*"

"Right," said Kate. "Sleepy Hollow, Washington Irving's home. It's in Tarrytown, New York. I've been there."

"Tarrytown," said Murphy. "Where Beatrice Larsen lived."

Kate nodded, thinking once again it was information gleaned too late. "It's in the other painting, too." *Also too late*, she thought.

They moved to the other painting, the one that had been retrieved from Beatrice Larsen's trash can. The lab had done a good job, the globs and streaks of acrylic paint had been completely stripped from the surface, revealing all of the images.

The lab report, several pages long, included a breakdown of a variety of fibers and hairs that had been extracted from both paintings' surfaces, a chemical analysis of the acrylic paint—a high percentage of pigment in the polymer, which both Kate and Murphy knew meant the paint was

good quality—and the type of canvas, Belgium linen, and even the weave count.

"So it's the same kind of linen in all the clue paintings so far," said Murphy.

"And fairly high-grade. A lot better than painting on cotton duck. Our boy wants these to last."

They looked at the imagery, once again at the fragment replicated from Larsen's own painting—Madonna and Britney—and the building painted beside it, Sleepy Hollow, then at the lower half of the painting, previously obscured.

"An apple?" said Murphy, scratching at his stubble. "What do you think? Something to do with the next painting our psycho is targeting?"

Kate's adrenaline was already pumping. "An apple? A still life? What about that Magritte painting? You know, the famous one of the man with the apple in front of his face?"

"Should we try and find out who owns it?" asked Murphy.

"Hold on." Kate slid her magnifying glass over a tiny mark on the picture. "Look at this."

"It's some sort of bug," said Murphy. "Magritte doesn't paint bugs on his apples, does he?"

"No. But there are bugs, ants, insects, in other surrealist works." Kate closed her eyes, pictured Salvador Dalí's famous 1929 film, *Un Chien Andalou*, a scene where a man stares at a cut in his hand, and ants crawl out. She ran the magnifying glass back over the spidery critter. It didn't look like an ant, but there was something familiar about it. "I feel like I should know this."

"Something for Mert Sharfstein to look at?"

"Maybe. Give me a minute." It was irking the hell out of her that she could not come up with it. "The Institute should revoke my degree."

"It might come to you if you stop trying so hard." Murphy slid the painting out of her view. "Let me distract you with some news. I spoke to Tarrytown PD. Beatrice Larsen's will—the niece, Darby Herrick, inherits half of everything."

"Who gets the other half?"

"Brother, in Florida. Herrick and her brother are the offspring of Larsen's only sister. Parents are both dead. Herrick lives in their house."

"And now she's got another house," said Kate, "which she has to split with her brother—not to mention all of the aunt's paintings. Once the art establishment reevaluates Larsen, those paintings will be worth plenty. The woman was a part of history."

"How come when *you* say the old lady's art is gonna be worth more now that she's dead, it's fine, but when *I* said it, I was an asshole?"

"Some of us are just born with class, Murphy. What can I tell you?"

"Not from what I know about your humble origins." Murphy snapped his rubber band. "So, okay, if Herrick inherits, that gives her *motive* as well as *opportunity.*"

"True," said Kate. "But why destroy three paintings that she would have inherited?"

"You forgetting inheritance taxes? The IRS estimates tax *per* painting. That's three less paintings to pay taxes on."

"If that's the case, why destroy only three? If I were Darby Herrick and I wanted to cut down on the tax, I'd choose the best twenty or thirty paintings, take them somewhere safe, then I'd burn the place down to get rid of the mediocre paintings—while my aunt was still in it. It makes more sense that way, doesn't it?"

"Only if it was premeditated," said Murphy.

"Come to think of it," said Kate, "we don't *really* know that those three paintings were slashed. We only have Darby Herrick's word for it. She could be hiding them."

"Or . . ." Murphy was plucking out a discordant tune on his rubber band. "Suppose Herrick is sick of waiting around for the old girl to kick, goes nuts for a minute, kills the aunt, panics, decides to slash a few paintings to make it look like the psycho the tabloids have been writing about."

"Maybe," said Kate. "But wouldn't it have been a lot easier to make it look like an accident? Larsen smoked like a fiend. She falls asleep, sets the place on fire. End of story."

"Maybe Herrick wanted the house, too," said Murphy. "And maybe she might not know about the inheritance tax."

"Darby Herrick didn't strike me as stupid, or someone who would act on impulse. I think she'd do her homework." Kate thought about her meeting with the woman, tried to imagine her holding a pillow over the old woman's face, then pictured the ratty pillow on Beatrice Larsen's studio chair, the insides coming out.

They had contacted the Tarrytown PD right after Larsen's autopsy, asked that they collect every pillow in the house, send it to the One Police Plaza lab to compare with the stuff in Larsen's lungs and nose. "I want to see what our lab makes of the pillow stuffing, if it's the same as what the ME plucked out of Beatrice Larsen's nose and lungs."

"Right," said Murphy. "And we should be getting blood work back any minute. See if the bloodstains at the various crime scenes belong to anyone other than the vics, and if they find a common link. That would be nice."

"*Nice* is not the word," said Kate. She laid the magnifying glass back over what looked like a bug in that painting. *Damn.* It was right there, just below her consciousness.

What is it?

A *fake?*

The caller must have been playing a hoax—one Gregory Sarkisian did not appreciate. He had tried to dismiss it, but then the guy started giving him a bunch of statistics, some of which Sarkisian recognized as true. And then, when he said that Gorky hadn't started painting his series of *Garden* pictures until the year *after* the painting Sarkisian owned was made, it sounded as if he knew what he was talking about. But he didn't. It just couldn't be true. Could it? He tried to recall which arts organization the guy said he was with, but couldn't.

Sarkisian stared at the painting. It was the genuine article, he was certain of it. Still, the call had unnerved him. He would at least listen to what the man had to say—if he actually showed up.

Today was the three-month anniversary of the painting's purchase, a bit too public for Sarkisian's taste, the Christie's auction, the interview in the *Times* the next day, spending so much money for one painting—$7.3 million, a new record set, the highest price ever paid for an Arshile Gorky.

But to Sarkisian—a descendant of Armenian immigrants who had come to the States to escape the Turkish invasion—the spending of all that money for a painting made by one of his countrymen, an immigrant just like his grandparents, was well worth it. His grandfather had filled his head with stories of hardship and oppression, taught him about hard work and dedication, all of which had paid off: Sarkisian, at fifty-one, was CEO of a major investment firm, and in many ways he had bought the painting as much for his grandfather as for himself.

He glanced back at his prize. *Fake? No way.*

If the man had the nerve to show up, he was going to give him a piece of his mind, crush even the whisper of a rumor that his painting was bogus.

He regarded the painting's mostly gray tonality, which some might call depressing, though Sarkisian saw it as beautifully melancholy, a condition that had afflicted his people for centuries, and obviously Gorky as well, the artist having committed suicide at the age of forty-four. But there was more to it, a playfulness in the wavy lines and odd-ball doodles that skittered across the washy gray surface which continued to intrigue him. A day had yet to pass when Sarkisian did not look at his painting and smile. Right now his plan was to keep it for a few years, then donate it to his favorite New York museum in honor of his grandfather and get a hefty tax deduction at the same time—a transaction his grandfather would surely have appreciated.

What was the word the guy on the phone had used? Now that Sarkisian thought about it, the guy had not said the painting was a fake, he'd said something about the painting being a *phony,* or had he said that about Gorky himself?

Well, he would clear that up. It was absurd. Infuriating. He pictured the back of the canvas plastered with museum and gallery receipts, all the previous owners, a testament to the painting's authenticity. There had never been a question.

Sarkisian leaned closer to the painting. He was studying the unmistakable Gorky signature when his secretary buzzed.

———

"I've got it!"

Kate had been staring at the strange buglike image on and off for the past hour.

"It's what the surrealist painters called a nonspecific symbol. Something odd to hook the viewer into the painting as they try to inter-

pret it, or figure out what it is—a spider, a roach, a crawling eyeball? I'd say this is either early Joan Miró or Arshile Gorky." She sat down at Murphy's computer. "You're hooked up to all the art sites, right?"

"*Wrong.* You think the NYPD is going to pay for them?"

"Not even for the Art Squad?"

Murphy shook his head and scratched his stubbly cheeks. "Pathetic, I know."

"We need to get you a grant," said Kate. "And a shave."

Murphy drew his hand over his chin, raised an eyebrow, then turned to peruse his bookcase, tugged out two big books and plunked them onto his desk—one on Gorky, one on Miró. "These are the complete works of

each artist," he said. "It may be old-fashioned, but it'll have to do."

Kate and Murphy flipped pages quickly, trying not to tear them, each of them with a magnifying glass in hand.

It took them almost a half hour, but Kate eventually found what they were looking for. "Here it is. Arshile Gorky."

Kate read the print under the painting. "It's at the Museum of Modern Art, Houston, Texas."

Murphy immediately had the museum's registrar on the phone, asking about the painting and getting an answer in minutes. "The museum sold the painting at auction a few months ago."

"Did they say which auction house sold it?"

"Christie's."

"**Your five-o'clock is here,**" Sarkisian's secretary said through the intercom.

"Thank you, Iris. You can go now, if you'd like."

But the moment the guy walked into his office, Gregory Sarkisian was sorry. Why had he bothered? He knew his Gorky painting was authentic. Who was this guy, anyway? Face half hidden by a wide-brimmed hat, collar of his long black coat turned up, bushy mustache the only discernible feature. He looked ridiculous, like something out of an old Humphrey Bogart/Peter Lorre movie. Sarkisian would have laughed, but something stopped him. "Listen here . . ." Sarkisian tilted his head toward the painting above his desk. "My painting is *no* fake, despite whatever information you may *think* you have." He glanced at his watch, and the guy took note of it.

"Don't worry, I won't stay long."

Good. "Who did you say you were with, which arts organization?"

"You got my warning, didn't you?" The words a rasped whisper.

"What are you talking about?" Sarkisian was losing patience. "I have absolute proof this is genuine. The signature. The provenance. Everything about it has been authenticated. And I've already checked— Gorky produced an early *Garden* series as well as a later one, so what you said . . ." He sniffed. "Never mind. I'm sorry I agreed to this meeting in the first place. It's obviously a waste of time for us both. We're finished here."

But the guy strode past him, not stopping until he was only inches from the Gorky painting. He reached out to touch it.

"Now hold on—"

The move was so fast, Sarkisian wasn't sure it had happened, the knife in and out of his body in two fast strokes. In shock, he pressed his hands over the wounds and noticed that one of his Hermès suspenders had been slit and was flapping free, a gift from his latest girlfriend, a Brazilian model half his age.

He was trying to think of what to do or say—cry out for help, reach for the phone, his thoughts and actions jumbled—fear, pain, shock— tumbling over each other in his brain like dominoes. But when he looked up again and saw what was happening—the lunatic carving up his Gorky—the sheer audacity of the act so infuriated him that he forgot his wounds. He snatched the silver letter opener off the desk, and brought it down between the man's shoulder blades, though it did not go deep, hitting bone and stopping.

The guy whipped around, in almost as much shock as Sarkisian, plucked the opener from his flesh, holding it, staring at the blood, then dropped it to the floor.

Sarkisian reached out again, managed to get a grip on the guy's fedora, which he knocked off as he fell backward. As he was going down, he caught a glimpse of his prized painting in tatters, and the guy's face, mainly the bushy mustache, which, oddly enough, reminded him of the artist Arshile Gorky.

Calm now. Very calm. You can do this. One foot in front of the other.

A quick check of the coat. Other than the tear, it's okay, bloodstains obscured by the black fabric.

Hat back in place, collar turned up. All very *Spy-versus-Spy* or maybe *Austin Powers.* That's a good role, goofy and funny. Life as a spoof.

Gloved hands wedged deep in pockets, fingers wrapped around Sarkisian's silver letter opener, Mike Myers grin imagined on the lips.

The outer office is quiet, no secretary. A slight disappointment. It had been exciting to think of her out there during the act, only a few feet away. *Where did she go? For help? No, there was no screaming or calling out.*

Down the long hallway, offices on either side, a few with open doors. *Don't look, just keep walking. That's it.*

No one seems to notice; no one bolts out of an office, shouting, *You, there, stop!*

At the end of the hallway, the receptionist sits behind a large wooden island.

Keep going, head down, nod politely.

The receptionist does not bother to look up, mumbles, "Bye," on automatic.

Out the door, elevator button pressed. *Come on. Come on.*

The doors open, the elevator, remarkably, is empty.

The doors close.

A deep breath, audible, almost a sob. Hands shaking in pockets now, body covered in sweat, noticed for the first time, along with a palpable excitement.

I did it!

The elevator doors open. A man in a dark suit and a woman in a dress the color of blood step in, chatting: "Do you believe Harry said . . ."

They do not bother to check out the stranger with the hat pulled down and coat collar up. No more Austin Powers grin. Now it's a serious mien, something out of an espionage novel or old black-and-white movie.

The doors open. More people crowd in. Easier now to hang in the back, be invisible.

That's me. A ghost.

The doors open into the lobby.

Hang back. That's it. Now follow, just on the edge of the crowd, not quite one of them, but maybe, maybe taken as one of this elite, well-dressed business crowd. Why not?

A new role: successful entrepreneur.

Through the front door. Out on the street.

Another deep breath: The air smells like freedom.

Night. City lights illuminate the dark street, changing the screenplay into something gritty, but with humor, a superhero flick, *Spider-Man* or

The Hulk, the idea of scaling a building or simply walking right through it imagined, almost believed, for a moment.

Just keep walking. Better to merge with the crowd moving along the busy city street like a swarm of bees.

The back has begun to throb, but it is nothing compared with the normal daily pain. A Band-Aid and a pill, that's all it needs.

Down the subway stairs, hat still in place, though that bushy mustache is plucked off with the simple swipe of a hand—*Now you see it, now you don't; and for my next trick, ladies and gentlemen*—dropped into a trash container, the spy character along with it.

The subway platform is cold and the role has become something sadder now, closer to real life, unrehearsed and painful.

The train barrels down the tunnel, screeches to a stop, its doors open.

The curtain falls.

CHAPTER 21

FINANCE CEO GETS FINAL CUT

The murder of Gregory Sarkisian, 51, CEO of Financial Services Worldwide, just could be the latest in a string of bizarre art-related crimes. Though authorities are reluctant to tie the fatal attack on the financier to other recent attacks, the similarity to the fatal stabbings of wealthy art collectors Nicholas Starrett, on Long Island, and Gabrielle Hofmann Lifschultz of Greenwich, Connecticut, seem eerily alike—all three victims were found dead below million-dollar works of art, which had been slashed to ribbons.

Sources close to the investigation are speculating a connection, but . . .

What sources? Floyd Brown did not bother to finish the article. He tossed the *Post* onto his desk. Bad enough the psycho had finally made his way into his jurisdiction, but did the newspapers have to have a contest as to who could come up with the goddamn tackiest headline? No surprise. Good taste never sold newspapers. But didn't these people know that the victim was somebody's brother or father or husband? Didn't they care?

Brown knew the answer to that one.

He glanced back at the paper. Of course they were right. The similarity between the cases seemed to be more than coincidence, the MO pretty much a lock. And he knew the media would not let it go. Slashing an expensive painting was news, but slashing expensive people was *big* news. The newspapers and TV news would be stoking the flames as long as there was a spark. By now, every news station's research department was looking into the three victims' personal lives, hoping for something juicy; reporters rooting through fact and innuendo, not particularly caring which was which, just looking for the best story. Brown hadn't seen the *Times* or the *News*, though he'd caught a bit of CNN's sober reporting, *thank God*. But he didn't dare look at *Fox News*, which was guaranteed to be sensational.

He sagged into his chair and regarded the jacket on the Sarkisian homicide that had been sent over to him from Midtown North. Somehow he'd been waiting for it, knew in his gut that it was only a matter of time.

Damn. Why did his instincts always have to be right?

The easy cases usually broke fast. This damn case had gone into overtime before he'd even gotten it. It didn't mean they wouldn't break it, just that it was not going to be one of the easy ones.

Brown stood, swiped a stack of papers and folders off his desk and headed for the conference room.

FBI criminal psychiatrist and profiler Mitch Freeman had stayed up late reading through the material—the slashed de Kooning and Pollock paintings, the murder of Nicholas Starrett, the incomplete autopsy report on Beatrice Larsen, and the latest art-related murder, Gregory Sarkisian. The FBI had taken an interest in the case, and Freeman did not have to be persuaded to be part of it. In fact, he had volunteered. He'd worked with the NYPD on several cases, and with Kate McKinnon on two, the Death Artist and then, last year, the Color Blind case—and had been looking for an excuse to see her again. He thought he had established something more than a working relationship with her, but after a half dozen unreturned calls he figured he was wrong. He took his reading glasses off and looked up as Floyd Brown cut into the room.

"Hey, Mitch." Brown slapped the folders onto the table. "You look tired."

"Thanks a lot, Floyd. So do you." Freeman smiled at Brown. The two men liked each other. Not always the case with the Bureau and local police.

"You get briefed by Chief Tapell?"

Freeman nodded. "Conferenced with her yesterday, along with my Bureau chief. I ran what I could about your unsub through the Violent Criminal Apprehension Program, VICAP, but no similar case came up. It's a strange one." He shook his head. "By the way, the Bureau wants everything passed through them. You'll have to duplicate reports for FBI Manhattan and Quantico. My associates back at Behavioral Science will want to see what we turn up on this guy."

"Why? BSS planning another psycho survey?"

"Just our way of having a good time." Freeman smiled. "For the moment the Bureau is sticking to research and fieldwork, but there could be agents on your doorstep any day."

Just what we need, thought Brown, the FBI—*the G*, the cops called them—telling us what to do. "Figured as much," he said. He slid into a chair and checked the clock on the wall. "Murphy will be here soon."

"Art Squad, right?" He hesitated before he asked, "And, uh, McKinnon, too?"

Brown tried not to smile. He suspected the shrink was carrying a torch. "She'll be here."

"She okay?" Freeman tried to seem casual. "I mean, since her husband, and you know—"

"Hard to tell," said Brown. "McKinnon keeps things to herself."

Freeman nodded. "I was surprised she wanted in on the case."

"Nicholas Starrett, first vic—at least the first we know of—was a friend of hers. You know McKinnon."

Freeman did. Or thought he did. A woman on a mission, the way he always saw her, someone who would not quit until she got results. Last time, the special agent in charge, guy named Grange, a real tough nugget, hated having an ex-cop like McKinnon on the case, but he had softened, ended up respecting her, maybe even having a bit of a crush on her. Freeman pictured Kate the last time he'd seen her—long streaked hair, elegant wardrobe; the woman was pure class, though he suspected something hotter and sexier burned under that cool exterior. And he'd hoped to find out. They'd had coffee, then dinner, once. But nothing had happened. It had been too soon. Freeman knew the psychology of mourning. He wouldn't push her. But maybe now, a year later . . .

His reverie was broken by Nicky Perlmutter, who gave him a friendly whack on the back. "You know it's gotta be weird if they're sending *you* in."

"A psycho who slashes paintings *and* people? I'd say that's weird enough." Freeman shook hands with the six-foot-four detective, took in the guy's carrot-red hair and freckles, the Huck Finn face on a big man's body. "By the way, I can always make room for you in my schedule, private therapy sessions—which I *know* you need."

"Thanks, Doc. But my astrologer says to beware of shrinks bearing free advice."

"Who said it was free?"

The men were laughing when Kate walked in, Murphy just behind her.

She looked from Brown to Freeman, then Perlmutter, who popped out of his chair and embraced her. "Still the most gorgeous fucking woman in New York!"

"Who told you I was fucking?" Kate laughed, then pulled back and eyed Perlmutter. "What is it—you have a closetful of khakis and blue shirts? I swear this is *exactly* what you were wearing the last time I saw you." Thoughts of that last time rippled through her psyche, but she maintained her smile.

"Can't say the same about you." Perlmutter returned the once-over. "You've turned into fucking Patti Smith!"

"Again you've got me fucking? Your mind's in the gutter, young man." Kate ran a hand through her new spiky hair, suddenly self-conscious. She could feel all three sets of eyes on her.

"If the lovefest is over," said Brown.

Freeman pushed a hand through his sandy gray hair, managed a quiet hello, and Kate returned it, her eyes meeting the FBI shrink's for a moment before looking away.

"I have full reports from Suffolk, Greenwich, and Tarrytown," said Brown. "But I think everyone's up to snuff, yes?" He looked at Murphy. "I'll get you the Homicide report on Sarkisian—if you want it."

"Why wouldn't I?" said Murphy.

Kate glanced from Brown to Murphy, wondered why there seemed to be some animosity between them.

Brown distributed Xeroxes. "The pictures found at the scenes." He nodded at Murphy, seemed to be trying to make nice. "Monty, why don't you take over?"

Murphy cleared his throat. "These paintings have turned up at every scene. Not left at the scenes, but sent or delivered earlier—we think. We don't have an exact time frame, but it looks like each of the victims received them a few days before they were attacked."

"And you're thinking they're some sort of code," said Freeman.

"Right," said Murphy. "You want to explain them, Kate, or should I?"

Freeman caught the first-name basis, didn't much care for it.

Kate explained how the paintings indicated the artwork about to be hit as well as predicting the next one, then interpreted the artists and symbolism in each picture.

"But why send a warning?" asked Perlmutter, once she'd finished.

"These guys love their games," Freeman offered. "And some of them like to get close. He's taunting authority. Sending clues to the next attack, it's like saying 'Come on, I dare you. Try and catch me.'" He looked from Murphy and Kate to Brown. "I read the files. Looks like the same MO in all cases."

"Except for the slashed painting at the Modernist Museum," said Murphy. "No body there. Only a slashed painting."

"Maybe there was no one around to kill," said Brown.

"Or too many," said Kate. "If the painting was slashed at the opening, there were hundreds of people around, right in the next room." She turned toward Murphy. "By the way, the Guerrilla Girls we spoke to— one of them called me. Says they've canvassed their membership and no one admits to being at the Modernist Museum that night, or to putting stickers on people's backs."

"*Gorilla* girls?" said Perlmutter. "Like King Kong gorillas?"

"Feminist group," said Murphy. He spelled out the name, then explained what the Guerrilla Girls had been accused of the night the de Kooning was slashed. "So if they weren't there, who was putting the stickers on people's backs?"

"My guess? Whoever slashed the painting," said Kate. "Good way to distract the guards—and it worked."

"So, it was probably our guy," said Perlmutter.

"Means he's a planner," said Freeman. "*Organized.*" He regarded the files. "I'd say *very* organized. He had to watch and learn his victim's routine."

Murphy nodded, then went back to the fact that the earlier crimes had no bodies. "Like the Modernist attack, same thing with the Jackson Pollock at the law firm. No people harmed."

Freeman shuffled through the case papers. "But now you've got three crime scenes with very human victims."

"Right," said Brown. "Guess the question is: Is it the paintings he's after, or the people?"

"Could be that the vics just showed up at the wrong time," said Murphy.

"Okay." Brown dragged a hand over his skull. "Let's say, hypothetically, that the perpetrator, the unsub, starts out with the intent to only destroy the paintings. Then, at the Starrett scene, Starrett wakes up, catches him, and he kills him. But if that's the case, then you'd figure the guy would lie low after that. Or he'd take more precautions next time, right, Mitch?"

"Not necessarily," said Freeman. "You've obviously got a highly unsta-

ble person to begin with, a risk taker, an omnipotent personality, someone who sneaks into places and slashes paintings, gets a thrill out of
destroying something valuable. But let's say your scenario is right, that
Starrett interrupts the act and the guy kills him out of necessity. But
then he realizes something—he *likes* it, the killing part, even more than
he likes destroying the paintings. And why not? Think about it. Can a
painting scream or beg? It's not half as sexy to slash canvas as it is to slash
flesh. Lots of psychopathic personalities work their way up to murder."
Freeman perused the Xeroxes of the black-and-white paintings. "Just
wish we could figure out why he attacks the paintings in the first place."

"Well, that's the key, isn't it?" said Kate.

Freeman nodded. "I'd say it's your *ritual*."

"Right," said Kate. "And what connects all the cases. None of the victims knew each other. All they had in common were the paintings."

"So what do we know about the paintings that were attacked?" asked
Perlmutter. "Is there a link between them?"

"They're all blue-chip works of art," said Murphy. "Except for
Beatrice Larsen, there's been nothing valued under several mil—and all
of the artists are long dead, except for Larsen, again, who was killed at
the same time as the slashing of her paintings. Unless Larsen's murder
was made to look like the others."

"A copy cat?" asked Brown.

"It's possible," said Murphy. "The slashed paintings have been all
over the news."

The *Post* wasn't the only newspaper to suggest a link between the
murders of Gregory Sarkisian, Nicholas Starrett, and Gabrielle
Hofmann—the idea of a serial killer was too delicious, though the
police would not confirm it.

"But Larsen was part of the same group as Pollock, de Kooning,
Kline, Hofmann, and Gorky," said Kate. "All New York School
painters."

"They went to school together?" asked Brown.

"No. It's just a name, the umbrella that connects them. They all
painted during the same period, all of them were part of the abstract

expressionist movement." A chill rippled through Kate's body. *All of the paintings slashed by members of the New York School. The group I'm writing about. Could there be a connection?* It was the same feeling she'd had when she'd heard about Beatrice Larsen's death—as if there was something that tied her to these crimes. Though she couldn't imagine what.

But she did not have time to consider it, as Freeman asked, "Was there something special about the time, about that group?"

"Well, they were mostly European immigrants," said Kate. "Settled in New York in the thirties and ended up becoming the first important group of American artists. They made New York the center of the art world. Stole it away from Europe."

"Maybe there's something there," said Freeman. "A deranged European artist, someone who was infuriated by that?"

"Unlikely," said Kate. "He'd have to be in his eighties or nineties."

"And it's not really much of a motive," said Brown.

"These guys," said Freeman. "It doesn't take much. They can invent whole scenarios in their mind that have nothing to do with reality. Motive is easy if you're a paranoid schizophrenic."

"Anything else connect them?" asked Perlmutter.

"They all became rich and famous," said Murphy.

"That's true of de Kooning, Kline, Hofmann, and Pollock," said Kate. "But Gorky died *before* he got acclaim, and Beatrice Larsen had a brief flurry of fame in her youth, then lost it."

"I'm not sure where this is taking us," said Brown.

Everyone was quiet a moment, then Kate asked, "So where is the clue painting that *should* have been with Sarkisian?"

"Crime Scene didn't turn up any black-and-white painting like you're looking for," said Brown. "Not in the man's office. Not in his home."

"Is it possible this vic didn't get one?" asked Perlmutter.

"If it's the same perpetrator, the ritual should be the same," said Freeman.

"I'd be willing to bet there's a painting," said Kate. "And we'd better find it. If we're right, then it will point the way to the next strike—the next victim." Kate thought a moment. "Did Sarkisian have a wife?"

"Ex-wife. And she lives abroad," said Brown. "But there's a girlfriend. Her statement's in the jacket. We can check with Sarkisian's friends— see if he ever mentioned getting such a painting or maybe even gave it to one of them. I'll send more troops to go through Sarkisian's home and office again to make sure nothing was missed."

"I'd like to check it out personally," said Kate.

"Okay," said Brown. "But I'm sending a couple of uniforms with you."

Kate and Perlmutter walked out together, his arm flung over her shoulder. "So, you doing okay?"

"Yeah. Sure." She gave him a broad smile. "I'm great."

He gave her a look. "You don't have to try so hard."

"*Who says?* What about you? You still with—sorry, I was about to call him Spike Hair."

"That's sort of the pot calling the kettle black, no?" Perlmutter eyed her new hairdo. "And his name is Bobby—and he got a crew cut. Or I should say *zie* got a haircut."

"Excuse me?"

"GNP."

"Again: Excuse me?"

"Gender-neutral pronoun. *Zie* instead of he or she."

"Bobby doesn't know which he is?" asked Kate. "Or *you* don't?"

"Funny," Perlmutter deadpanned. "Bobby's into the new language politics. Works for LGBT." He held up a hand. "I'll translate before you ask: Lesbian Gay Bisexual and Transsexual—and also transgender, I guess. Not that Bobby is one, a transsexual or, well, you know."

"When on earth did you get so politically correct?"

"Me? Never. But I'm trying, you know—anything for love." He grinned. "It's called tolerance speech, and Bobby's all over me about it—gender neutrality, gender nonspecific pronouns—says that the old pronouns keep people in their assigned roles. I'm trying to learn the lingo—*zie* for he or she and *zir* for his or her, *per* for person, and *em*."

"*Em?*"

"Like: Tell *em* I'll see *em* later."

"Oh, brother."

"No good. Neither is, 'Oh, *sister.*'" He laughed. "Bobby says that not everyone is male or female, some people are *intersexual*, like they have both male and female characteristics."

"Don't look at me," said Kate. "Or *zie*. Or . . . whatever the fuck." She shrugged her shoulders. "God, I'm so out of it—and too old to learn."

"You got used to *Ms.*, didn't you?" Perlmutter raised an eyebrow. "But don't worry, you won't see me using *zie* around the station house. I'd rather not have my balls handed to me and join the ranks of the *neutersexual.*"

"Isn't that an oxymoron?" said Kate, and they both cracked up.

"What are you guys laughing about?" asked Freeman.

"*Guys?*" said Kate. "I beg your pardon."

"Sorry. Guys and *gals.*"

"Even worse," said Kate, and laughed again. "Sorry, Mitch. Nicky here was just giving me a lesson on nonspecific gender pronouns."

"I'll *zie* you later," said Perlmutter, and headed off, leaving Kate and Freeman standing alone together. There was an awkward silence. Finally Kate spoke. "I meant to call, Mitch, but . . ."

"It's okay. I was worried about you, that's all." He touched her hand.

Kate looked into his gray eyes, but she quickly looked away. "Thought I could use a little therapy, huh?" She tacked on a smile.

"More like a shoulder."

Kate's smile faded. "Look, Mitch, I'm just not . . ." *Not what?* She wasn't sure, but came up with a reasonable answer. "Not ready."

"Hey." Freeman's smile made up for Kate's, large and forced. "I'm not pushing you, honestly."

Another look into his compassionate eyes confirmed it. "I know," she said, then quickly shifted gears. "So you think we're looking at an organized killer?"

"Precise planning. Very little trace at the scenes. Gloved and careful. I'd say so."

"The worst kind to catch. Because they're so damn careful and methodical."

"True," said Freeman. "But the organized ones are also compulsive and very tightly wound, often completely obsessed by status and power, which leads to fury and therefore, to put it in layman's terms, prone to fucking up."

"Let's hope so." She gave Freeman another smile, then glanced at the folder on Gregory Sarkisian in her hand. "I've got to go do this," she said. "Later, okay?"

"Yeah, sure," said Freeman. "Later."

CHAPTER 22

Gregory Sarkisian's office, sealed since the murder, was dry and over-heated in that New York winter way with the stale, sickly sweet and slightly metallic odor of dried blood in the air. Kate opened her coat, pulled on a pair of latex gloves, and surveyed the room—sleek modern furniture, an orderly desk soiled by the remnants of fingerprint powder, a spectacular bird's-eye view of Times Square signage and neon, rooftops and sky-high slabs of glass and steel.

The rug was a deep wine color stained darker inside the taped out-line of where Sarkisian's body had fallen, though, in places, the stain had leached beyond the perimeter, giving the outline a mutating, almost living quality.

Kate stepped around it for a closer look at the Gorky painting, slashed so badly, a few pieces lay on the floor. The destruction was much worse than with any of the other paintings, and Kate wondered if Sarkisian had said something to incite his attacker.

She tried to imagine the intruder coming in, slashing the man and his art. *Had Sarkisian tried to stop him? Did they fight?* And what had been said to gain entrance? *Did he call first?* Kate couldn't remember if that was in the case report, and made a note to ask the secretary.

She did another slow three-sixty. It was all here—the reason for the crime, why this painting, this man, had been chosen. When Brown had asked the question—"Is it the paintings he's after, or the people?"—Kate was pretty sure of the answer: the paintings.

But why?

She closed her eyes, tried again to imagine it—the door opening, the attacker entering.

Which was hit first, the man or his artwork?

She guessed the man. Unlikely Sarkisian would stand by and watch the destruction of his painting.

She could practically see it now—the struggle, the stabbing, the shock on the man's face when he realized he was going to die.

Kate felt the slight buzzing sensation she used to feel when she was on a case, the hairs on the back of her neck, electric.

She opened her eyes and was staring at the slashed Gorky, which no amount of restoration could save. With her gloved fingers she gently lifted the torn flaps of canvas until she found it—that odd, buglike symbol that had been painted on that apple in the clue painting found at Beatrice Larsen's studio—the image that predicted this attack.

So where was the black-and-white painting Sarkisian should have received?

Twenty minutes of going through drawers and bookcases produced nothing.

But there had to be one; Kate was certain of it.

In the outer office, one of the uniforms was sitting on the edge of the secretary's desk, asking questions.

"I've already answered that," said the woman, "and I have no idea. *Honest.*"

There was no belligerence in her tone. More guilt, Kate thought. But why guilt—for letting the man into her boss's office? She did a quick review of the woman's statement, asked the uniform to take a break, and pulled a chair up to her desk.

"I've really gotta get into Mr. Sarkisian's office." The secretary tugged a tissue out of the wrist of her lace-trimmed blouse and dabbed at her eyes.

"I understand." Kate patted the secretary's arm. "And you will, soon." Another pat. "Iris, right?"

The secretary nodded.

"Had you worked for Mr. Sarkisian long, Iris?" A question Kate knew the answer to.

"Four years next week."

"And he was good to work for?"

"The best." A tear streaked black mascara down the secretary's cheek. "He treated me like"—she choked back tears—"a person, you know. I've had other jobs where, well . . . never mind."

"I've had my share of nasty bosses," said Kate. "And I know when I have a good one. It makes all the difference in the world."

"You can say that again." The secretary nodded and smiled.

"So, just a few questions, Iris. I know this must be difficult for you."

"Nobody else seems to think so."

"Well, *I* do." She offered the woman a sympathetic smile. "So, you saw the man?"

"Only for a minute. It was at the end of the day, and I had an appointment with the podiatrist, and Mr. S said I could leave, so . . . I didn't pay much attention. I—"

"Just tell me what you remember."

"I don't think I remember anything. I'm—I'm so . . . confused." Her eyes flickered and her lower lip began to tremble.

"It's okay, Iris." Kate laid her hand over the secretary's. "Close your eyes. Now, take a breath and relax. Let it all go. That's it. Now think back. The man showed up. Did he call first?"

The secretary's eyes were fluttering behind her blue-shadowed lids. "Yes."

"What did he say?"

"Um . . . That he needed to tell Mr. S something about his painting, the Gorky painting. Mr. S really loved that painting, you know. It meant a lot to him."

In the end, too much, thought Kate. "Did you get a name?"

"He didn't give his name—or maybe he did, but I . . . I'm sorry—I can't remember."

"That's okay. And then what?"

"Mr. S took the call. They didn't speak long because a minute later Mr. S told me the man would be coming over at the end of the day to see the painting and that I could leave after he got here."

"And Mr. Sarkisian didn't mention the man's name either?"

The secretary's eyes flipped open. "I don't remember. I don't think so."

"That's okay. You're doing great." She patted the woman's hand. "Close your eyes again. So, it's sometime later. The man shows up. What does he say?"

"Um, that he was here about the painting. That's all he said, or something like that."

"And you sent him in?"

"Yes."

"Can you remember what he looked like? Just let your mind form a picture; don't force it."

The secretary took another deep breath, and let it out. "He was wearing a hat, one of those old-fashioned kinds, you know, felt, I think, with a brim, like men used to wear in the movies, and it was low on his forehead; and, oh, his coat collar was turned up, which was also like in the movies. I remember thinking the guy looked like he stepped out of *Casablanca*, you know, that old movie with Humphrey Bogart and Ingrid Bergman? I just love that movie."

"Me, too," said Kate. "So, the man, was he tall?"

"It's hard to say because I was sitting."

"And he was white?"

"Yes. But I couldn't see much of his face with the collar up and the hat and all. Oh, wait. He had a mustache. A big, floppy one that covered his mouth."

"That's great. You see, you do remember. Was there anything else?"

"No, not really."

"Did you hear anything from inside the office?"

"No. I was only around for a couple of minutes, and Mr. S's door is very thick. I can't hear anything through it."

"And you were gone when the man left Mr. Sarkisian's office?"

She nodded, eyes open now. "I feel so bad, like . . . I could have done something if I was here."

"It's not your fault. You had no way of knowing." Kate patted the secretary's arm and stood to go, then stopped. "Do you know if Mr. Sarkisian received any sort of painting by mail or messenger?"

"A painting? Like what?"

Kate unfolded a Xerox of one of the black-and-white clue paintings and laid it on the woman's desk. "Something like this."

The secretary wound her soggy tissue around her finger. "Um, no."

"This is very important, Iris." Kate used her teacher-to-a-young-student voice. "If you ever saw a painting like this—"

"I'm not a thief."

"I never said you were. I'm sure you're a very honest person."

"I am."

"But, Iris, you must tell me the truth."

The secretary glanced up at Kate like a kid caught with her hand in the cookie jar. "Mr. S threw it out. I swear I didn't steal it. It was in the trash and I thought it was sort of interesting, you know, so I took it. But I didn't steal it! I *swear*."

"I'm sure he *did* throw it away." Kate's heart was beating fast. "But we're going to need it back—and right away."

Martin Dressler rearranged the pages on his desk for what seemed like the hundredth time, loose galleys for the catalog of his next show— Painting the Unconscious, Abstract Art After Freud.

The show was scheduled to open in less than six months and several museums and collectors were now—with all the publicity about slashed paintings—refusing to lend their pictures.

Damn the media, thought Dressler.

Although there was an odd flip side—the Modernist Museum had seen an increase in attendance since the reporting of the slashed de Kooning, and Dressler wondered if it might not behoove the institution to destroy one of their lesser paintings each month.

Ordinarily, that sort of perverse idea would have cheered the curator, but not with his exhibition falling apart after years of work. Half of the artwork for the show had been collected—pieces by the surrealists Dalí, Magritte, and Masson, and a few early expressionist paintings by de Kooning, Gottlieb, Reinhardt, and Motherwell.

But these would make up only a fraction of the exhibition.

Dressler sagged into the chair behind his desk. His boss, Colin Leader, the museum's director, had implied that the show would certainly be canceled if all the paintings were not available, and he suspected Leader had been looking for an excuse to cancel *him* as well. The two men had never got along, and the fact that Dressler had been at the museum longer than the director hardly seemed to matter.

Dressler sighed, this time more from anxiety, his mind replaying the meeting with Kate McKinnon and that cop, Murphy, who had asked him about that damn black-and-white painting: *Why'd you keep it?*

The question had been reverberating in his head for days.

He pictured the cop—messy black hair, penetrating blue eyes, crooked nose that lent the man an air of menace. Just the kind of man he liked, and usually had to pay for. Had the cop picked up on that, too?

Why'd you keep it?

Just plain stupid, he thought.

Colin Leader felt like throwing his goddamn cordless phone right out the window. The press just would not quit. For days reporters had been calling about the de Kooning, and now they wanted his opinion on everything from the Starretts' slashed Kline to Sarkisian's Gorky, to his fears about this lunatic—or gang of lunatics—that might break into his, or any other museum, destroy all the artwork, kill the guards, loot the storage bins, pillage and burn—as if the Spanish Inquisition had come to town, and he alone knew what to do about it.

Several board members who had lent artworks to the museum were insisting they be placed in storage or returned—though Leader had skillfully pointed out that the paintings would be safer in the museum, and the collectors safer without them.

Leader crossed the room, swung open the doors of an elaborately carved seventeenth-century armoire—recently converted into a liquor cabinet—and poured himself a tumbler of single-malt Scotch. What he really wanted was to smoke a little of that great Mexican weed or take a hit of crack, but with an important meeting coming up he didn't dare.

He drank the Scotch in a gulp, then poured another, his mind swinging from guilt to paranoia.

Was he under suspicion? Why and how had he allowed this to happen?

He mulled the questions over, but did not like the obvious answers, and sloughed off the moment of personal introspection like a snake shedding its skin. The real question now was: *How to get out of it?*

He finished off the second Scotch, hoping it would clarify his thoughts rather than muddle them.

Now was a time for prudence. It was simply too risky to continue with so many eyes focused on the museum, and him.

Leader closed the liquor cabinet, straightened his tie, smoothed his hair, and popped a handful of Tic Tacs.

Right now, he had to get through this meeting.

Later, he would make the call to say he was through.

CHAPTER 23

Kate stood in the small living room of the secretary's one-bedroom walk-up, staring at the painting in a ready-made frame. It was half the size of the other paintings that had been found at crime scenes. "Please tell me the rest of the painting is hidden under the frame," she said, knowing it wasn't possible.

The secretary chewed her lip. "No, I—I cut it down to fit the frame. I—" She prattled on. "I, uh, really only liked the top half, you know, the apple, though I wish that weird bug wasn't in it. Uh, was that wrong, to cut it down?"

Fuck, yes! Kate took a breath. *Be calm.* "Do you have the rest of it?"

"No, I—I threw it out."

Another deep breath so she would not rip the woman's head off. "Can you tell me what was in the bottom half?"

"No, I—"

"This is important. *Try.*"

The woman's lower lip was trembling. Any minute she'd be in tears. Kate stroked her arm. "It's okay. But let's try, okay? Close your eyes, like you did before, and picture it, the entire painting. Are you trying?"

"Yes, but . . . I can't remember." Her eyelids flipped open. You see, it was in the trash, like I said. Mr. S had thrown it away, and the bottom half was sort of crumpled, and so, when I got home and it didn't fit, I just cut off the bottom and—"

"And you're sure you don't remember the images on the bottom?"

"No, I—"

"What did you do with it, the other half?"

"I threw it out, like I said. I didn't think it was important. I mean, Mr. S had thrown it out, right? So, I thought, how important could it be?"

You have no idea. "How long ago? Could it still be around?"

"I put it in the trash bin, outside, days ago. It must have been picked up by now."

Kate stared at the remaining half of the painting—the Gorky "bug" on the apple, big and clear now, no mistaking it—a Gorky painting in the Big Apple, New York City. But what was that heavy black design behind the apple? Another painting? *What is it?* A landscape? Another Kline? She wasn't even sure if this indicated the next painting to be attacked.

"I'm sorry. I didn't know it was important," the secretary said, clearly holding back tears.

Kate patted her shoulder and tried not to cry along with her—or scream—then took a card from her wallet and handed it to the woman. "In case you remember anything."

Kate had spent an hour with Mert Sharfstein going through the possibilities—a landscape? A Kline? A Motherwell? They finally agreed that the painting behind the apple was most probably a Robert Motherwell, though neither he nor Kate could figure out exactly *which* Motherwell—it looked more like a generic version of a Motherwell, possibly a takeoff on one of the artist's *Elegy* paintings. But with no clue to its whereabouts, they were stumped. Still, Sharfstein's staff was doing an Internet search for which museums owned works by Motherwell, and Murphy was checking auction houses to see about any recent sales, while Kate sat with Brown and Perlmutter.

"Stupid woman," said Perlmutter.

"She had no idea what she was doing," said Kate. "We can't blame her."

"Maybe *you* can't." Perlmutter brought his fist down hard on the table.

"Take it easy," said Brown. "I don't need you adding to my headache. I just got off the phone with Tapell, and my ear still hurts."

"The mayor is probably making her ear hurt, too," said Kate.

Brown knew she was right. Street hookers and homeless people could die left and right and no one cared, but a high-profile victim always got attention. The rich liked to feel secure in their homes, and who could blame them?

Brown hated to play the cover-your-ass game—though it was a game every cop learned straight out of the Academy—and right now his ass felt pretty vulnerable.

The newspapers continued to play up the crimes, just as he'd thought, the *News* going so far as to include the NYPD tip line, and the phones had been ringing off the hook, the confessions pouring in. So far, none of them had described the clue paintings. That was the NYPD's holdback, the pertinent piece of information that would tell them which callers were phonies. They would have to keep that from the media as long as possible, though it wouldn't be long before a determined reporter sniffed it out. But the confessors were not the only ones calling. Anyone who owned what they considered to be art—a painting on velvet or a megamillion antiquity—was calling.

Midtown North, which covered the area where Sarkisian had worked and died, was running out of men and patience. Since Brown's Special Investigative Squad had been brought in, Midtown North got stuck with the shit work, and they were not happy. No one was happy.

Perlmutter said, "The receptionist confirms the secretary's description of the unsub who attacked Sarkisian—hat, trench coat, mustache. And the lab's come up with some blood that does not match the vic's. Looks like our boy spilled a bit of his own."

So Sarkisian did fight back, thought Kate. She'd been right.

"But we have nothing to type it against," said Brown. "Not yet.

According to forensics, there was no blood at any of the scenes that did not belong to the vics."

Murphy interrupted. "The auction houses, Sotheby's and Christie's, have put me in touch with the two main galleries that sell Motherwell paintings. They're both going to fax us lists of anyone who bought a Motherwell in the past two years anywhere in the Metropolitan area, including Westchester and Connecticut. But they both warned the lists will be long."

Moments later the fax machine began to spit out page after page of names of collectors' who had purchased Robert Motherwell paintings.

"I'm giving these to Midtown North to check out," said Brown. "But Perlmutter, you head them up." He nodded at Kate and Murphy. "And you two go along to let them know what we're looking for."

Kate and Murphy shared a car, Murphy talking to the lab, one hand on the cell phone, one on the steering wheel. Kate didn't bother to tell him it was illegal.

"Results of the pillow from Beatrice Larsen's studio," he said, clicking off. "Lab says the pillow was filled with old-fashioned foam rubber. Generic stuff. Lab says it's a match for the stuff in the old lady's nose and lungs, but they picked up every pillow in the house, and they're all pretty much the same. The pillows Larsen slept on were identical, also old and torn, maybe leaking that shit. Lab says it's *possible* she inhaled bits of it in her sleep over time. Plus, she had emphysema and a bad heart."

"In other words, it's going to be hard to prove murder," said Kate.

"Exactly. But there's something else. Lab says the residue on the old lady's eyelids was from masking tape. And there were traces of talc, too."

"Someone taped her eyes shut?"

"Or open," said Murphy.

"There was no tape on her eyes when they found her, right?"

"Far as we know."

"Talc?" said Kate. "From latex gloves, maybe."

"Could be."

"So the attacker, wearing gloves, tapes Larsen's eyes open, or shut. Why?"

Murphy shook his head. "Either way, what do we got? Nada. If the unsub hadn't been wearing gloves, maybe; or if he'd touched his skin and then her eyes, also maybe; if he was a secreter, which he doesn't seem to be. Lab didn't find any sweat deposits, so there's nothing to DNA."

Kate tried to picture it. "Maybe he taped her eyes open to watch while he slashed her paintings." The idea chilled her. *Had the killer wanted Beatrice Larsen to suffer?*

"Tarrytown PD is going to pay the niece a visit, make her a little nervous, see what she says."

Kate was trying to imagine Darby Herrick taping her aunt's eyes open, pressing a pillow over her face, listening to the woman suffocate and choke. *Was she capable of it?*

Murphy angled a look at Kate. "You like the Herrick girl for this?"

"I don't know. Seems to me, if it was the niece, she'd opt for something quick and simple." She was thinking again about the usual crime scene motto—you take something with you and leave a bit of yourself behind. But it would not apply in this case because Herrick had spent so much time in her aunt's studio that her hair and fibers would naturally be all over the place. "What do you think?"

"Doesn't really matter what I think. I'm just the art guy, remember?"

"What's that supposed to mean?" Kate narrowed her eyes in his direction. "Something going on between you and Brown?"

"What makes you think that?"

"Hey, you don't want to talk about it," said Kate, "that's okay with me."

Murphy was quiet for a few minutes, then finally said, "I used to work homicide, a few years back, with Brown. We weren't partners, but in the same unit. There was an accident, and . . . I killed a kid." Murphy's eyes turned dark, inward, his voice robotic. "I was taking down a coked-up scumbag who'd shot a seventy-five-year-old grocery clerk. My bullet ricocheted off a metal freezer compartment into the kid's head. Dead in seconds. Not quite four years old." He stared ahead at the traffic.

"IA cleared me. Determined it was accidental. But I couldn't sleep after that. Had trouble looking at my daughter, too . . ." Murphy swallowed and took a deep breath. "Whole slew of bad feelings after that. You know—guilt, remorse, depression." He listed them without any emotion, but his face was screwed up with pain. "Guess that's what drove my wife away—that and a Southampton millionaire in a Jaguar." He laughed, but there was no humor in it. "I took a year off, tried to *find* myself. Did a little time on the couch, too. Didn't think I could be a cop again, you know."

Kate did know. It was the reason she had left police work—the first time. Not that she'd killed anyone. Not directly. But an error in judgment had cost a teenager, Ruby Pringle, her life. Kate replayed one of her own bad movies: Finding the girl's body in a Dumpster, a day too late. If only she'd been paying attention . . . The Starrett's Kline painting winked in her mind. One more item she could add to her TOO LATE file.

"I guess Brown thinks I fucked up."

"Brown's not the judgmental type."

"All cops are judgmental. It goes with the job."

"Sounds to me like it's your own guilt you're reacting to."

"I thought your degree was in art, not psychology."

"Forget it," said Kate.

They were both quiet a minute, Murphy staring through the windshield as if he were looking for something. "When the art thing came along, I grabbed it. A second chance, you know."

"I've heard more than one artist say that art can save your life."

"Hasn't done it so far. And I even tried painting, once." Murphy grumbled a laugh.

"Try getting yourself a big lump of clay, and really dig your hands in."

"Here we go again. What is this, art therapy 101?"

"Better than lying on a couch, no?"

Kate's cell phone rang. It was Sarkisian's secretary.

"I remembered something," she said. "The bottom half of the painting? It was a tunnel—a picture of a tunnel. I cut it off because tunnels always scare me. I guess I sorta blocked it, you know."

"A tunnel," Kate repeated, the idea taking root. "Do you remember if there was anything with it—a picture of a wedge of cheese perhaps?"

"Yes! Exactly. Except I remember thinking at the time it was a piece of pie. Pretty weird, huh?"

The museum board meeting had been excruciating, Colin Leader feeling as though he might actually leap up out of his seat at any moment and tell them what he'd been up to.

Why on earth was he having this sudden urge to come clean? Was it the reporters who would not stop calling or the cops who kept coming by?

Damn. He had to get a grip. He was losing it, forgetting himself, the respectable role of museum director that he had molded and perfected.

Leader caught his reflection in the armoire's mirror, his elegant but understated suit, the perfect cut of his hair. He looked down and admired his Italian oxfords, enjoyed the fact that they were absurdly expensive.

Jesus, am I going to blow it all? Now?

It wasn't like he wanted to, but he had to stop, didn't he?

But it's all a sham, man, you know that.

His inner voice. A Cockney lad, someone he used to know, someone with a conscience and a heart whom he had long ago given up.

He had to get it over with, put an end to it. Right now.

Another drink, that's what he needed, something to soothe his nerves.

He opened the armoire, got ahold of that bottle of Scotch, caught a glimpse of his shaking hand.

A drunk. That's what I've become.

A lot worse than that, mate.

"Oh, shut up," he said, staring at his reflection, pouring the Scotch into a glass.

The pressure was too much. He couldn't take it anymore. He could not live like this. It had to be finished, over, and right now.

He swallowed the Scotch and shut the armoire doors. He was ready.

"I've got to call the museum," said Kate. "Right away." She retrieved her cellular and waited for the wireless operator to connect her. "Come on." It seemed to be taking forever.

Murphy turned the car around in the middle of the street, switched on the siren and beacon, and headed south. "You think our perp would have the balls to hit the same place twice?"

"The museum has already displayed itself as an easy target. And if the guy is after a Motherwell painting, I know the museum has at least one, maybe more." Kate was hoping the psycho did *not* have the balls for another attack on the Modernist Museum, but the clues in the painting—the tunnel, the cheese—indicated otherwise. "You heard what Mitch Freeman said—that the guy is taunting authority, saying 'Come on, I dare you, try and catch me.' What better way than to attack the same place twice?" Kate let out a breath, listened to the phone ring, then an automated voice told her she had reached the Modernist Museum, and the list of numbers to push for each department.

"Shit! Can't you ever get a *person* on the phone anymore?"

CHAPTER 24

Murphy cut the siren and beacon as he brought the Crown Victoria to a stop beside a dozen other police cars and EMT vehicles outside the Modernist Museum. He and Kate did not exchange a word as they made their way through the blockade of uniforms.

Inside, a dozen cops were taking statements from museum staff, and Kate recognized a young woman, an intern, who had just started working at the museum. She was crying.

Just outside the curator's office, Nicky Perlmutter was questioning the museum director, Colin Leader, who had blood on his hands.

While Kate listened to Perlmutter, she stared into the office and took in the scene—the smallish Robert Motherwell painting in tatters, a man on the floor in a kidney-shaped pool of blood. She swallowed hard and took a deep breath.

"So you came in and he was on the floor, already dead," Perlmutter said.

"Yes," said Leader. "I already told you that."

"And you didn't touch the body, didn't try to revive him?"

"No. As I said, I could tell that he was dead."

"Oh? How could you tell?"

"Well, it was . . . obvious. The blood, and . . . he wasn't breathing."

Kate would have to agree. The curator, Martin Dressler, appeared to be very dead.

Crime Scene was crawling all over the office, Floyd Brown conferring with an ME who had just plucked a thermometer from Dressler's body.

Perlmutter could smell booze on the museum director's breath. "And before that, you say, you were in a meeting?"

"That's right." Leader licked his lips. He felt as if he could use another drink. "Is it really necessary to go over all of this again, Officer?"

"*Detective.*" Perlmutter gave him one of his Huck Finn smiles. "Yes, it is important we go over it. You want it to be correct, don't you?"

Leader could feel sweat trickling from his armpits. He glanced over at Kate with a look that said *What are you doing here?*

The ME came out of the office, Floyd Brown beside him. They pulled off their gloves and booties. "Body's still warm," said the ME. "Vic hasn't been dead for more than a couple of hours."

Brown turned to Leader. "Does Dressler have a secretary?"

"An assistant, yes, but she was out today. The flu. It's going around."

What was it that Brown was picking up from the guy, an odor—and it wasn't just the booze, which was strong; there was some guilt there, too. *The Nose*, what they used to call him. Not his favorite nickname, but it was true. According to Brown, guilt had a smell. He looked hard at the museum director—clearly, the guy had had opportunity, though he didn't know if there was a motive. But he'd find out. He looked into Leader's eyes. "Just answer my detective's questions and you can go home, Mr. Leader. I'm sure this has been a terrible ordeal for you." He did not want to frighten the guy into calling a lawyer before Perlmutter finished with him. He took hold of Kate's arm, moved a few feet away, and whispered, "Just stand here and pretend to talk to me."

Just behind them, Perlmutter asked Leader, "So, you're sure you never went over to see if Mr. Dressler was breathing?"

"I already explained that." He sighed deeply. "No, I did not check Mr. Dressler's breathing. I could see that he was dead. There was no need to check his pulse."

Perlmutter held his pen over his notepad. "Was that pulse or breath?"

"*Pulse.* Does it matter? I was using it as an expression. But I did not check either his pulse or his breath. I . . . I did not see the need. I . . ."

"Take it easy, sir." Perlmutter laid a hand on the director's shoulder.

"I'm perfectly fine," said Leader.

"Good." Perlmutter took a moment to make a note in his pad—or pretended to. "Did not check pulse or breathing," he said. "Got it. Great." Another Huck Finn smile. "But then, hm, I'm wondering, sir, how did you get the blood all over your hands?"

Leader stared at his hands as if noticing for the first time. "Oh. Well . . ." He swallowed hard. His tongue felt thick. He really did need that drink. "I thought I'd explained that, hadn't I?"

Perlmutter made a show of flipping pages in his notepad. "It's probably in here, but tell me again."

Leader stopped, forced a laugh. "Should I be calling a lawyer?"

"Only if you think you need one, sir."

"No, I . . . why should I? I mean . . ."

"Right," said Perlmutter. "Why would you?" He smiled.

"Well," Leader took a deep breath. "There was blood on the wall. And when I came in and saw Martin . . . like that, well, I felt a bit sick and I must have put my hand against the wall to steady myself."

"So, the handprints on the wall, those would be *yours.*"

Leader took another deep breath. "What I'm saying is . . ." *Jesus, what am I saying?* His head was spinning. ". . . that I placed my hand on the wall—into the blood that was already there. I don't know how it got there. I guess . . . it was Martin's."

Perlmutter scribbled in his notepad. "Hand on the wall. Check." He looked down at Leader's hands. "But what about the other one?"

"The other one—*what?*"

"Your other hand. I was wondering why it had blood on it, sir."

"Well, I, I guess I rubbed them together," said Leader. "I can't be sure. It was, well, it was very upsetting finding the body like that."

"Of course it was. So, tell me again: You came down to Mr. Dressler's office to talk to him about . . .?"

"An exhibition."

"You didn't normally call, or use interoffice e-mail?"

"Well, yes, sometimes I do, but I wanted to see him, Martin, in person."

"Because . . ."

"Because I had bad news. I was going to cancel a show he was planning."

"And that would have been upsetting to Mr. Dressler."

"I suppose."

"But you didn't get to tell him."

"No. As I have already said, he was . . . dead."

"I see. So you came into Mr. Dressler's office to deliver bad news and you found him dead on the floor. Then you backed up into the wall, covered one of your hands with the victim's blood. Then you rubbed your hands together. Is that about right?"

"You know," said Leader, suddenly feeling very sober, "I think I'd like to talk to a lawyer."

They were all back at the station house, gathered around the conference table: Perlmutter and Brown, Kate and Murphy, along with Mitch Freeman and two field agents the Bureau had sent over from FBI Manhattan. Brown was surprised they had waited this long.

The two agents had distributed several sheets of paper, which everyone was now studying.

"Before we get to the specifics of the latest attack, thought we should go over the vics' stats, see if there's anything to add." This from a young crew cut in a standard-issue gray suit named John Bobbitt, who had swaggered into the conference room and said, "No relation to John *Wayne* Bobbitt, thank you very much, heh, heh, heh," so that Kate had thought, *Where the hell is Lorena and her scissors when we need her?*

"Standard victimology report," said the other agent, a slightly older guy, same gray suit, heavyset, balding, name tag read Vincent Moroni. "CID did the workup. And we've run all your case reports through NICS, CJIS, UCR, the usual."

Kate was racking her brain to remember what they all were. *NICS: National Instant Criminal Background Check System. CJIS: Criminal Justice something-or-other.* But *UCR?* That stumped her for a moment, though she wasn't about to ask. Then she remembered: *Uniform Crime Reporting.*

"FYI," said Agent Bobbitt. "This is still in formation, and any details you can add will be greatly appreciated."

Brown knew he was full of shit. When the G stepped in, they did not want your opinion. They wanted control. And they wanted the credit.

Kate looked down at the sheet of paper, noted the heading: "Preliminary Victim Report. The Slasher. BSS 107-CS278." "The Slasher?" she asked.

"That's right," said Bobbitt. "Every investigation gets a code name. We thought 'the Slasher' was a good one." He almost smiled.

"I'm sure the media will agree with you," said Brown. "They're going to soil themselves over that one."

"Who says they're going to get it?" said Bobbitt.

"You're kidding, right?" said Brown. "They get everything. Sometimes faster than we do."

"The Slasher," said Perlmutter. "I like it. I can see it on a marquee."

Bobbitt gave him a counterfeit smile. "Hey, it wasn't up to me. Came out of UCR. But you're stuck with it."

Kate looked again at the report, a list of the victims and their particulars.

1. Starrett, Nicholas. Water Mill, NY. Homicide.
   WM. DOB: 4/26/46.
   Weapon: Knife (long-handled X-Acto)
   POD: residence.
   No witnesses (wife on scene; statement in CR)
2. Hofmann-Lifschultz, Gabrielle. Greenwich, CT. Homicide.
   WF. DOB 7/11/60
   Weapon: Knife (long-handled X-Acto)
   POD: residence
   No witnesses

3. Larsen, Beatrice. Tarrytown, NY. Homicide.
   WF. DOB: 2/12/24
   Weapon: Knife (long-handled X-Acto)
   POD: residence (semi-attached garage)
   No witnesses
4. Sarkisian, Gregory. New York, NY. Homicide.
   WM. DOB: 8/13/54
   Weapon: Knife (long-handled X-Acto)
   POD: office.
   No witnesses (descriptions from co-workers in CR)
5. Dressler, Martin. New York, NY. Homicide.
   WM. DOB: 6/18/56
   Weapon: Knife (long-handled X-Acto)
   POD: Modernist Museum, NY, NY
   No witnesses (co-workers' statements in CR)

Oh, how the cops and feds love their paperwork, thought Kate. Nothing new here.

"Common denominators?" Bobbitt asked, and answered his own question. "The knife, for one."

Already knew that, thought Brown. The G had simply taken the info from the NYPD case reports, tried to make it their own, giving it back in G-speak.

"Well," said Kate. "I'd say the common denominator is the paintings, the slashed artwork. That's the only thing that links them."

"Right," said Brown. "None of the vics knew each other."

Bobbitt gave them each a cheesy smile. "Thanks. We know that. What else?"

"Three art collectors, one artist, one curator," said Murphy.

"Right," said Moroni. "Which brings us to the latest, Dressler." He nodded in Perlmutter's direction. "You filed the CR, correct?"

Perlmutter nodded back.

Moroni slid Perlmutter's case report out and scanned it. "So what'd you make of Leader, the museum director? Seems pretty odd, the place being hit twice."

"Leader was at a meeting and plenty of co-workers saw him," said Perlmutter, going through the notes he'd gathered from the director's assistant as well as statements from the museum staff that the uniforms had collected. "But there was a solid half hour between the end of the board meeting and the time when Leader says he discovered Dressler's body. Claims he returned to his office after the meeting and made some notes, alone. His assistant went off on an errand after the meeting, so she could not verify whether or not her boss actually came back to his office, or what he was doing for that half hour. But when she got back, Leader was not in his office."

"Anyone see Leader arrive at the scene, at Dressler's office?" asked Moroni.

"Nada," said Perlmutter. "Dressler's office is at the end of a long hallway and there's an exit door just opposite. Anyone could easily slip in or out, use the stairs rather than the elevator, avoid the hallway, and not be seen."

"And Leader used the stairs?" asked Crew Cut Bobbitt.

"That's what he says."

Kate was having trouble imagining the museum director actually murdering his curator. Though she and Dressler were not friends, she had known him in the art world for years, and she could not get the image of the man dead on the floor from her mind.

"And it was Leader who called it in, right?" Murphy had removed a rubber band and was fashioning a makeshift cat's cradle on his fingers.

"Right," said Perlmutter.

"Doesn't mean crap." Brown laid his palms onto the desk. "How many perps you know call in the crime, think it's going to make them look good? And there was definitely something off about the guy."

"I'll say," said Bobbitt, skimming Perlmutter's report. "The guy's got the vic's blood on his hands and his prints on the wall. Either he's real sloppy or real stupid, or both."

"Not stupid," said Kate.

Bobbitt regarded her with another one of his cheesy smiles. "Thank you for your insight, *Ms.* McKinnon."

Was he intentionally trying to piss her off? Though it could have been worse; he could have said Miss or Mrs.

Brown cut in. "Lab will tell us if they exchanged fibers or anything else," he said. "But the question is motive." He leaned toward Kate. "You knew the vic. You have a take on this?"

Kate thought a moment. She truly did not. "No."

"Bureau's doing a full background check on Leader," said Moroni.

"Tell you one thing," said Perlmutter. "Guy had booze on his breath."

"Booze on his breath, blood on his hands. I say we bring him in," said Bobbitt.

"Maybe." Brown sat back, laced his fingers behind his head and waited till they were all watching him. "I agree with Detective Perlmutter. There was definitely something off about the man. But I say we cut him loose."

The two FOs started to speak at once, but Brown spoke over them. "Sure, we could pick him up, probably build a case. But what have we really got? Plenty of circumstantial—but no motive." He looked from one agent to the other. "I say we let him think he's off the hook, let him feel real secure. But we watch him. Twenty-four/seven tail. See where he goes. Who he sees."

"Suppose he splits," said Agent Moroni.

"Any trips to the airport, we're on him like ants at a picnic."

Moroni looked at Bobbitt. "I like it. Could be there's others involved. Better to get the whole nest."

Perlmutter said, "Maybe Dressler and Leader were involved in something together, and Leader killed him to keep him quiet."

"What do you mean, involved in something?" Bobbitt listed toward Perlmutter. "You pick up a vibe on the guy's, uh, sexual orientation, that what you're implying?"

"Not at all," said Perlmutter. "Why?"

"Oh, you know, art museums and all." He waved a limp wrist. "I was thinking maybe you thought he and his curator had a lovers' quarrel."

Kate leaned across Perlmutter. "Well, Agent Bobbitt, you're right about one thing—Martin Dressler was gay, and perfectly open about it. But I have no idea about Colin Leader. And if you are suggesting that men in the arts are effeminate, well, I can think of a dozen very macho artists who could arm-wrestle you—and win." She tried to imitate his smile. "But for the record, Dressler and Leader didn't even like each other."

"And you know that because . . ."

"Because when we first interviewed Dressler," Murphy answered for her, "it was really obvious that he disliked his boss."

"Just trying to examine all the avenues," said Bobbitt. "Hey, here's one for you. How do you know when your boyfriend is gay?" He looked at Perlmutter, then the others. "When he brings you flowers and then he *arranges* them."

No one laughed.

Bobbitt glanced around the table. "Get it?"

"I'm not sure," said Kate. "Are you telling us that your boyfriend brings you flowers, or just arranges them?" She raised her eyebrows. "Either way, I think it's sweet." She went on before he could speak, shifting into a serious question. "Did Crime Scene find anything resembling one of those black-and-white clue paintings in Dressler's office?" She paused a moment. "Though he'd already received one—the one that predicted the attack on the de Kooning painting—so unless he got it only minutes before he was killed, or he never saw it, I think he would have reported it to the police. At the very least called me, or Murphy."

"There was nothing like it in the office," said Perlmutter.

"Then we need to search his home. It's possible it was sent there, and maybe it's still there, unopened," said Kate. "An approximation of a Motherwell painting was in the last clue painting, and that's what was slashed in Dressler's office. There should be a clue painting—somewhere. And we have to know where he plans to strike next."

"You want to handle that?" Bobbitt asked Brown. "Or should we?"

"I think we can handle it," said Brown.

"Wait a minute." Kate rubbed her eyes, which felt tired and itchy. "Something doesn't make sense to me. At the moment, Leader is our number one suspect for killing Dressler, right? But then why would Leader intentionally send a painting with clues to indicate he was going to kill a colleague?"

"Valid question," said Freeman. "But if Leader *is* the Slasher, he's got a major psychosis going. It's possible that the idea of killing someone close to him really got him off. Plus, he's taunting us again, showing us how clever he is." He looked from Kate to Perlmutter. "What was your take on Leader? Intelligent? Egotistical? Arrogant?"

"I'd go with all three," said Perlmutter.

"Fits the profile," said Freeman.

"You run your profile through BSS stats?" asked Bobbitt.

"Don't worry," said Freeman, "I will."

"I'm with McKinnon," said Murphy. "First priority: We've got to find that missing painting."

"Could be Leader chickened out. Took the painting back when he killed Dressler," said Perlmutter.

"And if Leader's our man, we might not need the painting because we'll be watching him," said Brown.

"Okay, so we watch him," said Bobbitt. "Twenty-four/seven. Starting now."

"Just to complicate things," said Kate, "I think someone better keep an eye on Beatrice Larsen's niece, Darby Herrick. She had motive and opportunity for killing her aunt. I wouldn't rule her out. I'm not saying she's our killer here, but she could have arranged her aunt's death to look like the others."

"I'll have the Bureau authorize Tarrytown PD to put a tail on her," said Agent Moroni. "Meanwhile, I'll see what's turned up in Leader's background check. He's a Brit, so we're checking with Interpol, too."

Kate remembered something. "Colin Leader was at the Starretts' party the night Nicholas was murdered. At least I think so. He was invited, I know that much."

"We'll check and see if he showed up," said Brown. "And if anyone saw him leave."

Bobbitt was already up from the table, whispering into his cell phone. His cohort, Moroni, joined him.

Brown eyed them, sighed, and looked away.

Paulina Zolcinski, forty-seven years old, a widow who cleaned rich people's apartments by day and the Modernist Museum offices by night, was exhausted, swollen feet up on two pillows as she watched David Letterman ramble on about New York's top ten something-or-other, which she did not understand or find funny, though the audience was howling with laughter. She figured it was because her English was not so good, or maybe because she lived out in Queens, and the jokes were about Manhattan. She didn't understand the allure of the city, though she certainly wouldn't mind having one of those apartments she cleaned, which were like small palaces among the dirt and grime and traffic.

Zolcinski massaged her aching feet, looked past the television and David Letterman's toothy grin, and caught a glimpse of the painting she had pinned to the wall.

After what had happened, there was no question she would have to throw it away.

Zolcinski, a teacher back in Kraków, where she had made less money trying to get teenagers to understand the basics of algebra and geometry than she did using Fantastic and Tidy Bowl to clean up after the American rich, had never stolen a single thing in her life. The envelope, part of a large stack of unopened mail cluttering the curator's desk, had slipped from her hands and tumbled to the floor, the flap popping open, half the painting sliding out.

At first glance, she thought the initials were a design, and then, for just a second, a swarm of bees, but she never would have taken it had it been any of those things. It was when she looked closer and realized they were initials—her initials—that it became too tempting to pass up. *Her* initials. In a painting.

But now, according to the news, he was dead. And she had just cleaned his office and taken the painting. The envelope had been unopened until it fell off the desk; the curator had not yet seen it. But still, the police might question her, and then they would be taking inventory of his things, and someone else might know about the envelope, and after that would undoubtedly come Immigration, and she could kiss the United States good-bye. No more American dollars to send home to her mother in Kraków. She would be on the next plane back to Poland.

Zolcinski pushed herself up, crossed the room in stocking feet, and stopped a moment to regard the painting.

It wasn't that she even liked it that much. It was just the initials. Looking at it now she decided it didn't make much sense, and certainly was not worth the risk.

She stared at the echoing repetition of her initials for a moment and wondered what it could possibly mean, then yanked the painting off the wall, lumbered into the kitchen, balling it up as she did so, stuffed it into a Hefty bag, twisted the top into a knot, and took it outside to the garbage.

CHAPTER 25

The ice in Miranda Wilcox's drink was melting and she was getting antsy for the Colombian to leave—they had concluded their deal almost an hour ago. The Colombian had made an offer—fifteen percent discount if he took both the Gorky and the lesser-known expressionist painting—and Wilcox had agreed. In fact, she had anticipated the request and had built an additional twenty percent into the asking price, and was therefore still five percent ahead.

But the Colombian was working on his second Mount Gay rum and Coke, and it did not look like he was in any hurry to get moving. He shimmied closer to her on the couch and laid his hand on her thigh. She felt like swatting it off, but did not want to queer the deal. She forced herself to smile as the Colombian's fingers crawled up past her mini and toyed with the edge of her lace thong; but she stopped smiling when he tugged so violently that the lace came away in his hand and the throng got wedged in her ass.

"I would have taken it off—*if* you'd asked."

"I don't like asking," he growled. To her ear, his garbled English sounded like: *I don lick assing.*

Wilcox sighed. She guessed she would have to fuck him.

The Colombian was standing in front of her now, leering. "How about a tip?" He pronounced the word "teep." "You know, babee, sales tex." He grinned.

"I'm not a whore," said Wilcox.

He arched one thick, black eyebrow as if to say, *Oh, no?*

She wanted to tell him to go fuck himself, add something like *I know that won't be possible with your little breakfast sausage dick*, but didn't dare. The Colombian scared her. Plus, he was already unzipping his fly, tugging that unremarkable equipment out of his pants, which was only half hard, even less impressive than usual.

He grabbed the back of her head and pushed her face into his crotch, and said, "Suck eet."

It wasn't that Wilcox didn't enjoy a bit of the rough stuff—she did—but only when she was in charge. Plus, the Colombian had a bit of a hygiene problem, and she was breathing through her mouth, which was going to make the act impossible.

"Suck eet!" He exerted more pressure to the back of her head, but Wilcox pulled away.

"I'm just not . . . in the mood."

"In dee moot?" He laughed, yanked her up by her hair, carted her into the bedroom, threw her on the bed, tore her blouse open and pushed her skirt up. A minute later he was on top of her, grunting away and driving himself inside her like a tiny jackhammer.

Miranda Wilcox stared at the ceiling, calculating her share of the profits from the two sales.

By the time the Colombian had finished, rolled off, and was panting beside her like a dog on a hot day, she had figured it out to the penny.

After the meeting, Mitch Freeman tagged along with Kate, who had decided to walk home, though she had not invited him.

It was one of those clear December nights, the really cold months still ahead of the city, Eighth Avenue bustling, couples arm in arm, people hanging out, talking, laughing.

In less than two decades the area had been transformed from a dreary landscape of unwashed brownstones, tenements, delis, and bodegas into one of Manhattan's most desirable neighborhoods.

"It's nice here," said Freeman.

"I love it," said Kate. "I'm always running into artists and writers I know, and the Chelsea art galleries are only a few blocks over, not to mention Whole Foods, which is only four blocks from my home and means I never have to cook again—if I don't want to."

"Sounds good," he said.

They passed restaurant after restaurant, a hip card store, a gourmet food shop, tried to maneuver through a pack of men laughing and shouting in front of a coffee bar called Big Cup, two of them engaged in a deep, soulful kiss.

"Plus, it's the gay capital of the world," Kate whispered. She took in Freeman's square jaw, graying sandy hair flopping into his eyes. "Bet you'd score," she said, and laughed.

"Is it okay if I stick with girls?"

"Try calling them *women* and you might do better."

Freeman smiled.

Kate had wanted to see the baby before he was put to bed, but she was feeling okay with Freeman, which surprised her. When he suggested a drink, she steered them into one of the neighborhood's hip-looking eateries, where they chose a small table, Kate opting for a martini rather than her usual Scotch, Freeman for a beer.

"I'm really sorry about not calling back," she said after a minute. "It was . . . a difficult year, and now I've got Nola and the baby living with me, that plus the book I'm trying to write, and my television show, and this case—"

"Are you listing excuses why you can't see me?" Freeman added a smile. He had to stop himself from leaning across the table and kissing her mouth.

Kate took in the curve of his lips, the dimple in his chin. It had been a long time since she'd looked at a man that way and it stirred up a variety of unexpected emotions. She was suddenly crying. "Jesus." She fumbled with the cocktail napkin, blotting her tears. "I don't know what's wrong with me. Sorry."

Freeman touched her hand with his fingertips. "Don't apologize."

"Why? You like to see women cry?" She managed a smile.

"It's good to get your feelings out."

"Now you sound like a therapist."

"Occupational hazard." He reached across the table and wiped a tear off her cheek. "One question: If you're so busy, how come you took this case on?"

"Because my friend asked me to," she said, knowing that was not exactly the truth.

"You sure you're doing it for your friend?"

"Okay. If you insist upon making this a therapy session . . ." Kate sighed. "I have these dreams where I'm walking down that alleyway and there's this moment when I see Richard . . . and he's still alive, and I have a chance to save him and I reach out, but . . . it's too late."

"There was no way you could have saved him, Kate."

"I know that. But maybe finding out who did this to Nicholas Starrett will help."

"Maybe," said Freeman.

"You don't think so, do you?" She looked into his eyes, and continued before he could answer. "When I went after Richard's murderer I had a very specific idea in my mind—to kill him. I wasn't interested in a trial or bringing him to justice. I just wanted revenge."

"A natural enough emotion."

"Yes." Kate sighed. "Though it didn't make me feel any better."

"Loss, revenge—complicated stuff." Freeman touched her hand. "So you're looking for a second chance?"

"Maybe. Though I'm not looking to kill anyone this time. Not yet, anyway."

"A step in the right direction."

Kate had had enough personal revelation and switched gears. "I was thinking before, in the meeting, about the Slasher." She tossed her head. "Can't believe I actually used the code name."

"Kind of catchy, you've got to admit."

Kate nodded. "So what's motivating him? I really think it has to have something to do with the art."

"Yes. Unless the art is just a symbol for something else—power, prestige, success?"

Kate wasn't sure.

"What do you make of the museum director, Leader?" asked Freeman.

"We've met at museum events, but I can't say I know him. And I can't imagine him committing murder right on his doorstep."

"Jeffrey Dahmer killed in his own house and buried the victims under the floorboards," said Freeman. "I hate to tell you how many psychopaths hunt on their own turf—and none of them think they're going to get caught. They're all detached from any set of normal feelings, not to mention reality, and almost all of them think they're smarter than everyone else."

"But why the paintings?" said Kate. "Why *kill* paintings?"

Freeman could not come up with an answer.

I've done this before. There is no need to panic. No need to panic . . . No need to panic . . .

A mantra as Leader wrapped the four artworks he had "liberated" from the museum's basement. Still, his hands were sweating and the tape kept tangling, and he kept seeing that tall redheaded cop and hearing the guy's words: *How did you get the blood all over your hands, sir?*

But they had let him go—and they would not have if they'd suspected anything. He was being paranoid, that's all.

He wrapped a bit more tape around the stolen artwork and thought, *Just because you're paranoid doesn't mean they're not out to get you.*

Leader took a deep breath and let it out slowly. He'd get rid of these tonight, and that would be that. Tomorrow, he would be finished with this life, the role of dignified museum director, all of it becoming a big bore.

He glanced about the room, at the furniture and knickknacks, his personal art collection—or what was left of it. He had, since last week, been choosing his favorites and sending them on ahead. The rest would have to remain behind. Better if it looked like he'd simply taken a vacation. By the time they realized he was not coming back, he'd be settled into a new home and a new identity.

He'd always known this day would come, and he had made plans for it. There was plenty of money waiting for him.

His carry-on suitcase was open on the bed, the Internet e-ticket beside it, the flight set for tomorrow night. He just needed something to get through the night, and found it in the medicine cabinet—two aspirin with codeine, washed down with a shot of Scotch.

For a moment he thought about calling, just to check on the plans. But he knew everything was in order; it always was. And the damn phone system was computerized these days. *Why ask for trouble?* Anyway, these last four artworks were his farewell gift, all arranged, the usual routine.

He checked his watch. It was time. Cart the artwork to the public garage where he'd left his car, then a short drive to the park and back, and that would be it.

Tomorrow a new life would be waiting for him. No job this time. *Country squire*, he thought, a role he was born to play.

CHAPTER 26

Maurice Jones worked for Jamal Youngblood, whom he'd never met, who worked for some white guy—or was it a white woman? He'd never been told, and never would be, which was just fine with Maurice, who had learned early on that asking questions just got you into trouble. Maurice, whose nineteenth birthday was only a month away, had been living on the streets and by his wits since he was ten. For the last couple of years he'd been a freelance runner—delivering drugs or driving stolen goods across state lines without asking what it was he was carting. Tonight, he was driving a gray SUV up the New York Thruway, according to the instructions he'd gotten from Jamal that morning.

The SUV would be waiting in a municipal parking lot on 102nd Street and First Avenue. Keys under the front seat. Ticket to get out of the lot in the visor. He was to pick up the car at 8 P.M. Head out of the city via the Willis Avenue Bridge. Take I-87 North to Exit 9. From there, drive 1.3 miles along White Plains Road until he came to the Starlight Diner. There, he would be met by another car. He was not to get out of the SUV or to interact with the other driver while the merchandise was placed in the back of the SUV. On his way back he was to make another stop, this one in Central Park. After that, it was back to the parking lot, leave the car. Go home.

Maurice figured it was drugs, but had not asked. He never asked. As Jamal always said, "Better you don't know."

As he merged onto I-87, Maurice lit up a joint, turned on the radio, and bopped to the beat of Kanye West, the producer turned rapper, who, according to what he'd just read in *Spin*, was the son of a Black Panther, some sort of cool black power thing way back when. He didn't exactly know what the Black Panthers did, but he liked the name, thought about getting himself a tattoo of a black panther. Maurice was feeling good. He'd gotten his usual fee—five hundred in cash, up front. Kanye West had just finished up his rousing *Jesus Walks*, and Maurice was down to his last toke when he spotted the sign: EXIT 9—TARRYTOWN.

Darby Herrick was nearly finished taping the bubble wrap around the paintings. To her surprise, the first painting she'd delivered had been sold immediately—and they wanted more. It was almost too easy. Though now, after the Tarrytown police had questioned her about her aunt's death, she was nervous. But they didn't know anything. It was that McKinnon woman who had unnerved her, acting all friendly with her bullshit camaraderie while she asked all those questions. But what could she possibly know?

Herrick strapped another piece of tape around the painting and set it with the others. They were not big paintings, but good ones—all from her aunt's most successful period, the late fifties, when she'd been the pretty young woman artist among the famous men painters. She'd heard her aunt's stories. A thousand times.

Herrick had tried to break into the New York art scene—all those artists clamoring after careers—but it just made her anxious. She had lasted less than a year, retreated to the small house and studio not far from her aunt, and had been painting in isolation ever since, living on the tiny inheritance she had received when her parents died, now about to run out.

But that was all going to change.

The phone call had been unexpected; the conversation convincing—

Sell off a few of your aunt's paintings before the taxes are assessed—and Herrick had agreed. A way to get something before Larry got his share. Why split the profits with a brother who hadn't earned them?

Darby Herrick glanced at the paintings pulled from the racks and stacked around the perimeter of her aunt's studio. There were plenty of them. Who was going to miss three or four?

Did you see her last night? Kate McKinnon, asking when she'd last seen her aunt, the question replaying in her mind.

Did the woman suspect something—or was she just fishing?

But how could McKinnon know?

And it was just a few paintings. Didn't she deserve to get something for all the shit she had put up with?

Herrick pulled back the curtain and peered through the window at the dark street, then gathered the paintings and slid them into the back of her Ford station wagon.

A minute later, with her heart beating fast, she slipped into the front seat, lit up a cigarette, turned the key in the ignition, and took off.

She did not notice the unmarked car that followed her.

The Tarrytown PD that witnessed the exchange at the Starlight Diner immediately called the NYPD with a description of the gray SUV, and when Maurice Jones crossed the Willis Avenue Bridge back into Manhattan, a car was tailing him. The Tarrytown PD was, by then, following Darby Herrick's Ford station wagon.

Within minutes, the NYPD and the FBI had sent out the order: "Follow everyone, but do not intervene."

The surveillance team that had been assigned to watch Colin Leader had called in the moment he'd left his apartment, followed him to the parking lot, and were now watching his silver BMW roll into Central Park.

Fifteen minutes later, when the SUV and the BMW came out of the park, each at a different exit, there were over a dozen unmarked police cars idling. Leader was followed back to his apartment; Maurice Jones, to the municipal lot, then on foot, as he headed uptown.

The Central Park PD kept watch on the SUV for several hours, but no one showed up.

Had the cops been spotted? They weren't sure.

In the morning, Tarrytown PD arrested Darby Herrick, the NYPD picked up Maurice Jones, and FBI Manhattan seized the SUV and its contents—three paintings from Beatrice Larsen's studio and several small artworks obviously taken from the storage bins of the Modernist Museum—though Colin Leader had not yet been arrested.

"I say we leave Leader out there," said Brown, setting his hands onto the conference table. "Clearly, the man was working with someone else and we need to see who that somebody is—who he's selling to."

"The kid, Maurice, isn't talking," said Agent Bobbitt. "Says he's just an errand boy. Says he didn't know what he was carrying. Says he gets a call, does the pickup. That's it."

"Probably true," said Brown.

"But you're going to keep him in lockup," said Bobbitt. "Can't afford to have him on the street, talking."

"He'll still be missed," said Brown. "And so will the art. That's why I say leave Leader out there. Let him think it all went down just fine."

"He's bound to hear from the other end that it didn't." Murphy went for his rubber band, caught Bobbitt's eye, and stopped.

"True," said Brown. "And then *we* hear who calls, where he goes—or who comes to him. His phone's tapped and surveillance is back in place."

"You think Leader is behind the murders?" asked Perlmutter. "A way to cover up the art theft?"

"Could be," said Brown.

"Maybe the curator, Dressler, got wind of it," said Perlmutter. "Confronted Leader, and Leader killed him."

"Or maybe Dressler was in on it," said Agent Moroni. "Maybe he got greedy, or was going to blackmail Leader."

Kate had been listening to all of it, and she just wasn't sure. "What about Darby Herrick?"

"What about her?" Bobbitt asked.

"Tarrytown has her in custody," said Brown. "She says she never met the buyer for her aunt's art. Claims she got a phone call. We checked her phone records. There's one from a public phone, another from a cell that we have to trace. The deal was strictly cash. Herrick admits she'd already sold one piece. Same drill. Also swears she never heard of Colin Leader."

Kate was trying to think it through. Had Darby Herrick killed her aunt for the inheritance, or was it a lucky coincidence—an opportunity to make some cash?

"The Bureau has asked Tarrytown to keep Herrick in custody," said Bobbitt. "We can't have her talking. Not to anyone. Not even a lawyer. Not yet."

"So much for her civil rights," said Kate. "Let me guess—this some-how falls under the Patriot Act?"

"Funny," said Bobbitt. "I didn't think you cared for jokes."

"I love jokes," said Kate. "When they're funny."

"Okay," said Bobbitt. "I got one you'll like. What do you call an anorexic woman with a yeast infection?"

"I'm sure you'll tell me," said Kate.

"A quarter-pounder with cheese." He slapped the table and laughed.

Kate knew what he was doing, showing her it was a boys' club, but she already knew that, had known it the first time she'd put on the ill-fitting blue uniform, and she knew it wouldn't change, either. "You know, Agent Bobbitt, you're really wasting your talents with the Bureau. You should quit, start doing stand-up."

Brown cut in before she had a chance to get herself in trouble. "Leader's probably been doing this for some time."

"Right," said Murphy, "I'm having the museum check any missing inventory."

"But we still have to see where he might lead us," said Brown.

"No way he's working alone," said Agent Moroni. "But whoever it is, they might lie low when the art doesn't show up, figure we're onto them."

"It's too late to put the art back in the SUV," said Brown.

"True," said Agent Bobbitt. "But I have another idea." He unbuttoned his suit jacket, sat forward, and folded his hands on the table. "Suppose we leak a few news items, something like . . . 'A recent group of artworks stolen from a few prominent museums have turned out to be . . . forgeries.'" He looked up and smiled. "You get my drift?"

"Yeah," said Brown. "You want to stir the shit."

"With a great big spoon," said Bobbitt.

"It could cause a lot of trouble for Leader," said Perlmutter.

"Exactly," said Bobbitt. "But you have a car on him twenty-four/seven. We can see who comes to complain to him."

"It's too risky," said Brown.

"Only for the felons," said Bobbitt. "We turn the rats against each other."

"Agent Bobbitt." Kate met the cocky young agent's eyes. "I see your point, and it may, in fact, produce results, but saying a museum had forgeries in its collection will put its credibility in jeopardy."

"Hey," said Bobbitt. "It won't be the first time someone lied to the press. And we don't have to say *which* museum."

Kate looked away from Bobbitt, to Perlmutter and Brown. "You guys know me, and I'm not exactly Snow White, but am I the only one here who thinks this is bordering on a serious moral issue?"

Bobbitt turned toward his colleague. "You have a problem with this, Moroni?"

Brown answered before the other agent could. "McKinnon could be right," he said. "And the papers won't print it unless they believe it, and when they find out it's a lie—"

"So there will be a few pissed-off reporters," said Bobbitt.

"Could be plenty of shit to clean up later," said Perlmutter.

"So we buy them a mop," said Bobbitt. "Look, you guys don't want to dirty your hands, fine. I'll feed the stories through the Bureau's connections."

CHAPTER 27

Urban Legend has it that the reporters who work for New York's tabloids have a lottery for best—that is, worst—headline. One of the finalists for the fabricated art forgery story was Art Fart, risky business even for the *Post*. In the end, they settled on:

PHONY BALONEY!

Under the headline, the smaller banner read:

No Honor Among (Art) Thieves

Who has the last laugh now? According to reliable sources, a number of New York's more prestigious museums have reported artworks missing from their storerooms over the past few years—many of which have turned out to be fakes or forgeries, including a late-period Arshile Gorky and a Monet *Haystack*.

Naturally, the authorities will continue to pursue the matter, though this reporter cannot resist noting the irony of art thieves stealing what turns out to be fake art. Among the museums implicated were the Modernist, Guggenheim, and Whitney— though none would comment . . .

The *News* ran a similar article, one that reveled in making fun of anyone and everyone who collected modern art, alongside a photo of a Monet *Haystack* with the caption: "Could be a fake—and it only costs a couple of mil!"

The *Times*, which ran the story on the first page of its Metro Section, did a more serious reporting job, questioning how museums could be so lax in both collecting and then losing artworks—whether they were forgeries or not.

Agent Bobbitt had also leaked the story to CNN and Interpol, both of which had, in turn, spread the story to newspapers in Europe, South America, Asia, as well as the Internet, and every television news station.

Colin Leader read the *Times* article twice, then called the museum's PR department to tell them to stand by their "No comment" policy or simply deny all allegations. He had made one statement to the press: To his knowledge, there were no paintings missing from his museum. A lie.

But forgeries?

It just could not be true. The artwork he had so carefully selected, work that would not be immediately missed—forgeries? *No way.* Who could be spreading such malicious gossip—and why?

He reached for the phone to call the *Times* and give them a piece of his mind, then put it back down. What could he say: *How dare you call those pieces I stole from the museum fakes?*

The minute he put the receiver down, it was ringing—a reporter. He let the answering machine pick it up. This one inquiring about Martin Dressler's murder.

Jesus. What could he say about that?

The phone rang again. Another reporter about the forgeries.

Was the story true or false? Leader was not convinced, but there was little time to consider the story's validity—his plane left tonight and he intended to be on it. But had the artwork he delivered to the van in the park made it to its destination? If it had, his cash should have been delivered as well, and it had not been.

He went back to the *Times*. There was nothing in the article about intercepting any stolen works of art. It was simply a story about missing artworks believed to be fakes.

Leader reached for the phone, and once again stopped. He and his contact rarely spoke on anything but public telephones.

Would the police be calling him? Leader started to sweat, thoughts skittering around his brain like a ball in one of those pinball arcade games.

But wouldn't the coppers have called by now if they suspected him of something? Sure. He was okay. He needed a drink, something to calm down, that was all. He shook a Valium into his palm, washed it down with Scotch. If the police had questions, he could answer them. Wasn't he the one to champion the idea of more security for storeroom artwork at the museum? A brilliant ruse, he'd always thought—though he'd never hired anyone to do the job. And there was no way to connect him to the stolen artworks. He was sure of it. He'd been careful.

After a minute, the booze and drugs kicked in and Leader felt better. He turned off his phone and lay down on the couch. He'd wait just a little bit longer for that cash.

An hour earlier, the Colombian had picked up the *Post* and the *News*, something to read while being driven out to New Jersey's small Teterboro Airport, where his private plane awaited. He was only halfway through the *Post* story when he asked his driver to turn around.

Now he was standing across the room from Miranda Wilcox, who had been stripped naked and tied to her bed by his driver and bodyguard, two men whose combined IQ was somewhere in the range of sixty.

Legs spread apart, arms stretched over her head, Wilcox was shivering and crying, eyelids puffy, small clusters of blue-purple bruises appearing only minutes after her nose had been broken. She was swallowing blood and feeling nauseated.

"Carlos," she said with all the emotion she could muster, "I have never cheated you. *Never.*" She had been repeating variations on this theme for the past half hour, swearing that she had never sold the Colombian a forgery, although the *Post's* listing of the Monet *Haystack*, and the *News* photo, were more convincing than she was.

What the Colombian now wanted was the names of Wilcox's contacts. He promised he would set her free if she delivered the information and she did not hesitate. If asked, she would have given up her mother. She was quick to supply Colin Leader's name as the source of many of the Colombian's purchases, including the Monet *Haystack* and the recent Gorky painting, and Darby Herrick as the source of the Beatrice Larsen painting, though she swore—to her knowledge—all of the paintings were one hundred percent genuine. If any of the artworks she had sold to the Colombian were indeed forgeries, the blame, she insisted, fell on her suppliers.

The Colombian—who enjoyed the way human beings betrayed one another—had returned to Wilcox's apartment with the two paintings she had just sold him—the Larsen and the Gorky—and despite Wilcox's averring to their authenticity, had slashed them into ribbons and demanded the return of his money. Wilcox claimed that all but her small percentage had been turned over to her sources, Leader and Herrick, when, in fact, the money was still sitting in a small safe-deposit box. She hoped the Colombian would go after Leader and Herrick, and she could keep the cash—some of which she would use for her inevitable nose job.

The Colombian had no idea whether she was lying or not, but did not care. At the moment, the burgundy-tinted saliva that oozed out along with her words had turned him on. He unzipped. When he had finished his business, he gave his two henchmen a few simple but specific directions about their next assignment, then leaned over Miranda Wilcox and cut out her tongue.

The detectives, in the unmarked Crown Victoria outside Colin Leader's apartment, had been there since before dawn, rear ends going numb, feet falling asleep, eyes fighting sleep.

"I gotta get me some coffee," said Michael Carney, a seasoned detective who was sick to death of one more boring stakeout in a long line of boring stakeouts.

His new partner, Jennifer Tyson, a young woman recently promoted to detective (too fast, if you asked Carney), was disappointed to have drawn such a dreary assignment with an equally dreary partner, who had dandruff and a slight case of BO. She was happy to have the car to herself for a few minutes.

"You want one?" he asked, stepping out and shaking his legs.

"A soy latte," she said.

"A *what?*"

"You're going over to Starbucks, aren't you?" She pointed across the street.

"Three bucks for a cup o' joe? Fuck that shit. There's a deli two doors down. You take it black or *colored?*" He laughed at his bad joke.

"Forget it," said Tyson.

"Suit yourself." Carney scuttled away.

Tyson watched him cross the street, rolled her window down for air, then closed her tired eyes and thought about her six-month-old baby girl who stayed with her mother all day, and now tonight, too, because she'd been assigned this boring stakeout—an easy way to rack up brownie points provided she did not complain. Her husband, a handsome, aspiring actor, would be gone by the time she got home, bartending at a Queens club, and he was going to be pissed as hell.

The Colombian, now driving himself, had turned off the New Jersey Turnpike toward Teterboro Airport just as his two gorillas approached Colin Leader's building. They didn't know much, but they knew a cop car on surveillance when they saw one. They split up, the driver heading openly toward Leader's building, while the bodyguard crossed to the other side of the street.

Jennifer Tyson opened her eyes and saw a menacing-looking character marching toward Leader's building. In fact, the Colombian's driver was making quite a show of himself, moving stealthily but obviously, eyes darting back and forth, like a silent-screen villain, and Tyson could not take her eyes off him. She went for the phone to call for backup just as the Colombian's bodyguard reached through the window, grabbed her by the hair and slit her throat. She struggled a minute, hands at her neck in a futile attempt to stanch the blood spewing from her jugular, as the man crawled into the backseat, crouched down, and waited.

A few minutes later, Carney—concentrating on balancing a Danish and a cup of coffee as he got into the car—did not have time to notice his partner before the bodyguard reached over the seat and plunged the knife into his windpipe.

Afterward, the Colombian's bodyguard laid both cops' bodies down onto the car seat so that passersby would not immediately notice, then joined his partner, who was waiting in the lobby of Leader's building after having hit every buzzer on the intercom and repeating the two words the Colombian had made him memorize, "Con Ed," until someone buzzed him in.

They repeated "Con Ed" again at Leader's door, and when he did not answer, the bodyguard threw his full weight against it and the lock snapped as if it were made of tin. This was followed by a punch in the face that sent Leader's glasses flying, and his body to the floor. The bodyguard then sat on him while the driver searched the premises for the cash Miranda Wilcox had promised would be there. Despite Leader's protests that there was no money in the house other than the cash in his wallet, the men did not believe him, nor did they want to disappoint their boss.

When neither cigarette burns nor kidney punches produced the money, the gorillas tugged Leader's pants to his ankles, relieved him of his testicles, left him on the floor to die slowly, and made their escape worrying how the Colombian might punish them for failing to come up with the cash.

CHAPTER 28

When Colin Leader did not report to work or call in, his assistant went to his apartment. She found his body, curled into a ball, surrounded by a puddle of semicongealed blood, which she later told her friends made it look as if the man were floating in black-cherry aspic.

At approximately the same time, Miranda Wilcox's maid was announcing her arrival with a cheerful "Hello-o," as yet unaware of the fact that the lady of the house had choked to death on her own blood.

The crime scene photos were scattered across the conference table, the squad, along with Agent Vincent Moroni, attempting to put together what had gone down. Agent John Bobbitt was conspicuously missing.

"MO is pretty much the same—both tortured and left to die," said Floyd Brown. "It will take a while for DNA, but the lab will tell us if the saliva and hairs found at both the Leader and Wilcox scenes match."

"If it weren't so sloppy, I'd have guessed mob-related," said Nicky Perlmutter.

"Agreed," said Brown. "But a hired gun would be in and out of there, fast. These animals took their time, enjoyed themselves."

Kate was still absorbing the bad news—Colin Leader and Miranda Wilcox dead. And those two cops. She thought everyone knew why, though no one was saying. She turned to Moroni and asked, "Where's Bobbitt?"

"Still at the Bureau" was all he said.

"Right," said Kate, barely able to contain herself from saying, *Of course he's not here, the cowardly fuck!* She stared at Moroni, who had conveniently shifted gears.

"The errand boy," he said, "Maurice Jones, gave us a name—Jamal Youngblood. He was the dispatcher. We ran him through CJIS. Has a juevy record: petty theft, assault. His lawyer's cutting a deal with the DA for more info. So far, Youngblood's told us that the paintings in the back of the SUV were headed for a warehouse storage bin, which, it turns out, was rented by Miranda Wilcox. OLEC got her bank records, turned up canceled checks for two other storage locations over the past ten years. She obviously moved her inventory around."

"So the paintings Leader put in the SUV were on their way to Wilcox," said Perlmutter. "Which means Leader and Wilcox were definitely connected."

Murphy handed everyone a couple of pages of printed matter. "The story on Miranda Wilcox," he said. "Clearly our art fence. Had a front business selling art to corporations, but didn't earn nearly enough to maintain the Park Avenue apartment, Mercedes in the garage, and the house in the Hamptons." He turned to Kate. "You ever come across her?"

"No. Never."

Moroni distributed another set of papers, these on Colin Leader. "CID put this together. As you can see, the guy had a history. Fired from his first job—small museum in England, suspicion of theft, though they couldn't prove it. Name was *Ledder* at the time, which is what it says on his birth certificate. After England, there was a short stint in Greece on an archaeological dig—until a few pieces of rare pottery disappeared. After Greece, he spent a few years at a small museum in Australia, where he worked his way up from curator to director, made a name for himself. And chose a new one—*Leader.*"

Kate thought back to the talk with Cecile Edelman, remembered the woman had been impressed with what Leader had done at the

Australian museum. She guessed that was as far back as the board members had checked. "Do we know how many pieces disappeared from the Modernist Museum during Leader's tenure?"

"The museum's registrar is still checking," said Murphy. "But it looks as though Leader altered inventory sheets. Made it look like pieces were loaned out to small museums—but they never came back."

"You think Wilcox was always his fence?" she asked.

"Could be," said Moroni, interrupting. "But Leader wasn't her only client. We've got Darby Herrick's phone records, too, which show several calls that we've linked to Wilcox's cell phone."

"See if there were any calls to either Gabrielle Hofmann or her husband, Henry Lifschultz," said Kate. "According to Cecile Edelman, Leader and Gabrielle's husband were friends. It seems like a connection we should know more about, especially since Lifschultz is the only one of the three who's still alive."

"Got it," said Moroni. "We have a field agent at Greenwich PD keeping an eye on Lifschultz."

"So, do we know who actually killed Leader and Wilcox?" asked Murphy.

"According to Crime Scene, there are at least three sets of prints at the Wilcox place," said Brown.

"Quantico lab already ran them," said Moroni. "Two of them came up blank, but the third set belongs to one Carlos Escobar."

"What the hell was Miranda Wilcox doing with a drug lord?" asked Perlmutter.

Kate ventured a guess. "Having an affair? Selling him art? Probably both."

"I don't see Escobar as an art lover," said Moroni.

"Art can be just another status symbol," said Kate, though she hated to think of it like that. "To some people it's like a fancy car or a Rolex watch, only better. Plus, it's a nice way to launder your excess cash."

"So where is Escobar now?" asked Perlmutter.

"According to CJIS, he hightailed it back to Colombia ASAP," said Moroni.

"Jesus," said Kate. "Do you people ever speak in anything but initials?"

"Figured you knew what they stood for," said Moroni, then slowly enunciated: "Criminal . . . Justice . . . Information . . . Services. Do I need to spell out ASAP, too?"

Assholes aplenty, she thought, but did not say.

"Escobar has a huge spread in Colombia. Interpol has had its eye on him for years, but he's slippery. Has his own plane, too." Moroni frowned. "Goddamn airports are supposed to be reporting any and all flights, especially these days, but—"

"So we have the shady art dealer, Wilcox. The crooked museum dealer, Leader. And a drug dealer who buys art." Perlmutter listed them on his fingers. "What about the curator, Dressler? How was he involved?"

"Maybe Dressler was aiding and abetting Leader, and some shit went down," said Moroni. "They all could have been working together. Maybe there wasn't one murderer either—just a bunch of art thieves covering their tracks. It could have gone down any number of ways. All I'm saying is that this little nest of vipers—they all could have been killers."

"But why'd they kill Nicholas Starrett?" asked Kate.

"Suppose he got wind of what Leader was doing," said Murphy. "It's possible. He was on the board of Leader's museum." He tugged on his rubber band as he talked. "Say Nicholas Starrett stumbles upon the fact that there are paintings missing from the museum. He doesn't know it's Leader, but he makes the mistake of *telling* Leader. Now Leader KNOWS that Starrett KNOWS, so Leader goes to the party with the intent of silencing Starrett before Starrett figures out it's *him*."

"Okay," said Kate. "But what about Gabrielle Hofmann?"

"Leader could have been involved in selling the paintings from her private collection—maybe with her husband, Lifschultz. Remember, Leader and Lifschultz were seen on the golf course—they knew one another. Maybe Lifschultz gives the paintings to Leader, his wife finds out, and Lifschultz tells Leader, and Leader kills her—or Lifschultz killed her himself."

"He has a solid alibi," said Moroni. "And the Bureau did a background check on him, pretty much came up empty."

Kate wanted to go through each victim; she wanted answers. "What about Sarkisian? Do we know if there's any connection between Sarkisian and Leader?"

Brown shook his head.

"I can have the Bureau run a check," said Moroni. "See if they find any connection between Sarkisian and the others—Leader, Wilcox, or Lifschultz."

"Bureau can do just about anything, can't they?" Kate shot Moroni a look, though it was not him it was meant for—it was meant for Bobbitt, his absent partner. "While you're at it, check on Darby Herrick? We know she was funneling her aunt's artwork through Wilcox, but do we think she played a bigger role? Like, did she kill her aunt?"

"That's one we may never be able to prove," said Murphy. "You saw the lab reports. The foam rubber, the tape residue. But there's no way to link it to Herrick. Sure, her prints were in the studio, along with yours, your cameraman's, and a dozen others'. All of them, run through IAFIS, and nothing." Murphy had the rubber band off his wrist, winding it around a finger.

"Now I have a question." Brown reached for one of the Wilcox crime scene photos where the destroyed Gorky and Larsen paintings were clearly visible. "These two paintings were slashed at the scene. Why?"

"Could be Leader decided Wilcox knew too much, went to her place, they fought, he slashes her paintings to make it look like the psycho, and kills her," says Moroni.

"You want to know what I think happened—which is what we *all* think happened, but for some fucking reason no one wants to say it?" Kate leveled a stare at Moroni, then slapped her hand down hard on the crime scene photos. "Wilcox sells the paintings to Escobar, who reads the phony news items that says they were forgeries. He goes ballistic, slashes the paintings, tortures Wilcox, gets her to give up Leader, then goes and kills Leader."

"We don't know that." Moroni shifted in his chair. "And Escobar's prints haven't turned up at Leader's place. Anyway, it was NYPD cops who let whoever it was get through to Leader—not the Bureau."

"Oh, nice touch, Moroni," said Kate through clenched teeth. "Hey, folks, anyone here want to take the goddamn responsibility for four murders? *Four.* One of them a young mother?"

They were all quiet a moment. Kate let out a deep breath but kept her eyes on Moroni, and when she next spoke the anger had drained from her voice. "Look, I know it was Bobbitt and not you who made the decision to plant those stories, but the Bureau obviously helped carry it out, and hell, we all let it happen; so please, let's just admit it, okay, guys?" She looked from one to the other. "Two victims tortured to death—on the same day—and they're linked by stolen art. The prints of a known drug lord were at one scene, and even if his prints didn't show up at the other, you know, I know, and everyone in this room knows they were connected, and sooner or later—and I'm guessing sooner—we'll get the proof. And then some reporter is going to find out those newspaper stories were a plant—and a lie—and the shit is going to hit the fucking fan."

"Trust me." Moroni sighed. "Bobbitt's been locked up with a 'Professional Standards' since this story broke, and my guess . . . you won't be seeing him again."

Kate headed north on the New York State Thruway, the whole ride thinking how they had screwed up, allowing those bullshit stories to be planted in the papers, and what had happened—all those people dead. *Damn it.* Why hadn't she fought harder?

She knew the answer to that—she had wanted to break the case, too. Just not like this.

According to Moroni, Bobbitt would be taking the fall, and he deserved it. But they had all gone along, under protest, sure, but they were complicit, if not exactly guilty; and none of it—not her guilt, not Bobbitt's job—was going to bring the victims back.

Kate turned off the thruway at the Newburgh Beacon Bridge and followed Route 9 until she found the Beacon Correctional Facility for Women.

What she needed now were a few answers. Maybe, if she was lucky, she'd get some.

Darby Herrick looked like shit. Skin ashen, eyes red-rimmed, curly hair gone dry and limp, the gray uniform hanging on her thin frame. She'd been awaiting pretrial for three counts of interstate art theft and could not afford bail. The funds from her aunt's estate were frozen, though it seemed unlikely she would ever see any of the money. Her brother was now petitioning for all of it. Herrick had been assigned a public defender, a skinny guy with acne on his cheeks who did not look old enough to vote, let alone practice law. He was just leaving as Kate made her way into the visitors' room.

"You here to gloat?" asked Herrick as Kate took a seat.

"No. I'm here because I want to know the truth."

"The truth is those paintings belonged to me. I earned them."

"Because you took care of her all those years?"

"You have a cigarette?"

Kate pushed a pack of Marlboros—her old brand—across the table.

"You don't look like a smoker."

"I'm not. Not anymore. These are for you." She waited as Herrick lit up and sucked the smoke into her lungs.

"Can I ask you something off the record?"

"Is there such a thing?"

"Probably not," said Kate. "But this is for my own curiosity." She paused a moment. "Did you kill your aunt?"

"No." Herrick met Kate's gaze. "But you don't think I'd say yes, do you? My lawyer wouldn't like that." She exhaled a long plume of smoke. "But I *didn't*. You may not believe me, but I loved that cantankerous old bitch."

Kate saw a flickering of emotion in Herrick's eyes, but it could have been an act.

"It's exactly like I said. I found her like that, dead, and those paintings, slashed."

"But you were selling off some of her paintings the minute she died. You think your aunt would have condoned your selling her work on the black market?"

"Beatrice?" Herrick's mouth curled into a sardonic smile. "She would have *loved* it."

Kate could imagine Beatrice Larsen getting a kick out of people illegally trading her artwork for cash, cutting out the art establishment that had not treated her kindly. "How did you meet Miranda Wilcox?"

"Why should I tell you?"

"Because maybe I can help."

Herrick took a deep draw on her cigarette, held it a moment, then exhaled slowly. "I never met her. Had never even heard of her. She called me out of the blue. Made it seem easy. Said everyone did it, that it was no big thing. She made all the arrangements."

Kate pictured Miranda Wilcox scouring the obits for the deaths of artists, then contacting the heirs.

"She said she could help me sell a few paintings before I was hit with taxes, that the sales would help pay them."

"Of course you knew that was illegal."

Herrick shrugged.

"Do you have any idea who killed your aunt?"

"Who says she was killed?"

Kate stared at Herrick, waiting.

"If she was killed, I guess that Leader guy killed her, right?"

"Did your aunt ever meet him?"

"I don't know."

"And you never met him?"

"No. Why would I?" Herrick peered through the cigarette smoke at Kate. "You trying to set me up here?"

"Not at all. I was just curious."

"I never met the man." Herrick squashed her cigarette into a metal ashtray. "Now how the hell are you going to help me?"

———

Kate pondered Herrick's question as she drove back to the city, her instincts telling her that Herrick was guilty only of trying to make a few quick bucks. In her time, Kate had questioned enough guilty people to know one, and Herrick did not fit the profile. She was angry and scared, and Kate didn't like her, but there was none of those telltale ticks that exposed a liar, no cool indifference or overdone histrionics.

But somebody had killed Beatrice Larsen. Kate was sure of it. She wasn't buying the heart failure—Larsen's heart may have been broken more than a few times, but she was a strong woman. As for the "slow aspirations of foam rubber" theory that the lab proposed, well, they may not be able to make a case out of it, but it sure as hell felt like murder to Kate.

The cops were looking for rational solutions to irrational situations— Leader killed Dressler, Escobar killed Wilcox and Leader, maybe Wilcox killed Larsen—all very possible, even plausible. But who killed Gregory Sarkisian and Gabrielle Hofmann? And what about her friend, Nicholas Starrett?

CHAPTER 29

The newspapers were having a good time picking over the corpses of Colin Leader and Miranda Wilcox—flesh peeled back, personal histories exposed—all in the name of freedom of the press.

One of the lower-rent tabloids had even gotten hold of an obscene crime scene photo of Miranda Wilson savagely beaten, and printed it along with as much minutiae as they could dig up about the art dealer's shady business dealings and deadly sex life.

A day after the murders, the papers reported that the bodies of two brawny Latinos were found dumped in a Staten Island landfill, each with a shot to the back of the head. There was enough trace evidence—strands of Wilcox's ash-blond hair and fibers from the rug in Colin Leader's foyer—to link them to the murders, though the press hadn't a clue about that. The headlines screamed: MOB HIT, which the NYPD and FBI allowed them to believe. They had no intention of divulging the fact that these were Escobar's henchmen, another secret that, in all likelihood, would surface soon enough. As for the up-and-coming Agent Bobbitt, he was, according to Agent Moroni, down-and-out and looking for a new job. He deserved it, thought Kate, though she felt they had all played a part in the mess, and had said as much to Brown.

Chief of Police Clare Tapell was trying her best to keep a lid on the phony art story as long as possible. She knew, once it broke, there would be the inevitable question of accountability and hoped she could make that stick to the FBI rather than the NYPD.

The Modernist Museum had released a statement denying allegations that Colin Leader had been pilfering from the museum's collection. Clearly a defensive move—no one in their right mind would donate artwork to a museum that could not guarantee the safety of its inventory—and the other museums accused of having forgeries in their collections were protesting loudly. Kate knew it was simply a matter of time before they discovered the truth.

Meanwhile, the story of the two dead cops vied for the public's attention—and certainly won its sympathy—with reporters relishing such details as Michael Carney's long career and Jennifer Tyson's six-month-old child. Photos of the pretty cop with her baby girl were splashed across all three New York dailies. The *News* even ran an interview with Tyson's husband, the out-of-work actor, who had obviously supplied them with one of his head shots, hoping perhaps to catch the eye of a talent agent or casting director.

Kate could not look at the pictures of the young detective Tyson and her baby without tearing up or wanting to scream. Reporters, having gotten wind of her involvement in the case, had barraged her with calls for an interview—all declined. She had also been dodging calls from Mitch Freeman, despite her promise not to. The case had opened a wound rather than healed one—the idea of *dating*, possible.

She was torn between getting answers to a case that would not end, or disappearing into her work, and turned her attention back to her life, like tonight, a concert at PS 167, by the foundation kids.

Rudy Musanti had been working in the evidence room of the Sixth Precinct for close to twenty years, a desk job given to him after he had failed his detective's test three times and decided that going for a fourth would just be embarrassing. His wife, Dottie, who had been pissed at him for at least eighteen of those twenty years, had lately been threatening to leave him if he did not come up with a way to bring home more money, and though she made his life hell, Rudy did not like to be alone. He had considered moonlighting—late-night security guard, telemarketing—but never got around to it, and now, with less than a month to go till retirement, there wasn't much point.

Now he had a retirement plan.

The newspapers had been clamoring for a peek at the Slasher's clue paintings ever since someone—probably another cop who needed money—had leaked the news of their existence, and here they were, bagged and stored, no less than six feet from Rudy's desk.

Rudy pulled himself out of his chair—no small feat having recently gone past the two-hundred-pound mark, not pretty on his five-foot-eight frame, the result of years spent sitting behind a desk—and slogged over to the flat file. He lifted one of the paintings out by a corner and glanced at it. He had a feeling someone, somewhere, would pay top dollar for these dumb-ass paintings. There was always a freak out there willing and wanting to buy anything. Like the gruesome crime scene photo of that art dealer he'd sold to that supermarket tabloid. But selling an image and selling an original were two different things. He could always deny he leaked the picture, but if the original paintings disappeared under his watch, well, that could be trouble.

Copies would have to do. And why not? Homicide and Art Squad had copies. The FBI had copies. Why deny the public? This was America, after all—land of the free, home of the voyeur.

Musanti slid the paintings out of their plastic bags, carried them over to the Xerox machine, and made a full set of copies.

Now, all he had to do was call a few of those reporters who were always sniffing around for something juicy. He'd try the *Post* first, then the *Trib*. If they declined, he'd go back to the supermarket tabloid. He was planning on asking for a grand apiece. Six pictures. Six grand— unless someone offered more.

As soon as he made the deal he would break the news to Dottie over a double order of spareribs at their favorite Chinese place.

José Medina's mother had fixed herself up—lipstick and eyeliner, hair bobbed—and Kate could see where José got his looks. His sisters were there, too, ribbons in their dark hair, talking and giggling. Anita Medina waved Kate over.

"For once," she said, "I am at the school and it is not about José being in trouble." She smiled as Kate settled into the auditorium seat beside her, and Kate returned the smile, though thoughts of this case would not stop playing in her mind—the slashed paintings and slashed people, the odd connections between the victims—none of it making any sense.

But the thoughts receded when the curtains parted to reveal a blue-black backdrop spray-painted with Day-Glo graffiti, and José's quasi-jazz-hip-hop group started playing—two kids on guitars, one on piano, a sassy teenage girl singing a sort of Ella Fitzgerald scat, sixties Motown, and rap, all rolled into one. José, hair slicked like he was in a road-show version of *West Side Story*, moved fluidly even with one arm in the cast, working the turntable for one song, the drums for another, singing backup in all six numbers as if he'd been doing it his entire life.

Afterward, there was a reception, soda and cookies, though Kate knew the teens would have preferred harder stuff. She was surprised to learn that José had not only written five out of the six musical numbers but had designed the backdrop as well.

"I'm impressed," she said. "A musician *and* an artist."

José shrugged, tried to play it cool, but he was smiling, glowing, even, surrounded by his sisters and friends—the big man, the star.

Kate suggested he come with her when she next visited Phillip Zander's studio, meet the artist and his musical assistant, and José agreed, and she left the performance feeling good—though it didn't last.

CHAPTER 30

Cecile Edelman was not the sort of woman easily given to feelings of guilt, but she was feeling awful. It would have been one thing if Colin Leader had been fired, or quit, but to be murdered? On top of that, the idea that the man had been stealing artworks from the museum! It was all too much. After all, she had been part of the search committee that hired the man! True, she had, of late, been arguing for Leader's dismissal, but shouldn't she have seen it immediately, the signs of decadence and immorality?

No question the museum was in trouble—and this was the kind of stain an institution could not easily wash away.

A few weeks ago she had happily resigned from the board, but now she felt responsible, that somehow she had to help them out, maybe give them a donation—a significant work of art that would get media attention and deflect some of the bad publicity, show that a serious collector still believed in the museum.

Maybe, she thought, she should rejoin the board, help them steer out of this mess. Her late husband, Morton, surely would have approved—after all they had done to turn the Modernist into a respected establishment, he would have been dismayed to see it crumble.

Yes, she would swallow her pride, become a board member again, and help them find a new director. Someone dynamic with a spotless reputation, someone intelligent, an art historian with a high enough profile to bring in new donors and new money, someone like . . . Kate McKinnon. Of course. She'd be *perfect*!

But would Kate be interested? She had no idea. She hardly knew the woman, though Kate certainly had the profile from her television show, and the Ph.D., plus looks and style—though that kooky new hairdo would have to go. She would give her a call, feel her out, try to convince her at least to consider the notion.

But a moment later, when she thought about those brash new board members—men like Henry Lifschultz—Cecile deflated. They hadn't gone along with any of her ideas in the past. Why would they listen to her now?

Edelman stared at the painting her late husband had commissioned for her sixtieth birthday, a stenciled Warhol portrait of her, all gold and purple, glamorous, if a bit flat—but it captured the determined woman she had always been and always would be, and it gave her confidence. She could convince Henry Lifschultz and his board member cronies what was good for the museum. It was obvious they needed her guidance, now more than ever.

She would call Henry Lifschultz right away, before her confidence failed, and tell him that she intended to rejoin the board, and her idea about finding a new director. At the same time she could offer condolences for his wife—which she should have done sooner. She dialed his number thinking she should probably offer condolences about Colin Leader as well; after all, the two men had been golfing buddies, maybe even friends.

Henry Lifschultz stared at the answering machine, listening to Cecile Edelman.

What did she mean, she wanted back on the museum board? And what the hell was she implying when she said she was sorry about Colin Leader—that she knew they had been *friends*? Was that some sort of threat? Was she implying blackmail? Why the hell was she even calling him? Offering condolences about his wife? *Yeah, right.*

"Fuck you!" Lifschultz shouted at the machine.

Edelman was a troublesome old bitch who had to have her own way; he'd seen that more than once and he wasn't buying this routine of hers—whatever it was.

But did she know something?

Like what?

Lifschultz paced across the living room of his Greenwich, Connecticut, home. He had to remain calm. He was just being paranoid. After all, what could she know?

Plenty.

Truthfully, he had no idea what anyone knew—not Cecile Edelman, not the police.

Lifschultz picked at his shirt. He was sweating and the cotton was sticking to his chest and back.

Had the police made the connection yet? It didn't seem so—not yet, anyway. Though his gut told him it was just a matter of time.

He tried to think . . . Was there anything tangible that connected them? Certainly there was no paperwork. And the calls had been made from a cell phone he had already disposed of. But was that information logged somewhere? Probably. Wasn't everything these days? And what about *her* cell phone?

He told himself to be calm, to practice his lines, to prepare the answers to the questions that would inevitably be coming his way. *Well, yes, we did some business. No, I had no idea there was anything illegal going on. How could I?*

Even to his ear it sounded a bit lame.

He glanced around the room, taking in what remained of the art and antiques his wife had collected, talismans that brought her to life, the frail birdlike woman who had never much appealed to him.

He needed to stick to his plan. Get out of town. Take up permanent residence in the house he'd been constructing in San Miguel for the past four years—which, if those goddamn Mexican serfs would move their fucking asses, would have been finished a year ago. But he could live in it while they finished tiling and painting the frescoes. Maybe he'd even get into it, the role of expat; better still, overlord: *You there, peasant, tile that wall like you mean it!*

Lifschultz laughed. It was all going to be fine.

Gaby hadn't had much interest in Mexico; she disliked the heat and the sun, always hiding under straw hats and sunglasses, but what she liked, or did not like, no longer mattered.

Lifschultz pictured himself in a chaise with a local senorita, or two.

But would it make him look guilty, leaving town so soon after Gaby's death?

Hell, he *was* guilty—and if he hung around long enough for someone to figure that out, he was also a goddamn fool.

Lifschultz moved to the bedroom, exchanged the sweaty shirt for a fresh one with his initials monogrammed on the top of the pocket. He would have to stay for the memorial service. After that, it was splitsville. *Hasta la vista, baby!*

Everything was set. The Park Avenue apartment on the market, his business ready to be closed. No big loss there, he had to confess. Then he remembered Kate McKinnon and her proposal for a dream house in Rhinebeck. At first, he'd been excited—the idea of a new client and a new project, of spending time with the sexy widow, imagined getting her alone amid the I-beams and two-by-fours—until he thought it through. It was a ruse, for sure. After all, she was involved with the police, isn't that what he'd just read? And now, when he thought about it, that guy with her, he must have been a cop.

Were they onto him? Had she been sent to check him out? Or was he being paranoid again? Maybe she did have land she wanted to build on.

Fuck it. Whichever it was—it was never going to happen. He had to get out. Now.

He looked over at the Doberman curled in the corner of the room. Poor beast looked fucking depressed, and had since Gaby's death. He wondered if dogs actually got depressed. He had no idea, didn't really care either. He hated the dog and the dog hated him. He stared at the creature, trying to see inside its brain. Did the dog know? *Jesus.* He *was* losing his mind—worrying what a dog did or did not know.

Get a grip.

One more day, that was all. The memorial service, tie up a few loose ends, then gone.

I had to get away. You understand. After what happened to Gaby, well, I just couldn't stay here.

An image flashed across his mind: Miranda, bound and tortured, the picture from that supermarket tabloid that he'd had the good and bad luck to have seen. It seemed so real, like it was happening in front of his eyes. Had he actually seen it? In real life? No, it was just a picture. But it was having that effect again—he was hard. He was hard and he was definitely losing his mind.

If Miranda were here, he'd fuck her and she'd fuck him and at least he'd forget about all of this shit that was driving him crazy. Of course Miranda was a big part of the worry.

Had he erased all of their e-mails?

He checked his computer. Yes. All gone. But hadn't he read that any hacker worth his weight in megabytes could recoup anyone's e-mail? And what about his office computer? He wasn't sure about that.

God, the stuff they had written to each other. He tried not to think about it, but was getting hard again, and the irony was that Miranda wasn't here to berate him for his bad thoughts, or spank him for his naughty-boy ways.

Damn it. How was he supposed to think clearly with all this shit running through his head?

He had to concentrate on getting out of here without being noticed. No question the Greenwich police had been watching him. He'd spotted the same unmarked car for the past two days. Though they had already missed the good stuff—at least he hoped so. They hadn't arrested him yet, so they must not know anything. And by the time they did, if they did, he'd be gone.

Cecile Edelman's phone message replayed in his mind. What was he going to do about *that*?

For now, calm down, pop a Valium, and do something constructive—like write the damn speech he was surely expected to give at his wife's memorial service.

He'd deal with Edelman later.

Lifschultz pulled a chair up to his wife's antique desk and uncapped his Mont Blanc pen. But what could he say? *Gaby was a nice girl who would never strap on a dildo and fuck me in the ass?* Oh, God, he was going straight to hell. But the thought of it made him laugh because Miranda always said hell was the right place for him.

He wondered: Was she there now, enjoying herself without him?

Detective Eric Kominsky hadn't liked the guy from the get-go, but right now he was bored, stomach grumbling from too much lukewarm thermos coffee, bladder aching to pee. He peered through his dark windshield at the gated driveway that led up to the Hofmann-Lifschultz home.

He was parked in the neighbor's driveway, the only way to avoid suspicion. One could not very well have a Chevy Caprice parked on the side of a Greenwich country road without arousing suspicion. Hell, if it wasn't a Mercedes, a Jaguar, or a Jeep, you'd be arousing suspicion just driving in this neighborhood.

Kominsky had been on this stakeout for what seemed like forever. His Greenwich chief worried that Lifschultz was going to sue, and never would have agreed to the surveillance if it had not been ordered by the FBI. But as far as Kominsky was concerned, it was a case of locking the barn door too late. He'd figured Lifschultz as a bad apple from their first conversation—the way the guy had been sweating, and more worried about himself than the fact that his wife had just been murdered.

Kominsky wasn't sure how long he'd be sitting here, but he was willing to wait, anything to catch this rich motherfucker. He just hoped the neighbors would not mind if he used their bathroom.

CHAPTER 31

Kate was working in the PBS editing room, eyes flicking from one small screen to another, when the phone rang. Two different tapes of Phillip Zander interviews were playing simultaneously and her eyes hurt from several hours of the work. After ten rings the phone went silent.

The station was getting antsy, applying pressure on her to finish the series on the New York School. The promos had been playing—for weeks—the first installment due to air in February. She had shirked her responsibility; even delayed her trip to Rome to meet with Sandy Resnikoff's daughter to see her father's paintings, and put together the promised segment on the *artist-who-got-away*—all because of this case. Resnikoff, thought Kate, who had been there at the beginning, friends with de Kooning, Kline, and Zander—all of the greats—but had given it up. *Why?*

But how could she go to Rome with the case still pending?

The phone rang again. "What?" she said, sounding more irritated than she'd meant to.

It was Murphy.

"Some asshole leaked the killer's paintings—to the *Trib*," he said. "Brown's throwing a shit fit, and naturally, Tapell's in a fury. Take a look and call me back."

Kate hung up and went to the waiting room, riffled through all the dailies, and found a copy of the *Trib*. She could see why Brown and Tapell were freaked.

With the killer's paintings on display, anyone with enough talent could duplicate one, use it to "copycat" a crime and throw the police off—not to mention the fact that it put the NYPD on display, showed they could not keep their house clean.

THE KILLING ART
Killer's Paintings, see page 3.

Kate opened the newspaper across the desk.

All of the paintings, even the one that had been cut down by Sarkisian's secretary, were splashed across a double-page spread, more obscene, she thought, than anything in a pornographic magazine—paintings that represented destruction and death displayed for the reader's entertainment.

Kate looked from one image to another. Was there anything new to see, something about them collectively they had failed to notice individually? If so, she wasn't seeing it now.

She glanced up at one of the video monitors—Phillip Zander talking about spontaneity and accidents, then looked again at the images in the newspaper, grainy and stark.

Madonna and Britney, a piece of pop trivia, an image Beatrice Larsen had used in a couple of paintings, the depiction of Sleepy Hollow beside it, Washington Irving's home in Tarrytown. Clues to where the crime—the murder of Beatrice Larsen and destruction of her paintings—would take place. The apple below, with the practically microscopic Gorky symbol embedded in it. That was the next prediction—a Gorky painting, in New York. *Nothing new in here,* thought Kate, turning to the painting beside it, many of the same clues—Sleepy Hollow, the portrait of Washington Irving, Madonna and Britney, and then the Hans Hofmann painting, the state symbol of Connecticut—these predicting the attack on Gabrielle Hofmann. Below that, the painting from the law firm with the Jackson Pollock. Again, nothing new.

The other page was more of the same—the painting that predicted the attack on her de Kooning at the Modernist and on the Starretts' Kline on Long Island. Kate lingered a moment on the depiction of Michael Jackson. *Why him?* They'd never determined that, and the image had no relation to any of the slashed paintings. She thought about the tragic pop star, the little boy with the amazing talent, who had grown up—or had he?—and become a freak. Had Beatrice Larsen ever put Michael Jackson in a painting? Kate could not remember seeing any, if she had.

She turned to the grainy reproduction of the Starretts' clue painting with its portrait of Franz Kline, and the Sarkisian clue painting below it, which had been cut down by his secretary.

There was something else in these paintings. Something she was missing, but she just couldn't see it. Kate rubbed her tired eyes, closed the newspaper, and tucked it under her arm.

The Chelsea loft building did not have a doorman, and there wasn't much of a lobby either, just a small entrance, walls and floor striated pinkish marble, stained and cracked in a few places, but Kate didn't care about the dirty marble or the lack of a doorman—she liked the anonymity of coming and going. She got her mail, unlocked the elevator, and rode up to the fifth floor. The elevator opened directly into her loft. It was unusually quiet tonight, Nola and the baby in Mount Vernon, visiting Nola's favorite aunt.

Kate stripped off her boots, looked up, and saw it immediately: a piece of fabric lying on the floor.

It wasn't like Nola to leave things lying around, but perhaps she had been in a hurry, and the baby had been fussing and she had dropped it without realizing it.

But it wasn't a diaper, or a cloth, or anything of Nola's. It was a blouse. And it was hers. A favorite silk one.

What the—

Kate didn't think, reached for it, and when she did, saw it had been torn, threads of fine silk like wispy hairs sending a charged electric current through her fingertips.

But it had not been torn. It had been slashed—and with a sharp knife—the cuts clean and fine.

Oh my God.

Kate froze.

Her first thought: *Was he here?* Quickly replaced by another: *Is he still here?*

She snatched her bag off the small table beside the elevator, and got her gun.

The heat pipes were clanging, blood pumping in her ears.

She took a few slow steps forward and saw them—bras, panties, skirts, and blouses—all of them carefully laid out and arranged down the length of hallway.

Kate's breath caught in her throat, the shock of seeing her things on the floor terrifying.

She took another step, her socks swishing against the hard wood floors, senses attenuated.

A clicking of heels against wood, slightly echoing.

Footsteps?

Kate aimed her gun, pivoted slowly, and when she heard them

again—*Yes, they were footsteps*—she realized they were from the floor above.

She let out her breath, went for her phone, managed to push the right buttons with trembling fingers, and called the station house.

Now another step, slowly, stopping at each article of clothing, staring at it without disturbing it. One of her lacy bras, neat circles sliced out where her nipples would be, then peach-colored panties sheared in half—split up from the crotch—and put back together, followed by hacked panty hose carefully rearranged into its recognizable shape. And with each step, each piece of ruined clothing observed, the fact that he had been here—*in my house!*—registered more deeply and profoundly on Kate's psyche. Fear set in, her entire body tingling as she followed the trail into her bedroom. She stopped in the doorway, stared into the room, careful not to touch anything, barely breathing as her eyes adjusted, and the dim room came into focus like a photograph in a bath of developer, areas filling in, details sharpening.

A surreal tableau: On her bed, blouse and pants with the under-clothes on top of them, all arranged in perfect order, a flat, empty man-nequin, but when she came closer she saw they'd been slashed and reassembled, like a cadaver stitched back together after an autopsy.

And just above her pillow, where her head would be, was a black-and-white painting, stabbed into the wall.

The lock on your back door has been completely detached," said one of the Crime Scene cops, displaying it to Kate. "He obviously came up the back staircase, took his time, too."

How much time had passed since she had come home and found her clothing slashed and displayed? Kate had no idea. She nodded at the cop, her adrenaline starting to ebb, leaving her drained and exhausted, the only thought in her mind, which would not quit: *My God, he's been here, in my house.*

There were detectives from Robbery, and a dozen crime scene tech-nicians dusting, spraying, and bagging.

Brown was there, Perlmutter, and Murphy, too, and they were all staring at the black-and-white painting above Kate's bed.

"There's nothing new in this painting, is there?" asked Murphy.

Kate took a deep breath and attempted to act cool as she took stock of
the images, identifying each. "That's the Hans Hofmann in the upper

left, the Motherwell beside it. Then the Franz Kline below the Hofmann, and the Britney-and-Madonna image from Beatrice Larsen's painting beside it. Below those two there's the Jackson Pollock on the right, and the de Kooning from the Modernist Museum on the left."

My de Kooning, she thought, *which is what got me involved to begin with, and now this—he's been here, in my goddamn house. Why?*

"You okay?" asked Murphy.

"Of *course* I'm *not* okay," Kate snapped. "The fucking psycho has been in my loft and—" She stopped, took a deep breath. She felt violated and terrified, but she did not want to show it, or take it out on Murphy. "Sorry, I'm just a little—oh, fuck it, I'm not sorry. I'm . . ." A deep breath. A moment to collect herself. She felt as if she were about to jump out of her skin, but knew she had to stop acting it, had to try and stay calm. "Fuck. I *am* sorry." She took another deep breath. "Okay," she said, going back to the painting. "I'd say that's the Jackson Pollock painting replicated in the bottom right. In all, it's just a recap of the paintings from the various crime scenes."

"And no clue to the next one," said Brown.

One of the Crime Scene crew leaned in. "Everything's been wiped down. Can barely find *any* prints at all."

Kate's dresser drawers were open, clothes spilling out onto the floor, most of them slashed or torn, another one of the Crime Scene crew bagging the items.

Kate stared at them, pictured the guy here, in her bedroom, going through her things, touching them, pawing over them, slashing them. She could almost feel him here now, and shivered.

Perlmutter put his hand on her shoulder, but it didn't do much good. She was working overtime to keep up the mask of calm, but her hands were shaking. Her only comfort was that Nola and the baby had not been here. *But what if they had been?* Kate shook her head against the thought.

"If we're lucky he used his teeth," said the crime scene guy, sliding a pair of her panties into a Ziploc bag, "and we'll get some DNA."

Kate doubted it. He was too smart for that. She wanted to grab her underwear out of the cop's hands, tell him, and everyone else, to get the hell out of her home—that she had been violated enough for one night. She thought she finally knew what rape victims went through—first getting attacked and then having to go through it again for the cops. No, she had not been raped, she knew that and tried to feel fortunate, but he had been here, and she could not shake the feeling that the hands that had caressed and mutilated her clothes had somehow been on her.

The crime scene crew was dusting around the black-and-white painting, flakes of powder sprinkling all over her pillows and bedspread like day-old New York snow.

"Gotta take these, too," one of them said, scooping up her bedspread, pillows, and sheets. "Check for any fibers."

Kate nodded dully, watched as they stripped her bed.

Another one of the CS crew dusted the knife, then removed it with a pair of plastic tongs. "Knife's been wiped clean," he said, inspecting it. "Maybe there's something on the blade, but doubtful." He dropped it into a bag, then laid a piece of plastic onto Kate's bed and placed the black-and-white painting on top of it. He was about to wrap it up when Murphy stopped him.

"Give us a few minutes, okay?" He squinted at the painting. "It looks like our guy's work. But now, after the newspaper, it could be anyone, right?"

"If he worked fast," Kate managed to say.

"Paper came out last night," said Perlmutter.

Brown dragged a gloved hand across his forehead. "Your name's been all over the newspapers with this case, McKinnon. Any fool trying to get attention might have done this."

"A fool with a paintbrush and some ability," said Kate. "But to what end?" *And why me?* She was trying to think it through. The artists she was writing about, their paintings attacked, one of them even killed. And now this. He was trying to get her attention—and he'd been successful.

"You know Musanti, in Evidence? We think he's the asshole responsible for leaking the pictures to the press," said Brown. "The only one with real access. He claims they were stolen, but I don't buy it. IA is looking into it."

"So we have him to thank for this," said Murphy.

"And any others that might show up," said Brown.

Kate could see they were trying to make her feel better—maybe themselves as well—trying hard to believe that the painting on her bed was the work of some loony copycat. For a moment she tried to believe it, too, but it didn't work. "This is no copycat," she said. "And you know it." *Why*, she thought, *does it always crawl in through my goddamn door? Do I invite it in?*

Hadn't she worked hard to quit being a cop, to create a quiet, comfortable life? And she'd been successful, too. Until the Death Artist and the Color Blind cases. But with those cases there hadn't been time to stop and question—*Should I do this?* She'd simply reacted. And afterward, she had tried again, and though she carried the scars, she'd managed to get back to some sort of normal life. And now this.

Do I intentionally put myself in these life-and-death situations? Do I have a death wish?

She thought about her mother's suicide, the history of depression and instability. Sure, her mother's suicide had left a mark, but that was history. She had a future now, Nola and the baby, and wanted to live for them, didn't she?

Kate watched the crew finish bagging her bedsheets.

Damn it, she was an intelligent, accomplished woman, an art historian, TV hostess, and a writer. Wasn't that enough to keep her from chasing felons and risking her life?

Perlmutter laid his hand on her arm and she tried to smile, to show him she was okay. But she was still taking stock of her emotions and compulsions. Maybe, she thought, after all these years, I'm just another cop in that long line of McKinnon cops. And maybe, if she was completely honest with herself, she'd have to admit that she liked the work, testing her ability, the sense it gave her of being alive, of living in the moment—no matter how dangerous. But the rational thought did not calm her.

Kate stared at the painting, trying to steady her nerves. "So why is this just a recap—a collection of paintings that have already been destroyed? I just don't get it. There's nothing new here, right?"

"Nothing that I can see," said Murphy, working up a jittery tune on his rubber band.

"Maybe it's a calling card," said Brown.

"Right," said Perlmutter. "His way of saying *hello*."

"Oh, great," said Kate.

"You can't stay here," said Brown. "You'll have to check into a hotel."

Kate had been thinking the same thing. But the idea of a hotel made her feel lonely, deserted. She shook her head.

"Then go to a friend's," said Brown.

She did not want to do that either. There was no one she wanted to bother—or burden. There was just one person she wanted to be with. *Richard*. Her husband. Her companion of ten years. Who was dead, and never coming back. And the thought of it—of Richard never coming back—suddenly made her feel more alone than she had ever felt.

"I'm not going to a hotel," she said. "Or a friend's. I'm staying here." Even to her ears it sounded crazy, to stay in a place that had been invaded, violated, that might never again feel safe. "I'm staying," she said, "because it's my home, and I will not be forced out of it by some goddamn psycho." The statement brought with it a bit of unexpected calm—that she would stand her ground, that she would not be intimidated—and even some clarity. "If he'd wanted to actually do me harm he'd have come when I was home, but he didn't."

"Maybe," said Brown. He wasn't sure. Could be the psycho *had* come to kill her and, when she wasn't there, had settled for scaring her. But he did not want to frighten her any more, and he knew she was acting tough, but she meant it. "Okay," he said. "I'll put uniforms outside the building and in the lobby."

"I'm staying," said Murphy.

"Forget it," said Kate.

Murphy looked her in the eye. "I *said*, I'm staying."

CHAPTER 32

Silky fabric pressed to cheek, the scent of perfume, eyes closed trying to discern all the sensations, to absorb them, to become the part. Now here was a role to play: Elegant, beautiful, smart. Though maybe not so smart.

That remains to be seen.

A glance at Kate's picture—cut from the newspaper—resting on a nearby table. Then a pill for the pain, though really there wasn't much, this pill more for pleasure.

How easy it had been. Waiting outside for them all to leave—the young black woman and her baby; the other woman, the nanny; observing their good-byes in front of the nondescript building, waiting another minute, then presto! the postman, a sad sack of a man, who even held the front door open. A quick mumbled *thank you*, hat pulled down, collar up, straight ahead, as if one belongs. Then up the back staircase, and not a soul on them, not with an elevator right there; New Yorkers so lazy, probably wouldn't use the stairs unless there was a power outage, a blackout.

What a thought—constant darkness and shadows. *If only.*

The silky garment, a pale peach-colored camisole, tugged over the head, a pair of lacy panties pulled on. They stretch to fit the form, feel like a smooth second skin.

Madonna is singing in the background. One of her techno tunes, overlaid with something vaguely Eastern. Kabbalah-influenced? *What the hell was she calling herself these days? Esther? Well, you had to give it to her, such a gift for reinvention. Something we share.*

A glance in the mirror, a shiver of excitement.

But a second glance brings reality and a different kind of shudder.

Lights out! Darkness. Better this way, the silk and perfume able to sustain the illusion—the fantasy always so much better than reality.

The scene replays . . .

The back staircase, old steel door, slowly working on the lock, finally standing in the loft—patience paying off in the end.

The biggest temptation had been all those paintings—to slash or not to slash?

Of course there were none of the official offenders, no reason to commit the act, nor reason to hang around.

The message had been made loud and clear: *I know you. Pay attention! You're a part of this now.*

Beneath the stretchy silk and lace, the skin takes on a new life, while the mind commits to the next step with renewed purpose.

Murphy sat at the kitchen table trying to act relaxed. When Kate wasn't looking he slipped the two rubber bands off his wrist so he wouldn't play with them; he knew it annoyed her. He thought Kate was doing a good job of acting cool, but he knew she'd been rattled. Who wouldn't be? He watched her make a show of straightening up, wiping off the kitchen counter for the third or fourth time.

"So," he said, "you like living down here, in Chelsea?"

"I *did*," said Kate. "Until tonight."

"Right," said Murphy.

"Sorry," she said. "That was a totally legit question." She gave it some thought. "Yes, I like it. It's totally different than living uptown. It makes me feel—now don't laugh, Murphy—young."

"What? You think I'd go near that line?" He smiled.

Kate smiled, too, maybe for the first time since she'd stepped into the loft and found her underwear on the floor, cut up.

"So . . ." Murphy had never been good at small talk, particularly with women. Something his wife had complained about. You want small talk, he'd always said, call someone small.

Kate wiped the table again. She didn't really want to talk, though she was glad Murphy had stayed, however awkward it might be to have the detective here, in her home. "Listen," she said. "I'm exhausted. I'm going to lie down, try to sleep. You okay out here?"

"Fine," he said, his fingers going for the missing rubber bands. "If I get tired I'll sack out on the couch."

Kate put new sheets on the bed, tossed around on them for a couple of hours, but it was no use. Every time she shut her eyes she pictured her slashed clothes laid out like a body. Finally, she gave up.

Murphy, stretched out on her couch, shoes kicked off, reading one of her art magazines, looked up as she came into the room. "Couldn't sleep?"

She shook her head and headed for the kitchen, Murphy following. "I'm going to make some coffee," she said, setting about the task as if it were crucial, carefully tucking the filter into the coffeemaker, measuring the grinds and water precisely. She didn't really want to talk, was afraid that once she did she would make a fool of herself, start telling Murphy how frightened she was, how she had been trying to get past Richard's murder for a year, but couldn't, and how lonely she felt, an emotion that embarrassed her, and the fact that right now she wanted nothing more than to be held.

But when Murphy smiled up at her, she cut out of the kitchen fast.

"You okay?" he called after her.

"Fine," she called back, letting her body sag onto the living room couch, feeling as if she was going to scream or cry, the tragedies in her life washing over: her mother's suicide and her father's battle with cancer, her surrogate daughter's death, and then Richard's. She felt alone, confused, and scared.

Why has he come after me?

That damn question would not quit—why had the psycho targeted her?

Kate listened to the garbage trucks outside her loft and stared at the dark windows without seeing them. What she saw was the rest of her life stretched out in front of her. She had never imagined herself like this, a single woman, alone.

Yes, there was Nola, and the baby, both of whom she adored. But eventually Nola would leave and take her son with her, and the thought of it tore at her heart as if someone had actually reached into her chest.

Murphy came in and said, "How's it going?" and his words—innocuous but kind—were enough to shatter her.

"Fine," said Kate. She stood quickly and headed for her bedroom because she did not want him to see her like this, and somewhere, deep inside, refused, absolutely rejected the idea that she was scared and vulnerable, and managed to get to her room in one piece, at least physically, telling herself: *You can do this; you're okay, you're strong,* but felt it coming and knew there was no way she could stop it. She slammed the door behind her so that Murphy could not hear, and there, with her mind alternating images of her slashed clothes with crime scene pictures of her husband's brutalized body, she fell back onto her bed and let go, sobbing for Richard, and the other loved ones she had lost, and yes, for herself, alone now, and scared.

A magnifying glass slides into the frame and captures it, a fragment of . . . something—but only for a second. Like an insect, it skitters away and creeps across her brain.

Kate jerked awake.

Had she actually been asleep?

The clock beside the bed confirmed it was 6 A.M.

Kate rubbed her eyes and it all came back—the slashed clothes on the floor and arranged on her bed, the fact that the psycho had been in her home. She pulled herself out of bed and heard Murphy, in the other room, and called out and he asked how she was, and she said okay.

She stood under the shower, hot water loosening her shoulder muscles, then found one of her few pairs of underwear left intact, slipped into her jeans and was pulling an old sweatshirt over her head when the nightmare replayed—that flickering, skittering image crawling across her brain.

What is it?

She tried to see it again. Was it the Gorky symbol, the one buried on that apple? She wasn't sure, but didn't think so.

Back in the kitchen, she finished making the coffee she'd started hours ago. "You look awful," she said, taking in the dark pouches under Murphy's eyes.

"Thanks a lot."

"All I meant was you look tired, and that I'm sorry I kept you up."

"Forget it." Murphy waved a hand.

Kate smiled. She had to admit she was glad he was still here.

Sunlight was streaking into the loft and she realized she felt a bit better; stronger, too, strong enough to tell Murphy to finish his coffee and get going—to call a replacement to babysit her so he could get some rest.

Murphy protested, but Kate made the call. When the other cop arrived, she patted Murphy on the top of his disheveled hair and told him to go home.

Kate offered the uniform who'd taken Murphy's place—a kid who looked fresh out of the Academy—a cup of coffee, then poured herself another, carried it into the living room, took a sip, and closed her eyes.

There it was again. But just for a second. No, it wasn't that symbol from the Gorky painting. It was something even less specific, just a piece of something, a fragment of an image. But what? Something she had once seen—or had she?

But she must have seen it—or why would she be seeing it now?

Eyes closed again. *Relax. Let it come.*

But it was no good. She couldn't force it.

Still, something had happened after she'd cried, something had broken and now seemed repaired, though she suspected it was Scotch-taped and could fall apart.

But she felt determined. Determined and committed to find out what was going on, and who was doing it.

She was heading down the hall to her office when she saw it, the *Trib*, exactly where she'd left it, opened to the pictures of the killer's artwork splashed across its pages.

It was in here, somewhere, what it was she was trying to remember.

Kate found her magnifying glass and drew it across the pictures, but the grainy newsprint revealed nothing.

Copies of the originals were in an envelope on her desk, and she took them out, laid each one on the floor, stood back, and took it all in.

Together they were *what?*—a collection of black-and-white paintings made by a lunatic who enjoyed leading the cops around by their collective noses.

But was there something else about them as a group?

Yes. They were all paintings by the New York School, America's foremost group of abstract expressionists—the group she was writing about. Kate glanced back at the newspaper. Once again she considered that it was more than a coincidence—the fact that she was writing about the group whose paintings were being attacked. But now the coincidence could not be denied.

He was here. In my home.

It had to have something to do with her.

She gazed at one newspaper image after another, reviewing the same paintings and same clues they had gone over, broken down, and analyzed dozens of times, then crouched down and slowly moved her magnifying glass over one of the pictures. There was the Gorky *bug,* too tiny to see with the naked eye, but now she was certain that wasn't what she was looking for.

She moved to another picture—the very first painting she and Murphy had seen, the one from the Modernist Museum with her de Kooning painting in it, and Michael Jackson's face. Slowly she covered every inch. There it was—the image from her dream.

But this was no dream. It was here, in black and white. And she remembered now the first time she had seen it, in Mert Sharfstein's gallery, under the magnifying glass he had drawn across the painting, this tiny little doodad, just a fragment at the edge of the painting that they had dismissed as something left over or unfinished—a scribble the painter had neglected to fix.

But did it mean anything?

Looking at it now, Kate wasn't sure.

She moved to another painting, examining every inch, and there it was again, the same little fragment, though no, when she compared it with the first, she realized they were not the same—though they seemed connected.

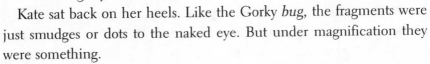

Now Kate's magnifying glass was moving quickly from one picture to another, sliding over the familiar images in search of these odd fragments at the outer edges.

And she found them. In every painting. Each one slightly different.

Kate sat back on her heels. Like the Gorky *bug*, the fragments were just smudges or dots to the naked eye. But under magnification they were something.

But what?

One by one, Kate laid the pictures on her desktop scanner, isolated the fragment, increased the magnification by three hundred percent, and printed them out. When she was finished she pushed the papers around, trying to make sense of them, but the pages were too clunky.

Scissors, that's what she needed. Seconds later, she'd cut them out and laid them on her desk.

Kate's hands were shaking as she moved the pieces around like a jigsaw puzzle. There were two pieces of the puzzle missing, but the image, to Kate, was unmistakable.

CHAPTER 33

I t's a Phillip Zander," said Kate. "I'm certain of it." She looked from Floyd Brown to Murphy, whose eyes were still ringed, hair a mess, then Nicky Perlmutter and Mitch Freeman, finally Agent Moroni. She was trying to act calm, but she was anything but. Still, she'd had the sense to call the Suffolk PD the moment she'd figured it out, and they had promised to get over to Zander's place. Her first thought: *If it's about the New York School and the fact that I'm writing about them,*

Zander is next! She'd called Zander, too, told him a cop would be knocking on his door any moment.

Now Kate focused on the fragmented picture and explained how she had arrived at it. There were two gaps in the image. She guessed that one could be found in the recent painting left on her pillow—and indeed, they had found it, a tiny fragment at the outer edge, scanned and enlarged it, then cut it out and added the piece to the puzzle.

"So now we know it wasn't *just* a recap of the images," said Kate. "He wanted me to have this, to find it—all the little fragments that would add up to his next victim. This proves it's our guy. Someone else might have been able to copy the paintings, but no one would have known about this."

Brown nodded.

Agent Moroni went back to the picture puzzle Kate had put together. "What about the missing corner?"

"My guess," said Kate, "it's in the painting we never turned up—the second one from the Modernist Museum, the one that should have been at the Dressler scene." She had another thought, this one, chilling. "In the past, the people who received these became the next victim."

"But there was always a clue to that," said Murphy. "And there's nothing in this that indicates you."

"There's the de Kooning that once belonged to me."

"Old news," said Perlmutter. "It's already been hit."

"So then . . . why?"

"Maybe he didn't want to send it to the NYPD and you were the next best thing," said Brown.

"The way I see it," said Mitch Freeman, "he's sending a message: Hello, there, I'm still here—and you can't catch me. He's toyed with us before, why not again?"

"That, plus he figured you'd be the one who would have the art knowledge to put this thing together," said Murphy.

Everyone agreed, and Kate thought it made sense, though it did not make her feel better. *He's chosen me for some reason*, she thought.

"So what does this say about Leader?" asked Perlmutter, switching gears. "Did we peg it wrong?"

"Leader was involved, no matter what," said Kate. "We know that he was stealing paintings."

"We never really liked him for the murder, though," said Brown.

"Could have been a partnership," said Perlmutter. "And now that Leader is out of the way, our boy is going solo."

Kate looked at the image again. "But the fact that there was one of these fragments in each one of the previous clue paintings would seem to indicate that Zander has always been a target—maybe the ultimate target."

"Why?" asked Brown.

A good question, thought Kate—and one she wanted answered.

Brown got a call from Suffolk PD saying everything was quiet at Zander's place, that they had a car at the entrance to his property, and a man inside.

"That's not enough protection," said Kate.

"East Hampton PD is a small operation," said Brown. "The other towns are cooperating, but they're only on standby."

"What about some field officers from the Bureau?" she said to Moroni, who nodded.

"And I want to go out there," she said. "Now."

The memorial service had gone smoothly, the speech a success—he'd even managed a few tears—though he had carefully avoided eye contact with Gaby's longtime lawyer, Lapinsky. Clearly, the man hated him.

And now that damn Greenwich cop, Kominsky—who had stood at the back of the chapel throughout the service—was blocking his exit.

"Just paying my respects," said Kominsky.

Respects, my ass, thought Lifschultz. He'd been right to think they were watching him. *The fucking balls of this guy to show up at his wife's memorial service.* He didn't say anything to the cop, just pushed past him.

Kominsky followed Lifschultz with his eyes.

Greenwich PD had gotten orders from the G to keep a close watch on the man, and though he was exhausted and could have asked for a replacement, Kominsky wanted this guy so bad his teeth hurt. He just hoped Lifschultz would make his move soon. He was leaving for Florida in two days—his first vacation in over four years—had been practicing his golf swing for months, and did not want this bastard Lifschultz to ruin it.

Kominsky rubbed a hand over his two-day growth of beard and watched as Lifschultz crossed the parking lot.

The man was as smooth as his slicked-back hair, thought Kominsky— at least *he* thought so.

Kominsky slid back into his unmarked Chevrolet Caprice and waited for Lifschultz to get into his Jag. When Lifschultz pulled out, he followed.

"**All of the paintings** have been by New York School artists, and now it appears that you've been a target all along." Kate tried to catch Zander's eye, but he'd turned away. "If you know of a reason—you have to tell me."

There were two Suffolk police cars at the end of the dirt road that led directly to Zander's home, a uniform and two field agents from the Bureau posted by the front door, more at back. Brown had lobbied Chief Tapell successfully for an NYPD helicopter to take Kate out to Long Island, Nicky Perlmutter along with her.

Zander stared past Kate, avoiding her questions.

Henry Lifschultz peered through a slit in his living room curtains. It was just getting dark, the winter sun preparing to slide behind the soft hills of his property. No doubt he would miss his Greenwich home, but there were sacrifices to be made, and he had prepared to make them.

He had already shifted funds from the Swiss account he'd set up without his wife's knowledge—the one he had been transferring money into since a month after their marriage—to a small family-owned bank near the Texas-Mexico border; the owner, with whom he had done business before, thrilled to earn the interest on several million dollars even for a couple of days. The money would be waiting for him, in cash and coupons.

He had packed nothing. He would leave the house without suitcase or briefcase. His flight was later that evening, but he had a stop to make before he took off—loose ends to tie up, nothing incriminating left behind.

Lifschultz let the curtains fall back into place, stepped away from the window, and considered his plan . . .

The necessary trip to the city, the rather circuitous route out to East Hampton, the twelve-seat prop plane—a puddle jumper back to JFK—then a plane for Texas. In Texas, he would pick up his cash and his rental car, cross the Mexican border, and head for San Miguel de Allende.

Lifschultz enjoyed this baroque plan, though there was nothing illegal about his trip—he hadn't been told not to leave the country. Still, he had more than a strong feeling the authorities would not be pleased.

Well, fuck that! He wasn't going to wait until they decided to charge him with . . . *something*. It was time for a new life. The San Miguel house was nearly ready, and if not, he could easily check into a hotel and wait it out.

He figured Kominsky would be following, though it did not worry him. He had no doubt that his Jaguar XK could easily give a two-year-old Chevy Caprice the slip.

Detective Kominsky was dreaming about his vacation, sunny skies and sinking a hole in one, when he heard gravel sputtering and the engine of Henry Lifschultz's Jaguar coming down the drive. He rubbed his eyes, turned the ignition key, and edged his car out of the neighbor's driveway, then called the station to report that Lifschultz was on the move—something he had done at least a dozen times over the past two days.

The desk cop called the NYPD and the FBI.

Zander's hands were shaking, and Kate could not blame him for being nervous, cops and FBI agents surrounding his house, and a psychopath looking to kill him, but she wanted answers and would not coddle him. She had explained about the paintings with their predictions, and the fragments she had put together, all of which had added up to his painting. Then she asked if there was anyone he knew who wanted him dead—simple as that.

"Me? Of course not! It's ridiculous." Zander shook his head.

"What about back then, in the early days? Is there something you're not telling me?"

"There's nothing to tell," said Zander. "We were friends, we were enemies. We laughed and got drunk and yelled at each other. It was such a long time ago and . . . they're all dead."

"All of them, but not *you*. And I'd like it to stay that way—wouldn't you?"

Zander sighed. "You said this person—this psychopath—has been targeting New York School artists. Maybe he's after me because I'm the only one left?"

"Maybe," said Kate, but it did not strike her as a strong enough argument. "Tell me about Sandy Resnikoff; why he left the group."

"Who knows? He left. Maybe it was because we all liked to dress like businessmen and Sandy didn't. We didn't want to be seen as *bohemians*." Zander forced a grin.

Kate did not return it. "So you've told me. Why is it that every time I ask you about Sandy Resnikoff you change the subject?"

"Who cares about Resnikoff?!" He brought his fist down onto his paint table, rattling tins of oil and cans of turp.

Kate waited until Zander had collected himself. When he continued, his voice was quieter. "Maybe Resnikoff couldn't take the pressure of all the attention that was coming to the group. Maybe he just wanted a quiet life."

"There's got to be more to it than that."

"Do you think we tied him up and put him on a plane to Rome?"

Kate did not know what she thought. "I was hoping you would supply some answers—and I think you'd better because your life is at stake."

Zander looked up, something flickered in his eyes, and Kate waited.

"There was a meeting," he said. "A group of us, in Robert Motherwell's studio . . . and an argument . . ." He looked down at his hands, the swollen knuckles, nails chipped, years of paint embedded in the toughened flesh. "But it was so long ago I can't tell you what it was about."

"Then why tell me about it at all?"

"Because it was after that meeting that Resnikoff took off." Zander rubbed at his eyes as if trying to smudge away a memory.

"So Resnikoff was angry?"

"I suppose."

"You *suppose*, or you *know*?"

"I can't remember what was said. It was over fifty years ago. But . . . yes, Resnikoff was angry, something had upset him."

"Like what?"

"It's all jumbling in my mind—all the fights and disagreements. I just know this one was the end for Resnikoff. After that meeting he left the country, and I never saw him again. I can't tell you what happened . . . I don't remember."

Kate did not believe him. The man had demonstrated the sharpness of his memory too many times.

But Zander closed his eyes and Kate could see he had shut down.

Now, more than ever, she needed to know why Resnikoff had left the group. She was thinking it was time she went to Rome to find out, when Perlmutter's police phone crackled to life.

CHAPTER 34

Clare Tapell's office resembled a beehive, detectives and agents crowding the room, all of them on cell phones, pacing, buzzing.

Floyd Brown had received the call that Henry Lifschultz was on the move and had passed on that information.

Now Tapell was coordinating with Suffolk PD, who were standing by with troops, and the FBI was talking to field agents ready to jump in.

No one was sure where Lifschultz was heading or what part he played in this drama, but they intended to find out. His wife had been murdered; Leader, his probable business partner, and Miranda Wilcox, possibly his lover, also both dead. He was the sole surviving suspect, and they were not going to lose him.

Kate had been rephrasing her questions to Zander for a half hour and her frustration was turning to anger.

"Why," she asked for what seemed like the hundredth time, "would *your* painting be indicated in all of the previous clue paintings?"

"Who knows? Some lunatic who hates my artwork? Like those crazies who stalk movie stars and politicians." Zander was changing his tactic, anger exchanged for incredulity.

Kate wasn't buying it. It was possible but unlikely. As a cop, she had seen plenty of crimes that made no sense, but they were the anomalies. Usually it was the husband who killed the wife, the wife who'd poisoned her philandering husband, the ex-boyfriend who shot his girlfriend and her new fiancé. Revenge, thought Kate, was a powerful motivator—and her gut was telling her that someone had targeted Phillip Zander for a reason.

"You know," she said, "without more information, the cops will eventually give up trying to protect you, which means . . . a week from now, say, you just might have to face this psycho alone."

"I'm an old man," said Zander.

"Meaning what? That you're ready to die?" Kate did not like saying it, but she wanted him to know there were consequences to hiding the truth. "Because that's what will happen. He's already struck several times, each one of them predicted—and now he's targeted you. And I don't think he's simply going to go away."

"Do you think you're scaring me? I've told you all I know. I have no enemies. I don't even have any friends." He shook his head. "They're all dead. There's no one, I tell you."

"Maybe no one that you know of." Kate looked into his eyes. Perhaps he was telling the truth. She couldn't tell. "But what about in the past?"

Zander let out a long sigh. "There was a time we were all friends, all comrades working together to change an idea about art, and then . . . it ended. That's all." Zander glanced up at Kate and she thought she saw something in his eyes—not fear or anger, but shame.

"But you must know why it ended—you were there."

"All things end. Good things. Bad things. They have their moment, and then they end. Ours was a wonderful, beautiful moment, but it ended. We split apart as so many things do. Friendships ended, and some people were hurt." He swiped a hand across his eyes. "Resnikoff was not the only one to be abandoned by the group. There were others."

"What do you mean—abandoned by the group?"

"Oh, did I say that? I meant he, Resnikoff, abandoned the group. He left."

"But that's not what you said."

Zander took a deep breath. "Is this an interview or an interrogation?"

Kate answered with a question. "What about these others you mentioned—who were abandoned by the group, like you said?"

"That's not what I meant. I already told you. They *left*. And that's that. There is nothing more to say. I'm finished." He planted his hands firmly on the arms on his chair and began to push himself up. Kate offered a hand to assist him, but he ignored her. She watched him move slowly across the studio, and realized it was true. He was—at least for now—finished talking.

Lifschultz kept his speed to a law-abiding thirty miles per hour along the Greenwich country roads, and Kominsky had no trouble staying with him, hanging back just enough to remain somewhat less than obvious, though he was certain Lifschultz knew he was on his tail. When Lifschultz turned onto the Hutchinson Parkway, Kominsky followed. Traffic was moderate and he allowed two cars between them. The Jaguar picked up speed, switched lanes, and Kominsky did the same. They drove like this, on and off, the Jaguar looping back and forth across lanes, for ten minutes.

A mile ahead, two highways converged with options for the Whitestone Bridge or George Washington Bridge, and it was then Henry Lifschultz cranked the Jag up to seventy, still weaving in and out of lanes, but Kominsky managed to stay with him, able to play the game.

The Jaguar slowed and headed toward the George Washington Bridge, and Kominsky decided it was a good time to call in with his location and Lifschultz's obvious destination.

Kominsky was just reaching for his phone when Lifschultz cut across all six lanes of traffic—horns blaring, tires screeching as cars hit their brakes—and when he looked up he had approximately three seconds to stop short and be rear-ended by a Jeep Cherokee he saw barreling toward him in his rearview mirror, or crash into the car in front of him. He opted for the Jeep, hoping it had good brakes and the driver decent reflexes.

But at that precise moment, the woman driving the Cherokee was studying her nails and complaining into her cell phone about the terrible manicure the Korean girl had given her, and the last thing Kominsky saw was the Jeep's headlights, followed by the sickening sound of collapsing metal.

Seconds later he was propelled through his windshield.

Henry Lifschultz heard the crash and caught a glimpse of it in his side-view mirror as he once again switched lanes and headed toward the George Washington Bridge. He tried not to smile, but could not help himself. He figured that Kominsky had called in earlier to report that he had left his home, and assumed there was another car waiting up ahead. At the next exit he cut off the highway, drove a few blocks until he found the gas station and garage, pulled in, and parked. There was an old MG up on a lift, two mechanics beneath it.

"Boss around?" he asked.

One of the mechanics tilted his head toward a door in the back of the garage and Lifschultz pushed it open.

The boss, a fat man staring at an eight-inch TV propped on his desk, did not look up when he entered.

Lifschultz explained that his car—the practically brand-new XK Jag out front—was giving him trouble, had stalled on the highway, and he couldn't chance driving it into the city. He then opened his wallet, laid three hundred-dollar bills in front of the man, said he was in no hurry to have the car fixed, but needed to get into Manhattan for an important meeting, and there was another hundred in it if one of the mechanics could give him a lift. He did not give his name or address, and though the car could easily be traced back to him, he had a feeling the fat man wouldn't try very hard to return it if he never showed up.

True, he would miss his beautiful car, but a motorcycle would be better on the dusty cobblestone streets of San Miguel, and the Jag wasn't even an option, as he was flying, not driving, to Texas.

The mechanic, Hector, knew all the back roads and shortcuts to avoid the highway traffic. He also had a stash of marijuana, and by the time he dropped Henry Lifschultz in Manhattan—in just under thirty minutes—they were both stoned. Lifschultz gave him another fifty for a couple of joints. He was feeling mellow, magnanimous, and lucky. As he got out of the car he checked his watch. He had plenty of time to do what he needed to do.

Cecile Edelman reached for her phone, then replaced it. She could not decide whether to call Henry Lifschultz again. She was certainly not going to beg for his support. Still, Morton would have wanted her to try. If she did not hear from Lifschultz in a day or so, she would try again.

She crossed the room, plucked a Sotheby's catalog off an antique table, and flipped pages until she found what she was looking for, a de Kooning painting—one of the artist's *Women* series, this one on paper mounted on board, not quite the quality of the one the museum had lost, but the reserve price was good. She thought she might bid for it and, if she won, donate it to the Modernist Museum as a way to deflect attention from all their bad publicity—plus it would take care of her taxes for the year.

She was thinking this when she heard the light tapping noise coming from the direction of her kitchen—someone at the service entrance. The maid, no doubt, who was forever losing her keys.

She walked across the kitchen, turned the dead bolt, and opened the door.

CHAPTER 35

By the time the ambulance reached the scene, Detective Kominsky was dead.

The news was delivered to Floyd Brown, who was still at One Police Plaza. The FBI was now going through everything they had collected on Lifschultz: tax returns, driving history, even his high school and college transcripts. Plus the recent wireless telephone bill that confirmed not only outgoing calls to Colin Leader, but an incoming call the day after Lifschultz's wife's murder, which had been traced to Miranda Wilcox's cell phone.

They were fairly certain Lifschultz had been stealing his wife's artwork and fencing it through Wilcox, though they had no way to know whether or not Gaby Hofmann had found out. Though Lifschultz had an alibi for the night of his wife's murder, he could easily have had Leader or Wilcox do the job, or have farmed it out—and they were looking for something to prove that.

The NYPD issued an APB. The FBI called their Critical Response team. Cops and agents were getting ready to move. Helicopters were idling.

But at that moment, Henry Lifschultz had managed to slip under the radar.

Kate had been calling the station house every half hour from Zander's studio. When she finally reached Floyd Brown, he brought her up to speed on Henry Lifschultz, and told her to sit tight.

Sit tight? How, thought Kate, with the killer out there, somewhere, and now the NYPD and the FBI tracking Henry Lifschultz?

She stared at one of Zander's paintings, one of the artist's typically distorted figures, and thought it pretty much summed up the way she was feeling—lacking any sort of emotional coherence, and certainly the way she had felt since she had stumbled into this case—confused and disjointed. She hoped they would arrest Lifschultz soon and get some answers.

It had been easier than he'd imagined, slipping in and out of the city, doing what he needed to do—all of it according to plan. He had cleaned up any evidence that would link him to the paintings he'd sold from his wife's collection. Whatever else they might find—phone calls at best— wouldn't prove anything. And by the time these were discovered he'd be in Mexico.

Henry Lifschultz dragged on the joint and stared at the taxi's glass divider trying to decide whether or not to ask the driver to take him all the way out to Long Island. He just wasn't sure. Would the cabbie remember him later? He closed his eyes, imagined himself as the Polish film director Roman Polanski, who'd fled the States to avoid a statutory rape charge. He was thinking about whether or not he'd exchange his slicked-back look for a more casual hairstyle, and how, when he got to Mexico, he was going to find a couple of unfortunate, and very young, Mexican girls and pay their families a little something to have them come live with him.

He had a sudden wave of paranoia (possibly brought on by that third or fourth joint), just as he spotted the sign for West Side Budget Car Rental, asked the driver to stop, and went in.

He presented two pieces of ID in the name of Adam Weinstein, his part-time business associate, a credit card and driver's license, both of which he had, less than an hour ago, slipped out of the man's wallet. He held his breath while the girl ran the card through the machine, and released it when it went through. He declined the insurance, thinking, *Live dangerously*, and almost laughed out loud.

Minutes later, he pulled on his black racing gloves—absurd, he realized, in this Tinkertoy of a car, a beige Ford Taurus, of all things—then headed east toward the Midtown Tunnel feeling free, happy, and clever as hell.

Agent Moroni thanked Sharnise Vine—Employee of the Month at the West Side Budget Rental Car Company—and hung up. He turned to the group still buzzing around Tapell's office and quieted them down.

"I think we've found him," he said. "A car's just been rented in the name of Lifschultz's business partner, Adam Weinstein. A beige Ford Taurus. License plate number X67901." Moroni's associates back at FBI Manhattan had been running Lifschultz's name, along with the names of every relative, friend, and associate of the man that they could dig up through every available credit card system, and it had paid off. "Woman at Budget Rental describes the guy as fortyish, good-looking, slicked-back hair."

"Sounds like a match for Lifschultz," said Brown.

A call to Weinstein confirmed that he had not rented a car, and, in fact, was just about to call his credit card companies to report his loss.

Within seconds, the Bureau alerted the bridge and tunnel authorities, and unmarked cars were dispatched. The word went out not to stop him—they wanted to see where he was going.

Tapell and Brown added a couple of NYPD unmarked vehicles to the pursuit, then Brown checked in with Kate and Perlmutter.

All remained quiet at Zander's. He told them to stay where they were until further notice. He had planned to join them on Long Island, but right now he needed to see what developed with Lifschultz.

Henry Lifschultz was still feeling good as he followed the stream of cars into the Midtown Tunnel, his mind replaying the events of the past few hours—the crash that had taken care of that Greenwich cop, dumping his car, taking care of all those loose ends in Manhattan. Just a bit more to do and he'd be free to start his new life.

He had no idea that a convoy of unmarked cars was behind him.

"Where do you think he's heading?" Moroni asked Brown.

Everyone's guess: the airport.

But that hypothesis did not pan out.

When Lifschultz passed the exits for LaGuardia, then JFK, there was more debate about arresting him, but both the NYPD and the FBI were curious: Were there more snakes to be unearthed? A stash of artwork hidden in some out-of-the-way storage bin? Was Lifschultz the brains behind the entire operation? All questions they needed answered.

The helicopter pilot was sitting on Zander's front porch with a couple of Suffolk uniforms, the tips of their cigarettes glowing on and off like fireflies in the dark night.

Zander was napping on his studio couch—or pretending to, thought Kate. Anything to avoid her questions.

Nothing had happened for hours, and it was too damn quiet. She and Perlmutter had been drinking coffee for too long, taking turns hitting the bathroom, both of them on edge.

Kate had spoken to Brown every fifteen minutes, and he'd said they would be arresting Lifschultz soon—though not soon enough for Kate, who was hoping the man would supply answers to this tangled case of who-was-stealing-from-and-selling-art-to-whom—and why.

Nicky Perlmutter came out of the bathroom and took a turn calling

Brown. "Not much more info," he said, shutting his cell. "They're still tailing the guy."

"Why the fuck don't they just arrest him?" Kate took a deep breath but could not calm down.

"They want to see where Lifschultz goes," said Perlmutter. "Make sure they don't miss anything."

It made sense, but it did not soothe her. She was thinking it through again—Lifschultz selling his wife's artwork by way of Wilcox; Leader and Lifschultz being friends. Yes, there were connections between all of them, which should not be difficult to prove. But who was the pivotal player, and who was the murderer?

She glanced over at Zander, thought again about the puzzle she had put together of his painting, and could not stop asking herself the same question: *Why Phillip Zander?*

Lifschultz's Taurus passed over the Suffolk County line, and when he cut off the Long Island Expressway at Manorville, it was clear he was headed for the island's east end.

"Does Lifschultz have a summer house in the Hamptons?" asked Tapell.

The answer: No.

The question of the moment: Then where was he going?

Was he heading toward Phillip Zander's studio?

No one had yet to say it, but they were all thinking it: *This could be the guy. The Slasher.* Could it be that he planned to make Zander—the last living legend of the New York School—his final victim?

Appearances of cooperation notwithstanding, both the FBI and the NYPD wanted the collar: The Bureau, trying to recoup from the back-firing and embarrassment of Agent Bobbitt's plan, needed the arrest badly; Tapell, with the mayor breathing down her neck, needed it, too. All of the cars following Lifschultz had him clearly within their sight and could arrest him at any time, but neither agency was going to make a move until they thought it would be their men or women who would be putting the cuffs on Lifschultz.

The air in Tapell's office had gone dry and electric.

The two teams had split apart, the G on one side, the NYPD on the other. Everyone waiting.

When Lifschultz's car approached the two-lane road that would take him through the various Hampton towns, Tapell notified each of the local police departments, and one by one, cars joined the caravan.

Not to be outdone, Agent Moroni gave the word for the helicopter to start its engine—but Floyd Brown demanded he go along for the ride.

Henry Lifschultz, listening to an oldies station and singing along to the hits of his youth, was stoned out of his mind. He was doing a pretty good imitation of Abba's "Dancing Queen," smoking the very last reefer he'd bought from Hector, and was perfectly on schedule for the East Hampton plane ride reserved in the name of Adam Weinstein that would take him to JFK. Had he not been stoned, he might have noticed the long line of cars that had been following him since he'd left the Long Island Expressway.

He had, twice during the ride, considered cutting off the L.I.E. and heading directly to the airport, but since he had plenty of time, and wanted his disappearance to be as confusing as possible, he had decided against it. If you're going to disappear, he thought, *disappear.*

He squashed the tiny roach out in the rental car's ashtray. The marijuana had made him hungry. He could practically taste the burritos and margaritas.

"Henry Lifschultz? The Slasher?" Kate stared at Perlmutter and shook her head.

Zander stirred and opened his eyes. "What's going on?"

Kate dragged a chair up beside him. "Do you know a man named Henry Lifschultz?"

Zander shook his head.

"What about his wife, Gabrielle? She was Hans Hofmann's granddaughter."

"I knew Hans, of course, but no, I have no idea who his granddaughter is, or this man—what was his name?"

"Lifschultz. Henry Lifschultz." She looked into Zander's eyes. *Was he lying?* "Why would a man you don't know come after you?"

"I have no idea."

Perlmutter's cell phone rang and when he got off he looked from Zander to Kate. "Lifschultz is only minutes away," he said.

Lifschultz had switched to one of those mellow rock stations and was singing along with Rod Stewart, who was warbling a sandpaper-voiced rendition of the old standard "You Go to My Head." He was singing loudly about bubbles in a glass of champagne as the helicopter carrying Agent Moroni and Floyd Brown caught up to him, now hovering in the sky above his head. He did not bother to put on his turn signal when he took the abrupt turn toward the airport, also a well-known back route to East Hampton and Springs.

The cop behind him—a nervous rookie who had joined the Westhampton PD only weeks before—hit the breaks hard to avoid slamming into the Taurus, his brakes screeching loud enough to cut through Rod Stewart's singing, and Lifschultz glanced in his rearview mirror and noticed, for the first time, something like twelve Crown Victorias making the same identical turn. This, he realized, could not be a coincidence.

For a moment, forgetting that this was not his Jag, Lifschultz laid into the accelerator, gripped the steering wheel with his racing-gloved hands, and the Taurus lurched forward, kicking up rocks and clouds of dirt.

Seeing this, the Suffolk cops—no one later knew who it was who did it first or gave the order—started flipping on sirens and bubble lights.

From above, Brown and Moroni watched, helpless, as the lights popped on.

Now, with the sirens in his ears and lights flashing in his mirrors, an irrational voice fueled by Valium and marijuana urged Henry Lifschultz on. He pressed the accelerator to the floor and swerved the car onto a rutted dirt road that brought him into the woods.

He had gained perhaps a quarter-mile lead when he heard the pop and felt the tire deflating, and while the car was still in motion, flung his door open and pitched himself out, tucking his body into a ball and rolling. For a moment he lay there stunned; then, amazed to find himself in one piece, he pulled himself up and ran.

The sirens were somewhere behind him, blips of red light casting about in the trees. Was he losing them? He did not consciously think where he would go or what he would do, though his drugged mind was playing absurd scenes of hiding out in abandoned cabins and living off wildlife he would kill with his bare hands.

Above him, the helicopter's blades were whipping up the winter trees, and from somewhere behind there were bullhorns blaring warnings, though he could not make out the words between the noise of the chopper and the blood pounding in his ears.

The trees opened into a barren field and Lifschultz tore across it like a deer pursued by hunters.

The cops had abandoned their cars and were on foot now, adrenaline pumping through their veins, weapons drawn.

Lifschultz dared a look over his shoulder and saw them coming across the field, his mind—too stoned and too scared to think clearly—trying to process it, though with the helicopter's spotlight suddenly on him, he realized it was over, stopped, turned toward them, and raised his gloved hands. But to at least one of those uniforms, his black-gloved fists looked like guns.

The cop raised his rifle and fired. Instantly, two dozen Long Island cops—who rarely, if ever, had used a weapon on anything other than a garden rabbit—followed suit.

From above, Brown shouted "No!" But it was hopeless. He and Moroni were merely witnesses to the scene—Henry Lifschultz's body jitterbugging in the staccato helicopter light as bullets riddled his body.

When the firing stopped, there was smoke in the air and the odor of burned matches. Later, when the coroner was attempting to count the number of gunshot wounds Lifschultz had sustained, he gave up at eighty.

"It's over," said Perlmutter, once he'd gotten the news. "Lifschultz tried to run and they killed him."

"Damn it," said Kate. "Now we'll never know." She glanced away from Perlmutter to Zander, who looked tired and very, very old. She took a deep breath. "Do you think the Suffolk PD can stay the night?"

"Why?" asked Perlmutter.

"Because . . ." Kate could not come up with an answer and could not explain it. "I just want them to stay, that's all."

Zander protested, but Perlmutter had already gone outside and was arranging it with the cops.

As Kate said good night to the old man, an unexpected, almost overwhelming flood of emotion overcame her. She patted his hand and hurried out of the house toward the waiting helicopter.

CHAPTER 36

Everyone was exhausted from the night before. Kate and Perlmutter from their vigil at Zander's; the rest of the team from the chase.

But it had not ended last night.

They were back at the station house and dealing with the latest development: Cecile Edelman, dead, her artwork slashed—Motherwell, Rothko, Zander—all the paintings replicated in the gray-and-white acrylic found beside her body.

That canvas, bagged and numbered, was now pinned to the corkboard wall in the conference room. The squad, along with Agent Moroni and Bureau psychologist Mitch Freeman, was back around the table.

"It's all the major paintings in her collection." Kate stood and came in for a closer look. "Including the Phillip Zander painting."

"Just like the one you put together from the fragments," said Brown.

"Yes." Kate reached for her magnifying glass. "Look at this. It's a street sign," she said. "Park. Like Park Avenue. But it says, *Park Z.*" Kate

thought for only a second. "Park Z. P. Z. Phillip Zander. The next victim."

"Right," said Moroni. "Obviously, Zander was the intended next victim." He drummed his nails on the conference table. "But where was the painting indicating that Edelman was the next in line? I mean, the one *before* Zander?"

"Our missing painting," said Kate. "The one that should have been at the curator's, Dressler's, scene—the one we never found."

Moroni nodded. "It looks as if one of Edelman's last telephone calls was to Lifschultz. CID's provided both of their phone records, and this . . ." He passed out a transcript of the message Cecile Edelman had left on Lifschultz's phone machine. "It's hard to know exactly what she meant—wanting to be back on the museum board, sending him her sympathy about his *friend*, Leader—but it sounds as if she knew about Leader and the art-theft ring, and suspected Lifschultz was in on it. Sounds like she was leaning on him."

"How would she know that?" asked Perlmutter.

"Edelman's been involved with the Modernist Museum from the beginning," said Murphy. "She could have found out."

"Maybe that was the real reason she quit the board," said Kate. "But she didn't want to tell us when we talked to her because she didn't want to hurt the museum's reputation. I know the museum meant a lot to her, and to her late husband."

"So she figured she'd handle it by herself," said Brown. "Obviously a mistake."

"So this is how we're seeing it." Moroni folded his hands onto the table. "Lifschultz kills Edelman, then drives out to Long Island to take care of Zander. Two for one—Edelman, then Zander." He scanned a page of notes. "There are close to three hours not accounted for after the crash on the Hutchinson Parkway that killed Detective Kominsky. Enough time for Lifschultz to do everything—dump his car, cab into Manhattan, kill Edelman, rent the car, and head out to Long Island. We know from his partner that he went to his office and shredded papers and erased e-mails—which LEO retrieved."

"LEO?" asked Kate, trying not to sigh from exasperation.

"Law Enforcement Online," said Moroni. "The e-mails absolutely link him to Wilcox, without question. From the tone of them it's clear that Lifschultz and Wilcox were more than *professionally* involved. You've got the transcripts in your folder. Makes for nice bedtime reading." Moroni grinned, but it quickly morphed into a frown. "The partner, Weinstein, puts Lifschultz at the office for about an hour. Says Lifschultz came into his office for a chat, nothing important, which is when he must have lifted the credit card and license. Weinstein is stunned by the whole thing, says Lifschultz was a real charming guy, a regular Cary Grant."

"Last time I heard that comparison," said Mitch Freeman, "it was someone talking about Ted Bundy."

"But Lifschultz led a normal life," said Perlmutter. "Had a wife, a job."

"Hey, Bundy was working in Washington," said Freeman. "Co-workers loved him. He was handsome, charming, and had a girlfriend he was living with who had no idea he was raping and murdering girls, sometimes several a day. You only see the monster through the violent acts. Otherwise, he can be that super-charming guy Lifschultz's associate saw. These guys have a tremendous ability to compartmentalize. A psychopath can wear a mask of perfect sanity—almost too perfect, because it's been worked on and studied. Someone said about Bundy: 'he was always so *sincere*.'"

"The part that bothers me," said Kate, "is why go after Zander? If Cecile Edelman had something on Lifschultz, okay, I can see why he might need to eliminate her. But after he killed her wouldn't he just want to get away? And Zander didn't have anything on him."

"I think that's where the psychopath theory kicks in." Brown glanced over at Freeman. "Question: Did Lifschultz want to get caught?"

"From all the elaborate plans he'd made, I'd have to say no. I think it was more of a game to him, and one he thought he could get away with. *Grandiose narcissism*—a trait shared by many sociopaths. They think they're smarter than everyone else, above the law. My guess would be that Lifschultz did not start out as a killer. But something happens, he's interrupted, kills, and that's it—"

"He develops a taste for it," said Brown. "I've seen that before."

"Right," said Freeman. "A serial killer is someone who becomes addicted to killing. Not everyone who kills becomes addicted, of course. There are crimes of passion and convenience. But a serial killer is an *addict*—someone who becomes obsessed with killing. The more they kill, the more they want to kill. It's a compulsion, a need. Once they've tasted murder it's all they can think about. To quote Bundy again, he said he thought about killing twenty-four hours a day."

"Jesus," said Kate.

"Of course there has to be some predisposition for this. A shattered, violent childhood. Tremendous loss. Sexual abuse. Something. The creating of alternate personae begins early—a way to escape an unbearable situation." Freeman plucked his reading glasses off and sighed. "One day they'll isolate the brain chemistry that makes for a serial killer. They've already got pictures of criminal brains versus normal ones."

"Paging Dr. Frankenstein," said Kate.

"So Lifschultz is at his office getting rid of evidence," said Brown. "Then he goes to Edelman's and takes care of her because she was onto him, or he thought so."

"Her apartment is only a few blocks from his office," said Murphy.

"Anyone recognize him there?" asked Moroni.

"Nada," said Perlmutter. "Detectives have been showing his photo around the building. Doorman says he must have followed someone in through the service entrance. And he came in through the back entrance of Edelman's apartment, so that's a good guess." He glanced at Kate. "Same as he did at your place."

"I'm not quite seeing it," said Kate. "What about the clue paintings? Do we have any proof Lifschultz was making them?"

"The guy was an architect," said Murphy. "He had the art school training. He was capable of making them."

"Capable of making them is different from *actually* making them," said Kate.

"Maybe not," said Moroni. "It's true nothing like them has turned up at his home or office, but he did have acrylic paint and brushes in both places."

"Question," said Perlmutter. "According to the report, Lifschultz had a seat reserved in the partner's name on a plane at the East Hampton airport. So he could have been heading toward the airport."

"Right," said Moroni. "He was going to finish up his plan to kill Zander—then get on a plane. Otherwise it doesn't make sense."

Brown rubbed a hand across his forehead. "Nothing that guy did makes sense."

"Okay," said Kate. "But why take a plane from East Hampton *back* to JFK when he could have turned off the L.I.E. and gone directly to JFK?"

"That's what leads us to believe he was going to take care of Zander first," said Moroni.

"Is that rational?" asked Kate.

"Only a rational person would ask that," said Freeman. "But these guys aren't rational. No matter how much we learn about them, they're always changing the rules on us, reinventing the genre. Sometimes their motivation isn't clear. It's what makes this job so damn frustrating."

"And interesting?" Kate managed a smile.

"You could say that." Freeman returned her smile.

"Check out Toxicology," said Brown, directing the group back to Lifschultz's case report. "Guy was stoned on tranquilizers and weed."

"But cogent enough to take care of everything," said Moroni. "Cleaning up his office e-mails and killing Edelman—before making his getaway to Mexico by way of Texas." He switched to the Bureau's

CID report. "You can see he'd already transferred a shitload of money into the First National Bank of Texas. Believe it, that guy was never coming back."

Kate sat forward. "So either the guy was stoned and not making sense, or he was a premeditated killer who had all his ducks in a row. Which is it?"

"Sorry," said Freeman. "But they're not mutually exclusive. Plenty of psychopaths kill while they're on drugs. In fact, it can act as a stimulant—a way to facilitate murder. Would the Manson family members have been so willing to stab a pregnant starlet if they hadn't been drugged? Would those kids have beaten Matthew Shepard to death if they hadn't been strung out on crystal meth?"

Kate saw his point. Henry Lifschultz had struck her as more of an arrogant playboy than a psychopath, but everything did point to the guy having killed Edelman, and that he was heading toward Zander's. If only they had taken him alive.

She took another look at the Edelman clue painting—she wanted to be sure she was not missing anything. She recognized again each of the various paintings depicted: Motherwell, Rothko, Warhol, Zander, and Resnikoff. She had seen them all in the Edelman apartment. She dragged her magnifying glass over the surface. There were no little fragments that might add up to another painting, but something else stopped her.

"What's this?"

"Shouldn't the initials be PZ on a reproduction of a Phillip Zander painting?" she asked. "And not . . . DH."

"Maybe he was playing with us," said Perlmutter. "Trying to throw us offtrack."

"But offtrack for a reason, right?" Kate tapped her lip. "DH. I can't, off the top of my head, think of an artist with those initials."

"We can try an Internet search," said Murphy. "See if we come up with anything."

"And if we come up with an artist who matches?" asked Moroni. "Then what?"

"I don't know," said Kate. "But maybe it's another prediction—an artist who is on the hit list."

"*Was* on the hit list, you mean," said Moroni. "Lifschultz is dead, remember? They're all dead." Moroni came in for a closer look. "Just looks like part of the design to me. It doesn't have to be initials, does it? He's already made the PZ initials clear with the PZ in the Park Avenue sign, right?"

True enough, thought Kate. She glanced back at the overall painting, her eyes settling on another image, the painting by Sandy Resnikoff. The artist who had fled the New York School. *Why?* She still wanted to know.

Resnikoff was not the only one to be abandoned by the group. There were others. The statement Zander had made, then tried to retract.

What others? And why had they been abandoned? And how was she going to find out? It no longer appeared to matter to the case, but it still mattered to her, and to her book. She looked around at the men. They were probably right. But she still needed some answers—and perhaps Resnikoff's daughter could provide them.

"That's it for now," said Moroni, pushing away from the table. "Let's all go home."

You go home, thought Kate. *I'm going to Rome.*

CHAPTER 37

The hotel was nowhere near the four-star affairs Kate was used to staying in with Richard, but those days were over. For the moment she was happy to be out of New York, though the case kept resurfacing at the back of her mind like acid reflux. *Let it go,* she told herself. *You've been working too hard.*

Still, it continued to plague her while she took a shower, and would not quit as she put on makeup and pulled on a turtleneck and jeans, and was still there as she stepped into her boots and threw on a black leather jacket and headed out into the gorgeous Roman light with weather more like September than December. And it clung to her like a bad odor as she crossed the street and headed into the beautiful Piazza Navona, crowded with closed-up stalls that would be selling toys and miniatures for the Christmas holiday later in the day.

She tried hard not to think about the case, filling her mind with details from her undergrad Roman Art and Architecture—that the plaza had originally been the site of the enormous Domitian Stadium used for festivals, jousts, and open-air sports, then a marketplace in the fifteenth century, and later, from the seventeenth until the nineteenth century, flooded every August weekend to become an artificial lake—a sight she would have liked to see.

Kate could hardly wait to speak with Daniella Resnikoff, but the meeting was set for the afternoon. She needed distraction, and found it, in the church of San Luigi dei Francesi, which housed one of her all-time favorite paintings, Caravaggio's *The Calling of St. Matthew.*

Inside, it was cool and dark as Kate dropped a few coins into a slot and the painting was illuminated—a Roman tavern scene, men huddled at a table in the dress of their day, one of them Matthew, the tax gatherer, with a look of *Who, me?* as Christ aims a languid, but clearly beckoning arm in his direction, all of it brought to life by a dazzling shaft of painted light that transformed the banal scene into something truly spiritual.

Caravaggio: an artist with an amazing gift, and . . . a murderer.

Kate recalled his brief life.

The artist, she knew, had been in and out of prison for brawls and assault, then killed a man over a disputed score in a game of court tennis. After that, he'd fled, hiding in one city after another, landing in Naples for a while, where he made some of his most dramatic paintings. But with the authorities on his trail, he'd taken off again, this time to Malta, where he painted in exile until he was finally captured. Imprisoned for only a few days, the now infamous artist received a pardon from the pope. But the years of running and hiding had taken their toll. When the boat that was to take him back to Rome left without him, he collapsed on the beach and died. He was thirty-nine.

The lights flicked off, the painting slid back into the shadows, and Kate suddenly craved the sun, and a hit of caffeine, and found them both at a small café where she stood in the sunlight and drank an espresso. Afterward, she forced herself to stroll, to let the beauty of Rome distract her eyes, if not her mind, and when jet lag finally hit, she retraced her steps back to the hotel and slept fitfully until the alarm startled her awake.

Daniella Resnikoff was a mix of her New York Jewish father and Neapolitan mother, dark-eyed and olive-skinned with a hook nose that added striking glamour to what would have been just another pretty face. About the same age, she and Kate had hit it off immediately when they'd first met a year ago, and when Daniella heard about Richard's death, she'd written, and now they talked of it a bit more until Kate switched the topic to Daniella's father. They made their way to his former studio, crossing the Tiber River to Trastevere, the old section of Rome, a neighborhood favored by artists and artisans since the Middle Ages, Kate taking in the sights. But when they passed the church of Santa Cecilia, her Catholic school education kicked in and she remembered the saint's story—the patrician lady shut into her bath to be scalded to death, emerging days later unscathed, to be incompetently beheaded. Kate tried to dislodge the images, forced herself to take in the cobblestones and soft light suffusing the buildings.

Daniella bought panini and a bottle of Chianti and they headed up to the top floor of the old four-story building which housed her father's studio.

Inside, the late afternoon sun was spilling through windows and skylights, gilding the floors and Resnikoff's paintings that leaned against the stained plaster walls, and Kate took them in. The hand of the artist and his style were still there, but the figure had disappeared in favor of landscape. Kate pictured the 1950s painting that Cecile Edelman had owned, and a few others from that period which she remembered from art school—all of them wild figure paintings akin to de Kooning and Zander.

"When did your father abandon the figure?" she asked.

"From the time I was old enough to be aware of his paintings—and I was very young—I do not remember there being any figures in his work."

"Did he ever say why he gave it up?"

"There was one time, when I saw pictures of his early paintings. He said he'd given up the figure because . . . there had not been room."

Not been room. Kate considered the remark. "Had he meant there were already too many artists working with the figure?"

"Perhaps." Daniella shrugged. "I am not certain."

"Well, there was de Kooning and Zander. And your father would have made three."

"Ah, but . . . there was another . . . a friend of my father's." Daniella glanced up at the skylight and made one of those Italian gestures, hands waving in disgust. "But I cannot remember his name."

Kate was curious. She couldn't recall a fourth figure painter among the New York School painters, certainly not a major player.

"I have been meaning to clear out his space since he died, but have not been able to." Daniella regarded the paintings. "Do you think there might be a market for them in the States?"

"Absolutely," said Kate. "The art world is always looking for someone to rediscover, and your father has a history that any savvy art dealer could exploit." She smiled. "I didn't mean to sound so crass. I'd be happy to speak to some people for you." Sandy Resnikoff was still a name among those who knew, and after Kate's book and television show appeared, it might be even bigger.

"A gift I could give to my father," said Daniella. "That would be nice. He never had much success."

"He did at the beginning."

"Yes, but that was a long time ago."

Kate perused the walls and noticed that, like most artists, Resnikoff had, for inspiration, pinned images of other art in between his own—Tintoretto, Raphael, a faded reproduction of Leonardo's *Last Supper*.

Daniella followed Kate's eyes. "That was always one of my father's favorite paintings."

"I hope they can save it," said Kate. She knew that Leonardo's masterpiece had been in trouble almost since the moment the High Renaissance artist had finished it. Many blamed the wall, but art historians and restorers knew that Leonardo had painted it alfresco, directly on the wall, not in the standard fresco manner of working pigment into small areas of wet plaster.

Impatient man, thought Kate.

"Did your father ever say why he left New York?"

"He spoke of fighting among the artists, that he could not tolerate it. He was a gentle man. An artist."

"But *all* artists aren't necessarily gentle." Kate flashed again on Caravaggio.

"True," said Daniella. "He once described Jackson Pollock as a brute, and that it proved to him how unfair the gods were that such a man would be the one to become the most famous of them all." Daniella lit a cigarette and blew gray clouds toward the fading sun of the skylight. "My father was never interested in fame."

"And yet it came to him. You must have seen some of the early pieces written on him, the one in *ArtNews*: 'Sandy Resnikoff Paints a Picture.'"

"Of course. I have read it a hundred times."

"It was a rare honor, bestowed on only the best painters of that period—and he was one of them—though he left it all behind."

"He once told me that he could not tolerate the scene, all the jealousy and competition."

A common enough theme in the art world, thought Kate.

"He spoke once about a meeting—and an argument. I believe it was the last meeting he ever attended with the other artists in New York."

"Did he say what they fought about?"

"No, but . . . I think it may have had something to do with a picture, one in *Life* magazine."

"The famous one, *The Irascibles*, you mean?"

"Yes, the picture of all the artists together."

"Why wasn't your father included? He was as famous as any of them at the time."

"I have no idea. I did not see the picture until much later. I found it in an art history book, and asked him about it. He became furious, said it was a foolish picture. A bunch of peacocks, he called them, pretending to be what they were not."

Kate pictured the famous photo, then looked up and saw the faded Leonardo reproduction tacked to the wall, and remembered when Zander had been supplying her with the various nicknames for the artists—*Rothko the Rabbi, Reinhardt the Monk*—he had referred to himself as *Judas*. Had he betrayed Resnikoff in some way?

"Did your father ever speak of Phillip Zander?"

"One time . . . it was after I had returned from my first semester of school in the States . . . I was telling my father about a wonderful painting I had seen in a museum, and it was a Phillip Zander. I had never heard the name mentioned by my father. Ever. But then he told me they had shared a studio together, somewhere in Greenwich Village, as young men, and how they would pool their money to buy a pack of cigarettes, and the parties they would have with other painters. It sounded like a wonderful time. When I asked him why he had not stayed in touch with this Phillip Zander, he told me the man was dead. And later, when I learned that this was not true, I asked my father why he had said such a thing and he said, 'Because he is dead to me.'"

Kate wondered if she could dare to bring this up to Zander when she got home. Of course the artists were always fighting in those days, and she imagined Zander would give her some story, another anecdote that told her nothing. But clearly, this fight had been major—*Because he is dead to me*—something that would not easily be forgotten.

The sun had quit, and a soft rain was playing a tune on the skylight. Daniella related a few more stories about her father's life, things he had passed on about the early days, and Kate took notes. She asked that Daniella repeat certain of them for the camera tomorrow, explained about her crew and when they would arrive to film the studio and paintings. They finished the panini and drank the bottle of wine, and it was past midnight when Kate was ready to leave.

Daniella offered to walk her back to her hotel, but Kate protested.

Outside, the rain had stopped, leaving a light mist behind, turning street lamps into shimmering candles, and Trastevere into an impressionist painting. It was still unusually warm, and Kate thought the walk might sober her up.

She passed a church she did not recognize with an odd facade—a tiara of obelisks disappearing into the mist like a crown of thorns, and she pictured Jesus on the cross, then the *Last Supper* on Resnikoff's wall, and again thought of Phillip Zander. *Judas.* Why had he called himself that? And what had they fought about? *He is dead to me.* Strong, bitter words.

Kate was lost in thought when a shadow fell across her path. She caught her breath as a monk in a long dark smock, the street lamp highlighting his hawkish profile, turned and offered a smile.

She quickened her step past the church of Santa Cecilia, felt like that foolish young girl in a Catholic school uniform as an image of the saint, alive, head practically severed, crawled into her psyche. She turned into a small piazza; old houses and restaurants closed up for the night.

It brought her back to another time not so long ago, in Venice, a night not unlike this one, when she had pursued the Death Artist—or he had pursued her. She hugged her leather jacket to her body, and shivered. She was feeling light-headed and tired. Time for a cab, she thought. But the streets were nearly deserted.

She cut out of the piazza, found herself on a dark street—and the feeling she was not alone. She stopped and listened. Somewhere, not far away, was the soft purr of traffic, but that wasn't what she'd heard. She peered down the street. Had she imagined it? Either way, her nerves were starting to fray. She started up again, her boot heels echoing— *Maybe that's what I heard?*—passed under a small arch, and into another square.

That's when she saw them, two silhouettes, coming from opposite ends of the piazza, approaching fast.

Kate lurched one way, then the other, reached for the gun she did not have, while images of Colin Leader and Henry Lifschultz and a dozen other crime scene pictures flashed across her brain as the two figures came toward her. For a moment, her eyes and the mist played a trick on her and she thought it *was* them—Leader and Lifschultz—and then they snapped into focus: two young men, black leather jackets, caps pulled down to just above their eyes. The one on the right lunged and Kate spun toward him as the other slipped behind. A shove and she was falling. She reached out, but too late. As she hit the ground, a young couple turned into the piazza, and the two men raced out of the square, dissolving into shadows.

"Fuck!"

The young couple helped her up, asking in Italian if she was okay, and Kate patted various parts of her body to make sure she was, and it was then she realized they had stolen her bag.

Fucking purse snatchers!

She puffed out a breath, stood and slapped dirt and dust from her pants, feeling sober now, thanking the couple for scaring off her attackers.

She took the next few blocks quickly, found the river and then the bridge, eventually her hotel.

Locked in her small room, her identity stolen, Kate could not stop shivering.

Was it just a weird coincidence, those two guys attacking me?

Two teens had stolen her purse. That was all. But even here, across the ocean, her paranoia would not let go. Had someone sent them to scare her? If so, they'd done a good job.

Kate checked the time. She wanted to call the station, talk to Brown, make sure everything was still quiet and Zander was okay. She did the calculation and realized it was 8 P.M. in New York, but called anyway, got a desk cop who sounded grumpy and couldn't tell her anything.

She hung up, adding frustration to her paranoia and fear, and when she got into bed she could not stop replaying the image of the two men coming out of the mist, and the identities she had attached to them—Leader and Lifschultz—and when she finally managed to exhaust that, she replayed the things Daniella Resnikoff had said about her father leaving the New York art scene because he could not take the jealousy and competition, that there wasn't room for another figure painter, and his comment about Zander: *He is dead to me.*

Just before sleep arrived, she wondered again what had happened between the two men to create such enmity.

In the morning, Kate felt hungover and exhausted, and three hours at the American consulate to get a temporary passport and a separate photo ID did not help.

She had finally made contact with Floyd Brown, who told her that nothing had changed, Zander was safe, and they were still awaiting lab results from various crime scenes, and there was no reason to hurry home.

Oh, sure, she thought, trying to make light of her innate paranoia, *they would rather have me out of the country where I can't annoy them and tell them they might be wrong.*

By the time she got to Resnikoff's studio, her crew had filmed the interior and the paintings.

Kate clipped a mike on Daniella, who reminisced about her father, then began the interview asking questions about the man's artwork, and though she thought she would have an interesting segment for her series, when she was finished she still felt frustrated.

She was about to leave when Daniella suddenly said, "Hopson. That is the name. The fourth figure painter. I remember my father speaking of him and his work, and the fact that they had both painted the figure."

The name sounded vaguely familiar to Kate, and she made a note of it, but she could not place the man, or his work. Another forgotten artist, she thought.

"I know that at some point my father tried to convince him to come to Rome."

"When was that?" asked Kate.

"A long time ago. I was a young girl at the time. I recall my parents discussing whether or not they could afford to send him a ticket. Perhaps he was very poor. But it did not happen. At least I do not remember ever meeting him."

CHAPTER 38

Only one day back in New York and already Kate felt as if she had dreamed the three-day excursion to Rome. There were tourists crowding Manhattan monuments, bottleneck traffic in the streets, stores filled to capacity.

Christmas shopping. And Kate attempting to do it all in one morning. Infuriating, but distracting—a way to avoid thinking about the case.

There had been a very recent development, but according to Brown, nothing that would change anything. Still, Kate wanted to hear it. She craved the details, and called the station house every half hour, a lesson in futility: Brown in a meeting with Chief Tapell; Murphy investigating an art gallery robbery; Perlmutter simply missing in action. More time to kill, more shopping: the Strand Bookstore, Virgin Megastore, Macy's, Bloomingdale's, Baby Gap.

A lightweight sweater for Richard's mother—why she needed a sweater in Florida was a mystery, but Edie kept saying she needed a new one; two blouses and jewelry for Nola; clothes and toys for the baby, books, too; a couple of sing-a-long DVDs; an iPod for José, and a pair of earrings Kate thought would look good on his mother.

Still standing, and with an hour and a half to go before her meeting with the squad, she ran over to Black Orchid books, chatted with the owners Joe and Bonnie, took their recommendations for a half dozen books, then raced around Barneys men's department, choosing things for each of the squad—leather gloves for Brown, a cashmere scarf for Perlmutter, a pair of socks and a plain brushed-silver wristlet for Murphy, though she wasn't sure he'd wear it.

On Madison Avenue there were twinkling lights and store windows done up for the season, and Kate juggled packages the stores would not send, while trying to hail a cab. After twenty minutes, she gave up and hauled her packages down the street to the subway.

A quick pit stop at home, a call to Phillip Zander to see if he was okay and confirm their date for the following day, then to José, to make sure he was still on board for the trip. She had told him about Zander, the famous artist, and his musical assistant Jules, but it was more the idea of a ride out to this place called Long Island that seemed to entice José. "Can we see the water all around it?" he asked, and Kate had to explain it was a bit larger than that, but they could stop at the beach, if he liked, and if it wasn't too cold, take a walk, and that seemed to do it.

Someone at the Sixth Precinct had made an effort, albeit a pathetic one, to enliven the place for the season: a string of blue Christmas lights suspended above the central booking desk (several bulbs burned out), and a fold-out cardboard HAPPY HOLIDAYS pinned to the wall.

Perlmutter met her in the hall, greeted her with a kiss, and together they went into Brown's office.

Murphy was there, chair tilted back, front legs off the floor, head leaning back against the wall.

"Didn't your mother ever tell you that was a good way to break your neck?" said Kate, taking a seat beside him, forcing herself to make small talk when all she wanted was facts and details: *So what is this "new development"?*

"What my mother told me was 'Don't be a cop like your father.' And I didn't listen to that either." He plucked the rubber band at his wrist a couple of times. "So how was Rome?"

"Fine. Where's Brown?"

"Getting coffee," said Perlmutter, just as Brown came in balancing a tray of Starbucks.

"Wow," said Kate. "Who won the lottery?"

"I couldn't take another cup of the house sludge," said Brown, handing out the cups.

"This my decaffeinated double espresso grande soy mocha frappuccino?" asked Perlmutter.

"Aka coffee, black," said Brown.

Kate spent a minute handing out the gifts in their sleek black Barneys boxes, enjoying the surprised looks on the guys' faces as they opened them. "To replace those goddamn rubber bands," she said to Murphy. He was studying the bracelet as if he couldn't figure out its purpose.

Mitch Freeman cut into the office. "Am I breaking up a party?" He smiled at Kate, and she felt embarrassed that she had not gotten him a gift. There had been a moment, at Barneys, when she'd seen a pair of gold cuff links and thought of him, but had immediately decided against it; a bit too intimate, and the kind of gift she might have bought for her husband on their anniversary, and that was it, she just couldn't buy them after that.

The guys were acting a bit goofy, making awkward jokes . . . "Those socks are too good for your flat feet, Murphy . . ." "Yeah, like that scarf's not too good for your fat neck, Perlmutter . . ."

Little boys, thought Kate. She should have gotten them G.I. Joes and Erector sets.

Brown rewrapped his soft leather gloves as if they were made of glass, then reached behind him, plucked a folder off his desk, and handed it to Kate. "Guess this is what you want to see. The latest wrinkle."

Kate tried to make sense of a long column of lab test statistics, but couldn't. "What is it?"

"DNA results," said Brown. "On the curator, Dressler, over at the museum. He had a little something under his nails."

Kate sat forward. "And—"

"It was a woman."

"Who was a woman?"

"The DNA from under Dressler's nails—it belonged to a woman."

"Does that mean Miranda Wilcox?"

"That's what we're figuring," said Brown. "Coroner has plenty of samples from Wilcox's autopsy that can be tested, but it will take a while. This only came in yesterday. Quantico lab is duplicating the tests. The G never trusts us."

"Dressler must have found out something he wasn't supposed to, and Leader and Wilcox took care of him," said Perlmutter. "Or . . . Leader didn't have the stomach for it and Wilcox did the whole job. Maybe she took care of the others, too. Could have been her who did Beatrice Larsen. She was anxious to get her hands on the old lady's art, right?"

"Did anyone at the museum ever see Wilcox there?" asked Kate.

"Sent a couple of detectives over there with her picture," said Brown. "Nothing yet."

"I don't know." Kate was trying to picture it—Miranda Wilcox stabbing Dressler to death. "I never pegged her for more than a shady businesswoman."

"Is it that you can't picture her doing it because she was a businesswoman, or because she was a woman?" said Murphy. "You thinking, women—they're the gentler sex, right?"

Kate threw him a look. A naive part of her wanted to believe that women were, indeed, gentler. "Women don't start wars," she said, for lack of anything better to say.

"Really?" said Murphy. "You must have missed those pictures from the Abu Ghraib prison. Looked to me like that young G.I. Jane was having herself a hell of a time."

Perlmutter was about to say something—a discourse on gender politics, perhaps—but Freeman stepped in. "It's not about gender, or nature. It's about *nurture*. Read about the early life of Aileen Wuornos, and you'll see how a woman can come to kill as well as any man—and without feeling."

"Saw the movie," said Perlmutter. "*Monster*. Beautiful actress plays ugly. Guaranteed her the Academy Award."

Freeman didn't let Perlmutter's digression stop him. "As an infant,

Wuornos was abandoned by her mother, father committed suicide, and she was molested. Pregnant at thirteen. Lived in the woods like a wild animal. Traded sex for money."

"So what do we know about Miranda Wilcox's history?" asked Kate.

"Not anything more than the Bureau's CID trace that we already have."

"Can we place her at any of the other scenes?"

"Crime Scene never turned up any DNA at the other scenes," said Brown.

They went on like that for a while, hashing over the details of the case, whether the killings were a joint effort—Leader, Wilcox, and Lifschultz—and if they'd turned on one another, like rats in a cage, but there were no conclusions.

"Maybe we'll figure it out one day," said Brown. He tossed the lab report onto his desk.

"So that's it?" Kate's frustration felt like something that could burst right out of her, like one of those movie monster aliens.

"What do you want me to do, McKinnon?" Brown eyed her with his own mix of frustration and annoyance. "Make up a couple of false leads, tie a ribbon around the case so you can feel better?"

"No. I just want to feel like this isn't being tossed into a cold-case file before its time."

"It's not *cold*," said Brown. It's *over*. Official version: Lifschultz was our man. And if it turns out Wilcox aided and abetted . . ." He shrugged. "It won't matter. Right now, I've got a couple of very live cases." He laid his hand down onto a set of files on his desk. "These came in while you were pitching pennies into the Trevi Fountain. A Swedish couple attacked in Union Square—never good for tourism, especially at Christmastime. And a rape down by Chelsea Piers—which Tapell, and the mayor, are making priority. So I'm sorry if the Slasher isn't delivering for you—which, since he's dead—would be hard."

Kate didn't bother to tell him about her interview with Resnikoff's daughter. What was the point? "Forget it." She couldn't think of anything else to say, though the words felt inadequate, and sounded, even to her ears, petulant. She turned out of Brown's office feeling disappointed she had come.

Murphy followed her into the hall. "Sorry about that."

"Nothing to feel sorry about," said Kate. "Brown's right. You can't follow a lead when there's no lead."

Murphy nodded. "Thanks for this." He displayed the bracelet.

"You ever going to wear it?"

"Sure." He slipped it on beside his rubber band.

"It's supposed to replace those, not be part of a set."

"I still need something to play with."

Kate raised an eyebrow. "I think I'll let that one go."

Murphy shifted his weight from one foot to the other. He wasn't sure what it was he wanted to say. The case, working with Kate, hadn't exactly made him the hero he'd hoped to be, but he had enjoyed being back in the action. He tapped the silver bracelet. "Not only will I be wearing this out to Southampton tomorrow, but I'll carry the Barneys box. Might help me fit in with that crowd."

"Going to see your daughter?"

Murphy nodded, thought about Carol, who looked more and more like him all the time—dark hair, light eyes, becoming a young woman while he became the man who saw her every other weekend.

"I hate going out there. Always makes me feel so poor."

Kate pictured the East Hampton house she and Richard had owned, and their life together, already starting to feel unreal, more like a dream than something actually experienced. "I'll be out there, too, in Springs, but just for the day. Hey, you want to drive out with me?"

"I would, but only if you give me your Mercedes for keeps. I'm going to spend a couple of days, and I'll need a car, so . . . You visiting Zander?"

"My last interview, I think."

"How's he doing?"

"He sounds okay." Kate recalled Daniella Resnikoff repeating her father's words about Zander: *He's dead to me.*

Murphy extended his hand and Kate took it in hers and they stood there a moment and then he said he had to go.

Mitch Freeman was waiting at the entrance to the station house.

"Walking home?"

"Thought I might."

"Mind if I tag along?"

Kate nodded, though she wasn't sure she wanted company. They walked to Eighth Avenue and headed north, the blue sky streaked with gray, the air chilly.

"Do you really think Lifschultz was the Slasher?" she asked.

"You're asking because you don't?"

"I'm just trying to understand why he would go after Zander when he could simply have escaped?"

"Compulsion, for one. But sometimes it's impossible to explain. Psychopathic personalities are the most complex and difficult to know. The best way I can explain it is that the psychopath is . . ." He glanced up at the sky. " . . . an impostor. It's not just that he or she will mimic normal behavior, they actually *live* the part—or parts. Some of them are so adept at acting it's impossible to detect the charade until they crack— especially if they're intelligent."

"Lifschultz didn't strike me as all that smart. Smooth, for sure, but intelligent . . . I don't know."

"Well, maybe that's the good news. The smart ones often elude detection. Could be that Lifschultz suffered some remorse after his wife's death and that led him to take more risks."

"Could be," said Kate, though she was still thinking Zander had been targeted as the ultimate victim, and had trouble connecting that to Lifschultz. "I just keep waiting for the other shoe to drop. Lately, I seem to always imagine the worst possible scenario."

"A cop's psychology. It's natural, and protective."

Kate thought about that. Was she still a cop? It seemed so. *Once a cop, always a cop.* How many times had she heard that?

"And you've had more than your share of bad news," said Freeman.

"And one comes to expect it, right?"

Freeman nodded, then offered up a small square box. "Maybe this is the wrong moment, but . . . Merry Christmas."

"Oh, shit."

"Is that what people are saying instead of thank you these days?"

"Sorry." Kate laughed. "Thank you. Really. It's just that I didn't get you anything. I was going to, but—"

"I didn't expect you to." He smiled, and Kate took in the appealing crows' feet at the corners of his eyes. "Go on, open it. It's nothing big."

An antique Christmas ornament, frosted glass, and filigreed.

"Oh, it's beautiful. Now I'll have to get a tree—which I was going to, for the baby."

"How is he?"

"Wonderful. Nola took him up to her aunt's place in Mount Vernon again. The loft feels really quiet, a little lonely." She hadn't meant to say that out loud, even admit it to herself.

"Christmas always makes me feel lonely," said Freeman. "Maybe because I'm Jewish, and all my Christian friends go to their families and I imagine they're just having the best time."

"Christmas fun? Are you kidding?" Kate laughed. "It's a nightmare. Well, maybe not for Episcopalians, but I wouldn't know about that. But for Catholics?" She stopped a moment. "It's funny, Richard always loved doing the Christmas thing with my aunts and uncles." The thought of all those Christmases past, she and Richard, sobered her, and Freeman saw it and for lack of a better subject he went back to the DNA sampling, and the fact that the killer—at least Dressler's killer—was a woman, probably Miranda Wilcox. They kicked that back and forth for a while, and when they were only a few blocks from her loft Kate felt anxious and lonely, and asked Freeman if he'd like to come up to see her new place and have a drink. The way his face lit up gave her a moment's hesitation, but it was too late to take back the invitation.

Kate opened a bottle of Pinot Noir, and after a glass she relaxed and then realized an hour had passed and they had been chatting comfortably. She was happy she'd asked him in, and offered to whip up some pasta and tomato sauce. The dinner went well, and later, when they had finished, the conversation ebbed and there was that uncomfortable moment when Kate thought it might be best if Freeman just left, though she wasn't sure she wanted him to.

Freeman broke the ice. "Guess I should be going."

Kate nodded and led him down the hallway as images of her clothes, slashed and arranged along the floor, winked in her mind.

"What is it?" Freeman asked.

"Nothing. Just that, well, I'm still a little jumpy—since the break-in, I mean. It's silly, I know, but—"

"It's not one bit silly, Kate. Your space, your home, your safe zone was invaded. If you didn't feel uncomfortable with that you'd be an android."

"Thanks for saying that."

"It's the truth, that's all." He smiled again. "And I have a feeling you're anything but an android."

"Sometimes I wish I were an android. It'd be simpler."

Freeman smiled. "Can we do this again sometime, dinner, I mean?"

Kate nodded, plunged her hands into the pockets of her jeans, felt awkward, like a teenager on a first date.

Freeman slipped into his jacket, then stopped, leaned forward, pecked her cheek lightly, pulled back and looked into her eyes, and she knew what was coming, and when he moved toward her again, she put her hand on his chest to stop him, then took it away and closed her eyes.

Freeman's lips were soft, light on Kate's, until she kissed him back, thinking—*Do I really want to do this?*—then she parted her lips and the kiss became real. She could smell his aftershave, something lemony-lime, nothing like Richard's, *Thank God*, though the thought of Richard was there now, with Freeman's lips on hers, and his hand caressing her back.

Freeman broke the embrace. "You okay with this? I'll stop if you want me to, go home, see you another time when you feel—"

"Shhh." Kate put her finger to his lips, and kissed him again.

He started undressing her in the hallway, kissing her shoulders and neck as he did, and when they finally made it into Kate's bed she felt breathless and light-headed and asked if they might lie there a moment, not speaking or touching, and Freeman took a deep breath and rolled off to the side, and after a few minutes she reached for his hand and moved it to her breast and their lips connected again, and slowly their bodies took over, and when he entered her she wrapped herself around him, confused and excited, pushing aside images of herself with Richard, and let the act take her away, and when it was over she rested her head in the crook of his neck and hoped he did not feel her tears on his shoulder.

Afterward, when Freeman brushed a tear off her cheek and asked if she was okay, she nodded, though she wasn't sure; her emotions felt like dried leaves that had fallen from a tree, lying around her, fragile, and easily scattered. She had not had sex with another man in the ten years she'd been with Richard and sleeping with Mitch Freeman had been unexpected, a bit terrifying, and had confirmed two things: one, that she was alive, and two, that her husband was dead.

Freeman knew better than to stay the night. It was awkward when he left, but they kissed again, and Kate managed a smile, and when he was gone she knew there was no possibility of sleep, and did what she always did—went to work.

By 1950, each member of the New York School had found his own style and abstract expressionism had divided into two groups. On one side were the "action" painters, like Kline and de Kooning, who defined expression through a loaded brush and a fierce muscular hand. On the other side were painters like Rothko and Newman, who defined it through color. But not everyone fit the mold. Painters like Clyfford Still had a foot in both camps, and in retrospect the artists of the period are much more distinct than they appeared to be at the time.

One might ask: Are Jackson Pollock's "drips" at all like Willem de Kooning's dynamic brush strokes? Are Rothko's somber veils of color a match for Barnett Newman's immense expanses of pure flat color, or Ad Reinhardt's minimal black canvases?

Kate stopped writing a moment, an image of Freeman's naked body unexpectedly surfacing in her mind.

Did I actually do that?

A part of her felt anxious and guilty, but another part felt languorous and excited, which surprised her. She wasn't sure where it would go, or if she was ready, but a moment later that excitement was replaced by the conversation she and Freeman had had about psychopaths being impostors, and the next minute she was thinking about Henry Lifschultz, Colin Leader, and Miranda Wilcox—three people who had worked hard to conceal a secret. *Acting*, she thought. Something we all do.

Kate leaned her elbows onto the desk and thought about the various roles she had played: cop, wife, art historian, socialite, and now . . .what? She wasn't entirely sure. *A work in progress?*

But those roles had been real. There had been no covert life, no secrets.

She glanced up, her eyes falling on the reproduction of the Zander painting pinned above her desk.

Was he playing a role? She didn't know, though, to her mind, he was guarding a secret.

Thinking about Zander led her back into her writing.

And what about abstraction versus figuration? There were only two major figure painters in the group, Willem de Kooning and Phillip Zander. For a brief moment there was a third figure painter, Sandy Resnikoff, whose work was similar to both de

Kooning and Zander, though Resnikoff added implications of landscape along with his figures, and though he continued to paint, and paint well, he gave up the group, and left both the figure and the New York scene.

Kate's fingers were poised above the keyboard.

What else did she want to say about Resnikoff? What else had his daughter said?

Life magazine. *The Irascibles.*

Kate plucked a book off the shelf, flipped pages until she found the famous black-and-white photograph from 1950, an assembly of fifteen select members of what was to be known as the New York School. The Rebel, Jackson Pollock, in the center, riveting gaze, cigarette poised; behind him the inscrutable Monk, Ad Reinhardt, buttoned up in his black suit; Willem de Kooning, the King, glowering from the back row; Mark Rothko, the Rabbi, down front, looking, to Kate, more like one of the Marx brothers; behind him a boyish Robert Motherwell; and beside him a young Phillip Zander.

A bunch of peacocks . . . pretending to be what they were not. How Resnikoff, who was not in the picture, had described them.

But they had been friends—Zander and Resnikoff—that much had been confirmed.

He is dead to me.

Had Zander betrayed Resnikoff in some terrible way?

If it hadn't been a big deal, wouldn't Zander simply have told her?

Oh, you know, I called Resnikoff an idiot.

Or . . .

I told him his work was no good and he got furious and never spoke to me again.

The kind of thing Kate knew happened among creative people all the time. But this seemed more serious, something Zander did not want to admit to her—or maybe to himself.

But what could be so bad?

Kate doubted she'd get Zander to tell her—though maybe now, after the threat against his life, he might want to unburden himself. Maybe. But not likely.

Another hour of work and Kate felt exhausted.

When she slid into bed she thought about Mitch Freeman and was surprised to find herself smiling. But just as she was drifting off to sleep she remembered those initials DH, which she had forgotten to look into.

CHAPTER 39

José leaned back against the car's headrest, his old Discman earphones in place, the new iPod in his one good hand, the other still in the removable cast. When Kate gave it to him his eyes widened and his smile was broader than she'd ever seen, though he was embarrassed he didn't know how to program it. Jules, she assured him, would help him do that.

After an hour of listening to the locustlike buzz emanating from José's earphones, Kate slipped a CD into the car's player and sang along with Annie Lennox, and they drove through Queens into Nassau County, the two of them in their own musical worlds.

At Manorville, Kate turned off the Long Island Expressway and had a thought of Henry Lifschultz's taking the same route out to the Hamptons. She tried to picture him behind the wheel, tried to imagine: *What had he been thinking?* If only they had taken him alive, she might know.

A light snow had begun to fall and she tapped José on the arm.

"Pretty, isn't it?"

A teenager's bored shrug. "I've seen snow before."

"I figured you had," said Kate, trying not to sigh.

"So, what's he like? This old man?"

"Like a grandfather. A very talented one. He does these wild paint-

ings, you'll see." Kate pictured Zander in his studio, and then the fragments of what had added up to one of his paintings.

"And the other guy, the one who's into music?"

"His assistant, Jules. A really nice kid. Well, to me he's a kid. He must
be in his twenties. He makes his own CDs, and, like I said, he'll help
you with your iPod."

José nodded and reset his earphones. A minute later, Kate exchanged
Annie Lennox for Nina Simone and was tempted to tell José to turn off
his Discman and listen to her sing, but didn't. And when the singer
started up with one of her sexy, sultry numbers, "I Want a Little Sugar
in My Bowl," Kate thought about Mitch Freeman, and felt a wave of
pleasure and guilt.

The back roads, woods, and fields were dusted with snow, glimpses of
the bay, flat and colorless, flashing between talc-white trees etched
against a gray sky. Kate tapped José again—his eyes were closed, though
he was not sleeping, head swaying to the music piped through his earphones—as she turned down the lonely stretch of road that led to
Zander's studio.

It was quiet. No cops or police cars, no helicopter this time. Still,
something about the hushed stillness was working its way under Kate's
skin. She shivered as she got out of the car and it had nothing to do with
the cold.

José hung back a moment, gazing up at the house and barn, modest
by Hamptons standards, and Kate saw it through his eyes, the tall naked
oaks and evergreens, the sprawling old house and converted barn
attached by a covered walkway. To José, she imagined, it must look like
something out of the movies.

Kate knocked and opened the door.

Zander was seated in front of a painting, brush in hand, but he
stopped working when they came in.

"José, this is Mr. Zander."

"*Mister?*" Zander screwed up his face. "Call me Phil." He laid his brush on the palette and extended one of his large, knobby hands, which was, at the moment, streaked with red and blue paint. "What did you do to your arm?"

"Fight," said José, with a cocky tilt of his head. "It doesn't hurt, and the cast comes off at night."

"That's good," said Zander. "I hear you like music—but probably not *this*." He flicked his head toward a large speaker in the corner, Ella Fitzgerald crooning "A Foggy Day in London Town." "Jules is your man. He went home to get a bunch of CDs he thought you might like. He'll be back in a minute."

José squinted at Zander's painting, asked, "Where's her other arm?"

Kate flinched. "José—"

"No, no," said Zander. "That's a damn good question. I swear it was there a minute ago." He looked at the floor as if it could have fallen off and José laughed, and Kate felt relieved, then he took a rag and wiped at an area of blue paint to reveal a fragment of a flesh-colored limb. "Ah, there it is. Sometimes I just forget." He shrugged and laughed. "Maybe I'll paint it back in, but you never know." He aimed his paintbrush at the canvas. "Here's a question for you. Is this a real figure, or not?"

José shook his head. "No."

"Exactly. It's a *painting* of a figure, and I can make her any darn way I want to make her. When you get to be as old as me no one tells you what to do. I can paint however I want. I can sleep late. Hell, I can sleep all day if I feel like it!"

"Or watch TV, like, anytime?"

"You bet." Zander winked at Kate, and she smiled. She'd never seen him quite like this and she was beginning to feel like a rat—thinking this kindly old man was concealing secrets, which she was once again about to probe.

The studio door swung open and Jules appeared, shaking white flakes from the slicker that covered his head and body, like a dog coming in from the rain. "Lot of snow out there," he said.

Kate glanced past the open door—it looked like a picture postcard— then made the necessary introductions.

Jules slipped off his slicker, though the omnipresent baseball cap remained in place, then led José over to the CD player. In minutes, they had attached José's iPod to the computer, and Kate heard words like "burning" and "downloading," and José was beaming. Ella Fitzgerald had been exchanged for hip-hop, and Kate was surprised she liked the music. She must have been moving to it unconsciously because Jules yelled over, "You go, girl," and he and José cracked up.

"Who is this?" she asked.

"Black Eyed Peas," Jules shouted over the track. "I'll burn a CD for your ride home."

Kate said, "Thanks," but Jules had already turned back to José, and she thought she heard José say something about the rapper 50 Cent, but with the music pumping, she couldn't make out much of what anyone was saying, though she didn't care—she had never seen that particular look on José's face: pure pleasure.

Zander clapped his big, knobby hands over his ears and signaled to Jules, who lowered the volume and plopped a pair of earphones over José's ears, and a set on himself.

"It's really good of you to do this," Kate said to Zander.

Zander waved his hand. "I'm already half deaf. Might as well go for a hundred percent. And it's good for Jules. He spends way too much time taking care of an old man like me."

"How are you? I mean, since—"

"Oh, *that*." Zander waved a dismissive hand. "I'm fine."

Kate looked into his eyes. Was he really fine? If a psycho killer had, only last week, targeted her for death, she would still be feeling it. Even now, seeing that Zander was all right, she could not shake a sense of unease.

She tugged the laptop out of her bag and forced a smile. "This is easier than a tape recorder. No transcribing," she said. "Just a few more questions."

Zander nodded and went back to his painting. "Maybe José is right—Where the hell *is* her other arm?" he said, which launched him into a solid half-hour description of his process.

Kate only half listened. She was waiting for Zander to finish his story so she could ask her questions.

"I was just in Rome, in Sandy Resnikoff's studio," she said, when he stopped talking, trying to make it sound casual. "His daughter showed me a lot of his work. His paintings had changed. The figure was entirely gone. He'd been painting abstract landscapes."

"Really?" Zander plucked the brush off his palette and swished it around in a can of turpentine.

"Yes. His daughter said he hadn't painted the figure in years—not since she could remember. Do you find that odd?"

"Artists change," he said.

"Yes, but Resnikoff was one of the originals, like you and de Kooning, who experimented with a new kind of figure. It seems strange to me that he would leave New York and totally give it up."

"Like I said, artists change."

"But *you* didn't."

Zander's hand froze in midstroke.

"I didn't mean that your work hasn't grown and matured, just that you continue to paint the same subject matter—the figure. You shared a studio with Resnikoff, didn't you?"

"Over fifty years ago." Zander's paintbrush was whipping the turpentine into a froth. "I remember one time . . ."

But it was not a memory of Resnikoff that Zander offered up; instead, it was another story, one Kate already knew, about the painter Ad Reinhardt calling sculpture ". . . what you bump into when you stand back to look at a painting." Zander relished all the details, and laughed at the end, but Kate refused to be deterred.

"Resnikoff's daughter mentioned that when she asked her father why he gave up the figure, he said, 'There wasn't room.' What do you think he meant by that?"

Zander let out a hissing sigh. "How can you expect me to remember such things?"

Because you remember everything else. But Kate didn't have a chance to say it as Zander proved it again by changing the topic, this time with a long-winded history of creating a WPA mural with the painters Arshile Gorky and George McNeil, what it was like, the day-to-day goings-on, even the bologna sandwiches they ate for lunch.

Oh, yes, his memory was just fine.

But he switched the topic again—stories about the writers and critics that gave words to the new American painting, how much they helped the movement and how powerful they became. Kate tried to bring him back to the subject of Resnikoff, this time bringing up the *ArtNews* article "Sandy Resnikoff Paints a Picture," but Zander only switched gears, speculating that Elaine de Kooning had slept with editor of *ArtNews*, either to further her husband's career or to torture him, then twenty minutes detailing the de Koonings' stormy marriage.

Again, Kate was not really listening—she pretty much knew the stories. She tuned in to the music; Aretha Franklin was just beginning "A Natural Woman."

"I love this," she shouted over to Jules and José—a way to show Zander that she was more interested in Aretha than his rehashing of the de Kooning marriage.

"Who is she?" asked José.

"Aretha Franklin? You're kidding me, right?" said Jules. "You gotta be. Tell me you're kidding before my heart breaks."

José only shrugged.

"The Queen of Soul? The ultimate diva?" Jules turned up the volume, Aretha slid up and down the scales, and he joined her: "You make me feel like a . . . natural woman." He rested a hand on José's shoulder. "You need a history lesson, young man. How about Elvis?"

"Elvis? Yeah. I've *heard* of him."

Jules rummaged through his CDs, came up with a compilation of greatest hits—a photo on the sleeve of Presley in decline, stuffed into gold lamé kung-fu garb, blue-black hair and matching muttonchops, enough eyeliner to stock a cosmetics counter. He struck an Elvis pose and sang, "You ain't nothin' but a hound dog."

José looked at him with surprise, and Kate laughed.

And the distraction had worked. Zander had stopped talking—and she resumed, while the real Elvis crooned "Heartbreak Hotel" in the background.

"There was a fourth figure painter, wasn't there—other than you and de Kooning and Resnikoff?"

"Not that I remember." Zander kept his eyes glued to his canvas.

"A painter named Hopson."

Zander's hand twitched, a straight vertical brush stroke of red suddenly a zigzag. "Oh yes. I remember him. Vaguely."

"What can you tell me about him?"

"Just that he was around the group."

"What about his paintings? What were they like?"

Zander was banging his brush around in that tin of turpentine so violently, Kate thought it might topple, but his voice remained calm. "I haven't any idea. I barely knew the man."

Kate thought a moment, an image of the initials flickering in the back of her mind. "And his first name? You wouldn't happen to remember it, would you?"

Zander took a deep breath, stared at his painting, the ceiling, the floor, as if the name were printed somewhere and he just had to find it. "Nope," he finally said. "Can't remember it." He glanced over at her and smiled the kind of smile that says *I'm finished talking about this.*

But Kate wasn't.

"Was it Donald? David, maybe?"

"What's that?"

"Hopson's first name. It started with a D, right?"

Zander wrinkled his brow as if giving it serious thought. "Sorry," he said after a moment. "As I said, he wasn't someone I knew well."

"Still," said Kate, "you'd have known his first name, wouldn't you?"

"Maybe at one time I did. But if so, I no longer remember." He turned back to his painting with a new intensity, scrubbing his paintbrush against the canvas so hard Kate thought he might tear it.

Zander was painting as if his life depended on it—or pretending to, thought Kate, probably to evade her questions, which didn't stop her from asking them all over again: his relationship to Resnikoff—*Yes, we*

were friends, though never that close; that last fateful meeting again—
Like I said, we argued, but about what, I can't remember; and finally: "So
why would someone want you dead?"

"I have no idea," said Zander. "The art world can be a cruel and spite-
ful place. I'm sure you know that. Success breeds resentment."

"Resentment is one thing," said Kate. "But murder?"

"I thought this man, what was his name, Lipshitz?"

"Lifschultz."

"Whatever. I thought he was some sort of psycho, and a psycho
doesn't really need a reason, does he?"

Kate sighed. Zander had a point. Plus, there was not even a consen-
sus that all the murders were committed by the same person. The curator, Martin Dressler, it appeared, had been killed by a woman. And
Lifschultz may have been many things, but he was not a woman.

Another half hour of questions that Zander ignored or deflected, and
Kate finally gave up, packed up her laptop, and signaled to José that it
was time to leave. Her book would have to survive without Zander's version of the demise of his friendship with Resnikoff, or exactly why
Resnikoff had given up a promising career and left New York—or anything from Zander about the fourth figure painter, Hopson.

But José was not ready to leave. He trotted over clutching his iPod,
one earphone still plugged in, going on about how they'd programmed
only ninety songs and didn't she know that an iPod could hold, like,
thousands.

Kate was surprised when Zander suggested she let the boy stay over.

"No," she said. "His mother's expecting him."

"She won't care," said José, and was on the phone getting his mother's
approval before Kate could stop him. Then he literally bopped his way
across the room to Jules, earphones back in place.

"I guess that's that," said Kate. "You sure he won't be any trouble?"

"I have four bedrooms and they're never used," said Zander, easing
back into his kindly grandfather mode. "And Jules will stay. He'll enter-
tain him."

The music had changed again, more of Jules's history lesson, Kate figured, Michael Jackson's "Man in the Mirror," and Kate commented that she was surprised to hear him play it.

"Why?" asked Jules, straining to be heard over the music. "You don't like the gloved one?"

"I'm just surprised you still do."

"Usher is a lot better," said José.

"Yeah, Usher's good, but he, like, stole all of Michael's moves," said Jules. "They all took from Michael—his music, his dancing. The rappers are into all that macho bullshit, to them everyone's a ho, a bitch, or a fag, but Michael was never like that. Listen to his words." He cocked his head, and sang along in his sweet, light voice.

Kate was impressed. But still, she had trouble separating Michael Jackson the man from his music.

"Yeah, Michael's cool with me," said José, smiling up at Jules.

But Jules tapped the CD player and "Man in the Mirror" was exchanged for some heavy-duty rapper, one of those macho guys he'd just been complaining about—rapping about bonin' the bitches—and that did it for Kate. She said her good-byes, and told José she'd be back for him in the morning.

Jules caught up with her at the door, handed over a CD. "Here you go, your compilation CD, courtesy of me and José. Black Eyed Peas, Christina Aguilera, Belle and Sebastian, some others you might like."

"Trying to make me cool, huh?" Kate smiled, and noted Jules's art handler's gloves. "If you're trying to keep the paint and resins at bay, you'd be a lot better off with latex."

"I know," said Jules. "But they make me itch and sweat. The cotton ones are a lot more comfortable."

"Me, I never wore gloves, ever." Zander displayed hands that proved the point.

"Right," said Jules. "But I don't want to ruin my health with your art supplies." He brushed the scraggly hair off his face with a gloved hand, then went back to José and the music. They replaced their headphones and got serious.

Kate said "Good-bye" again, but Zander was staring intently at his painting and the boys were downloading music, and no one was really listening. "Hey," she called out to José. "You have my cell number if you need to reach me."

José threw her a quick nod and smile.

Kate shivered though the studio was warm, her body anticipating the cold outdoors—at least that's what she told herself.

CHAPTER 40

The world had gone white, the trees lining Springs Fireplace Road sagging under the weight of the snow, the bay nearly invisible, Kate's windshield wipers working overtime, and losing, snow piling up faster than they could clear it.

The car's heater was turned up high, but Kate still felt chilled. *What is it?* Something seen, and not seen, a flickering impression that had registered on the outer fringes of her brain.

Kate peered through the windshield, hands gripping the steering wheel. Even at twenty miles per hour the narrow lanes were precarious, the thought of driving back to Manhattan more and more daunting; and when she skidded halfway across the road just past the Springs General Store—where Jackson Pollock had shopped and bought his liquor—she had an image of the artist who had died not far from here, his car smashed against a tree, and she did not want to join him.

There was no compelling reason for her to get home, particularly now that she'd be driving back tomorrow, and she hadn't been thrilled to leave José out here anyway. It made sense to stay. She made a quick call to her friends in East Hampton, arranged to spend the night, then made her way cautiously along the Old Stone Highway, replaying bits and pieces of those questions Zander would not answer: Resnikoff's abrupt departure from New York; that fourth artist, Hopson's first name; and she wondered what the old man was hiding, and why.

The railroad tracks were already under the snow, Kate's tires bumping over them, sliding a bit as she made her way along Amagansett's main street, everything closed up, a ghost town. On the narrow Indian Wells Highway the wind whipped the snow into a comet, the ocean, which Kate knew lay somewhere up ahead, invisible.

She finally turned onto Further Lane—that exclusive strip of prime ocean-view real estate—and passed Jerry Seinfeld's home, his own private baseball diamond buried beneath the snow; then Helmut Lang's summer getaway, his high-end designer clothes reminding her with a bittersweet pang of her former high life with Richard. At last she reached the private lane that led to her friend's home, just barely visible at the end of the road.

Jane and Jack Sands greeted her with hugs and a glass of red wine, and led her into the two-story living room, huge wooden beams imbedded in stone and concrete, Native American blankets, South American ponchos and pottery, all of it basking in the warm red-orange glow from the fireplace flames.

After a second glass of wine, Kate's unspecified anxiety began to abate. She and her friends brought one another up to date on recent events, Kate telling them about Nola and the baby; her friends beaming as they showed pictures of their grandchildren. At 7 P.M. they had to get ready for a dinner party just next door, and though they had called and made it clear to their hosts they would not go if Kate could not come with them, Kate begged off and insisted they go without her.

After they'd gone, she nibbled on some gourmet leftovers Jane had set aside for her, then retrieved her laptop, signed onto the Internet, went to a search engine, and started looking for artists with the initials DH.

Several contemporary painters popped up, but none that made sense. But when she typed in the name Hopson, a scant half page of links appeared along with that missing first name: Douglas.

Douglas Hopson, thought Kate. *DH*.

Now she recalled having seen the name before—an artist from the New York School period, though one who had never received any recognition, and was rarely, if ever, written about.

She hit the first link. It brought her to a 1941 exhibition, the American Moderns show organized by Sam Kootz, held at Macy's, of all places, a show she knew about and had even recently studied, though Douglas Hopson had not been mentioned in any of the literature. Like the rest of the world, Kate had pretty much ignored the fact that Douglas Hopson ever existed.

The second link was to another group show, at Peggy Guggenheim's revolutionary Art of This Century Gallery, with over forty artists, Hopson among them, along with several of the greats—Jackson Pollock, Willem de Kooning, and Phillip Zander. Amazing, thought Kate, that she had never come across Hopson's name in her other readings about Guggenheim's gallery, or if she had, had not taken notice.

The third link sent her to the Art Reference Library, which supplied background and limited statistics.

Douglas Hopson. Painter. Born 1911. Died 1978.

Kate did the math. Sixty-seven when he died, thirty-nine years old in 1950, the year the New York School painters were canonized by that *Irascibles* photo in *Life* magazine.

First Solo Exhibition: Eighth Street Gallery, NYC, 1948.

More math: Hopson had been thirty-seven years old, young by the standards of his day for a one-man exhibition. Both Franz Kline and Zander had been forty when they had theirs; de Kooning, forty-four. Nowadays, artists were showing directly out of graduate school, considered "mid-career" by forty, but not then.

Kate scanned the rest of Hopson's statistics—a smattering of group shows after 1948, no mention of him ever having another solo show, no list of his artwork in any public or private collections, and only one review, *ArtNews*, 1948. Kate clicked on the link, which brought her to the *ArtNews* archive.

DOUGLAS HOPSON
AT THE EIGHTH STREET GALLERY

The nine paintings Douglas Hopson showed at Eighth Street, all figural abstractions, are not soothing to the eye. Like many of his contemporaries, Hopson eschews beauty. His painted figures—mostly women—are wild picture-puzzle females with hacked-off heads, a leg here, arm there, brightly colored and exuberantly painted. One could say Hopson goes for the jugular—no pun intended.

With the possible exception of his contemporary, Willem de Kooning, who, lately, has been getting a lot of attention, I cannot think of another painter who uses the figure, or uses it so well. Naturally, if one is looking for any sort of realistic depiction of the body they will be disappointed. These figures do not abide by the rules of the real world. They are figures that exist only in a world of paint.

I can't say that Hopson's paintings are pleasing, and, in fact, I did not like them at first glance—they disturbed me. But for days I could not get them out of my mind.

These immediate and visceral works are painted from the heart and the gut, and this reviewer will be looking forward to seeing what Hopson has in store for us in future exhibitions.

A review filled with praise and expectation, none of it fulfilled. How many artists were there who had one great show and were never heard from again? Too many, thought Kate.

Picture-puzzle females with hacked-off heads, a leg here, arm there, brightly colored and exuberantly painted . . . figures that exist only in a world of paint. Kate sat back, closed her eyes, and a vision coalesced, a painting taking shape in her mind, and José pointing to it, asking: "Where's her other arm?"

Zander's painting. Not Hopson's painting.

Odd, thought Kate, that the *ArtNews* reviewer had compared Hopson to de Kooning, but not to Zander.

She sat forward and typed in the name "Phillip Zander." Page after page of links appeared, and she skimmed them until she found what she was looking for—a book: *The Early Work of Phillip Zander, Paintings made by the artist during his formative years, 1949–1950.*

But those were not his formative years—they were the years of his first solo exhibitions—the years that made him an international art star. His formative years would have been earlier, she thought, but there was nothing in the book before 1949.

Kate thought about the books she had on Zander at home—had any of them mentioned the man's artwork prior to 1949? She didn't think so. She hadn't really thought about it before, but now, as she scanned all the books on him, she realized they all told the same story: No paintings by Phillip Zander before 1949. It was as if he had burst upon the scene a fully matured artist, always making those wild signature figures of his.

But that couldn't be.

Kate sat back, reached for her wine, and took a sip. Had she ever seen a reproduction of an early Phillip Zander painting? She didn't think so.

But every artist made artwork before they became well known. There were dozens of books on de Kooning's work prior to his breakthrough *Women* series; likewise, Franz Kline's famous black-and-white abstractions, and Beatrice Larsen as well. Kate knew all of their early work. Funny she'd never even thought to ask Zander. Had he destroyed all of his early paintings? It was the logical answer. But if so, why?

Kate went back to her laptop, this time going to the Art Reference Picture Library, and once again typed in the name "Douglas Hopson."

A moment later an image filled the screen.

Kate was riveted. The painting of the figure was remarkably like a painting by another artist Kate knew well: *Phillip Zander.*

Kate went from Hopson's Internet site to Zander's, found a series of the artist's paintings, searched for one she knew best, which had been part of Cecile Edelman's collection, then double-clicked to enlarge it.

The similarity was uncanny, the way both artists created figures with

Douglas Hopson, *Pin-Up Girl*, 1947.

exaggerated hands, circular breasts, outlines of forms echoed by brush strokes.

Was Hopson just a derivative painter, copying the artists around him, or . . .

Kate went back to Hopson's Internet site to check a fact, and found it:

Douglas Hopson. First Solo Exhibition:
Eighth Street Gallery, NYC, 1948.

Then to Zander's:

Phillip Zander. First Solo Exhibition:
Charles Egan Gallery, NYC, 1949.

Hopson's show had been a year earlier than Zander's.
So it wasn't Hopson who was doing the imitating.

Was this why Hopson's initials, DH, had been in the corner of that replicated Zander painting—to let people know that Hopson had been the originator of the style, and not Zander?

But if Henry Lifschultz had made the black-and-white paintings—why would he care? And if it had been Leader or Wilcox, why would *they* care? Kate couldn't figure it out.

Clearly, the black-and-white paintings had been made as clues—preludes to vandalism and murder. But was there something more? What did any of them stand to gain by recognizing Douglas Hopkins's contribution to modern art—unless they were trying to sell the man's work, which, to her knowledge, they were not—none of Hopson's paintings had surfaced.

Kate just didn't get it.

But if it was any of them—Lifschultz, Leader, or Wilcox—who had made those paintings, then there had to be another reason.

Could one of them have been related to Hopson? Kate wondered.

She made three quick Internet searches—Leader, Lifschultz, Wilcox. But none of them turned up any link to Douglas Hopson.

Kate sat back again. So if not they, who would want to set the record straight on Douglas Hopson, a failed painter with one solo show to his name?

Kate returned to Hopson's vital statistics, but other than the few exhibitions, it revealed little.

So where else could she look?

Kate stared into the fire.

Of course. In one of her favorite everyday vices—the obits.

It took only a few seconds for the search engine to perform its magic.

THE NEW YORK TIMES, DECEMBER 24, 1978.
Douglas Hopson, 67, painter

Douglas Hopson, a painter associated with abstract expressionism, died in his East Fourth Street apartment in Manhattan, on December 22. He was 67.

The artist had early friendships with several artists of the New York School, such as Willem de Kooning and Phillip Zander, and exhibited beside them in the American Moderns show of 1941. After his one solo exhibition, at the Eighth Street Gallery, in 1947, Mr. Hopson's career stalled. Eking out a small living as a house painter, he received government assistance until the time of his death.

Mr. Hopson married the violinist Minnie Brill in 1940. They were divorced in 1963. Their one daughter, Robin, born in 1954, died in 1975. Mrs. Brill-Hopson passed away one year later.

Marcus Jacobson, a longtime friend of Mr. Hopson's, attested to the fact that the artist had continued to paint over the years. "He had an apartment filled with paintings," Jacobson said. "Everywhere you looked, paintings." Jacobson suggested that Hopson was extremely depressed by his failed art career, the deaths of his wife and daughter, and was drinking heavily.

The fire which ended Mr. Hopson's life apparently started sometime in the early morning hours of the 22nd. According to the Fire Department, it destroyed the apartment and all of Mr. Hopson's artwork.

The NYFD is speculating the fire was ignited by flammable artist products, and they called the fire suspicious.

Kate's fingers were moving rapidly on the keyboard now as she typed in the name Robin Hopson. There was only one link—to a news story in the *New York Daily News* in 1975.

COPS KILL
YOUNG MOTHER

Kate skimmed the article.

A drug sting gone bad. Alphabet City. Hippies selling and using. Several arrests. Two dead. One of them Robin Hopson.

Kate thought back to Hopson's obit, his daughter, dead in 1975, then his wife, dead one year later. Losing a mate was horrible enough, but a child? She didn't know how anyone survived that, and apparently Hopson's ex-wife had not—and neither had he.

Douglas Hopson's life had been a series of disasters: failed art career, failed marriage, the death of a child. Hardly a life at all.

She went back to the *Daily News* article, read it through one more time, the last line a sickening image: *One of the victims, Robin Hopson, was found with an infant in her arms.*

Jesus.

Kate went back over the article, but there was no mention of whether or not the baby had survived. She spent a few minutes surfing the Web, looking for a possible link, but found nothing.

As she closed her laptop, there it was again—that image, flickering at the periphery of her psyche. She stared into the fireplace, flames writhing like El Greco figures.

Figures. Fire.

Douglas Hopson had died in a fire.

A fire.

A song started playing in her head.

But it wasn't possible—what she was thinking—or was it?

No, she was being crazy, creating associations when there were none—the effects of two glasses of wine and not enough sleep.

But the song would not stop playing at the back of her mind—finger snapping, cymbals, drums, echo chambers, the chorus joining in, swelling, building toward a crescendo—and as it did, that image appeared again for a split second. Then everything mixed together— crime scene photos of slashed paintings and dead bodies, and Douglas Hopson, a man she never knew, dying in a fire, and this absurd image, not much more than a notation her optic nerve had photographed and stored, now playing it back along with that damn sound track, which was conjuring yet another picture—this one from one of those black-and-white clue paintings.

That was it. Kate was up. She grabbed her bag and her gun. She had to go. To prove that she was wrong. To prove that she was crazy. She had to be, because if she wasn't, she might already be too late.

Crazy?

Who, me? Prove it. Go on. I dare you.

Impossible.

The mask is perfectly in place.

A question—words that take a moment to be deciphered, processed, understood—interrupt the reverie.

"What? Oh, sure. Gotcha." *Go on, now, add a smile. That's it.*

Another question.

"Excuse me?" *Try not to sigh. Concentrate. Tilt the head, look quizzical.*

"Oh, right, right. Sure."

Yes, I can do this. Amazing, isn't it? To live in two worlds. To wake, to eat, to dress for the part, this role—Normal Life—well, not quite—and all the time knowing what I have done, this other part, this other me, that lives just a quarter inch below the surface.

"What?" A nod. A smile. "Uh-huh."

See? Everyone buys it. This act of normalcy, when another part of me just wants to scream: LOOK AT ME! SEE WHO I AM! SEE WHAT I HAVE DONE!

The Slasher?

Such a silly name. And the role, way too limited, too . . . common. They don't know me. But how could they?

One more smile, the acting flawless, smoothed over by pills, medication, and so many years of rehearsing.

But the time has come to quit acting. The actor knows this, is ready, and more than willing.

Another damn question.

"Uh-huh, sure. Me too. You have no idea *how* hungry I am."

It is a fact: The hunger has worked its way through the loins, into organs, and deep into the psyche.

The mask begins to crack.

CHAPTER 41

Outside, the snow had turned the sky an eerie silver. Jacket on, scarf covering half her face, Kate made her way to the car, wondering if she should call Floyd Brown. Would he think she was being ridiculous? She probably was. What about Murphy? He would be interested to hear about the initials—but should she bother him? He was with his daughter in Southampton. But she knew she should tell someone.

What the hell. She flipped open her cell phone, got Murphy's voice mail, left a message about the initials, where she was going, and asked him to give her a call, stressed that it was probably nothing urgent, though, as she closed her phone, she wasn't sure she believed her own words. She peered through her windshield at snowflakes the size of silver dollars, then got the cell phone to her ear again. No voice mail this time, just the phone, ringing.

Why don't they answer?

She drove back through the center of Amagansett, down Pantigo Road. The snow plows had been through, the road somewhat better, though the visibility remained poor. It hardly mattered—that other image was blotting out all others: *a flesh-toned stain suddenly appearing on white cotton?*

Had she actually seen it? After the year she'd had, all the loss and pain, nightmares, insomnia, all the meaningless violence, it was possible she was hallucinating. But she didn't think so.

At the end of town she crossed those snow-covered railroad tracks again, and went into a skid. Should she turn around? Was she being foolish? She did not answer the question, only tightened her grip on the wheel and drove on.

Minutes seemed like hours as she edged the car down the Old Stone Highway. As she reached the Springs, just past Barnes Hole, the driving became even more treacherous, the road all curves and turns, and when she passed Louse Point and turned onto Accabonic she hit a patch of ice that sent the old Mercedes skidding across the road, wheels sliding sideways, that feeling of utter helplessness as the car skated out of control.

Kate's hands were still locked on the wheel when the car stalled only inches from a thicket of trees, her breath coming in short, fast puffs. *Jesus. Will I make it in one piece?*

She loosened her grip on the wheel and turned the key. The engine sputtered and died.

No. Do not do this. Not now.

Another try. A stuttering gasp, like a dry cough.

Shit.

Kate took a deep breath, and sat back.

Give it a moment. Don't flood the engine.

The snow had covered the windshield, a blanket of blinding white.

She would give the car another minute, then try again.

If it failed, she would leave the car where it was and walk the rest of the way.

The skylights and windows have gone white with snow.

The painted figures appear to taunt, rising up from pigment and canvas, aiming distorted fingers, practically shouting: *Do it already. Get it over with!*

And yes, it is time, all the puzzle pieces have been set in place, all leading to here, and now.

A minute to contemplate the past—the frustration and pain that has culminated in this climactic moment, so carefully planned, lines and staging memorized and rehearsed, actually seen in the mind's eye dozens—no, hundreds—of times. And here it is, finally, about to happen.

A long look down the length of the studio, taking in the paint-stained floorboards, tables laden with tubes of oil color, bottles and tins of turpentine and resin, the smaller paint table on wheels, and all of those paintings, those bullshit paintings with their bullshit figures.

No one seems to notice. And why would they? *I am a ghost.*

The music, a pumping beat that gets the blood going—and soon there will be more blood.

A deep breath.

Ready. Set. Go.

Weapon drawn.

Ah, now they see me.

A moment to relish the looks of shock and fear, then a few steps, all that is necessary to get a hand around his throat.

The engine caught—*thank God*—and Kate edged the car back onto the road.

The bay was coming into view, lit up by the snow, a sleek onyx slab.

A couple more miles, that's all.

She was creeping, inching the car along the snow-covered road. She could not risk another skid.

It seemed like forever until she reached Springs Fireplace Road and then the turnoff to the private lane.

Small yellow rectangles—the lights of windows—flickered up ahead.

Here the snow had already formed drifts, easily a couple of feet deep, tires crunching, no sense of any traction. Kate held her breath until she reached the end of the drive, happy to cut the engine, and get out of the car. Her boots disappeared in the snow.

There was music coming from inside. She didn't know if it was a good sign or bad.

She dusted the snow off her jacket, and knocked.

No answer.

Could they not hear her over the music?

She knocked again, and tried the door. It was open.

The studio's bright spotlights were temporarily blinding—and that song—the same one she'd had in her mind, was actually playing, loud.

It only took a moment for Kate's eyes to adjust and see it—Zander's large painting—across the barn, the one he'd been working on, but the disjointed figure appeared more alive now, practically quivering. Was it the music—so loud that it seemed to shake the barn's foundation—that made it seem as if it were actually moving?

Kate took a few steps, and gasped. It *was* moving.

Oh my God.

José, strapped to the center of the slashed canvas, his arms and legs bound to the exposed wooden stretchers, a wide swath of clear tape across his mouth, his eyes wide with terror.

Beside him, Phillip Zander, in his paint-stained chair.

"The paintings were getting stale, the figures a bit stiff, don't you agree?"

The voice was just barely audible over the music.

Kate turned. And saw him. A shimmering scarecrow backlit by the studio's harsh spotlights, a pistol in his hand.

"Imitators and thieves need help when it comes to inspiration, don't you agree?"

He began to move around the perimeter of the studio as he spoke, emptying a gallon tin of turpentine, creating a liquid trail.

Kate's mind was reeling. *Talk to him. About anything. The music.* "You like him, Michael Jackson?"

"People don't understand him."

"But you do?" She was shouting over the music.

"We're alike, the two of us. No childhood. So much suffering. A ruined face. Constant re-creation to . . . to look . . . normal."

Kate was not entirely sure what he was talking about, just knew that she had to keep him talking. "Normal? What do you mean?"

"Think of him as my . . . self-portrait." He hit the CD player and Michael Jackson died in midsong. He was circling José with the turpentine, and Kate tried to telegraph the boy that it would be okay, that she would get them out of this. But how?

The acidic stench of turpentine filled the air as he made another loop, this time around Zander, who looked unconscious. There was a welt the size of an egg on the old man's forehead, and a gash, blood snaking its way through his wiry eyebrow.

"Do you have your tape recorder with you?"

"What? Yes. In my bag." *Along with my gun.*

Kate made a move, but he leaped forward, snatched the bag from her hand, dumped it, pens and pad, lipstick and atomizer, the small tape recorder, all scattering, along with her Glock, which hit the floor with a thud. He kicked it like a soccer ball, watched it skitter to the far end of the studio, hit the barn wall, bounce, and come to rest in a pile of paint rags. He kept his eyes on Kate as he plucked the small recording device off the floor and displayed it in his gloved hand, and she saw it again— the image that had set her off: *the gloved hand offering her the CD, then wiping his cheek, and the odd smear of tan-ocher pigment suddenly appearing on white cotton.*

She stared at the assistant's face, most of it hidden by long hair hanging limply over his cheeks, eyes shielded by large black-framed glasses, the droopy mustache.

Zander moaned. Like José's, his mouth was taped.

"Sad, isn't he—this charlatan." He nudged Zander with his pistol. "Wake up!"

Zander's eyes flicked open.

"That's better." He turned to Kate. "You. Sit. Over here. Beside him."

Kate did as she was told. She laid her hand on Zander's arm, which was taped to the chair.

"Do not touch him!"

Zander was fully awake now, his eyes alert with fear.

"Now . . ." He caught his breath and spoke calmly. "Phil is going to tell us all a story." He placed the tape recorder on the table between

Kate and Zander. "And later, you are going to write about it. Do you understand?"

Kate nodded. She thought she did understand. It was starting to make sense—some of it, though there were still so many questions waiting for answers.

He folded his angular body into a chair, balanced the gun on his knee, and aimed it at Zander. "Go ahead. Tell her."

Zander tried to move his lips, impossible under the tape.

"Oh, right." He laughed, high and shrill, stood and tried to remove the tape, but could not get ahold of it with his gloved fingers. Slowly, he tugged a glove off and displayed the hand, rotating it like a trophy, skin mottled and thickened, one finger gnarled, the pinky just a scarred nub.

"Nice, huh?" He got a grip on the tape and ripped it off Zander's mouth. The old man's lips split, blood appearing in the cracks, like overripe cherries.

Zander ran his tongue over his lips. "What do you want me to say, Jules?"

"Oh, you know. The truth? How about that? And don't leave anything out. The world needs to know. *She* needs to know—so she can fix it."

"Yes, I will," said Kate. "I'll do whatever it is you want me to do, whatever you want me to fix."

"Of course you will. You can't write a book about the New York School that's filled with lies, can you? I'm giving you an opportunity to tell the world the real story."

"And I will. But please just let José go."

"Sorry, I can't do that. The boy is my insurance." A glance over at José. "It's nothing personal, kid. I like you, really I do. You're cool. And it was fun, the music stuff and all, and oh—that reminds me—we have that CD still in the computer, just add those Jay-Z cuts we talked about and it will be finished, and make sure to take it home with you—that is, if your friend here does what I say."

"Of course I will." Kate thought a moment. "What is it you want—for me to write a book about Douglas Hopson, and his contribution to art? Is that it?"

A smile broke across his face, and when he pushed the hair away from his cheeks, Kate saw the flesh-toned makeup at the corners of his mouth tug and form tiny cracks. *A ruined face.* "So, you know."

Yes, she knew. Somewhere in the back of her psyche, as soon as she'd read the obituary, and about the fire, her mind had started telegraphing the image of that smear on the glove, and the split-second view she'd gotten of a scarred cheek. But it hadn't come together, hadn't really made sense until now. He had survived. Robin Hopson's baby, Douglas Hopson's grandchild, had survived. "Yes, but tell me."

"Tell you *what*?"

"All of it. So I understand it perfectly."

"No, *he'll* tell you." He aimed the gun at Zander's head. "Tell her how you killed my grandfather."

"I didn't kill your grandfather."

"Liar!" He pressed the gun against Zander's cheek. "I will kill you if you don't tell the truth."

Zander looked up. "You're going to kill me anyway, aren't you?"

There was a moment while he considered the question. "Yes. Yes, I will. But, I'll kill them as well if you don't tell the truth. That part is up to you."

"All this time," said Zander. "And I thought—"

"You thought *what*? That I . . . *liked* you. That I *cared*?" He laughed, and the fissures beside his mouth traveled like sidewalks cracking in an earthquake. "I brought your tea, and I readied your paints. I turned down the bed and delivered your pills. I listened. Pretended to care. And the more I did for you, the more you needed me." He moved closer to Zander, and whispered, almost tenderly, "How much sweeter is the betrayal when we think someone cares." He paused a moment, considering his own question. "But you know all about that, don't you? Betrayal." Another warped smile. "Oh, the games we play when we deceive ourselves, huh, Phil? So let's hear about your games. I've been waiting to hear you tell them, waiting so patiently. See, I learned all that, about patience, in a hospital bed, staring at the ceiling." He drew a scarred finger along his cheek; it came away caked with makeup. "Save the best for last, isn't that what they say?"

"Tell me about you—and what happened." Kate wanted all the facts, all the missing details. "Please."

"About . . . me?" Images like sheet music in a player piano looped across the brain, picking out the various roles and impersonations, the moments of reconstructed history which the actor believes to have lived. Which parts are real, which fantasized? The actor has trouble separating them, but it no longer matters.

He was about to speak when Kate's cell phone, on the floor, started ringing.

He kicked it away.

The message was unclear—something about the initials in the painting, McKinnon knowing who it was—an artist named Hopson—and she was going back to Zander's place, concerned about . . . something. Murphy wasn't sure what.

He smiled at his daughter. All afternoon they had been in the backyard of the Southampton mansion that belonged to the millionaire who was screwing his wife, who was off somewhere making more millions, and the one thing Murphy felt good about was that his ex-wife, Ginny, seemed miserable, and looked it, too.

For the first time in a long time, he and his daughter had been chatting easily—about school and friends, about how she hated the millionaire (which made him happy, though he did not show it). It was dark by the time they'd completed a snowman almost as tall as Murphy, with black rocks for eyes, a half-moon grin made of pebbles, and his own cap on its head. He hadn't cared if his hair got soaked with snow, anything for his daughter's smile.

But now, when he played McKinnon's message a second time, it nagged him. Exactly why had she called and left it? It wasn't like her. And there was definitely some tension in her voice, some anxiety about going back to Zander's place. He tried calling her back, listened to her cell phone ring, the voice mail pick up, then suddenly go dead.

He tried again, and when there was nothing, he turned to his daughter and said, "I gotta go, sweetie. But I'll be back later."

She asked where he was going and he said to help a friend, and promised not to be gone long, and kissed her cheek.

As he was leaving, his daughter called after him. "Daddy!" she said, plucking the woolen cap off the snowman. "It's cold. You'd better wear this."

"Why did you kill them?" asked Kate.

A moment's consideration. "I didn't mean to, not at first. It was the paintings I was after. I wanted, *needed* to get rid of them—the co-conspirators' artwork. It was a simple plan, really it was." He turned toward Zander. "You know what I'm talking about, don't you, Phil?"

"But you killed *people*," said Kate.

"Not at first. That wasn't the plan, but . . ." He glanced away a moment and when he looked back, his eyes were dark and hard. "It became a better plan, so much . . . more meaningful. You can see that, can't you?"

"Yes," said Kate.

"I was evening the score."

"For your grandfather?"

"Yes."

"But you were just an infant. How could you know?"

"I was four years old. And he was all I had. And I know everything. I read all about it. His own words."

"Whose words?" asked Kate.

"My grandfather's."

"He wrote about it?"

"I memorized it." He looked up a moment, and recited, "No one to trust the child to. No one. Not in this world. Better in heaven than here on earth, in hell." He glared at Zander. "I learned all about it. Everything you did. Everything that happened. And the rest I researched, studied, everything there was to know. I made it my life." He glanced at Kate. "Can you understand that? It was my raison d'être, my reason to live — to destroy them and their work, their reputations, too, the traitors, the so-called in crowd."

Beatrice Larsen was suddenly singing in Kate's head. *"I'm in with the in crowd . . ."*

"I only did what I had to do. You can see that, can't you? As for the others, well, to own those paintings made them just as guilty; you can see that, I'm sure."

What Kate saw was illness. But she wanted to keep him talking. The gun was across the room, she had to get to it. "Explain it to me."

"They were guilty. All of them. And I warned them — that man with his beloved Gorky, the other one with his Franz Kline, that stupid curator, and that Hofmann woman who owned all of those paintings, who had her grandfather's blood running through her veins. That was sweet. One grandchild confronts another, right? — she was the best one. No —" A glance in Zander's direction. "The best is yet to come." A crooked smile. "I didn't have to do that, you know, warn them. They were given a chance. And they failed. That's not my fault."

He had killed them all. It was not Lifschultz, nor Leader, or Wilcox. Here he was, the Slasher, and with the motivation Kate had been searching for — revenge.

"Why have you waited?" Kate looked from the studio assistant to Zander. "You could have killed him at any time."

"Of course. But that wasn't the plan. Taking my time, gaining his trust, that was the best part — the part that kept me going. I wanted this old fraud to feel like my grandfather must have felt — betrayed by a friend." He looked at the old man. "And we are friends, aren't we, Phil? You trust me, don't you?"

Zander managed a nod.

He turned the gun back on Zander. "Enough. It's your turn to speak."

"Just kill me," said Zander. "I don't care."

And Kate believed him. His face had collapsed, his spirit gone.

"Oh, I *will* kill you, but not yet — not until you've explained it, in detail. And if you don't . . ." He pivoted, aimed the pistol at José. "The boy dies. Then the woman. You will watch them die and it will be your fault—more blood on your hands—and then, only then, will you die, too."

Zander licked his bleeding lips, took a deep breath, and began to tell the story.

CHAPTER 42

t was that meeting . . . in Ad Reinhardt's studio," said Zander. "Was it Robert Motherwell who had put it together? I think so. All of us were there—de Kooning, Kline, Rothko, Resnikoff." He took another breath and started filling in the details, how the plan was put forth—that to become a part of history they had to become exclusive. Zander painted the scene with words, how he had looked around that room and watched the artists take in the information—that they must reduce their ranks to become famous, to become a *school*, one as famous as the School of Paris. "It was a simple idea," he said. "A simple plan. We would create a very small clique of very special artists that would become known as the New York School. But who would be part of it and who would not? That was the question." He sighed.

"We decided to push the others out—the artists who were not there, at the meeting. Some for no reason at all. Others, well . . . It wasn't difficult. We simply stopped inviting them to take part in our exhibitions, to be part of our world." He looked up, caught Kate's eyes. "I can see you judging me. But you weren't there—you don't know how it was."

No, she did not know how it was. But the cruelty astonished her.

"The art world was so small," said Zander. "And there was so little to go around, and we had been so poor. But it was starting to open up, the collectors sniffing around, buying and—"

"And you just had to be part of it, didn't you?" He tapped the pistol against Zander's cheek.

"Yes, I wanted to be part of it, I'll admit that. I was a young man then, and I wanted all of it—fame, wealth."

"What about Resnikoff?" asked Kate, knowing this time she would get the real answer.

"He was there, at the meeting, right beside me, listening to what was being suggested, and . . . he turned to me and said, 'You can't possibly go along with this, can you, Phil? You wouldn't do this to your friends, to other artists, would you?'" Zander's eyes clouded. "I didn't answer him, didn't say a word—and he got his answer. Then he shouted at me, and at the group, calling us peacocks and traitors, and he stormed out. And that was it for him. He was finished—and he knew it. He would be one of the outcasts. So he left New York and never came back."

Jules pressed the pistol into the old man's flesh. "Playing God must have felt good."

"No. It didn't."

"Liar."

"I'm not lying. I did it because . . . because I was afraid. I did not want to be an outcast."

"And what about my grandfather?"

"He wasn't there."

"And . . ."

"And he wasn't there—so he was out." Zander licked at the blood on his lips. "You know the rest."

"Yes, I do know." Lines of text play through the brain: *Why am I not part of it? Why? Why? Why?* "But there was more. Explain it to her. Go on. Tell her the rest."

"It was so long ago. How can it matter now?"

"It *matters*. To *me*! And to history." He swung the gun toward José. "Details, right now. For her—and for the history books—or he dies."

"*Please*," said Kate. She eyed her own gun across the studio. Could she make a dash for it?

"Douglas made a mistake. He criticized Kline one night, in public, at the Cedar Bar. Something about Franz cheating on his wife." Zander shook his head. "But those were the times, you see. We were free-thinkers, bohemians. We didn't care about bourgeois conventions."

"And Douglas Hopson did?" asked Kate.

"I suppose. I'm not sure. He'd had too much to drink—like the rest of us—when he said that to Franz, accused him of having weak morals. I remember de Kooning was furious, in a rage. You couldn't say anything about Kline when Bill was around. They were best pals." He took a deep breath. "Beatrice Larsen was there, with Franz. She was his girl at the time. She was the cause in some way. Franz had his arm around her, kissing her, you know. That's what must have prompted Hopson's com-ment, I suppose. I don't really know. But it got ugly, practically a brawl. And I think Hopson knew that was it for him." Zander paused. "Later, at that meeting, Hopson was the first to be excluded. No one wanted a prude, someone who was going to judge us. He was out. Everyone agreed. It was as simple as that."

"He wrote about it. In his journal. He knew," said Jules. "But he was your friend. How could you do that to him?"

"I—" Zander sighed. "Maybe I should have fought for him, but I was scared, like I said, *not* to be part of it. I didn't want to be ostracized. I wanted a career, to be included, part of them, part of the in crowd, a part of history."

"So you betrayed him, your best friend."

Judas, thought Kate. How Zander had described himself. And it was true.

"Douglas was not the only artist who suffered. There were the others, Beatrice, for one. We pushed her out, too."

"Too bad for Ms. Larsen. But she's at peace now. I helped her with that." Jules closed his eyes a moment, and Kate thought about striking, but the gun was still pressed against Zander's cheek.

"We kept them out of everything," Zander went on. "Our shows, gal-leries, even out of our parties. Like I said, the art world was small. We knew all the gallery owners, all the writers and critics. Once we spread the word that an artist was no longer important, no longer an integral part of the movement, they were finished. The critics stopped writing about them, the art dealers wouldn't show them. They were isolated, marginalized. They became pariahs, losers." He looked down at the floor. "I'm not proud of it."

Amazing, thought Kate, that artists could be so heartless to one another. *Gentle men,* the way Daniella Resnikoff had described her father and other artists. Not so gentle, these men, these artists.

"But there's more, isn't there? The most important part of this story," said Jules. "What they call . . . a motive."

"What do you mean?" asked Zander.

"Let's not play dumb, Phil. You wanted my grandfather out of the picture so you could steal his work."

"No, I—that's not true. Douglas and I, and Sandy, we worked together, shared ideas, and theories on the figure. We came to the style at . . . the same time."

"Liar!" He pressed the gun hard against Zander's temple.

"Don't!" Kate shouted. Though she knew he was right—that Zander *was* lying. The others—Resnikoff and Hopson—had come to the style before him.

"Do you want me to admit I'm a fraud?" Zander whispered. "Will that make you happy?"

"Nothing . . . will make me happy. But the truth is . . . the truth."

"Yes." Zander let out a deep breath, almost a sob. "I was an academic painter of still-life pictures and drawings from the model—but I was trying to open up. Resnikoff and Hopson showed me how to pour the paint first, like Pollock was doing, to let it suggest the image, and how to find the figure hidden within it." He glanced up. "There. I've said it. Your grandfather, and Resnikoff, they were first."

"And you pushed them out so you could steal from them. How easy it must have been to say, *Oh, that Hopson is such a prude. Who needs him around to judge us? I say he's out.* Isn't that why Resnikoff turned and left that meeting? Because you were the *first* to say it? Because *you* were the one to say that my grandfather, that Douglas Hopson was out?

Zander just barely whispered, "Yes."

"Resnikoff must have been shocked, sickened by your betrayal. But once Resnikoff was gone, too, well, who was to know, or to care?" He slid the tape recorder closer to Zander. "Say it now. For History. The real reason you pushed my grandfather out was to *steal* his work."

Another whispered "Yes."

"Say it: My grandfather was the original. *Say it.*"

"Yes, your grandfather, Douglas Hopson, was the original." Zander sighed again. "But it was like Resnikoff said—there wasn't room." He raised his head and locked eyes with Kate. "You see, de Kooning was painting the figure, and already becoming famous for it. How many other figure painters could there be in our small group? Maybe one. And Resnikoff had taken himself out, was about to move away. That left me and Hopson. And Hopson hadn't been there, at the meeting. And he'd offended the others. I knew he'd be pushed out, no matter what."

"And you made sure of it."

"Yes. No. It was the plan. Not just *my* plan. It was the group's plan. You see, each of us had to have something special, something to identify us, Pollock his *drips*, Rothko his moody veils of color, Clyfford Still his stalagmite abstractions, Motherwell his *Elegies* . . . but how many figure painters could there be other than de Kooning? I had tried to explain it to Hopson. I went to him. I did. I told him, 'Douglas, paint something else. The figure, it's taken.' I pleaded with him, even told him to make amends with Franz and Bill, too. Before it was too late. But he wouldn't listen. I was trying to help him."

"*Help him?* You fucking liar. You sit here, a king, a success, collecting fat checks for a painting style you *stole*—and you say you were trying to *help* him?" He moved the gun between Zander's eyes, his scarred fingers twitching on the trigger.

"I have always regretted it." Zander shut his eyes, took a deep breath, and said, "Do it."

"No, wait. I need to know more." Kate had to try and stall him. "What about the photograph in *Life* magazine? *The Irascibles.*"

"Another group idea," said Zander. "Something to canonize us for the history books—and we made sure who was in the picture—"

"And who was *not*." The gun was still trained on Zander's forehead. "You stole my grandfather's work and made him an outcast. No exhibitions, no attention, no money. He became a failure. His marriage collapsed—who would stay married to such a miserable flop?—then his daughter, my *mother*, the product of all that failure, lost to drugs, dead."

"You can't blame me for that," Zander whispered, but it was clear he did blame himself. Kate could see it in his eyes.

"You and your cronies changed the course of history. You set off a chain reaction. You ruined my grandfather's life, then my mother's life, then my grandmother, and . . . mine. You stole all of them from me— you stole my life—if you could call it that. I never really had . . . a life. I was there, you see, when my grandfather set the fire, and I . . . died along with him. He wanted me to die, but . . . I came to understand that, and I forgave him."

"Why?" asked Kate. "Why, if your grandfather knew you were there, in the apartment, and still he set the fire, do you forgive him?"

"He didn't mean it. He—he was drunk. Ruined. His mind . . . He *loved* me! He *did*. And I know why he did it. You don't understand. You couldn't."

Kate wanted to understand, and asked again, but he did not respond. He pressed the gun against Zander's cheek. "I forgave him, my grandfather, the man you destroyed," he repeated. "But not you. *Never* you."

"Listen to me," said Kate. "Even if it was his fault, it's over." She struggled to keep her voice calm. "There's no need to do this, to cause more pain and suffering."

"Pain and suffering? What do you know about pain and suffering? My grandfather suffered until the day he died . . . until the day he set his work on fire, himself on fire, *me* on fire!" Baseball cap thrown to the floor exposing a forehead of leathery skin, the scarred fingers of one hand pawing at the cheek, creating tracks in the heavy makeup. "This is suffering!"

Kate was torn—to lunge for the gun or to watch—but she couldn't move.

Shirt off, then pants, the pistol switched from one hand to the other.

Then the mustache plucked from the lip. T-shirt off, underpants discarded. "I'm tired. So tired of masks."

Kate was frozen, taking it in, the scarred naked body, tiny breasts, Robin Hopson's child, the baby in her lap when she had been killed, Douglas Hopson's grandchild—a granddaughter.

"Oh my God," said Zander.

"I knew you would never hire a woman assistant, not you, big macho man abstract expressionist. I studied you. Did my homework. You've had over a dozen assistants in the past twenty years. All young men. Did you know that? And, I thought . . . Why not? I can be that. When you have no life, you see, no identity, it's simple to become someone else. And I did it. I have lived as neither man, nor woman. So I can be . . . anything. The role became my greatest challenge. And, truthfully . . . anything is better than . . . being me." A pitiful shake of the head as all the roles and performances she had pretended to over the years, the make-believe that kept her alive in that hospital bed, cracked and dissolved. Her hand traveled up and down her body, over breasts and belly, and Kate took it all in—hair pushed aside to expose scarred cheeks, a misshapen ear, patches of puckered flesh against areas of smooth clear skin, a patchwork quilt, somewhat like the figures in her grandfather's paintings.

"Who would want me?" she asked. "Tell me."

"You're a person. A talented human being." Kate took another step, but the pistol was swung back toward her.

"I don't want to kill you. I've had enough killing. Enough pain. Years of pain, of drugs, of others tormenting me."

"I'm sure you have," said Kate, and she meant it. She took a small step forward, her voice warm, caring. "Tell me about it. Please."

"Hospitals. Drugs. One foster home after another. What more do you want to know? Can you imagine what it's like to be a freak, people staring at you, children pointing? But I learned how to conceal it, to pretend. You see, I can be anything, because he made me . . . nothing."

"You suffered," said Kate. "I can see that. But let me fix it. Let me correct history."

"Oh, yes. You will fix it—history. That's why I brought you in. Did you realize I'd arrange that? That I'd invited you to be part of this? You, the art historian, the chronicler. And you'll do your job, won't you?"

"Yes."

"But for me . . . it's too late." There were tears streaking down the scarred cheeks, and Kate saw it—her moment to strike—but the sight of all that pain had paralyzed her.

"You have so much talent," she said. "Your paintings—"

"Frauds. Like him."

"No. They're beautiful."

"Just games."

"And your music—"

"My only comfort. You could say it sustained me. I listened to every kind of music, all day and into the night. It took me away. Carried me. Soothed me. For so long it was all I had. But then . . . then I had revenge to sustain me."

"Your grandfather will be remembered," said Kate. "Revered. All you have done for him—let it mean something. I'll write it all. I promise you that." She looked over at José. "But let him go. *Please.*"

The young woman nodded, but there wasn't much heart in it, as if something inside of her had finally broken. She switched off the tape recorder and tossed it to Kate. "Take this. You won't have much time." She walked backward toward the far end of the studio, balancing the gun in one hand, and reached for a box of matches. "Time to finish what my grandfather started." She glanced back at Kate. "Promise me you will do your job, that you will set the record straight, and I will give you one minute to escape."

"I promise," said Kate.

She plucked a match from the box, and held it up. "One minute."

Kate swiped a straight razor off the paint table, chopped frantically at the tape that bound José's arms and legs to the stretcher bars. She had his one good arm free, then the one in the cast, and was slicing at the tape that held his legs when she heard the match strike. "No!" she screamed, but too late. She turned and saw the match had already dropped from the assistant's hand. Seconds later, there were flames racing down slender turpentine paths.

Kate hacked at the tape, José tumbling to the floor just as the fire reached him, shoes, pants smoldering. Kate whipped off her jacket, batted the flames. "Keep this around you," she said. "And run. *Run.*" She pushed José forward and watched as he cut through the flames, made it to the door, and tugged it open.

Cold air rushed in as he disappeared, oxygen offering life to the fire, flames inhaling and exhaling, spiraling toward the barn's rafters.

Just past the flames she could see Hopson's granddaughter on the other side of the studio, trapped, but not moving.

Zander was still taped to the chair, and Kate sliced at the tape, managed to get one of his arms free.

Around them, his paintings were blistering and turning black.

"Go," said Zander, "get out." He glanced up, and with his one free arm pushed her back as a beam broke loose from the ceiling and crashed down, a burning wall between them.

Kate could not get past the flames, and the burning log was impossible to move.

And then there was someone beside her, leaning into the beam, pushing it, and together they slashed the tape and got Zander free. They propped him between them, Kate and Murphy, each of them with an arm around his waist, and dragged him toward the door.

The studio was filling with smoke, Kate's eyes stinging and tearing, but she pulled the scarf from her neck and wound it around Zander's face.

She turned back once, and caught another glimpse of Hopson's granddaughter. She was standing naked as the flames reached her, arms stretched out as if beckoning them, her lips moving, speaking or reciting something, impossible to hear over the roar of the flames, which coiled around her pale thin body like white-hot snakes.

It was not until she was outside that Kate realized her shoes were sizzling. She kicked them off, wedged her feet into the snow, dropped to her knees and pressed handfuls of snow onto her face. The tape recorder had fallen from her pocket into the snow, and she dusted it off, stared at it for a moment, then glanced back at the barn as a part of the roof burst open and flames shot through, painting the sky with wild, expressionistic brush strokes.

José was there, beside her, and she hugged him to her.

Murphy still had his arm around Zander. He looked from the old man to José, and Kate wondered if perhaps he was recalling the accidental shooting of a young boy, and that it had come full circle, an odd sort of bargain with the devil—a child's life for the old man beside him.

"You okay?" Kate asked Zander.

He didn't answer. He was staring at his studio, his last series of paintings, the work for his exhibition in the spring being reduced to ashes, while the flames, like wild dancing figures, shimmered in his irises.

CHAPTER 43

Phillip Zander was lying in a hospital bed, hands bandaged, singed in the fire, and Kate could not help but think he would, for the rest of his life, see his assistant's scarred hands when he saw his own—and be reminded of what he had done, and all the pain he had caused.

The fire had completely destroyed his studio, and he did not, he told her, think he would rebuild. When she asked him where he would paint, he said he was not sure he would ever paint again.

He did not look or sound like the vital man she had been interviewing, and days later, when his son called to tell her that his father had died peacefully in his sleep, Kate was saddened, but not surprised. She hoped he had died at peace, and wondered if confessing what he had done had made that possible.

The Suffolk PD, the NYPD, and the FBI found all they needed in Juliet Hopson's small studio, only a few miles from Phillip Zander's home. Kate had accompanied Brown, Perlmutter, and Murphy, and there was no mistake—Juliet Hopson had been the Slasher. Books and research on all the victims, sketches for the black-and-white paintings, a closetful of costumes, a medicine cabinet stocked with theatrical makeup, vials of tranquilizers and painkillers—Percodan, Vicodan,

Oxycontin—that attested to a life of pure physical hell. But the psychic and emotional pain, the years of deprivation that cause a mind to break, to commit heinous crimes against humanity, these were something less easily quantifiable, something for the psychiatrists and criminologists to discuss and argue about perhaps in a similar way to the artists of the New York School, who had fought and debated beauty and ugliness, Freud and Jung, the conscious versus the unconscious, and freedom for artists to break the rules and do anything they desired—though the rules seemed to apply to some rather than all.

A picture of Hopson's painting, the one Kate knew, *Pin-up Girl*, had been printed out from a computer, and was pinned to the wall. There were other paintings in Juliet's studio as well, small abstractions with bits of collage, pictures of beautiful men and women cut from magazines and imbedded in the paint, gorgeous disembodied faces floating in pig-

ment that Kate could not help but see as projections and desires of the scarred young woman who wore disguises and lived in a make-believe world where she could be anything—anything but herself.

But there was one more painting, in progress, pinned to a wall that caught Kate's eye.

Kate stared at it. Not exactly sure what it was she was looking at, then it coalesced. It was a painting of flames, one of Zander's paintings behind them, burning.

The last clue painting, thought Kate, *the final prediction: A Phillip Zander painting, in flames.*

She had planned this, too: that Zander's work, like her grandfather's, would be destroyed.

Then Kate looked closer and saw something else, something beside the Zander painting, almost hidden in the expressionistic brush strokes that made up the flames: an inchoate figure, naked, the face almost blank, the sex just barely discernible.

The final prediction, thought Kate, to join her grandfather and his art.

Ashes to ashes . . .

Among Juliet Hopson's papers Kate had also found a worn, rather innocuous-looking spiral notepad, and after the lab went over it, she got to take it home, and read it through in a night—Douglas Hopson's journal. She wondered how the small child had come to own it, and how it had survived, but there was no one to ask. A fireman who had rescued it from the burning apartment, eventually turning it over? A family friend? Kate had no idea, except for the fact of its existence.

Perhaps there had been other such journals. She had no way of knowing that either. This one had been started in the early seventies, the date, in pen, on the first page, July 1972, picked up in what appeared to be mid-thought—about color and form, and the futility of making art—with other dated entries scattered throughout.

One earlier entry mentioned "a drunken night at the Cedar," and the insult he had so foolishly hurled at Franz Kline. *How could I be so stupid?* But for the most part, it was one man's musing on frustration and failure—*Why, I ask, over and over, why am I not part of it? Why? Why? Why? Why?* And the artist's own answer many pages later: that he had finally discovered it had all been a plan, that his friend, Phillip Zander, had betrayed him, though Hopson did not say how he had discovered it.

Kate read Hopson's ruminations on disillusionment and hopelessness—*Why do I do it? Keep painting? For who? For what?*—with entries after his daughter's death, which had Kate sobbing, followed by more depression and despair when the man's wife had died.

Toward the end, the journal began to lose coherence, the statements no longer about Hopson's specific frustration with art or the misery of being a failed artist. After those two deaths, it became a journal of ramblings, occasionally philosophical, but incoherent:

> I curse the gods, the spirit of flesh that has made me want to do
> this, that eats at me, and my brain—a life unlived—ants crawl-
> ing under my flesh—to paint is to live and die, but what sweet
> death, not worth living—singing, Oh, God, oh, my darling
> Robin, forgive me . . . And Minnie, dear Minnie, O painted
> house with no soul, losing sleep, seeing ghosts. The figure, arm-
> less, headless . . .

Page after page, the sentences making less and less sense, until the final entry—December 22, 1978—a mix of logic and insanity—*Time to go, take the paintings with me, an offering to God or the devil, whoever will have me, and bring the child with me as yet another, greater offering; this angel, who is too good for this world, and better off without it, better off dead.* These last words written in a shaky hand.

Kate wasn't sure what she should do with the journal—surely it was not meant for any sort of public scrutiny—but she could not destroy it. Finally, she donated it to a small museum that specialized in artists' books, where it would be archived and saved, a document of one artist's life and death.

As for the media, the story of Jules-Juliet Hopson's reign of terror was akin to a pig sniffing out a rich vein of rare truffles, and they dined on it for weeks, rehashing not only the recent murders, but Juliet Hopson's tortured past, as well as the story of her grandfather—the forgotten artist of the New York School. Douglas Hopson was finally getting attention, though the media's interest ran toward the prurient—poverty, failure, drinking, a daughter lost to drugs, self-immolation—rather than his contribution to the history of art.

Kate dodged reporters until she'd figured out there was something she actually wanted to talk about—the victims. The killers, she knew, were always remembered, but the victims—who would speak for them? And so she did. Beatrice Larsen, Martin Dressler, the little she knew of Gregory Sarkisian, or Cecile Edelman, or Gabrielle Hofmann, or her friend Nicholas Starrett. And though it did not make her happy, it did make her feel as though her time spent on the case had, in some small way, been worth it—though she once again retired her gun, this time turning it in to Floyd Brown when she went back to the precinct to fill out reports.

"I'll keep it till the next time," he said.

"There won't be a next time," said Kate, determined to channel her energy into her work, and she told Brown so.

"Yeah," he said, with a sweet but sardonic smile. "And I retired two years ago."

"It's not going to be pretty, Floyd, the two of us pursuing felons on walkers."

Brown laughed and said again that he'd keep her gun handy—"just in case"—and Kate told him to throw it out, and they talked for a while, and Brown mentioned that Murphy was up for a citation, and Kate was glad to hear it.

Possibly the most ironic coda to the case, which Brown passed on, was that Agent Bobbitt had not been fired, but moved to Quantico and put in charge of Marketing and Public Relations approximately five minutes before the various media discovered they had been used. Apparently, Bobbitt was now dealing with major lawsuits from three newspapers and four of New York's most prestigious art museums. Kate wondered who at the Bureau had the sense of humor, and justice, to give Bobbitt the job knowing the shit storm would be landing in his lap. She thought if Richard were here he would leap at the chance to defend the art museums, and when she pictured him in one of his trademark Armani suits, delivering a speech on the moral responsibility that went along with freedom of the press, she felt a mix of sadness and pride.

The Seventh Avenue subway was crowded and overheated and Kate was happy when she made it to the street. She walked the rest of the way to the Medinas' apartment.

She had been worried about José, was even paying for him to see a therapist, though he claimed to be fine, and had, in fact, become a hero among his friends, his name and picture in the newspapers.

"Something about José has changed," said his mother, peering at Kate above her coffee cup, the two women sitting in the Medinas' cramped kitchen. "He's settled down, you know. It's almost like . . . he has become a man."

Kate wondered if that was true or if he'd simply been traumatized into behaving. But later, when he came home, and they took a walk, he talked about his band—they were making their own CD—and he actually did seem fine.

They were crossing Broadway and talking about New Year's Eve— Kate trying to dissuade him from going to Times Square with his buddies—when he said, "This is going to sound crazy, but I really liked him."

Kate knew José was well aware of Jules's true gender, and did not bother to correct him. She watched as he inserted the tiny iPod earphones and hummed along to songs he had programmed with a killer.

The garbage trucks were making their usual late-night racket outside her loft, and Kate was back at her computer trying to put the finishing touches on her book about the New York School.

She had already added a chapter on that fateful meeting in Ad Reinhardt's studio, though she had learned history could be subjective, facts, over time, blurred, sometimes lost. Still, it was a necessary part of the story, and through it, she had inadvertently found what she was looking for, a theme—success and failure—and had worked hard to balance the story, giving equal time to the lesser-known artists of the period as well as the superstars. After all, who was to say what another fifty years would do for the various artists' reputations?

Her chapter on Douglas Hopson was nearly complete, dates in place to show he was an originator, not imitator. In his journal, she had found a few relevant quotes he'd made about his art, and added them to her text. She had also included a reproduction of his painting, *Pin-up Girl*, a painting that no longer existed. In fact, all of the artist's paintings had been destroyed in the fire set by his own hand.

But then, how many people ever got to see real masterpieces? One did not have to go to Paris to know that the *Mona Lisa* existed. It was the pictures of masterpieces, the replications, that most people saw and knew—and now Hopson's painting would be seen and remembered, and that seemed fair enough. An image, thought Kate, if it exists on the page—or in our mind—exists, doesn't it?

The thought stopped her, and for a moment she considered paintings that no longer existed—Courbet's famous *Stone Breakers* or the remnants of Mantegna's frescoes in Padua, artwork she had studied in school which had been sacrificed to the gods of war. But it was other kinds of pictures, not paintings, but rather images of lost loved ones who lived on in her mind, that she was thinking of.

She pictured her mother and father, and Elena, who had been like a daughter to her. How she kept them alive inside her—though sometimes it just wasn't enough to have someone live only in your mind and heart. She wanted them here, now, all of the people she had loved and lost. *God, how I miss them.*

And Richard.

Kate glanced over at the photo on her desk, a picture taken before they married, the two of them, arms around each other, hanging on for dear life, smiling, so young and happy, filled with hope for a future, and she did not realize she was crying until she saw the tears drop onto her desk.

Afterward, when she had dried her tears, she tiptoed into the baby's room and watched him breathe, and thought again about why she had let herself be dragged into this case, into danger, and though she still did not have an answer, she realized that back in Zander's studio—when the place had been set on fire and she had been faced not only with José's and Zander's imminent demise, but her own—she had wanted to live.

Kate leaned into the crib, inhaled the baby's fresh scent, and kissed him lightly on his cheek.

Minutes later, she climbed into her own bed and the next thing she knew there was sunlight streaking through her bedroom windows and it was morning.

New Year's Eve. Kate's least favorite holiday. Wasn't there a way to outlaw it? she thought, tugging on her jeans. Still, she had agreed, after much deliberation, to have dinner with Mitch Freeman.

In the bathroom, she tried doing something with her hair, but it only did what it wanted, and she couldn't decide whether or not she should get it cut again or let it grow. Maybe she was getting too old to look like Meg Ryan; maybe Meg Ryan was too old to look like Meg Ryan. Kate stared at her reflection in the mirror and sighed. Hell, there was nothing wrong with getting older—as long as everyone else thought you looked young! She put on a bit of lip gloss, and decided she—and Meg—both looked damn good.

Mitch Freeman met her at the restaurant, and they talked easily throughout dinner—the baby, Nola, Kate's book, a class Freeman was going to be teaching on criminology, in the spring—and the hours passed quickly. When coffee came, Kate asked a question.

"Do you feel successful?"

"Why do you ask?"

"Something I've been thinking about—because of my book, and the artists of the New York School, the ones who made it and the ones who didn't. Is success something reflected on us by the world?"

"Well, psychologically speaking . . ." Freeman put on his earnest shrink voice, then smiled. "Seriously, you can only be a success if *you* feel like a success. Otherwise, anything you achieve is worthless."

"I guess I knew that. It's just that we all tend to live in one another's reflections and shadows, don't we? I mean, we're always comparing ourselves and our accomplishments: Am I doing better than so-and-so? I know it doesn't matter, but it's impossible, in our world, not to fall into the trap."

"That's why we have therapists." Freeman grinned, and Kate laughed, then got serious again.

"But you can still be a success without society's approbation, can't you? I mean, my God, there are so many artists out there making beautiful work that hardly anyone will ever see. Isn't dedicating one's life to creating something beautiful or interesting or brilliant enough?"

"If they *feel* successful, absolutely."

Kate nodded. "I don't mean to sound as if I'm standing on a soapbox, but I think there's something deeply wrong with a culture that worships fame as if that alone was an accomplishment."

"I'm with you on that one," said Freeman. "But does that mean you don't think Paris Hilton is a major contributor to American culture?"

Kate laughed, lifted her coffee cup, then set it back down. "Douglas Hopson was possibly the first of his group to do something new in his artwork, but the world didn't see it, and then, finally, neither did he. The other artists got the attention and went on to do bigger and better work—to have bigger and better careers."

"You know what they say: Nothing succeeds like success."

"And nothing is more painful than failure."

"No." Freeman frowned. "Sometimes we put obstacles in our paths because we're afraid of succeeding."

"Please, don't look at me when you say that, Doctor."

"I didn't mean you."

"You sure about that?"

They were quiet a moment, then Freeman asked, "So what is it you want from life?"

The question threw her. What *did* she want from life? Though she didn't think about her answer, just said it—"Another chance"—and the words surprised her.

Freeman reached across the table, touched her hand, and looked into her eyes, and for a fraction of a second Kate saw another set of eyes—*Richard's*—but it did not flatten her as it would have, and did, only days ago.

"I can't promise where this is going."

"I don't remember asking for a promise," said Freeman.

"Mitch, about what happened, between us. I don't fall into bed with every man I meet."

"I didn't think you did."

"I'm serious. There's been no one, I mean, since Richard." Kate needed to tell him this. "My marriage wasn't perfect, but I loved my husband, and a part of him is still with me." She took a deep breath. "And I'm worried there will always be a ghost between us—and to be honest . . . I don't *want* to lose him—or what we had together. I guess I'm scared. I don't want to lose him, but . . ."

"Look, Kate. I don't expect you to forget the fact that you were ever married to another man who you loved, and who loved you. I'm not trying to take Richard's place. I couldn't."

For a moment, Richard's face flashed before her eyes, then Freeman's took its place, alive and clear.

"We can take it slow," he said. "Drinks, dinners, and . . . you know." He smiled.

"Okay," said Kate, drawing a deep breath. "Now I have something really important to ask you."

Mitch Freeman sat up straighter, his gray eyes serious. "What?"

Kate waited a beat, then smiled and said, "Do you want dessert? Or do you want to take me home?"

Acknowledgments

My gratitude and thanks to the wonderfully supportive team at Morrow/HarperCollins—Jane Friedman, Michael Morrison, Lisa Gallagher, Debbie Stier, Brian McSharry, Carl Lennertz, Carla Parker, Brian Grogan, Mike Spradlin, Libby Jordan, Lynn Grady, Juliette Shapland, Betty Lew, Jessica Heslin, Richard Aquan, Ervin Serrano, Darlene Delillo, Tom Egner, Adrienne Di Pietro, Jill Schwartzman—among others—and especially my editor, the warm, witty, and talented Dan Conaway. (And thanks to Erika Schmid for correcting my English in all three of my books.)

Thanks to . . . Janice Deaner, reader, writer, editor, and friend; Ward Mintz and Floyd Lattin, who lent me their peaceful home, and much more; likewise Jane and Jack Rivkin (and thanks for insisting we take that harrowing drive between East Hampton and Springs in a snowstorm, Jack); Adriana and Robert Mnuchin for an elegant book party; Reiner Leist, who no matter how busy he gets is never too busy to help me out; Bruce and Micheline Etkin; Kathleen Monaghan and Richard Shebairo; Sunny Frazier and the San Joaquin SinC; Jan Heller Levi, who taught me so much about writing; Eliza Griswold, Marcelle Clements, Lynn Freed, and Joseph Caldwell for their kind words of literary encouragement; Pavel Zoubok, Judd Tully, Jane O'Keefe, Susan

Crile, David Storey and Jane Kent, Graham Leader, Terry Braunstein, Ellen Page Wilson, Diane Keaton, Nancy Dallett and Richard Toon, Caren and Dave Cross, Christof Keller, Arlene Goldstine, S. J. Rozan— friends and supporters all; the Corporation of Yaddo, and Elaina Richardson, its director; and to the many booksellers and readers who have been kind and loyal.

As always, a big thank-you to the remarkable Suzanne Gluck.

More thanks to my daughter, Doria, who is responsible for Kate's recent makeover; my sister, Roberta; and to my wife, Joy, who reads dozens of versions of every manuscript, offers astute commentary, and is always there for me.

There are many wonderful books about the early years of New York's art world, which have been helpful and I recommend them for a deeper (and factual) understanding of the period: Irving Sandler's *A Sweeper-Up After Artists*, Clifford Ross's *Abstract Expressionism: Creators and Critics*, James E. B. Breslin's *Mark Rothko*; Mark Stevens and Annalyn Swann's *De Kooning, An American Master*, Dore Ashton's *The New York School: A Cultural Reckoning*; and Lee Hall's *Elaine and Bill*, to name just a few.

One final note: The late George McNeil, artist and teacher, inadvertently inspired some of this plot. Among the many wise things George told me was to put the insanity into my artwork and to keep my life sane. *(I'm okay with the first part, George, but keep my life sane? Please come back and explain how to do that.)*